Lord John and the Hand of Devils

DIANA GABALDON is the internationally best-selling author of eight genre-bending, prize-winning historical novels – *Cross Stitch*, *Dragonfly in Amber*, *Voyager*, *Drums of Autumn*, *The Fiery Cross*, *A Breath of Snow and Ashes*, *Lord John and the Private Matter* and *Lord John and the Brotherhood of the Blade*. *A Breath of Snow and Ashes* was a No. 1 bestseller in four countries and won both a Corine international literary prize for fiction and a Quill Award in 2006. She lives with her family and other assorted wildlife in Scottsdale, Arizona. Visit the author at www.dianagabaldon.com

Praise for Diana Gabaldon

'A blockbuster hit!' *Wall Street Journal*

'Stunning' *Los Angeles Daily News*

'Triumphant . . . Her use of historical detail and a truly adult love story confirm Diana Gabaldon as a superior writer' *Publishers Weekly*

'The writing is superb – lush, evocative, sensual, with a wealth of historical detail' *Library Journal*

Also by Diana Gabaldon
(in order of publication)

Cross Stitch
Dragonfly in Amber
Voyager
Drums of Autumn
The Fiery Cross
A Breath of Snow and Ashes

THE LORD JOHN GREY SERIES
Lord John and the Private Matter
Lord John and the Brotherhood of the Blade

DIANA GABALDON

Lord John and the Hand of Devils

arrow books

Published by Arrow Books in 2009

7 9 10 8 6

Copyright © Diana Gabaldon 2007
Book design by Virginia Norey

Lord John and the Hellfire Club first appeared with *Lord John and the Private Matter* in October 2003

Diana Gabaldon has asserted her right under the
Copyright, Designs and Patents Act, 1988 to be identified
as the author of this work

First published in Great Britain in 2007 by Century
The Random House Group Limited
20 Vauxhall Bridge Road, London, SW1V 2SA

www.rbooks.co.uk

Addresses for companies within The Random House Group Limited can be found at: www.randomhouse.co.uk/offices.htm

The Random House Group Limited Reg. No. 954009

A CIP catalogue record for this book is available from the British Library

ISBN 9780099278252

Penguin Random House is committed to a sustainable future for our business, our readers and our planet. This book is made from Forest Stewardship Council® certified paper.

MIX
Paper from
responsible sources
FSC® C018179
www.fsc.org

Printed and bound in Great Britain by Clays Ltd, St Ives plc

Typeset by SX Composing DTP, Rayleigh, Essex

To Alex Krislov,
Janet McConnaughey, and
Margaret J. Campbell,
sysops of the Compuserve Books and Writers Community
(http://community.compuserve.com/Books),
the best perpetual electronic literary cocktail party in
the world. Thanks!

Acknowledgments

The author would like to thank

... Maxim Jakubowski, for inadvertently launching Lord John on his solo career.

... Marte Brengle, whose mention of her infamous ancestor Sir Francis Dashwood supplied me and Lord John with the basis of his first adventure.

... Karen Watson, of Her Majesty's Customs and Excise, for patient sleuthing through the byways of London in search of plausibly revolting locales and interesting historical trivia.

... Laura Bailey and Becky Morgan, for helpful suggestions regarding clothing and daily practicalities.

... Barbara Schnell, for making sure the German bits are accurate (well, they started out that way; we hope they still are).

... Steven Lopata, Piper Fahrney, Janet McConnaughey, and Larry Tuohy, for useful information on explosions, cannon-loading, fracturing metal, and other violent phenomena of the battlefield.

... Lauri Klobas, Eve Ackermann, John S. Kruszka, and the dozens of other kind, intelligent people from the Compuserve Books and Writers Community (whose names I have unfortunately misplaced or forgotten over the last ten years), who are always on hand with suggestions and information ranging from the mundane to the bizarre, and then some.

. . . Silvia Kuttny-Walser, for the title of this book.

. . . the excellent editors who have worked with me on this book, both piecemeal and entire: Max Jakubowski, Betsy Mitchell, Bill Massey, and John Flicker.

. . . Virginia Norey, aka the Book Goddess, for her wonderful design.

and

. . . the unsung genii of the Random House art department, who came up with the marvelous covers for the new Lord John books. Thank you!

Contents

Foreword

In which we find A PUBLISHING HISTORY, BIBLIOGRAPHIC INFORMATION, AN AUTHOR'S NOTE, and A WARNING TO THE READER

Dear Reader—

PRELIMINARY WARNINGS

1. The book you are holding is not a novel; it's a collection of three separate novellas.
2. The novellas in this collection all feature Lord John Grey, not Jamie and Claire Fraser (though both are mentioned now and again), but
3. I did want to assure you all that there *is* another Jamie and Claire book to follow *A Breath of Snow and Ashes*. I usually work on more than one book at a time, and have been working on that one, too. It's just that this one is shorter, and therefore got finished first.

Awright. Now, for those of you still with me . . .

Lord John Grey has been largely accidental, since the day he rashly decided to try to kill a notorious Jacobite in the darkness of the Carryarrick Pass. His association with Jamie and Claire Fraser (and with me) dates back to that passage in *Dragonfly in Amber*. While he did have small but important parts to play in subsequent books of the Outlander series, I really didn't intend to write books about him on his own. (On the other hand, I never intended to show Outlander to anybody, either, and here we are. You never know, that's all I can say.)

Lord John began his independent life apart from the Outlander books when a British editor and anthologist named Maxim Jakubowski invited me to write a short story for an anthology of historical crime that he was putting together in honor of the novelist Ellis Peters, who had recently died. Now, I had never written a short story – barring things required for English classes in school, which tended to be pretty lame – but I was fond of Ellis Peters's Brother Cadfael mysteries, and I thought it would be an interesting technical challenge to see whether I could write something shorter than 300,000 words, so . . . 'Why not?' I said.

It had to be the eighteenth century, because that's the only period I know well, and I hadn't time to research another time adequately, just for a short story. And it couldn't involve the main characters from the Outlander series, because a good short story has high moral stakes, just as a novel does; thus, it would be difficult to write a short story involving the Frasers that would not include an event significant enough to have an impact on the plot of future novels involving them. Since I don't think up plots in advance, I thought I'd just avoid the whole problem by using Lord John; he's a very interesting character, he talks to me easily, and he appears only intermittently in the Outlander novels; no reason why he couldn't be having interesting adventures offstage, on his own time.

Enter Sir Francis Dashwood and his notorious Hellfire Club, plus the murder of a red-haired man, and Lord John made his first solo appearance in a short story titled 'Hellfire,' which was published in 1998 in the anthology *Past Poisons*, edited by Maxim Jakubowski, and published by Headline.

The stories for this anthology had a limit of 10,000 words. 'Hellfire' was a hair over 12,000, but luckily nobody complained. I thought the ending was a bit rushed, even so – and so later rewrote the ending, expanding it slightly. Things turn out the same way, but with a little more style and elegance, I hope.

'Hellfire' has had an interesting publishing history, since that first appearance in *Past Poisons*. That anthology went out of print within a couple of years (it's since been reprinted), which is the point at which U.S. audiences began to hear about 'Hellfire' and to express interest in Lord John's solo adventure. Unfortunately, there's really nothing you can *do* with a 14,000-word short story; it's too long for magazine markets, much too short to be published alone.

At this fortuitous point, a couple of online acquaintances of mine decided to start an e-publishing business, and asked me whether I had 'a boxful of old short stories under the bed' (Why do people think every writer begins with short stories? Or if so, that they would be willing to expose this juvenilia to the world?) that they might be able to publish.

'What the heck?' I said, figuring this was as good an opportunity as any to explore the brave new world of e-publishing. In addition to my friends' business, the e-publishing arm of my German publishing company also decided to offer an electronic German version of 'Hellfire,' and so Lord John ventured out into international cyberspace.

This was an interesting experience, and fairly successful in e-publishing terms ('success' in e-publishing terms does not generally mean quitting your day job, let's put it like that). That experiment ended when my friends decided to list all their titles with Amazon.com – a very reasonable decision – but informed me that owing to the Amazon.com discount required of publishers, they would have to sell 'Hellfire' at $6.50, in order to make any money. I couldn't countenance the notion of selling a 23-page short story for six dollars and fifty cents, so we cordially parted ways at that point.

At this point, I began to think what else might be done with the story. It occurred to me that I'd enjoyed writing it – I like Lord John, and the complexities of his private life tend to lead him into Interesting Situations – and what if I were to write two or three more short stories involving him? Then all the short pieces could be published together in book form, and everybody would be happy. (Well, Lord John and I would, at least.)

'Hellfire' next saw print – retitled as 'Lord John and the Hellfire Club' – as an add-in to the trade-paperback edition of the first Lord John Grey novel, *Lord John and the Private Matter.*

And here it is *again,* at last in book form, in company with two novellas: 'Lord John and the Succubus,' which was originally written for another anthology; and 'Lord John and the Haunted Soldier,' written specifically for this collection.

Other accidents happened – his lordship is prone to such things, I'm afraid – and I wrote *Lord John and the Private Matter,* under the delusion that this was in fact the second Lord John short story. I was informed by my literary agents, though, that in fact, I had inadvertently written a novel. (Well, how would I know? To me, a novel is just getting *started* at 85,000 words.) This was good, insofar as my assorted publishers were ecstatic at the revelation that I actually *could* write a 'normal'-sized novel, and promptly gave me a contract for two more Lord John Grey novels – but it still left 'Hellfire' sitting there by itself at 14,000 words.

But accidents continued to happen: I was invited to write a novella for a fantasy anthology, and presto! We had 'Lord John and the Succubus,' which came in around 33,000 words. This meant that one more novella of that length or more, and we'd have critical mass.

Here, things got slightly tricky, though. By sheer

happenstance, the short Lord John pieces alternated with the full-length novel: 'Hellfire,' *Private Matter,* 'Succubus.' And I had embarked on the second novel, *Lord John and the Brotherhood of the Blade.* All fine – but the German publisher, anxious to have the collection, asked whether I might be able to hurry up and write the final novella before finishing the second novel. Easygoing sort that I am, I said I reckoned I could do that – and I did. Allow me to note that writing a novella that follows a novel that isn't yet written is not the easiest thing in the world, but if I wanted an easy life, I suppose I'd clean swimming pools for a living.

This collection was originally to have been titled *Lord John and a Whiff of Brimstone* (because of the supernatural aspect common to all the stories), but the German publisher explained that they couldn't use that title, because my most recent Outlander novel, *A Breath of Snow and Ashes,* is titled *Ein Hauch von Schnee und Asche* in German – and German does not have separate words for 'breath' and 'whiff' – ergo, they'd have another *Ein Hauch . . .* and they thought one was plenty. They suggested instead, *Lord John and the Hand of Devils,* which I thought was wonderful, and immediately took for the English-language volume as well.

I hope you'll enjoy it!

Best wishes, *Diana Gabaldon*

LORD JOHN
and the
Hellfire Club

Part I

A Red-Haired Man

London, 1756
The Society for Appreciation of
the English Beefsteak, a gentleman's club

Lord John Grey jerked his eyes away from the door. No. No, he mustn't turn and stare. Needing some other focus for his gaze, he fixed his eyes instead on Quarry's scar.

'A glass with you, sir?' Scarcely waiting for the club's steward to provide for his companion, Harry Quarry drained his cup of claret, then held it out for more. 'And another, perhaps, in honor of your return from frozen exile?' Quarry grinned broadly, the scar pulling down the corner of his eye in a lewd wink as he did so, and lifted up his glass again.

Lord John tilted his own cup in acceptance of the salute, but barely tasted the contents. With an effort, he kept his eyes on Quarry's face, willing himself not to turn and stare, not to gawk after the flash of fire in the corridor that had caught his eye.

Quarry's scar had faded; tightened and shrunk to a thin white slash, its nature made plain only by its position, angled hard across the ruddy cheek. It might otherwise have lost itself among the lines of

3

hard living, but instead remained visible, the badge of honor that its owner so plainly considered it.

'You are exceeding kind to note my return, sir,' Grey said. His heart hammered in his ears, muffling Quarry's words – no great loss to conversation.

It is not, his sensible mind pointed out, *it cannot be.* Yet sense had nothing to do with the riot of his sensibilities, that surge of feeling that seized him by nape and buttocks, as though it would pluck him up and turn him forcibly to go in pursuit of the red-haired man he had so briefly glimpsed.

Quarry's elbow nudged him rudely, a not-unwelcome recall to present circumstances.

'. . . among the ladies, eh?'

'Eh?'

'I say your return has been noted elsewhere, too. My sister-in-law bid me send her regard and discover your present lodgings. Do you stay with the regiment?'

'No, I am at present at my mother's house, in Jermyn Street.' Finding his cup still full, Grey raised it and drank deep. The Beefsteak's claret was of excellent vintage, but he scarcely noticed its bouquet. There were voices in the hall outside, raised in altercation.

'Ah. I'll inform her, then; expect an invitation by the morning post. Lucinda has her eye upon you for a cousin of hers, I daresay – she has a flock of poor but well-favored female relations, whom she means to shepherd to good marriages.' Quarry's teeth showed briefly. 'Be warned.'

Grey nodded politely. He was accustomed to such overtures. The youngest of four brothers, he had no hopes of a title, but the family name was ancient and honorable, his person and countenance not without appeal – and he had no need of an heiress, his own means being ample.

The door flung open, sending such a draft across the room as made the fire in the hearth roar up like the flames of Hades, scattering sparks across the Turkey carpet. Grey gave thanks for the burst of heat; it gave excuse for the color that he felt suffuse his cheeks.

Nothing like. Of course he is nothing like. Who could be? And yet the emotion that filled his breast was as much disappointment as relief.

The man was tall, yes, but not strikingly so. Slight of build, almost delicate. And young, younger than Grey, he judged. But the hair – yes, the hair was very like.

'Lord John Grey.' Quarry had intercepted the young man, a hand on his sleeve, turning him for introduction. 'Allow me to acquaint you with my cousin by marriage, Mr. Robert Gerald.'

Mr. Gerald nodded shortly, then seemed to take hold of himself. Suppressing whatever it was that had caused the blood to rise under his fair skin, he bowed, then fixed his gaze on Grey in cordial acknowledgment.

'Your servant, sir.'

5

'And yours.' Not copper, not carrot; a deep red, almost rufous, with glints and streaks of cinnabar and gold. The eyes were not blue – thank God! – but rather a soft and luminous brown.

Grey's mouth had gone dry. To his relief, Quarry offered refreshment, and upon Gerald's agreement, snapped his fingers for the steward and steered the three of them to an armchaired corner, where the haze of tobacco smoke hung like a sheltering curtain over the less-convivial members of the Beefsteak.

'Who was that I heard in the corridor?' Quarry demanded, as soon as they were settled. 'Bubb-Dodington, surely? The man's a voice like a costermonger.'

'I – he – yes, it was.' Mr. Gerald's pale skin, not quite recovered from its earlier excitement, bloomed afresh, to Quarry's evident amusement.

'Oho! And what perfidious proposal has he made you, young Bob?'

'Nothing. He – an invitation I did not wish to accept, that is all. Must you shout so loudly, Harry?' It was chilly at this end of the room, but Grey thought he could warm his hands at the fire of Gerald's smooth cheeks.

Quarry snorted with amusement, looking around at the nearby chairs.

'Who's to hear? Old Cotterill's deaf as a post, and the General's half dead. And why do you care in any case, if the matter's so innocent as you suggest?' Quarry's eyes swiveled to bear on his cousin by marriage, suddenly intelligent and penetrating.

'I did not say it was innocent,' Gerald replied dryly, regaining his composure. 'I said I declined to accept it. And that, Harry, is all you will hear of it, so desist this piercing glare you turn upon me. It may work on your subalterns, but not on me.'

Grey laughed, and after a moment, Quarry joined in. He clapped Gerald on the shoulder, eyes twinkling.

'My cousin is the soul of discretion, Lord John. But that's as it should be, eh?'

'I have the honor to serve as junior secretary to the prime minister,' Gerald explained, seeing incomprehension on Grey's features. 'While the secrets of government are dull indeed, at least by Harry's standards' – he shot his cousin a malicious grin – 'they are not mine to share.'

'Oh, well, of no interest to Lord John in any case,' Quarry said philosophically, tossing back his third glass of aged claret with a disrespectful haste more suited to porter. Grey saw the senior steward close his eyes in quiet horror at the act of desecration, and smiled to himself – or so he thought, until he caught Mr. Gerald's soft brown eyes upon him, a matching smile of complicity upon his lips.

'Such things are of little interest to anyone save those most intimately concerned,' Gerald said, still smiling at Grey. 'The fiercest battles fought are those where very little lies at stake, you know. But what interests you, Lord John, if politics does not?'

'Not lack of interest,' Grey responded, holding Robert Gerald's eyes boldly with his. *No, not lack of interest at all.* 'Ignorance, rather. I have been absent from London for some time; in fact, I have quite lost . . . touch.'

Without intent, one hand closed upon his glass, the thumb drawing slowly upward, stroking the smooth, cool surface as though it were another's flesh. Hastily, he set the glass down, seeing as he did so the flash of blue from the sapphire ring he wore. It might have been a lighthouse beacon, he reflected wryly, warning of rough seas ahead.

And yet the conversation sailed smoothly on, despite Quarry's jocular inquisitions regarding Grey's most recent posting in the wilds of Scotland and his speculations as to his brother officer's future prospects. As the former was *terra prohibita* and the latter *terra incognita,* Grey had little to say in response, and the talk moved on to other things: horses, dogs, regimental gossip, and other such comfortable masculine fare.

Yet now and again, Grey felt the brown eyes rest on him, with an expression of speculation that both modesty and caution forbade him to interpret. It was with no sense of surprise, though, that upon departure from the club, he found himself alone in the vestibule with Gerald, Quarry having been detained by an acquaintance met in passing.

'I impose intolerably, sir,' Gerald said, moving close enough to keep his low-voiced words from the ears of the servant who kept the door. 'I would ask your favor, though, if it be not entirely unwelcome?'

'I am completely at your command, I do assure

you,' Grey said, feeling the warmth of claret in his blood succeeded by a rush of deeper heat.

'I wish – that is, I am in some doubt regarding a circumstance of which I have become aware. Since you are so recently come to London – that is, you have the advantage of perspective, which I must necessarily lack by reason of familiarity. There is no one . . .' He fumbled for words, then turned eyes grown suddenly and deeply unhappy on Lord John. 'I can confide in no one!' he said, in a sudden, passionate whisper. He gripped Lord John's arm, with surprising strength. 'It may be nothing, nothing at all. But I must have help.'

'You shall have it, if it be in my power to give.' Grey's fingers touched the hand that grasped his arm; Gerald's fingers were cold. Quarry's voice echoed down the corridor behind them, loud with joviality.

'The 'Change, near the Arcade,' Gerald said rapidly. 'Tonight, just after full dark.' The grip on Grey's arm was gone, and Gerald vanished, the soft fall of his hair vivid against his blue cloak.

Grey's afternoon was spent in necessary errands to tailors and solicitors, then in making courtesy calls upon long-neglected acquaintance, in an effort to fill the empty hours that loomed before dark. Quarry, at loose ends, had volunteered to accompany him, and Lord John had made no demur. Bluff and jovial by temper, Quarry's conversation was limited to cards, drink, and whores. He and Grey had little in common, save the regiment. And Ardsmuir.

When he had first seen Quarry again at the club, he had thought to avoid the man, feeling that memory was best buried. And yet . . . could memory be truly buried, when its embodiment still lived? He might forget a dead man, but not one merely absent. And the flames of Robert Gerald's hair had kindled embers he had thought safely smothered.

It might be unwise to feed that spark, he thought, freeing his soldier's cloak from the grasp of an importunate beggar. Open flames were dangerous, and he knew that as well as any man. And yet . . . hours of buffeting through London's crowds and hours more of enforced sociality had filled him with such unexpected longing for the quiet of the North that he found himself filled suddenly with the desire to speak of Scotland, if nothing more.

They had passed the Royal Exchange in the course of their errands; he had glanced covertly toward the Arcade, with its gaudy paint and tattered posters, its tawdry crowds of hawkers and strollers, and felt a soft spasm of anticipation. It was autumn; the dark came early.

They were near the river now; the noise of clamoring cocklesellers and fishmongers rang in the winding alleys, and a cold wind filled with the invigorating stench of tar and wood shavings bellied out their cloaks like sails. Quarry turned and waved above the heads of the intervening throng, gesturing toward a coffeehouse; Grey nodded in reply, lowered his head, and elbowed his way toward the door.

'Such a press,' Lord John said, pushing his way after Quarry into the relative peace of the small, spice-scented room. He took off his tricorne and sat down, tenderly adjusting the red cockade, knocked askew by contact with the populace. Slightly shorter than the common height, Grey found himself at a disadvantage in crowds.

'I had forgot what a seething anthill London is.' He took a deep breath; grasp the nettle, then, and get it over. 'A contrast with Ardsmuir, to be sure.'

'I'd forgot what a misbegotten lonely hellhole Scotland is,' Quarry replied, 'until you turned up at the Beefsteak this morning to remind me of my blessings. Here's to anthills!' He lifted the steaming glass which had appeared as by magic at his elbow, and bowed ceremoniously to Grey. He drank, and shuddered, either in memory of Scotland or in answer to the quality of the coffee. He frowned, and reached for the sugar bowl.

'Thank God we're both well out of it. Freezing your arse off indoors or out, and the blasted rain coming in at every crack and window.' Quarry took off his wig and scratched his balding pate, quite without self-consciousness, then clapped it on again.

'No society but the damned dour-faced Scots, either; never had a whore there who didn't give me the feeling she'd as soon cut it off as serve it. I swear I'd have put a pistol to my head in another month

11

had you not come to relieve me, Grey. What poor bugger took over from you?'

'No one.' Grey scratched at his own fair hair abstractedly, infected by Quarry's itch. He glanced outside; the street was still jammed, but the crowd's noise was mercifully muffled by the leaded glass. One sedan chair had run into another, its bearers knocked off balance by the crowd. 'Ardsmuir is no longer a prison; the prisoners were transported.'

'Transported?' Quarry pursed his lips in surprise, then sipped, more cautiously. 'Well, and serve them right, the miserable whoresons. Hmm!' He grunted, and shook his head over the coffee. 'No more than most deserve. A shame for Fraser, though – you recall a man named Fraser, big red-haired fellow? One of the Jacobite officers – a gentleman. Quite liked him,' Quarry said, his roughly cheerful countenance sobering slightly. 'Too bad. Did you find occasion to speak with him?'

'Now and then.' Grey felt a familiar clench of his innards, and turned away, lest anything show on his face. Both sedan chairs were down now, the bearers shouting and shoving. The street was narrow to begin with, clogged with the normal traffic of tradesmen and 'prentices; customers stopping to watch the altercation added to the impassibility.

'You knew him well?' He could not help himself; whether it brought him comfort or misery, he felt he had no choice now but to speak of Fraser – and Quarry was the only man in London to whom he could so speak.

'Oh, yes – or as well as one might know a man in that situation,' Quarry replied offhandedly. 'Had him to dine in my quarters every week; very civil in his speech, good hand at cards.' He lifted a fleshy nose from his glass, cheeks flushed ruddier than usual with the steam. 'He wasn't one to invite pity, of course, but one could scarce help but feel some sympathy for his circumstances.'

'Sympathy? And yet you left him in chains.'

Quarry looked up sharply, catching the edge in Grey's words.

'I may have liked the man; I didn't trust him. Not after what happened to one of my sergeants.'

'And what was that?' Lord John managed to infuse the question with no more than light interest.

'Misadventure. Drowned by accident in the stone-quarry pool,' Quarry said, dumping several teaspoons of rock sugar into a fresh glass and stirring vigorously. 'Or so I wrote in the report.' He looked up from his coffee, and gave Grey his lewd, lopsided wink. 'I liked Fraser. Didn't care for the sergeant. But never think a man is helpless, Grey, only because he's fettered.'

Grey sought urgently for a way to inquire further without letting his passionate interest be seen.

'So you believe—' he began.

'Look,' said Quarry, rising suddenly from his seat. 'Look! Damned if it's not Bob Gerald!'

Lord John whipped round in his chair. Sure enough, the late-afternoon sun struck sparks from a fiery head, bent as its owner emerged from one of the stalled sedan chairs. Gerald straightened, face set in a puzzled frown, and began to push his way into the knot of embattled bearers.

'Whatever is he about, I wonder? Surely— Hi! Hold! Hold, you blackguard!' Dropping his glass unregarded, Quarry rushed toward the door, bellowing.

Grey, a step or two behind, saw no more than the flash of metal in the sun and the brief look of startlement on Gerald's face. Then the crowd fell back, with a massed cry of horror, and his view was obscured by a throng of heaving backs.

He fought his way through the screaming mob without compunction, striking ruthlessly with his sword hilt to clear the way.

Gerald was lying in the arms of one of his bearers, hair fallen forward, hiding his face. The young man's knees were drawn up in agony, balled fists pressed hard against the growing stain on his waistcoat.

Quarry was there; he brandished his sword at the crowd, bellowing threats to keep them back, then glared wildly round for a foe to skewer.

'Who?' he shouted at the bearers, face congested with fury. 'Who's done this?'

The circle of white faces turned in helpless question, one to another, but found no focus; the foe had fled, and his bearers with him.

Grey knelt in the gutter, careless of filth, and smoothed back the ruddy hair with hands gone stiff and cold. The hot stink of blood was thick in the air, and the fecal smell of pierced intestine. Grey had seen battlefields enough to know the truth even before he saw the glazing eyes, the pallid face. He felt a deep, sharp stab at the sight, as though his own guts were pierced, as well.

Brown eyes fixed wide on his, a spark of recognition deep behind the shock and pain. He seized the dying man's hand in his, and chafed it, knowing the futility of the gesture. Gerald's mouth worked, soundless. A bubble of red spittle swelled at the corner of his lips.

'Tell me.' Grey bent urgently to the man's ear, and felt the soft brush of hair against his mouth. 'Tell me who has done it – I will avenge you. I swear it.'

He felt a slight spasm of the fingers in his, and squeezed back, hard, as though he might force some of his own strength into Gerald; enough for a word, a name.

The soft lips were blanched, the blood bubble growing. Gerald drew back the corners of his mouth, a fierce, tooth-baring rictus that burst the bubble and sent a spray of blood across Grey's cheek. Then the lips drew in, pursing in what might have been the invitation to a kiss. Then he died, and the wide brown eyes went blank.

Quarry was shouting at the bearers, demanding information. More shouts echoed down the walls of the streets, the nearby alleys, news flying from the scene of murder like bats out of hell.

Grey knelt alone in the silence near the dead

man, in the stench of blood and voided bowels. Gently, he laid Gerald's hand limp across his wounded breast, and wiped the blood from his own hand, unthinking, on his cloak.

A motion drew his eye. Harry Quarry knelt on the other side of the body, his face gone white as the scar on his cheek, prying open a large clasp knife. He searched gently through Gerald's loosened, blood-matted hair, and drew out a clean lock, which he cut off. The sun was setting; light caught the hair as it fell, a curl of vivid flame.

'For his mother,' Quarry explained. Lips tightly pressed together, he coiled the gleaming strand and put it carefully away.

Part II

Intrigue

The invitation came two days later, and with it a note from Harry Quarry. Lord John Grey was bidden to an evening's entertainment at Joffrey House, by desire of the Lady Lucinda Joffrey. Quarry's note said simply, *Come. I have news.*

And not beforetimes, Grey thought, tossing the note aside. The two days since Gerald's death had been filled with frantic activity, with inquiry and speculation – to no avail. Every shop and barrow in Forby Street had been turned over thoroughly, but no trace found of the assailant or his minions; they had faded into the crowd, anonymous as ants.

That proved one thing, at least, Grey thought. It was a planned attack, not a random piece of street violence. For the assailant to vanish so quickly, he must have looked like hoi polloi; a prosperous merchant or a noble would have stood out by his bearing and the manner of his dress. The sedan chair had been hired; no one recalled the appearance of the hirer, and the name given was – not surprisingly – false.

He shuffled restlessly through the rest of the mail. All other avenues of inquiry had proven fruitless so far. No weapon had been found. He and Quarry had sought the hall porter at the Beefsteak, in hopes that the man had heard somewhat of the conversation between Gerald and Bubb-Dodington, but the man was a temporary servant, hired for the day, and had since taken his wages and vanished, no doubt to drink them.

Grey had canvassed his acquaintance for any rumor of enemies, or failing that, for any history of the late Robert Gerald that might bear a hint of motive for the crime. Gerald was evidently known, in a modest way, in government circles and the venues of respectable society, but he had no great money to leave, no heirs save his mother, no hint of any romantic entanglement – in short, there was no intimation whatever of an association that might have led to that bloody death in Forby Street.

He paused, eye caught by an unfamiliar seal. A note, signed by one G. Bubb-Dodington, requesting a few moments of his time, in a convenient season – and noting *en passant* that B-D would himself be present at Joffrey House that evening, should Lord John find himself likewise engaged.

He picked up Quarry's note again, and found another sheet of paper folded up behind it. Unfolded, this proved to be a broadsheet, printed with a poem – or at the least, words arranged in the form of verse. 'A Blot Removed,' it was titled. Lacking in meter, but not in crude wit, the doggerel gave the story of a 'he-whore' whose lewdities outraged the public, until 'scandal flamed up, blood-red as the abominable color of his hair,' and an unknown savior rose up to destroy the perverse, thus wiping clean the pristine parchment of society.

Lord John had eaten no breakfast, and sight of this extinguished what vestiges he had of appetite. He carried the document into the morning room, and fed it carefully to the fire.

Joffrey House was a small but elegant white stone mansion, just off Eaton Square. Grey had never come there before, but the house was well known for brilliant parties, much frequented by those with a taste for politics; Sir Richard Joffrey, Quarry's elder half brother, was influential.

As Grey came up the marble steps, he saw a member of Parliament and the First Sea Lord, close in converse ahead of him, and perceived a considerable array of discreetly elegant carriages standing at a distance in the street. Something of an occasion, then; he was a trifle surprised that Lady Lucinda should be entertaining on such a scale, on the heels of her cousin's assassination – Quarry had said she was close to Gerald.

Quarry was on the *qui vive;* Grey had no sooner been announced than he found himself seized by the arm and drawn out of the slowly moving reception line, into the shelter of a monstrous plant that had been stood in the corner of the ballroom, where it consorted with several of its fellows in the manner of a small jungle.

'You came, then,' Quarry said, unnecessarily.

Seeing the haggard aspect of the man, Grey said merely, 'Yes. What news?'

Fatigue and distress tended merely to sharpen Grey's fine-cut features, but gave Quarry an air of snappish ferocity, making him look like a large, ill-tempered dog.

'You saw that – that – unspeakable piece of excrement?'

'The broadsheet? Yes; where did you get it?'

'They are all over London; not only that particular excrescence – many others, as vile or worse.'

Grey felt a prick of deep unease.

'With similar accusations?'

'That Robert Gerald was a pederast? Yes, and worse; that he was a member of a notorious sodomitical society, a gathering for the purpose of . . . well, you'll know the sort of thing? Disgusting!'

Grey could not tell whether this last epithet was applied to the existence of such societies, or to the association of Gerald's name with one. In consequence, he chose his words with care.

'Yes, I have heard of such associations.'

Grey did know, though the knowledge was not personal; such societies were said to be common – he knew of taverns and back rooms aplenty, to say nothing of the more notorious mollyhouses, where . . . Still, fastidiousness and caution had prevented any close inquiry into these assemblies.

'Need I say that – that such accusations have no truth – not the slightest pretention to truth?'

Quarry spoke with some difficulty, avoiding Grey's eye. Grey laid a hand on Quarry's sleeve.

'No, you need not say so. I am certain of it,' he said quietly. Quarry glanced up, giving him a half-embarrassed smile, and clasped his hand briefly.

'Thank you,' he said, voice rasping.

'But if it be not so,' Grey observed, giving Quarry time to recover himself, 'then such rapid profusion of rumor has the taste about it of an organized calumny. And that in itself is very strange, do you not think?'

Evidently not; Quarry looked blankly at him.

'Someone wished not only to destroy Robert Gerald,' Grey explained, 'but thought it necessary also to blacken his name. Why? The man is dead; who would think it needful to murder his reputation, as well?'

Quarry looked startled, then frowned, brows drawing close together in the effort of thought.

' 'Strewth,' he said slowly. 'Damme, you're right. But who . . . ?' He stopped, looking thoughtfully out over the assemblage of guests.

'Is the prime minister here?' Grey peered through the drooping foliage. It was a small but brilliant party, and one of a particular kind; no more than forty guests, and these all drawn from the echelons of power. No mincing fops or gadding henwits; ladies there were, to be sure, providing grace and beauty – but it was the men who were of consequence. Several ministers were in attendance, the sea lord, an assistant minister of finance . . . He stopped, feeling as though someone had just punched him hard in the belly.

Quarry was muttering in his ear, explaining something about the prime minister's absence, but Grey was no longer attending. He fought the urge to step back farther into the shadows.

George Everett was looking well – very well indeed. Wig and powder set off the blackness of his brows and the fine dark eyes below them. A firm chin and a long, mobile mouth – Grey's index finger twitched involuntarily, tracing the line of it in memory.

'Are you well, Grey?' Quarry's gruff voice recalled him to himself.

'Yes. A trifling indisposition, no more.' Grey pulled his eyes away from Everett's slim figure, striking in black and primrose. It was only a matter of time, after all; he had known they would meet again – and at least he had not been taken unawares. With an effort, he turned his attention back to Quarry.

'The news you mentioned. Is it—'

Quarry interrupted, gripping his arm and pulling him out from the shelter of the trees into the babble of the party.

'Hark, here is Lucinda. Come, she wishes to meet you.'

Lady Lucinda Joffrey was small and round, her dark hair worn unpowdered, sleek to the skull, and her ringlets fastened with an ornament of pheasant's feathers that went well with her russet gown. Her face was plump and rather plain, though it might have some claim to character, had there been much life to it. Instead, swollen lids drooped over eyes smudged with shadows she had not bothered to disguise.

Lord John bowed over her hand, wondering again as he did so what had caused her to open her house this evening; plainly she was in great distress.

'My lord,' she murmured, in response to his courtesies. Then she lifted her eyes and he found himself startled. Her eyes were beautiful, almond-shaped and clear gray in color – and despite their reddened lids, clear and piercing with intelligence.

'Harry tells me that you were with Robert when he died,' she said, softly but clearly, holding him with those eyes. 'And that you have offered your help in finding the dastard who has done this thing.'

'Indeed. I offer you my most sincere condolences, my lady.'

'I thank you, sir.' She nodded toward the room, bright with guests and blazing candles. 'You will find it strange, no doubt, that we should revel in such fashion, and my cousin so recently and despicably slain?' Grey began to make the expected demur, but she would not allow it, going on before he could speak.

'It was my husband's wish. He said we must – that to shrink and cower before such slander would be to grant it credence. He insisted that we must meet it boldly, or suffer ourselves from the stain of scandal.' Her lips pressed tight, a handkerchief crumpled in her hand, but no tears welled in the gray eyes.

'Your husband is wise.' That was a thought; Sir Richard Joffrey was an influential member of Parliament, with a shrewd appreciation of politics, a great acquaintance with those in power – and the money to influence them. Could the killing of Gerald and this posthumous effort to discredit him be in some way a blow at Sir Richard?

Grey hesitated; he had not yet told Quarry of Gerald's request at the club. *There is no one I can confide in,* Gerald had said – and presumably included his cousin by marriage therein. But Gerald was dead, and Grey's obligation was now vengeance, not confidence. The musicians had paused; with a tilt of the head, Grey drew his companions back into the privacy of the jungle.

'Madam, I had the honor of a very brief acquaintance with your cousin. Still, when I met him . . .' In a few words, he acquainted his hearers with Robert Gerald's last request.

'Does either of you know what his concern might have been?' Grey asked, looking from one to the other. The musicians were starting up, the strains of fiddle and flute rising above the rumble of conversation.

'He asked you to meet him on the 'Change?' A shadow passed over Quarry's face. If Gropecunt Street was the main thoroughfare for female prostitution, the Royal Exchange was its male counterpart – after dark, at least.

'That means nothing, Harry,' Lucinda said. Her grief had been subsumed by interest, plump figure drawn erect. 'The 'Change is a meeting place for every kind of intrigue. I am sure Robert's choice of meeting place had nothing to do with – with these scurrilous accusations.' Lady Lucinda frowned. 'But I know of nothing that would have caused my cousin such concern – do you, Harry?'

'If I did, I would have said so,' Quarry said irritably. 'Since he did not think me fit to confide in, though—'

'You mentioned some news,' Grey interrupted, seeking to avert acrimony. 'What was that?'

'Oh.' Quarry stopped, irritation fading. 'I've gleaned a notion of what Bubb-Dodington's invitation consisted.' Quarry cast a glance of unconcealed dislike toward a knot of men gathered talking at the opposite side of the room. 'And if my informant be correct, 'twas far from innocent.'

'Which is Bubb-Dodington? Is he here?'

'Indeed.' Lucinda pointed with her fan. 'Standing by the hearth – in the reddish suit.'

Grey squinted through the haze of hearth smoke and candle glow, picking out a slender figure in bagwig and rose velvet – fashionable, to be sure, but seeming somehow slightly fawning in attitude, as he leaned toward another of the group.

'I have inquired regarding him,' Grey said. 'I hear he is a political, but one of no great consequence; a mere time-server.'

'True, he is nothing in himself. His associations, though, are more substantial. Those with whom he allies himself are scarcely without power, though not – not yet! – in control.'

'And who are those? I am quite ignorant of politics these days.'

'Sir Francis Dashwood, John Wilkes, Mr. Churchill . . . Paul Whitehead, too. Oh, and Everett. You know George Everett?'

'We are acquainted,' Grey said equably. 'The invitation you mentioned . . . ?'

'Oh, yes.' Quarry shook his head, recalled to himself. 'I finally discovered the whereabouts of the hall porter. He had overheard enough of Bubb-Dodington's conversation to say that the man was urging Gerald to accept an invitation to stay at West Wycombe.'

Quarry raised his brows high in implication, but Grey remained ignorant and said so.

'West Wycombe is the home of Sir Francis Dashwood,' Lady Lucinda put in. 'And the center of his influence. He entertains there lavishly, even as we do' – her plump mouth made a small moue of deprecation – 'and to the same purposes.'

'The seduction of the powerful?' Grey smiled. 'So Bubb-Dodington – or his masters – sought to entice Gerald? To what end, I wonder?'

'Richard calls the West Wycombe assemblage a nest of vipers,' Lucinda said. 'Bent upon achieving their ends by any means, even dishonorable ones. Perhaps they sought to lure Robert into their camp for the sake of his own virtues, or' – she paused, hesitant – 'for the sake of what he might know regarding the prime minister's affairs?'

The music was starting afresh at the far end of the room, and they were interrupted at this delicate moment by a lady who, spotting them in their leafy refuge, came bustling in to claim Harry Quarry for a dance, waving aside all possibility of refusal with an airy fan.

'Is that not Lady Fitzwalter?' Buxom and high-colored, the lady now pressing Quarry's hand provocatively to her breast was the wife of Sir Hugh, an elderly baronet from Sussex. Quarry appeared to have no objections, following up Lady F's flirtations with a jocular pinch.

'Oh, Harry fancies himself a great rake,' Lady Lucinda said tolerantly, 'though anyone can see it comes to nothing more than a hand of cards in the gentlemen's clubs and an eye for shapely flesh. Is any officer in London greatly different?' A shrewd gray eye passed over Lord John, inquiring as to what his own differences might be.

'Indeed,' he said, amused. 'And yet he was sent to Scotland for some indiscretion, I collect. Was it not the incident that left him with that slash across the face?'

'Oh, la,' she said, pursing up her mouth in scorn. 'The famous scar! One would think it the Order of the Garter, he do flaunt it so. No, no, 'twas the cards that were the cause of his exile – he caught a Colonel of the regiment a-cheating at loo, and was too much gone in wine to keep a decent silence on the point.'

Grey opened his mouth to inquire about the scar, but was silenced himself by her grip upon his sleeve.

'Now, there's a rake, if you want one,' she said, low-voiced. Her eyes marked out a man across the room, near the hearth. 'Dashwood; him Harry spoke of. Know of him, do you?'

Grey squinted against the haze of smoke in the room. The man was heavy-bodied, but betrayed no softness of flesh; the sloping shoulders were thick with muscle, and if waist and calves were thick as well, it was by a natural inclination of form, rather than the result of indulgence.

'I have heard the name,' Grey said. 'A political of some minor repute?'

'In the arena of politics, yes,' Lady Lucinda agreed, not taking her eyes from the man. 'In others . . . less minor. In fact, his repute in some circles is nothing short of outright notoriety.'

A reach for a glass stretched the satin of Dashwood's broidered plum-silk waistcoat tight across a broad chest, and brought into view a face, likewise broad, ruddy in the candle glow and animated with a cynic laughter. He wore no wig, but had a quantity of dark hair, curling low across the brow. Grey furrowed his own brow in the effort of recall; someone had said something to him, yes – but the occasion escaped him, as did its content.

'He seems a man of substance,' he hazarded. Certainly Dashwood was the cynosure of his end of the room, all eyes upon him as he spoke.

Lady Lucinda uttered a short laugh.

'Do you think so, sir? He and his friends flaunt their practice of licentiousness and blasphemy as Harry flaunts his scar – and from the same cause.'

It was the word 'blasphemy' that brought back recollection.

'Ha. I have heard mention . . . Medmenham Abbey?'

Lucinda's lips pursed tight, and she nodded. 'The Hellfire Club, they call it.'

'Indeed. There have been Hellfire clubs before – many of them. Is this one more than the usual excuse for public riot and drunken license?'

She looked at the men before the fire, her countenance troubled. With the light of the blaze behind them, all individuality of lineament was lost; they appeared no more than an assemblage of dark figures; faceless devils, outlined by the firelight.

'I think not,' she said, very low-voiced, glancing to and fro to assure they were unheard. 'Or so I *did* think – until I heard of the invitation to Robert. Now . . .'

The advent near the jungle of a tall, good-looking man whose resemblance to Quarry made his identity clear put an end to the clandestine conference.

'There is Sir Richard; he is looking for me.' Poised to take flight, Lady Lucinda stopped and looked back at Grey. 'I cannot say, sir, what reason you may have for your interest – but I do thank you for it.' A flicker of wryness lit the gray eyes.

'Godspeed you, sir – though for myself, I should not much respect a God so petty as to be concerned with such as Francis Dashwood.'

Grey passed into the general crowd, bowing and smiling, allowing himself to be drawn into a dance here, a conversation there; keeping all the time one eye upon the group near the hearth. Men joined it for a short time, fell away, and were replaced by others, yet the central group remained unchanged.

Bubb-Dodington and Dashwood were the center of it; Churchill, the poet John Wilkes, and the Earl of Sandwich surrounded them. Seeing at one point during a break in the music that a good many had gathered by the hearth, men and women alike, Grey thought the moment ripe to make his own presence known, and unobtrusively joined the crowd, maneuvering to a spot near Bubb-Dodington.

Mr. Justice Margrave was holding the floor, speaking of the subject which had formed the meat of most conversations Grey had heard so far – the death of Robert Gerald, or more particularly, the rash of rumor and scandal that followed it. The judge caught Grey's eye and nodded – his worship was well acquainted with Grey's family – but continued his denunciation unimpeded.

'I should wish that, rather than the pillory, the stake be the punishment for such abominable vice.' Margrave swung a heavy head in Grey's direction, eyelids dropping half closed. 'Have you read Holloway's notion, sir? He suggests that this disgusting practice of sodomy be restrained by castration or some other cogent preventative.'

Grey restrained the urge to clasp himself protectively.

'Cogent, indeed,' he said. 'You suppose the man who cut down Robert Gerald to be impelled by moralistic motives, then?'

'Whether he were or no, I should say he has rendered signal service to society, ridding us of an exponent of this moral blight.'

Grey observed Harry Quarry standing a yard away, gleaming eyes fixed upon the elderly justice in a manner calculated to cause the utmost concern for that worthy's future prospects. Turning away, lest his acknowledgment embolden Quarry to open violence, he found himself instead face to face with George Everett.

'John,' Everett said softly, smiling.

'Mr. Everett.' Grey inclined his head politely. Nothing squelched, Everett continued to smile. He was a handsome devil, and he knew it.

'You are in good looks, John. Exile agrees with you, it seems.' The long mouth widened, curling at the corner.

'Indeed. I must take pains to go away more often, then.' His heart was beating faster. Everett's perfume was his accustomed musk and myrrh; the scent of it conjured tumbled linens, and the touch of hard and knowing hands.

A hoarse voice near his shoulder provided welcome distraction.

'Lord John? Your servant, sir.'

Grey turned to find the gentleman in rose velvet bowing to him, a look of spurious cordiality fixed upon saturnine features.

'Mr. Bubb-Dodington, I collect. I am obliged, sir.' He bowed in turn, and allowed himself to be separated from Everett, who stood looking after them, a faint smile upon his lips.

So conscious was he of Everett's eyes burning holes in his back that he scarce attended to Bubb-Dodington's overtures, replying automatically to the man's courtesies and inquiries. It was not until the rasping voice mentioned the word 'Medmenham' that he was jerked into attention, to realize that he had just received a most interesting invitation.

'. . . would find us a most congenial assembly, I am sure,' Bubb-Dodington was saying, leaning toward Grey with that same attitude of fawning attention he had noted earlier.

'You feel I would be in sympathy with the interests of your society?' Grey contrived to infuse a faint tone of boredom, looking away from the man. Just over Bubb-Dodington's shoulder, he was conscious of the figure of Sir Francis Dashwood, dark and bulky. Dashwood's deep-set eyes rested upon them, even as he carried on a conversation, and a ripple of apprehension raised the hairs on the back of Grey's neck.

'I am flattered, but I scarcely think . . .' he began, turning away.

'Oh, do not think you would be quite strange!'

Bubb-Dodington interrupted, beaming with oily deprecation. 'You are acquainted with Mr. Everett, I think? He will make one of our number.'

'Indeed.' Grey's mouth had gone dry. 'I see. Well, you must allow me to consult . . .' Muttering excuses, he escaped, finding refuge a moment later in the company of Harry Quarry and his sister-in-law, sharing cups of brandy punch at the nearby buffet.

'It galls me,' Harry was saying, 'that such petty time-servers and flaunting jackanapes make my kin to be the equal of the he-strumpets and buggerantoes that infest the Arcade. I've known Bob Gerald from a lad, and I will swear my life upon his honor!' Quarry's large hand clenched upon his glass as he glowered at Mr. Justice Margrave's back.

'Have a care, Harry, my dear.' Lucinda placed a hand on his sleeve. 'Those are my good crystal cups. If you must crush something, let it be the hazelnuts.'

'I shall let it be that fellow's windpipe, and he does not cease to air his idiocy,' said Quarry. He scowled horridly, but suffered himself to be turned away, still talking. 'What can Richard be thinking of, to entertain such scum? Dashwood, I mean, and now this . . .'

Grey started, and felt a chill down his spine. Quarry's blunt features bore no trace of resemblance to his dead cousin-by-marriage, and yet – his face contorted with fury, eyes bulging slightly as he spoke . . . Grey closed his eyes tightly, summoning the vision.

He left Quarry and Lady Lucinda abruptly, without excuse, and made his way hastily to the large gilded mirror that hung above a sideboard in the dining room.

Leaning over the skeletal remains of a roasted pheasant, he stared at his mouth – painstakingly forming the shapes he had seen on Robert Gerald's mouth – and now again on Harry Quarry's, hearing in his mind as he made them the sound of Robert Gerald's effortful – but unvoiced – last word.

'Dashwood.'

Quarry had followed him, brows drawn down in puzzlement.

'What the devil, Grey? Why are you making faces in the mirror? Are you ill?'

'No,' said Grey, though in fact he felt very ill. He stared at his own image in the mirror, as though it were some ghastly specter.

Another face appeared, and dark eyes met his own in the mirror. The two reflections were close in size and form, both possessed of a tidy muscularity and a fineness of feature that had led more than one observer to remark in company that they could be twins – one light, one dark.

'You will come to Medmenham, won't you?' The murmured words were warm in his ear, George's body so close that he could feel the pressure of hip and thigh. Everett's hand touched his, lightly.

'I should . . . particularly desire it.'

Part III

Christened in Blood

Medmenham Abbey
West Wycombe

It was not until the third night at Medmenham that anything untoward occurred. To that point – despite Quarry's loudly expressed doubts beforehand – it had been a house party much like any other in Lord John's experience, though with more talk of politics and less of hunting than was customary.

In spite of the talk and entertainment, though, there was an odd air of secrecy about the house. Whether it was some attitude on the part of the servants, or something unseen but sensed among the guests, Grey could not tell, but it was real; it floated on the air of the Abbey like smoke on water.

The only other oddity was the lack of women. While females of good family from the countryside near West Wycombe were invited to dine, all of the houseguests were male. The thought occurred to Grey that from outward appearance, it might almost be one of those sodomitical societies so decried in the London broadsheets. In appearance only, though; there was no hint of such behavior. Even George

Everett gave no hint of any sentiment save the amiability of renewed friendship.

No, it was not that kind of behavior that had given Sir Francis and his restored abbey the name of scandal. Exactly what *did* lie behind the whispers of notoriety was yet a mystery.

Grey knew one thing: Dashwood was not Gerald's murderer, at least not directly. Discreet inquiry had established Sir Francis's whereabouts, and shown him far from Forby Street at the time of the outrage. There was the possibility of hired assassination, though, and Robert Gerald had seen *something* in the moment of his death that caused him to utter that last silent accusation.

There was nothing so far to which Grey could point as evidence, either of guilt or depravity. Still, if evidence was to be found anywhere, it must be at Medmenham – the deconsecrated abbey which Sir Francis had restored from ruins and made a showplace for his political ambitions.

Among the talk and entertainments, though, Grey was conscious of a silent process of evaluation, plain in the eyes and manner of his companions. He was being watched, his fitness gauged – but for what?

'What is it that Sir Francis wants with me?' he had asked bluntly, walking in the gardens with Everett on the second afternoon. 'I have nothing to appeal to such a man.'

George smiled. He wore his own hair, dark and shining, and the chilly breeze stroked strands of it across his cheeks.

'You underestimate your own merits, John – as always. Of course, nothing becomes manly virtue more than simple modesty.' He glanced sidelong, mouth quirking with appreciation.

'I scarce think my personal attributes are sufficient to intrigue a man of Dashwood's character,' Grey answered dryly.

'More to the point,' Everett said, arching one brow, 'what is it in Sir Francis that so intrigues *you*? You have not spoke of anything, save to question me about him.'

'You would be better suited to answer that than I,' Grey answered boldly. 'I hear you are an intimate – the valet tells me you have been a guest at Medmenham many times this year past. What is it draws *you* to seek his company?'

George grunted in amusement, then flung back his head, breathing in the damp air with enjoyment. Lord John did likewise; autumn smells of leaf mold and chimney smoke, spiced with the tang of ripe muscats from the arbor nearby. Scents to stir the blood; cold air to sting cheeks and hands, exercise to stimulate and weary the limbs, making the glowing leisure of the fireside and the comforts of a dark, warm bed so appealing by contrast.

'Power,' George said at last. He lifted a hand toward the Abbey – an impressive pile of gray stone, at once stalwart in shape and delicate in design. 'Dashwood aspires to great things; I would join him on that upward reach.' He cast a glance at Grey. 'And you, John? It has been some time since I presumed to know you, and yet I should not have said that a thirst for social influence formed much part of your own desires.'

Grey wished no discussion of his desires; not at the moment.

' "The desire of power in excess caused the angels to fall," ' he quoted.

' "The desire of knowledge in excess caused man to fall." ' George completed the quote, and uttered a short laugh. 'What is it that you seek to know then, John?' He turned his head toward Grey, dark eyes creased against the wind, and smiled as though he knew the answer.

'The truth of the death of Robert Gerald.'

He had mentioned Gerald to each of the house party in turn, choosing his moment, probing delicately. No delicacy here; he wished to shock, and did so. George's face went comically blank, then hardened into disapproval.

'Why do you seek to entangle yourself in that sordid affair?' he demanded. 'Such association cannot but harm your own reputation – such as it is.'

That stung, as it was meant to.

'My reputation is my own affair,' Grey said, 'as are my reasons. Did you know Gerald?'

'No,' Everett answered shortly. By unspoken consent, they turned toward the Abbey, and walked back in silence.

On the third day, something changed. A sense of nervous anticipation seemed to pervade the air, and the air of secrecy grew heavier. Grey felt as though some stifling lid pressed down upon the Abbey, and spent as much time as possible out of doors.

Still, nothing untoward occurred during the day or evening, and he retired as usual, soon after ten o'clock. Dismissing the valet, he undressed alone. He was tired from his long rambles over the countryside, but it was early yet. He picked up a book, attempted to read, but the words seemed to slide away from his eyes. His head nodded, and he slept, sitting up in the chair.

The sound of the clock striking below in the hall woke him from uneasy dreams of dark pools and drowning. He sat up, a metal taste like blood in his mouth, and rubbed away the sleep from his eyes. Time for his nightly signal to Quarry.

Unwilling to allow Grey to risk such company alone, Quarry had followed Lord John to West Wycombe. He would, he insisted, there take up station in the meadow facing the guest wing each night, between the hours of eleven and one o'clock. Lord John was to pass a candle flame three times across the glass each night, as a sign that all was so far well.

Feeling ridiculous, Grey had done so on each of the first two nights. Tonight, he felt some small sense of reassurance as he bent to light his taper from the hearth. The house was silent, but not asleep. Something stirred, somewhere in the Abbey;

he could feel it. Perhaps the ghosts of the ancient monks – perhaps something else.

The candle flame showed the reflection of his own face, a wan oval in the glass, his light blue eyes gone to dark holes. He stood a moment, holding the flame, then blew it out and went to bed, obscurely more comforted by the thought of Harry outside than by the knowledge of George Everett in the next room.

He waked in darkness, to find his bed surrounded by monks. Or men dressed as monks; each wore a rope-belted robe and a deep-cowled hood, pulled far forward to hide the face. Beyond the first startled exclamation, he lay quiet. He might have thought them the ghosts of the Abbey, save that the reassuring scents of sweat and alcohol, of powder and pomade, told him otherwise.

None spoke, but hands pulled him from his bed and set him on his feet, stripped the nightshirt from his body, and helped him into a robe of his own. A hand cupped him intimately, a caress given under cover of darkness, and he breathed musk and myrrh.

No menaces were offered, and he knew his companions to be those men with whom he had broken bread at dinner. Still, his heart beat in his ears as he was conducted by darkened hallways into the garden, and then by lantern light through a maze of clipped yew. Beyond this, a path led down the side of a stony hill, curving into the darkness and finally turning back into the hillside itself.

Here they passed through a curious portal, this being an archway of wood and marble, carved into what he took to be the semblance of a woman's privates, opened wide. He examined this with curiosity; early experience with whores had made him vaguely familiar, but had afforded no opportunity for close inspection.

Once within this portal, a bell began to chime somewhere ahead. The 'monks' formed themselves into a line, two by two, and shuffled slowly forward, beginning to chant.

'Hocus-pocus,
Hoc est corpus . . .'

The chant continued in the same vein – a perversion of various well-known prayers, some merely foolish nonsense, some clever or openly bawdy. Grey restrained a sudden urge to laugh, and bit his lip to stop it.

The solemn procession wound its way deeper and he smelled damp rock; were they in a cave? Evidently; as the passage widened, he saw light ahead and entered eventually into a large chamber, set with candles, whose rough-hewn walls indicated that they were indeed in a catacomb of sorts. The impression was heightened by the presence of a number of human skulls, set grinning atop their crossed thigh bones, like so many Jolly Rogers.

Grey found himself pressed into a place near the wall. One figure, robed in a cardinal's red, came forward, and Sir Francis Dashwood's voice intoned the beginning of the rite. The rite itself was a parody of the Mass, enacted with great solemnity, invocations made to the Master of Darkness, the chalice formed of an upturned skull.

In all truth, Grey found the proceedings tedious in the extreme, enlivened only by the appearance of a large Barbary ape, attired in bishop's cope and miter, who appeared at the Consecration. The animal sprang upon the altar, where it gobbled and slobbered over the bread provided and spilled wine upon the floor. It would have been less entertaining, Grey thought, had the beast's ginger whiskers and seamed countenance not reminded him so strongly of the Bishop of Ely, an old friend of his mother's.

At the conclusion of this rite, the men went out, with considerably less solemnity than when they had come in. A good deal had been drunk in the course of the rite, and their behavior was less restrained than that of the ape.

Two men near the end of the line seized Grey by the arms and compelled him into a small alcove, around which the others had gathered. He found himself bent backward over a marble basin, the robe pushed down from his shoulders. Dashwood intoned a prayer in reverse Latin, and something warm and sticky cascaded over Grey's head, blinding him and causing him to struggle and curse in the grip of his captors.

'I baptize thee, child of Asmodeus, son of blood . . .' A kick from Grey's foot caught Dashwood under the chin and sent him reeling backward. A hard punch in the pit of the stomach knocked the breath from Grey and quieted him for the remainder of the brief ceremony.

Then they set him on his feet, bloodstained, and gave him drink from a jeweled cup. He tasted opium in the wine, and let as much as he dared dribble down his chin as he drank. Even so, he felt the dreamy tendrils of the drug steal through his mind, and his balance grew precarious, sending him lurching through the crowd, to the great hilarity of the robed onlookers.

Hands took him by the elbows and propelled him down a corridor, and another, and another. A draft of warm air, and he found himself thrust through a door, which closed behind him.

The chamber was small, furnished with nothing save a narrow couch against the far wall, and a table upon which stood a flagon, several glasses . . . and a knife. Grey staggered to the table, and braced himself with both hands to keep from falling.

There was a strange smell in the room. At first he thought he had vomited, sickened by blood and wine, but then he saw the pool of it, across the room by the bed. It was only then that he saw the girl.

She was young and naked and dead. Her body lay limp, sprawled white in the light, but her eyes were dull and her lips blue, the traces of sickness trailing down her face and across the bedclothes. Grey backed slowly away, shock washing the last remnants of the drug from his blood.

He rubbed both hands hard across his face, striving to think. What was this, why was he here, with the body of this young woman? He brought himself to come closer, to look. She was no one he had seen before; the calluses upon her hands and the state of her feet marked her as a servant or a country girl.

He turned sharply, went to the door. Locked, of course. But what was the point? He shook his head, his brain slowly clearing. Once clear, though, no answers came to mind. Blackmail, perhaps? It was true that Grey's family had influence, though he himself possessed none. But how could his presence here be put to such use?

It seemed he had spent forever in that buried room, pacing to and fro across the stone floor, until at last the door opened and a robed figure slipped through.

'George!'

'Bloody hell!' Ignoring Grey's turn toward him, Everett crossed the room and stood staring down at the girl, brows knit in consternation. 'What's happened?' he demanded, swinging toward Grey.

'You tell me. Or rather, let us leave this place, and then you tell me.'

Everett put out a quelling hand, urging silence. He thought for a moment, and then seemed to reach some conclusion. A slow smile grew across his face.

'Well enough,' he said softly, to himself. He turned and reached toward Grey's waist, pulling loose the cord that bound the robe closed. Grey made no move to cover himself, though filled with astonishment at the gesture, given the circumstances.

This astonishment was intensified in the next instant, as Everett bent over the bed and wrapped the cord round the neck of the dead woman, tugging hard to draw it tight, so the rope bit deep into flesh. He stood, smiled at Grey, then crossed to the table, where he poured two glasses of wine from the flagon.

'Here.' He handed one to Grey. 'Don't worry, it's not drugged. You aren't drugged now, are you? No, I see not; I thought you hadn't had enough.'

'Tell me what is happening.' Grey took the glass, but made no move to drink. 'Tell me, for God's sake!'

George smiled again, a queer look in his eyes, and picked up the knife. It was exotic in appearance; something Oriental, at least a foot long and wickedly sharp.

'It is the common initiation of the brotherhood,' he said. 'The new candidate, once approved, is baptized – it was pig's blood, by the way – and then brought to this room, where a woman is provided for his pleasure. Once his lust is slaked, an older brother comes to instruct him in the final rite of his acceptance – and to witness it.'

Grey raised a sleeve and wiped cold sweat and pig's blood from his forehead.

'And the nature of this final rite is—'

'Sacrificial.' George nodded acknowledgment toward the blade. 'The act not only completes the initiation, but also insures the initiate's silence and his loyalty to the brotherhood.'

A great coldness was creeping through Grey's limbs, making them stiff and heavy.

'And you have . . . have done this?'

'Yes.' Everett contemplated the form on the bed for a moment, one finger gently stroking the blade. At last he shook his head and sighed, murmuring to himself once more. 'No, I think not.'

He raised his eyes to Grey's, clear and shining in the lamplight. 'I would have spared you, I think, were it not for Bob Gerald.'

The glass felt slick in Grey's hand, but he forced himself to speak calmly.

'So you did know him. Was it you who killed him?'

Everett nodded slowly, not taking his gaze from Grey's.

'It is ironic, is it not?' he said softly. 'I desired membership in this brotherhood, whose watchword is vice, whose credo is wickedness – and yet had Bob Gerald told them what I am, they would have turned upon me like wolves. They hold all abomination dear – save one.'

'And Robert Gerald knew what you were? Yet he did not speak your name as he died.'

George shrugged, but his mouth twitched uneasily.

'He was a pretty lad, I thought – but I was wrong.

No, he didn't know my name, but we met here – at Medmenham. It would have made no difference, had they not chosen him to join us. Were he to come again, though, and see me here . . .'

'He would not have come again. He refused the invitation.'

George's eyes narrowed, gauging his truth; then he shrugged.

'Perhaps if I had known that, he need not have died. And if he had not died, you would not have been chosen yourself – would not have come? No. Well, there's irony again for you, I suppose. And still – I think I would have killed him under any circumstance; it was too dangerous.'

Grey had been keeping a watchful eye on the knife. He moved, unobtrusively, seeking to get the corner of the table betwixt himself and Everett.

'And the broadsheets? That was your doing?' He could, he thought, seize the table and throw it into Everett's legs, then try to overpower him. Disarmed, they were well-matched in strength.

'No, Whitehead's. He's the poet, after all.' George smiled and stepped back, out of range. 'They thought perhaps to take advantage of Gerald's death to discomfit Sir Richard – and chose that method, knowing nothing of his killer or the motive for his death. The greatest irony of all, is it not?'

George had moved the flagon out of reach. Grey stood half naked, with no weapon to hand save a glass of wine.

47

'So you intend now to procure my silence by claiming I am the murderer of this poor young woman?' Grey demanded, jerking his head toward the still figure on the bed. 'What happened to her?'

'Accident,' Everett said. 'The women are drugged; she must have vomited in her sleep and choked to death. But blackmail? No, that isn't what I mean to do.'

Everett squinted at the bed, then at Grey, measuring distance.

'You sought to use a noose for your sacrificial duty – some mislike blood – and though you succeeded, the girl managed to seize the knife and wound you, severely enough that you bled to death before I could return to aid you. Tragic accident; such a pity. Move a little closer to the bed, John.'

Never think a man is helpless, only because he's fettered. Grey flung his wine into Everett's face, then smashed his glass against the stones of the wall. He whirled on a heel and lunged upward, jabbing with all his might.

Everett grunted, one side of his handsome face laid open, spraying blood. He growled deep in his throat, baring bloody teeth, and ripped the blade across the air where Grey had stood a moment before. Half blinded by blood and snarling like a beast, he lunged and swung again. Grey ducked, was hit by a flying wrist, and fell across the woman's body. He rolled sideways, but was trapped by the folds of his robe.

The knife gleamed overhead. In desperation, he

threw up his legs and thrust both feet into Everett's chest, flinging him backward.

Everett staggered, flailing back across the room, half-caught himself, then froze abruptly. The expression on his face showed vast surprise. His hand loosened, dropping the knife, and then drew slowly through the air, graceful in gesture as the dancer that he was. His fingers touched the reddened steel protruding from his chest, acknowledging defeat. He slumped slowly to the floor.

Harry Quarry put a foot on Everett's back and freed his sword with a vicious yank.

'Good job I waited, wasn't it? Saw those buggers with their lanterns and all, and thought best I see what mischief was afoot.'

'Mischief,' Grey echoed. He stood up, or tried to. His knees had gone to water. 'You . . . did you hear?' His heart was beating very slowly; he wondered in a dreamy way whether it might stop any minute.

Quarry glanced at him, expression unreadable.

'I heard.' He wiped his sword, then sheathed it, and came to the bed, bending down to peer at Grey. How much had he heard, Grey wondered – and what had he made of it?

A rough hand brushed back his hair. He felt the stiffness matting it, and thought of Robert Gerald's mother.

'It's not my blood,' he said.

'Some of it is,' said Quarry, and traced a line down the side of his neck. In the wake of the touch,

he felt the sting of the cut, unnoticed in the moment
of infliction.

'Never fear,' said Quarry, and gave him a hand to
get up. 'It will make a pretty scar.'

'Lord John and the Succubus'

In 2003, I was invited to write a novella for an anthology edited by Robert Silverberg, titled *Legends II: New Short Novels by the Masters of Modern Fantasy*. I had slight reservations – as my World of War Craft–playing son asked, seeing the contract, 'Since when are you a modern master of fantasy, Mom?' – but (a) was very flattered to be asked to share a volume with George R. R. Martin, Terry Brooks, and Orson Scott Card, and (b) I'm inclined to regard the notion of literary genres in the same light as a Chinese menu, and (c) if I had a family motto, it would probably be 'Why not?' (the accompanying coat-of-arms being a stone circle quartered on a field of azure and crimson with rampant hippogriffs). So I did.

However, I had the same concerns regarding the main characters of the Outlander books that obtained when I wrote 'Hellfire.' Reflecting that it had worked once, so why not?, I decided to call Lord John into active duty once more.

The difficulty being, of course, that Lord John Grey is not a time-traveler, nor yet a telepath, a shape-shifter, nor even an inhabitant of an alternate universe loosely based on the history and culture of Scotland or Turkestan. But, on the other hand, there was no requirement that the main character of this putative novella be himself a creature of fantasy – and a story in which a perfectly normal (well, more or less) hero comes into conflict with supernatural creatures is a solid archetype. Hey, if it was good enough for Homer, it's good enough for me.

And so, 'Lord John and the Succubus' was published in 2004, as part of the *Legends II* anthology. In terms of Lord John's chronology, this story follows the novel, *Lord John and the Private Matter,* and in it, we renew our acquaintance with Tom Byrd, Lord John's valet, and his friend, Stephan von Namtzen. Set in Germany (which didn't actually exist as a political entity at the time, but was a recognizable geographical region) in the early phases of the Seven Years War, 'Succubus' is a supernatural murder mystery, with military flourishes.

LORD JOHN
and the
Succubus

Historical note: Between 1756 and 1763, Great Britain joined with her allies, Prussia and Hanover, to fight against the mingled forces of Austria, Saxony – and England's ancient foe, France. In the autumn of 1757, the Duke of Cumberland was obliged to surrender at Kloster-Zeven, leaving the allied armies temporarily shattered and the forces of Frederick the Great of Prussia and his English allies encircled by French and Austrian troops.

Chapter 1

Death Rides a Pale Horse

Grey's spoken German was improving by leaps and bounds, but found itself barely equal to the present task.

After a long, boring day of rain and paperwork, there had come the sound of loud dispute in the corridor outside his office, and the head of Lance-Korporal Helwig appeared in his doorway, wearing an apologetic expression.

'Major Grey?' he said '*Ich habe ein kleines Englische problem.*'

A moment later, Lance-Korporal Helwig had disappeared down the corridor like an eel sliding into mud, and Major John Grey, English liaison to the Imperial Fifth Regiment of Hanoverian Foot, found himself adjudicating a three-way dispute among an English private, a gypsy prostitute, and a Prussian tavern owner.

A little English problem, Helwig had described it as. The problem, as Grey saw it, was rather the *lack* of English.

The tavern owner spoke the local dialect with such fluency and speed that Grey grasped no more than one word in ten. The English private, who normally probably knew no more German than *'ja,'* *'nein,'* and the two or three crude phrases necessary to accomplish immoral transactions, was so stricken with fury that he was all but speechless in his own tongue, as well.

The gypsy, whose abundant charms were scarcely impaired by a missing tooth, had German that most nearly matched Grey's own in terms of grammar – though her vocabulary was immensely more colorful and detailed.

Using alternate hands to quell the sputterings of the private and the torrents of the Prussian, Grey concentrated his attention carefully on the gypsy's explanations – meanwhile taking care to consider the source, which meant discounting the factual basis of most of what she said.

'. . . and then the disgusting pig of an Englishman, he put his [incomprehensible colloquial expression] into my [unknown gypsy word]! And then . . .'

'She said, she said she'd do it for sixpence, sir! She did, she said so – but, but, but, then . . .'

'These-barbarian-pig-dogs-did-revolting-things-under-the-table-and-made-it-fall-over-so-the-leg-of-the-table-was-broken-and-the-dishes-broken-too-even-my-large-platter-which-cost-six-*thalers*-at-St.Martin's-Fair-and-the-meat-was-ruined-by-falling-on-the-floor-and-even-if-it-was-not-the-dogs-fell-upon-it-snarling-so-that-I-was-bitten-when-I-tried-to-seize-it-away-from-them-and-all-the-time-these-vile-persons-were-copulating-like-filthy-foxeson-the-floor-and-THEN . . .'

At length, an accommodation was reached, by means of Grey's demanding that all three parties produce what money was presently in their possession. A certain amount of shifty-eyed reluctance and dramatic pantomimes of purse and pocket-searching having resulted in three small heaps of silver and copper, he firmly rearranged these in terms of size and metal value, without reference as to the actual coinage involved, as these appeared to include the currency of at least six different principalities.

Eyeing the gypsy's ensemble, which included both gold earrings and a crude but broad gold band round her finger, he assigned roughly equitable heaps to her and to the private, whose name, when asked, proved to be Bodger.

Assigning a slightly larger heap to the tavern owner, he then scowled fiercely at the three combatants, jabbed a finger at the money, and jerked a thumb over his shoulder, indicating that they should take the coins and leave while he was still in possession of his temper.

This they did, and storing away a most interesting gypsy curse for future reference, Grey returned tranquilly to his interrupted correspondence.

To Harold, Earl of Melton
From Lord John Grey
The Township of Gundwitz
Kingdom of Prussia

My Lord—

In reply to your request for information regarding
my situation, I beg to say that I am well-suited.
My duties are . . .

He paused, considering, then wrote *interesting,*
smiling slightly to himself at thought of what
interpretation Hal might put upon that,

> *. . . and the conditions comfortable. I am quartered*
> *with several other English and German officers in*
> *the house of a Princess Louisa von Lowenstein, the*
> *widow of a minor Prussian noble, who possesses a*
> *fine estate near the town.*
>   *We have two English regiments quartered here:*
> *Sir Peter Hicks's 35th, and half of the 52nd – I*
> *am told Colonel Ruysdale is in command, but have*
> *not yet met him, the 52nd having arrived only*
> *days ago. As the Hanoverians to whom I am*
> *attached and a number of Prussian troops are*
> *occupying all the suitable quarters in the town,*
> *Hicks's men are encamped some way to the south;*
> *Ruysdale to the north.*
>   *French forces are reported to be within twenty*

miles, but we expect no immediate trouble. Still, so late in the year, the snow will come soon, and put an end to the fighting; they may try for a final thrust before the winter sets in. Sir Peter begs me send his regards.

He dipped his quill again, and changed tacks.

My grateful thanks to your good wife for the smallclothes, which are superior in quality to what is available here.

At this point, he was obliged to transfer the pen to his left hand in order to scratch ferociously at the inside of his left thigh. He was wearing a pair of the local German product under his breeches, and while they were well-laundered and not infested with vermin, they were made of coarse linen and appeared to have been starched with some sub-stance derived from potatoes, which was irritating in the extreme.

Tell Mother I am still intact, and not starving,

he concluded, transferring the pen back to his right hand.

Quite the reverse, in fact; Princess von Lowenstein has an excellent cook.
        Your Most Affec't. Brother,
                    J.

Sealing this with a brisk stamp of his half-moon signet, he then took down one of the ledgers and a stack of reports, and began the mechanical work of recording deaths and desertions. There was an outbreak of bloody flux among the men; more than a score had been lost to it in the last two weeks.

The thought brought the gypsy woman's last remarks to mind. Blood and bowels had both come into that, though he feared he had missed some of the refinements. Perhaps she had merely been trying to curse him with the flux?

He paused for a moment, twiddling the quill. It was rather uncommon for the flux to occur in the cold weather; it was more commonly a disease of hot summer, while winter was the season for consumption, catarrh, influenza, and fever.

He was not at all inclined to believe in curses, but did believe in poison. A whore would have ample opportunity to administer poison to her customers . . . but to what end? He turned to another folder of reports and shuffled through them, but saw no increase in the report of robbery or missing items – and the dead soldiers' comrades would certainly have noted anything of the kind. A man's belongings were sold by auction at his death, the money used to pay his debts and – if anything were left – to be sent to his family.

He put back the folder and shrugged, dismissing it. Illness and death trod closely in a soldier's footsteps, regardless of season or gypsy curse. Still, it might be worth warning Private Bodger to be wary of what he ate, particularly in the company of light-frigates and other dubious women.

A gentle rain had begun to fall again outside, and the sound of it against the windowpanes combined with the soothing shuffle of paper and scratch of quill to induce a pleasant sense of mindless drowsiness. He was disturbed from this trancelike state by the sound of footsteps on the wooden stair.

Captain Stephan von Namtzen, Landgrave von Erdberg, poked his handsome blond head through the doorway, ducking automatically to avoid braining himself on the lintel. The gentleman following him had no such difficulty, being a foot or so shorter.

'Captain von Namtzen,' Grey said, standing politely. 'May I be of assistance?'

'I have here Herr Blomberg,' Stephan said in English, indicating the small, round, nervous-looking individual who accompanied him. 'He wishes to borrow your horse.'

Grey was sufficiently startled by this that he merely said, 'Which one?' rather than 'Who is Herr Blomberg?' or 'What does he want with a horse?'

The first of these questions was largely academic in any case; Herr Blomberg wore an elaborate chain of office about his neck, done in broad, flat links of enamel and chased gold, from which depended a seven-pointed starburst, enclosing a plaque of enamel on which was painted some scene of historic interest. Herr Blomberg's engraved silver coat buttons and shoe buckles were sufficient to proclaim his wealth; the chain of office merely confirmed his importance as being secular, rather than noble.

'Herr Blomberg is bürgermeister of the town,' Stephan explained, taking matters in a strictly logical order of importance, as was his habit. 'He requires a white stallion, in order that he shall discover and destroy a succubus. Someone has told him that you possess such a horse,' he concluded, frowning at the temerity of whoever had been bandying such information.

'A succubus?' Grey asked, automatically rearranging the logical order of this speech, as was *his* habit.

Herr Blomberg had no English, but evidently recognized the word, for he nodded vigorously, his old-fashioned wig bobbing, and launched into impassioned speech, accompanied by much gesticulation.

With Stephan's assistance, Grey gathered that the town of Gundwitz had recently suffered a series of mysterious and disturbing events, involving a number of men who claimed to have been victimized in their sleep by a young woman of demonic aspect. By the time these events had made their way to the attention of Herr Blomberg, the situation was serious; a man had died.

'Unfortunately,' Stephan added, still in English, 'the dead man is ours.' He pressed his lips tightly together, conveying his dislike of the situation.

'Ours?' Grey asked, unsure what this usage

implied, other than that the victim had been a soldier.

'Mine,' Stephan clarified, looking further displeased. 'One of the Prussians.'

The Landgrave von Erdberg had three hundred Hanoverian foot troops, raised from his own lands, equipped and funded from his personal fortune. In addition, Captain von Namtzen commanded two additional companies of Prussian horse, and was in temporary command of the fragments of an artillery company whose officers had all died in an outbreak of the bloody flux.

Grey wished to hear more details regarding both the immediate death and – most particularly – the demoniac visitations, but his questions along these lines were interrupted by Herr Blomberg, who had been growing more restive by the moment.

'It grows soon dark,' the bürgermeister pointed out in German. 'We do not wish to fall into an open grave, so wet as it is.'

'Ein offenes Grab?' Grey repeated, feeling a sudden chill draft on the back of his neck.

'This is true,' Stephan said, with a nod of moody acquiescence. 'It would be a terrible thing if your horse were to break his leg; he is a splendid creature. Come then, let us go.'

'What *is* a s-succubus, me lord?' Tom Byrd's teeth were chattering, mostly from chill. The sun had long since set, and it was raining much harder. Grey could feel the wet seeping through the shoulders of his officer's greatcoat; Byrd's thin jacket was already soaked through, pasted to the young valet's stubby torso like butcher's paper round a joint of beef.

'I believe it is a sort of female . . . spirit,' Grey said, carefully avoiding the more evocative term 'demon.' The churchyard gates yawned before them like open jaws, and the darkness beyond seemed sinister in the extreme. No need to terrify the boy unnecessarily.

'Horses don't like ghosts,' Byrd said, sounding truculent. 'Everybody knows that, me lord.'

He wrapped his arms round himself, shivering, and huddled closer to Karolus, who shook his mane as though in agreement, showering water liberally over both Grey and Byrd.

'Surely you don't believe in ghosts, Tom?' Grey said, trying to be jocularly reassuring. He swiped a strand of wet fair hair out of his face, wishing Stephan would hurry.

''Tisn't a matter of what *I* don't believe in, me lord,' Byrd replied. 'What if this lady's ghost believes in *us*? Who is she, anyway?' The lantern he carried was sputtering fitfully in the wet, despite its shield. Its dim light failed to illumine more than a vague outline of boy and horse, but perversely caught the shine of their eyes, lending them a disturbingly supernatural appearance, like staring wraiths.

Grey glanced aside, keeping an eye out for Stephan and the bürgermeister, who had gone to assemble a digging party. There was some movement outside the tavern, just visible at the far end of the street. That was sensible of Stephan. Men with a fair amount of beer on board were much more likely to be enthusiastic about the current prospect than were sober ones.

'Well, I do not believe that it is precisely a matter of ghosts,' he said. 'The German belief, however, seems to be that the succubus . . . er . . . the feminine spirit . . . may possess the body of a recently dead person, however.'

Tom cast a look into the inky depths of the churchyard, and glanced back at Grey.

'Oh?' he said.

'Ah,' Grey replied.

Byrd pulled the slouch hat low on his forehead and hunched his collar up round his ears, clutching the horse's halter rope close to his chest. Nothing of his round face now showed save a downturned mouth, but that was eloquent.

Karolus stamped one foot and shifted his weight, tossing his head a little. He didn't seem to mind either rain or churchyard, but was growing restive. Grey patted the stallion's thick neck, taking comfort from the solid feel of the cold, firm hide and massive body. Karolus turned his head and blew hot breath affectionately into his ear.

'Almost ready,' he said soothingly, twining a fist in the horse's soggy mane. 'Now, Tom. When Captain von Namtzen arrives with his men, you and Karolus will walk forward very slowly. You are to lead him back and forth across the churchyard.

Keep a few feet in front of him, but leave some slack in the rope.'

The point of this procedure, of course, was to keep Karolus from stumbling over a gravestone or falling into any open graves, by allowing Tom to do it first. Ideally, Grey had been given to understand, the horse should be turned into the churchyard and allowed to wander over the graves at his own will, but neither he nor Stephan was willing to risk Karolus's valuable legs in the dark.

He had suggested waiting until the morning, but Herr Blomberg was insistent. The succubus must be found, without delay. Grey was more than curious to hear the details of the attacks, but had so far been told little more than that a Private Koenig had been found dead in his quarters, the body bearing marks that made his manner of death clear. What marks? Grey wondered.

Classically educated, he had read of succubi and incubi, but had been taught to regard such references as quaintly superstitious, of a piece with other medieval popish nonsense like saints who strolled about with their heads in their hands or statues of the Virgin whose tears healed the sick. His father had been a rationalist, an observer of the ways of nature and a firm believer in the logic of phenomena.

His two months' acquaintance with the Germans, though, had shown him that they were deeply superstitious; more so even than the English common soldiers. Even Stephan kept a small, carved image of some pagan deity about his person at all times, to guard against being struck by lightning, and the Prussians seemed to harbor similar notions, judging from Herr Blomberg's behavior.

The digging party was making its way up the street now, bright with sputtering torches and emitting snatches of song. Karolus snorted and pricked his ears; Karolus, Grey had been told, was fond of parades.

'Well, then.' Stephan loomed suddenly out of the murk at his side, looking pleased with himself under the broad shelf of his hat. 'All is ready, Major?'

'Yes. Go ahead then, Tom.'

The diggers – mostly laborers, armed with spades, hoes, and mattocks – stood back, lurching tipsily and stepping on each other's shoes. Tom, lantern held delicately before him in the manner of an insect's feeler, took several steps forward – then stopped. He turned, tugging on the rope.

Karolus stood solidly, declining to move.

'I told you, me lord,' Byrd said, sounding more cheerful. 'Horses don't like ghosts. Me uncle had an old cart horse once, wouldn't take a step past a churchyard. We had to take him clear round two streets to get him past.'

Stephan made a noise of disgust.

'It is not a ghost,' he said, striding forward, prominent chin held high. 'It is a succubus. A demon. That is quite different.'

'*Daemon?*' one of the diggers said, catching the

English word and looking suddenly dubious. '*Ein Teufel?*'

'Demon?' said Tom Byrd, and gave Grey a look of profound betrayal.

'Something of the kind, I believe,' Grey said, and coughed. 'If such a thing should exist, which I doubt it does.'

A chill of uncertainty seemed to have overtaken the party with this demonstration of the horse's reluctance. There was shuffling and murmuring, and heads turned to glance back in the direction of the tavern.

Stephan, magnificently disregarding this tendency to pusillanimity in his troops, clapped Karolus on the neck and spoke to him encouragingly in German. The horse snorted and arched his neck, but still resisted Tom Byrd's tentative yanks on his halter. Instead, he swiveled his enormous head toward Grey, jerking Byrd off his feet. The boy lost his grip on the rope, staggered off balance, trying vainly to keep hold of the lantern, and finally slipped on a stone submerged in the mud, landing on his buttocks with a rude *splat*.

This mishap had the salutary effect of causing the diggers to roar with laughter, restoring their spirits. Several of the torches had by now been extinguished by the rain, and everyone was thoroughly wet, but goatskin flasks and pottery jugs were produced from a number of pockets and offered to Tom Byrd by way of restorative, being then passed round the company in sociable fashion.

Grey took a deep swig of the fiery plum liquor himself, handed back the jug, and came to a decision.

'I'll ride him.'

Before Stephan could protest, Grey had taken a firm grip on Karolus's mane and swung himself up on the stallion's broad back. Karolus appeared to find Grey's familiar weight soothing; the broad white ears, which had been pointing to either side in suspicion, rose upright again, and the horse started forward willingly enough at Grey's nudge against his sides.

Tom, too, seemed heartened, and ran to pick up the trailing halter rope. There was a ragged cheer from the diggers, and the party moved awkwardly after them, through the yawning gates.

It seemed much darker in the churchyard than it had looked from outside. Much quieter, too; the jokes and chatter of the men died away into an uneasy silence, broken only by an occasional curse as someone knocked against a tombstone in the dark. Grey could hear the patter of rain on the brim of his hat, and the suck and thump of Karolus's hooves as he plodded obediently through the mud.

He strained his eyes to see what lay ahead, beyond the feeble circle of light cast by Tom's lantern. It was black-dark, and he felt cold, despite the shelter of his greatcoat. The damp was rising, mist coming up out of the ground; he could see wisps of it purling away from Tom's boots, disappearing in the lantern light. More of it drifted in an eerie fog round the mossy tombstones of neglected graves, leaning like rotted teeth in their sockets.

The notion, as it had been explained to him, was that a white stallion had the power to detect the presence of the supernatural. The horse would stop at the grave of the succubus, which could then be opened and steps taken to destroy the creature.

Grey found a number of logical assumptions wanting in this proposal; chief among which – putting aside the question of the existence of succubi, and why a sensible horse should choose to have anything to do with one – was that Karolus was not choosing his own path. Tom was doing his best to keep slack in the rope, but as long as he held it, the horse was plainly going to follow him.

On the other hand, he reflected, Karolus was unlikely to stop *anywhere*, so long as Tom kept walking. That being true, the end result of this exercise would be merely to cause them all to miss their suppers and to render them thoroughly wet and chilled. Still, he supposed they would be still more wet and chilled if obliged actually to open graves and perform whatever ritual might follow—

A hand clamped itself on his calf, and he bit his tongue – luckily, as it kept him from crying out.

'You are all right, Major?' It was Stephan, looming up beside him, tall and dark in a woolen cloak. He had left aside his plumed helmet, and wore a soft-brimmed wide hat against the rain, which made him look both less impressive and more approachable.

'Certainly,' Grey said, mastering his temper. 'How long must we do this?'

Von Namtzen lifted one shoulder in a shrug.

'Until the horse stops, or until Herr Blomberg is satisfied.'

'Until Herr Blomberg begins wanting his supper, you mean.' He could hear the bürgermeister's voice at a distance behind them, lifted in exhortation and reassurance.

A white plume of breath floated out from under the brim of von Namtzen's hat, the laugh behind it barely audible.

'He is more ... resolute? ... than you might suppose. It is his duty, the welfare of the village. He will endure as long as you will, I assure you.'

Grey pressed his bitten tongue against the roof of his mouth, to prevent any injudicious remarks.

Stephan's hand was still curled about his leg, just above the edge of his boot. Cold as it was, he felt no warmth from the grasp, but the pressure of the big hand was both a comfort and something more.

'The horse – he goes well, *nicht wahr*?'

'He is wonderful,' Grey said, with complete sincerity. 'I thank you again.'

Von Namtzen flicked his free hand in dismissal, but made a pleased sound, deep in his throat. He had – against Grey's protests – insisted upon making the stallion a gift to Grey, 'in token of our alliance and our friendship,' he had said firmly, clapping Grey upon both shoulders and then seizing him in fraternal embrace, kissing him formally upon

71

both cheeks and mouth. At least, Grey was obliged to consider it a fraternal embrace, unless and until circumstance might prove it otherwise.

But Stephan's hand still curled round his calf, hidden under the skirt of his greatcoat.

Grey glanced toward the squat bulk of the church, a black mass that loomed beyond the churchyard.

'I am surprised that the priest is not with us. Does he disapprove of this – excursion?'

'The priest is dead. A fever of some kind, *die rote Ruhn,* more than a month since. They will send another, from Strausberg, but he has not come yet.' Little wonder; a large number of French troops lay between Strausberg and the town; travel would be difficult, if not impossible.

'I see.' Grey glanced back over his shoulder. The diggers had paused to open a fresh jug, torches tilting in momentary distraction.

'Do you believe in this – this succubus?' he asked, careful to keep his voice low.

Rather to his surprise, von Namtzen didn't reply at once. At last, the Hanoverian took a deep breath and hunched his broad shoulders in a gesture not quite a shrug.

'I have seen . . . strange things from time to time,' von Namtzen said at last, very quietly. 'In this country, particularly. And a man is dead, after all.'

The hand on his leg squeezed briefly and dropped away, sending a small flutter of sensation up Grey's back.

He took a deep breath of cold, heavy air, tinged

with smoke, and coughed. It was like the smell of grave dirt, he thought, and then wished the thought had not occurred to him.

'One thing I confess I do not quite understand,' he said, straightening himself in the saddle. 'A succubus is a demon, if I am not mistaken. How is it, then, that such a creature should take refuge in a churchyard, in consecrated ground?'

'Oh,' von Namtzen said, sounding surprised that this was not obvious. 'The succubus takes possession of the body of a dead person, and rests within it by day. Such a person must of course be a corrupt and wicked sort, filled perhaps with depravity and perversion. So that even within the churchyard, the succubus will suitable refuge find.'

'How recently must the person have died?' Grey asked. Surely it would make their perambulations more efficient were they to go directly to the more recent graves. From the little he could see in the swaying light of Tom's lantern, most of the stones nearby had stood where they were for decades, if not centuries.

'That I do not know,' von Namtzen admitted. 'Some people say that the body itself rises with the succubus; others say that the body remains in the grave, and by night the demon rides the air as a dream, seeking men in their sleep.'

Tom Byrd's figure was indistinct in the gathering fog, but Grey saw his shoulders rise, nearly touching the brim of his hat. Grey coughed again, and cleared his throat.

73

'I see. And . . . er . . . what, precisely, do you intend to do, should a suitable body be located?'

Here von Namtzen was on surer ground.

'Oh, that is simple,' he assured Grey. 'We will open the coffin, and drive an iron rod through the corpse's heart. Herr Blomberg has brought one.'

Tom Byrd made an inarticulate noise, which Grey thought it wiser to ignore.

'I see,' he said. His nose had begun to run with the cold, and he wiped it on his sleeve. At least he no longer felt hungry.

They paced for a little in silence. The bürgermeister had fallen silent, too, though the distant sounds of squelching and glugging behind them indicated that the digging party was loyally persevering, with the aid of more plum brandy.

'The dead man,' Grey said at last. 'Private Koenig. Where was he found? And you mentioned marks upon the body – what sort of marks?'

Von Namtzen opened his mouth to answer, but was forestalled. Karolus glanced suddenly to the side, nostrils flaring. Then he flung up his head with a great *harrumph!* of startlement, nearly hitting Grey in the face. At the same moment, Tom Byrd uttered a high, thin scream, dropped the rope, and ran.

The big horse dropped his hindquarters, slewed round, and took off, leaping a small stone angel that stood in his path; Grey saw it as a looming pale blur, but had no time to worry about it before it passed beneath the stallion's outstretched hooves, its stone mouth gaping as though in astonishment.

Lacking reins and unable to seize the halter rope, Grey had no recourse but to grip the stallion's mane in both hands, clamp his knees, and stick like a burr. There were shouts and screams behind him, but he had no attention to spare for anything but the wind in his ears and the elemental force between his thighs.

They bounded like a skipping cannonball through the dark, striking the ground and rocketing upward, seeming to cover leagues at a stride. He leaned low and held on, the stallion's mane whipping like stinging nettles across his face, the horse's breath loud in his ears – or was it his own?

Through streaming eyes, he glimpsed light flickering in the distance, and realized they were heading now for the village. There was a six-foot stone wall in the way; he could only hope the horse noticed it in time.

He did; Karolus skidded to a stop, divots of mud and withered grass shooting up around him, sending Grey lurching up onto his neck. The horse reared, came down, then turned sharply, trotted several yards, and slowed to a walk, shaking his head as though to try to free himself of the flapping rope.

Legs quivering as with ague, Grey slid off, and with cold-stiff fingers, grasped the rope.

'You big white *bastard*!' he said, filled with the joy of survival, and laughed. 'You're bloody marvelous!'

Karolus took this compliment with tolerant grace, and shoved at him, whickering softly. The horse seemed largely over his fright, whatever had caused it; he could but hope Tom Byrd fared as well.

Grey leaned against the wall, panting until his breath came back and his heart slowed a bit. The exhilaration of the ride was still with him, but he had now a moment's heed to spare for other things.

At the far side of the churchyard, the torches were clustered close together, lighting the fog with a reddish glow. He could see the digging party, standing in a knot shoulder-to-shoulder, all in attitudes of the most extreme interest. And toward him, a tall black figure came through the mist, silhouetted by the torch glow behind him. He had a moment's turn, for the figure looked sinister, dark cloak swirling about him – but it was, of course, merely Captain von Namtzen.

'Major Grey!' von Namtzen called. 'Major Grey!'

'Here!' Grey shouted, finding breath. The figure altered course slightly, hurrying toward him with long, stilted strides that zigged and zagged to avoid obstacles in the path. How in God's name had Karolus managed on that ground, he wondered, without breaking a leg or both their necks?

'Major Grey,' Stephan said, grasping both his hands tightly. 'John. You are all right?'

'Yes,' he said, gripping back. 'Yes, of course. What has happened? My valet – Mr. Byrd – is he all right?'

'He has into a hole fallen, but he is not hurt. We have found a body. A dead man.'

Grey felt a sudden lurch of the heart.

'What—'

'Not in a grave,' the captain hastened to assure him. 'Lying on the ground, leaning against one of the tombstones. Your valet saw the corpse's face most suddenly in the light of his lantern, and was frightened.'

'I am not surprised. Is he one of yours?'

'No. One of yours.'

'What?' Grey stared up at the Hanoverian. Stephan's face was no more than a pale oval in the dark. He squeezed Grey's hands gently and let them go.

'An English soldier. You will come?'

He nodded, feeling the cold air heavy in his chest. It was not impossible; there were English regiments to north and to south of the town, no more than an hour's ride away. Men off duty would often come into town in search of drink, dice, and women. It was, after all, the reason for his own presence here – to act as liaison between the English regiments and their German allies.

The body was less horrible in appearance than he might have supposed; while plainly dead, the man seemed quite peaceful, slumped half sitting against the knee of a stern stone matron holding a book. There was no blood nor wound apparent, and yet Grey felt his stomach clench with shock.

'You know him?' Stephan was watching him intently, his own face stern and clean as those of the stone memorials about them.

'Yes.' Grey knelt by the body. 'I spoke to him only a few hours ago.'

He put the backs of his fingers delicately against the dead man's throat – the slack flesh was clammy, slick with rain, but still warm. Unpleasantly warm. He glanced down, and saw that Private Bodger's breeches were opened, the stuff of his shirttail sticking out, rumpled over the man's thighs.

'Does he still have his dick, or did the she-thing eat it?' said a low voice in German. A faint, shocked snigger ran through the men. Grey pressed his lips tight together and jerked up the soggy shirttail. Private Bodger was somewhat more than intact, he was glad to see. So were the diggers; there was an audible sigh of mass relief behind him.

Grey stood, conscious all at once of tiredness and hunger, and of the rain pattering on his back.

'Wrap him in a canvas; bring him . . .' Where? The dead man must be returned to his own regiment, but not tonight. 'Bring him to the Schloss. Tom? Show them the way; ask the gardener to find you a suitable shed.'

'Yes, me lord.' Tom Byrd was nearly as pale as the dead man, and covered with mud, but once more in control of himself. 'Will I take the horse, me lord? Or will you ride him?'

Grey had forgotten entirely about Karolus, and looked blankly about. Where had he gone?

One of the diggers had evidently caught the word 'horse,' and understood it, for a murmur of *'Das Pferd'* rippled through the group, and the men began to look round, lifting the torches high and craning their necks.

One man gave an excited shout, pointing into the dark. A large white blur stood a little distance away.

'He's on a grave! He's standing still! He's found it!'

This caused a stir of sudden excitement; everyone pressed forward together, and Grey feared lest the horse should take alarm and run again.

No such danger; Karolus was absorbed in nibbling at the soggy remnants of several wreaths, piled at the foot of an imposing tombstone. This stood guard over a small group of family graves – one very recent, as the wreaths and raw earth showed. As the torchlight fell upon the scene, Grey could easily read the name chiseled black into the stone.

BLOMBERG, it read.

Chapter 2

But What, Exactly, Does a Succubus Do?

They found Schloss Lowenstein alight with candles and welcoming fires, despite the late hour of their return. They were far past the time for dinner, but there was food in abundance on the sideboard, and Grey and von Namtzen refreshed themselves thoroughly, interrupting their impromptu feast periodically to give particulars of the evening's adventures to the house's other inhabitants, who were agog with curiosity.

'No! Herr Blomberg's *mother*?' The Princess von Lowenstein pressed fingers to her mouth, eyes wide in delighted shock. 'Old Agathe? I don't believe it!'

'Nor does Herr Blomberg,' von Namtzen assured her, reaching for a leg of roast pheasant. 'He was most . . . vehement?' He turned toward Grey, eyebrows raised, then turned back to the princess, nodding with assurance. 'Vehement.'

He had been. Grey would have chosen 'apoplectic' as the better description, but was reasonably sure that none of the Germans present would know the term and had no idea how to translate it. They were all speaking English, as a courtesy to the British officers present, who included a captain of horse named Billman, Colonel Sir Peter Hicks, and a Lieutenant Dundas, a young Scottish officer in charge of an ordnance survey party.

'The old woman was a saint, absolutely a saint!' protested the Dowager Princess von Lowenstein, crossing herself piously. 'I do not believe it, I cannot!'

The younger princess cast a brief glance at her mother-in-law, then away – meeting Grey's eyes. The princess had bright blue eyes, all the brighter for candlelight, brandy – and mischief.

The princess was a widow of a year's standing. Grey judged from the large portrait over the mantelpiece in the drawing room that the late prince had been roughly thirty years older than his wife; she bore her loss bravely.

'Dear me,' she said, contriving to look winsome, despite her anxiety. 'As if the French were not enough! Now we are to be threatened with nightmare demons?'

'Oh, you will be quite safe, madam, I assure you,' Sir Peter assured her. 'What-what? With so many gallant gentlemen in the house?'

The ancient dowager glanced at Grey, and said something about gentlemen in highly accented German that Grey didn't quite catch, but the princess flushed like a peony in bloom, and von Namtzen, within earshot, choked on a swallow of wine.

Captain Billman smote the Hanoverian helpfully on the back.

'Is there news of the French?' Grey asked, thinking that perhaps the conversation should be guided back to more earthly concerns before the party retired to bed.

'Look to be a few of the bastards milling round,' Billman said casually, cutting his eyes at the women in a manner suggesting that the word 'few' was a highly discreet euphemism. 'Expect they'll be moving on, heading for the west within a day or so.'

Or heading for Strausberg, to join with the French regiment reported there, Grey thought. He returned Billman's meaningful look. Gundwitz lay in the bottom of a river valley – directly between the French position and Strausberg.

'So,' Billman said, changing the subject with a heavy jocularity, 'your succubus got away, did she?'

Von Namtzen cleared his throat.

'I would not say that, particularly,' he said. 'Herr Blomberg refused to allow the men to disturb the grave, of course, but I have men ordered to guard it.'

'That'll be popular duty, I shouldn't think,' said Sir Peter, with a glance at a nearby window, where even multiple thicknesses of woolen draperies and heavy shutters failed to muffle the thrum of rain and occasional distant boom of thunder.

'A good idea,' one of the German officers said, in heavily accented but very correct English. 'We do not wish to have rumors fly about, that there is a succubus behaving badly in the vicinity of the soldiers.'

'But what, exactly, does a succubus *do*?' the

Princess inquired, looking expectantly from face to face.

There was a sudden massive clearing of throats and gulping of wine, as all the men present tried to avoid her eye. An explosive snort from the dowager indicated what *she* thought of this cowardly behavior.

'A succubus is a she-demon,' the old lady said, precisely. 'It comes to men in dreams, and has congress with them, in order to extract from them their seed.'

The princess's eyes went perfectly round. She *hadn't* known, Grey observed.

'Why?' she asked. 'What does she do with it? Demons do not give birth, do they?'

Grey felt a laugh trying to force its way up under his breastbone, and hastily took another drink.

'Well, no,' said Stephan von Namtzen, somewhat flushed, but still self-possessed. 'Not exactly. The succubus procures the . . . er . . . essence,' he gave a slight bow of apology to the dowager at this, 'and then will mate with an incubus – this being a male demon, you see?'

The old lady looked grim, and placed a hand upon the religious medal she wore pinned to her gown.

Von Namtzen took a deep breath, seeing that everyone was hanging upon his words, and fixed his gaze upon the portrait of the late prince.

'The incubus then will seek out a human woman by night, couple with her, and impregnate her with the stolen seed – thus producing demon-spawn.'

Lieutenant Dundas, who was very young and likely a Presbyterian, looked as though he were being strangled by his stock. The other men, all rather red in the face, attempted to look as though they were entirely familiar with the phenomenon under discussion and thought little of it. The dowager looked thoughtfully at her daughter-in-law, then upward at the picture of her deceased son, eyebrows raised as though in silent conversation.

'Ooh!' Despite the late hour and the informality of the gathering, the princess had a fan, which she spread now before her face in shock, big blue eyes wide above it. These eyes swung toward Grey, and blinked in pretty supplication.

'And do you really think, Lord John, that there is such a creature' – she shuddered, with an alluring quiver of the bosom – 'prowling near?'

Neither eyes nor bosom swayed him, and it was clear to him that the princess found considerably more excitement than fear in the notion, but he smiled reassuringly, an Englishman secure in his rationality.

'No,' he said. 'I don't.'

As though in instant contradiction of this stout opinion, a blast of wind struck the Schloss, carrying with it a burst of hail that rattled off the shutters and fell hissing down the chimney. The thunder of the hailstorm upon roof and walls and outbuildings was so great that for a moment it drowned all possibility of conversation.

The party stood as though paralyzed, listening to

the roar of the elements. Grey's eyes met Stephan's; the Hanoverian lifted his chin a little in defiance of the storm, and gave him a small, private smile. Grey smiled back, then glanced away – just in time to see a dark shape fall from the chimney and plunge into the flames with a piercing shriek.

The shriek was echoed at once by the women – and possibly by Lieutenant Dundas, though Grey could not quite swear to it.

Something was struggling in the fire, flapping and writhing, and the stink of scorched skin came sharp and acrid in the nose. Acting by sheer instinct, Grey seized a poker and swept the thing out of the fire and onto the hearth, where it skittered crazily, emitting sounds that pierced his eardrums.

Stephan lunged forward and stamped on the thing, putting an end to the unnerving display.

'A bat,' he said calmly, removing his boot. 'Take it away.'

The footman to whom he addressed this command came hastily, and flinging a napkin over the blackened corpse, scooped it up and carried it out on a tray – this ceremonial disposal giving Grey a highly inappropriate vision of the bat making a second appearance at breakfast, roasted and garnished with stewed prunes.

A sudden silence had fallen upon the party. This was broken by the sudden chiming of the clock, which made everyone jump, then laugh nervously.

The party broke up, the men standing politely as the women withdrew, then pausing for a few moments' conversation as they finished their wine and brandy. With no particular sense of surprise, Grey found Sir Peter at his elbow.

'A word with you, Major?' Sir Peter said quietly.

'Of course, sir.'

The group had fragmented into twos and threes; it was not difficult to draw aside a little, under the pretext of examining a small, exquisite statue of Eros that stood on one of the tables.

'You'll be taking the body back to the Fifty-second in the morning, I expect?' The English officers had all had a look at Private Bodger, declaring that he was none of theirs; by elimination, he must belong to Colonel Ruysdale's 52nd Foot, presently encamped on the other side of Gundwitz.

Without waiting for Grey's nod, Sir Peter went on, touching the statue abstractedly.

'The French are up to something; had a scout's report this afternoon, great deal of movement among the troops. They're preparing to move, but we don't yet know where or when. I should feel happier if a few more of Ruysdale's troops were to move to defend the bridge at Aschenwald, just in case.'

'I see,' Grey said cautiously. 'And you wish me to carry a message to that effect to Colonel Ruysdale.'

Sir Peter made a slight grimace.

'I've sent one. I think it might be helpful, though, if you were to suggest that von Namtzen wished it, as well.'

Grey made a noncommittal noise. It was

common knowledge that Sir Peter and Ruysdale were not on good terms. The colonel might well be more inclined to oblige a German ally.

'I will mention it to Captain von Namtzen,' he said, 'though I expect he will be agreeable.' He would have taken his leave then, but Sir Peter hesitated, indicating that there was something further.

'Sir?' Grey said.

'I think,' Sir Peter said, glancing round and lowering his voice still further, 'that perhaps the princess should be advised – cautiously; no need to give alarm – that there is some slight possibility . . . if the French *were* in fact to cross the valley . . .' He rested a hand thoughtfully upon the head of Eros, and glanced at the other furnishings of the room, which included a number of rare and costly items. 'She might wish to withdraw her family to a place of safety. Not amiss to suggest a few things be put safely away in the meantime. Shouldn't like to see a thing like that decorating a French general's desk, eh?'

'That' was the skull of an enormous bear – an ancient cave bear, the princess had informed the party earlier – that stood by itself upon a small, draped table. The skull was covered with gold, hammered flat and etched in primitive designs, with a row of semiprecious stones running up the length of the snout, then diverging to encircle the empty eye sockets. It was a striking object.

'Yes,' Grey said, 'I quite – Oh. You wish me to speak with the princess?'

Sir Peter relaxed a little, having accomplished his goal.

'She seems quite taken by you, Grey,' he said, his original joviality returning. 'Advice might be better received from you, eh? Besides, you're a liaison, aren't you?'

'To be sure,' Grey said, less than pleased, but aware that he had received a direct order. 'I shall attend to it as soon as I may, sir.' He took leave of the others remaining in the drawing room, and made his way to the staircase that led to the upper floors.

The Princess von Lowenstein *did* seem most taken with him; he wasn't surprised that Sir Peter had noticed her smiles and languishings. Fortunately, she seemed equally taken with Stephan von Namtzen, going so far as to have Hanoverian delicacies served regularly at dinner in his honor.

At the top of the stair, he hesitated. There were three corridors opening off the landing, and it always took a moment to be sure which of the stone-floored halls led to his own chamber. A flicker of movement to the left attracted his eye, and he turned that way, to see someone dodge out of sight behind a tall armoire that stood against the wall.

'Wo ist das?' he asked sharply, and got a stifled gasp in reply.

Moving cautiously, he went and peered round the edge of the armoire, to find a small, dark-haired boy pressed against the wall, both hands clasped over his mouth and eyes round as saucers. The boy wore a nightshirt and cap, and had plainly escaped from his nursery. He recognized the child, though he had seen him only once or twice before; it was the princess's young son – what was the boy's name? Heinrich? Reinhardt?

'Don't be afraid,' he said gently to the boy, in his slow, careful German. 'I am your mother's friend. Where is your room?'

The boy didn't reply, but his eyes flicked down the hallway and back. Grey saw no open doors, but held out a hand to the boy.

'It is very late,' he said. 'Shall we find your bed?'

The boy shook his head so hard that the tassel of his nightcap slapped against the wall.

'I don't want to go to bed. There is a bad woman there. *Ein Hexe.*'

'A witch?' Grey repeated, and felt an odd frisson run down his back, as though someone had touched his nape with a cold finger. 'What did this witch look like?'

The child stared back at him, uncomprehending.

'Like a witch,' he said.

'Oh,' said Grey, momentarily stymied. He rallied, though, and beckoned, curling his fingers at the boy. 'Come, then; show me. I am a soldier, I am not afraid of a witch.'

'You will kill her and cut out her heart and fry it over the fire?' the boy asked eagerly, peeling himself off the wall. He reached out to touch the hilt of Grey's dagger, still on his belt.

'Well, perhaps,' Grey temporized. 'Let us go find

her first.' He grasped the boy under the arms and swung him up; the child came willingly enough, curling his legs around Grey's waist and cuddling close to him for warmth.

The hallway was dark; only a rushlight sputtered in a sconce near the farther end, and the stones emanated a chill that made the child's own warmth more than welcome. Rain was still coming down hard; a small dribble of moisture had seeped in through the shutters at the end of the hall, and the flickering light shone on the puddle.

Thunder boomed in the distance, and the child threw his arms around Grey's neck with a gasp.

'It is all right.' Grey patted the small back soothingly, though his own heart had leapt convulsively at the sound. No doubt the sound of the storm had wakened the boy.

'Where is your chamber?'

'Upstairs.' The boy pointed vaguely toward the far end of the hallway; presumably there was a back stair somewhere near. The Schloss was immense and sprawling; Grey had learned no more of its geography than what was necessary to reach his own quarters. He hoped that the boy knew the place better, so they were not obliged to wander the chilly hallways all night.

As he approached the end of the hall, the lightning flashed again, a vivid line of white that outlined the window – and showed him clearly that the shutters were unfastened. With the boom of thunder came a gust of wind, and one loose shutter flung back suddenly, admitting a freezing gust of rain.

'Oooh!' The boy clutched him tightly round the neck, nearly choking him.

'It is all right,' he said again, as calmly as possible, shifting his burden in order to free one hand.

He leaned out to seize the shutter, trying at the same time to shelter the boy with his body. A soundless flash lit up the world in a burst of black and white, and he blinked, dazzled, a pinwheel of stark images whirling at the back of his eyes. Thunder rolled past, with a sound so like an oxcart full of stones that he glanced up involuntarily, half-expecting to see one of the old German gods go past, driving gleefully through the clouds.

The image he saw was not of the storm-tossed sky, though, but of something seen when the lightning flashed. He blinked hard, clearing his sight, and then looked down. It *was* there. A ladder, leaning against the wall of the house. Well, then. Perhaps the child *had* seen someone strange in his room.

'Here,' he said to the boy, turning to set him down. 'Stay out of the rain while I fasten the shutter.'

He turned back, and leaning out into the storm, pushed the ladder off, so that it fell away into the dark. Then he closed and fastened the shutters, and picked up the shivering boy again. The wind had blown out the rushlight, and he was obliged to feel his way into the turning of the hall.

'It's very dark,' said the boy, with a tremor in his voice.

'Soldiers are not afraid of the dark,' he reassured the child, thinking of the graveyard.

'I'm not afraid!' The little boy's cheek was pressed against his neck.

'Of course you are not. How are you called, young sir?' he asked, in hopes of distracting the boy.

'Siggy.'

'Siggy,' he repeated, feeling his way along the wall with one hand. 'I am John. Johannes, in your tongue.'

'I know,' said the boy, surprising him. 'The servant girls think you are good-looking. Not so big as Landgrave Stephan, but prettier. Are you rich? The Landgrave is very rich.'

'I won't starve,' Grey said, wondering how long the blasted hallway was, and whether he might discover the staircase by falling down it in the dark.

At least the boy seemed to have lost some of his fear; he cuddled close, rubbing his head under Grey's chin. There was a distinct smell about him; nothing unpleasant – rather like the smell of a month-old litter of puppies, Grey thought, warmly animal.

Something occurred to him then, something he should have thought to ask at once.

'Where is your nurse?' A boy of this age would surely not sleep alone.

'I don't know. Maybe the witch ate her.'

This cheering suggestion coincided with a

welcome flicker of light in the distance, and the sound of voices. Hastening toward these, Grey at last found the nursery stair, just as a wild-eyed woman in nightgown, cap, and shawl popped out, holding a pottery candlestick.

'Siegfried!' she cried. 'Master Siggy, where have you been? What has – Oh!' At this point, she realized that Grey was there, and reared back as though struck forcibly in the chest.

'*Guten Abend*, Madam,' he said, politely. 'Is this your nurse, Siggy?'

'No,' said Siggy, scornful of such ignorance. 'That's just Hetty. Mama's maid.'

'Siggy? Siegfried, is it you? Oh, my boy, my boy!' The light from above dimmed as a fluttering body hurtled down the stair, and the Princess von Lowenstein seized the boy from his arms, hugging her son and kissing him so passionately that his nightcap fell off.

More servants were coming downstairs, less precipitously. Two footmen and a woman who might be a parlor maid, all in varying degrees of undress, but equipped with candles or rushlights. Evidently, Grey had had the good fortune to encounter a search party.

There was a good deal of confused conversation, as Grey's attempt at explanation was interrupted by Siggy's own rather disjointed account of his adventures, punctuated by exclamations of horror and surprise from the princess and Hetty.

'Witch?' the princess was saying, looking down

at her son in alarm. 'You saw a witch? Did you have an evil dream, child?'

'No. I just woke up and there was a witch in my room. Can I have some marzipan?'

'Perhaps it would be a good idea to search the house,' Grey managed to get in. 'It is possible that the . . . witch . . . is still inside.'

The princess had very fine, pale skin, radiant in the candlelight, but at this, it went a sickly color, like toadstools. Grey glanced meaningfully at Siggy, and the princess at once gave the child to Hetty, telling the maid to take him to his nursery.

'Tell me what is happening,' she said, gripping Grey's arm, and he did, finishing the account with a question of his own.

'The child's nurse? Where is she?'

'We don't know. I went to the nursery to look at Siegfried before retiring—' The princess's hand fluttered to her bosom, as she became aware that she was wearing a rather unbecoming woolen nightgown and cap, with a heavy shawl and thick, fuzzy stockings. 'He wasn't there; neither was the nurse. Jakob, Thomas—' She turned to the footmen, suddenly taking charge. 'Search! The house first, then the grounds.'

A distant rumbling of thunder reminded everyone that it was still pouring with rain outside, but the footmen vanished with speed.

The sudden silence left in the wake of their departure gave Grey a slightly eerie feeling, as though the thick stone walls had moved subtly closer. A solitary candle burned, left behind on the stairs.

'Who would do this?' said the princess, her voice suddenly small and frightened. 'Did they mean to take Siegfried? Why?'

It looked very much to Grey as though kidnapping had been the plan; no other possibility had entered his mind, until the princess seized him by the arm again.

'Do you think – do you think it was . . . her?' she whispered, eyes dilated to pools of horror. 'The succubus?'

'I think not,' Grey said, taking hold of her hands for reassurance. They were cold as ice – hardly surprising, in view of the temperature inside the Schloss. He smiled at her, squeezing her fingers gently. 'A succubus would not require a ladder, surely?' He forbore to add that a boy of Siggy's age was unlikely to have much that a succubus would want, if he had correctly understood the nature of such a creature.

A little color came back into the princess's face, as she saw the logic in this.

'No, that's true.' The edge of her mouth twitched in an attempt at a smile, though her eyes were still fearful.

'It might be advisable to set a guard near your son's room,' Grey suggested. 'Though I expect the . . . person . . . has been frightened off by now.'

She shuddered, whether from cold or at the thought of roving intruders, he couldn't tell. Still, she was clearly steadier at the thought of action, and that being so, he rather reluctantly took the opportunity to share with her Sir Peter Hicks's cautions, feeling that perhaps a solid enemy such as the French would be preferable to phantasms and shadowy threats.

'Ha, those frog-eaters,' she said, proving his supposition by drawing herself up with a touch of scorn in her voice. 'They have tried before, the Schloss to take. They have never done it; they will not do it now.' She gestured briefly at the stone walls surrounding them, by way of justification in this opinion. 'My husband's great-great-great-grandfather built the Schloss; we have a well inside the house, a stable, food stores. This place was built to withstand siege.'

'I am sure you are right,' Grey said, smiling. 'But you will perhaps take some care?' He let go her hands, willing her to draw the interview to a close. Excitement over, he was very much aware that it had been a long day, and that he was freezing.

'I will,' she promised him. She hesitated a moment, not quite sure how to take her leave gracefully, then stepped forward, rose onto her toes, and with her hands on his shoulders, kissed him on the mouth.

'Good night, Lord John,' she said softly, in English. *'Danke.'* She turned and hurried up the stairs, picking up her skirts as she went.

Grey stood for a startled moment looking after her, the disconcerting feel of her uncorseted breasts still imprinted on his chest. Then shook his head and went to pick up the candlestick she had left on the stair for him.

Straightening up, he was overtaken by a massive yawn, the fatigues of the day coming down upon him like a thousandweight of grapeshot. He only hoped he could find his own chamber again, in this ancient labyrinth. Perhaps he should have asked the princess for direction.

He made his way back down the hallway, his candle flame seeming puny and insignificant in the oppressive darkness cast by the great stone blocks of Schloss Lowenstein. It was only when the light gleamed on the puddle on the floor that the thought suddenly occurred to him: Someone had to have opened the shutters – from the inside.

Grey made his way back as far as the head of the main stair, only to find Stephan von Namtzen coming up it. The Hanoverian was a little flushed with brandy, but still clearheaded, and listened to Grey's account of events with consternation.

'*Dreckskerle!*' he said, and spat on the floor to emphasize his opinion of kidnappers. 'The servants are searching, you say – but you think they will find nothing?'

'Perhaps they will find the nurse,' Grey said. 'But if the kidnapper has an ally inside the house – and he must . . . or she, I suppose,' he added. 'The boy did say he saw a witch.'

'*Ja,* I see.' Von Namtzen looked grim. One big hand fisted at his side, but then relaxed. 'I will perhaps go and speak to the princess. My men, I will have them come to guard the house. If there is a criminal within, he will not get out.'

'I'm sure the princess will be grateful.' Grey felt all at once terribly tired. 'I must take Bodger – the body – back to his regiment in the morning. Oh – in that regard . . .' He explained Sir Peter's wishes, to which von Namtzen agreed with a flip of the hand.

'Have you any messages for me to carry, to the troops at the bridge?' Grey asked. 'Since I will be going in that direction, anyway.' One English regiment lay to the south of the town, the other – Bodger's – to the north, between the town and the river. A small group of the Prussian artillery under Stephan's command was stationed a few miles beyond, guarding the bridge at Aschenwald.

Von Namtzen frowned, thinking, then nodded.

'*Ja,* you are right. It is best they hear officially of the—' He looked suddenly uneasy, and Grey was slightly amused to see that Stephan did not want to speak the word 'succubus.'

'Yes, better to avoid rumors,' he agreed, saving Stephan's awkwardness. 'Speaking of that – do you suppose Herr Blomberg will let the villagers exhume his mother?'

Stephan's broad-boned face broke into a smile at that.

'No,' he said. 'I think he would make them drive an iron rod through his own heart first. Better, though,' he added, the humor fading from his face, 'if someone finds who plays these tricks, and a stop to it makes. Quickly.'

Stephan was tired, too, Grey saw; his English grammar was slipping. They stood together for a moment, silent, listening to the distant hammer of the rain, both feeling still the chill touch of the graveyard in their bones.

Von Namtzen turned to him suddenly, and put a hand on his shoulder, squeezing.

'You will take care, John,' he said, and before Grey could speak or move, Stephan pulled him close and kissed his mouth. Then he smiled, squeezed Grey's shoulder once more, and with a quiet *'Gute Nacht,'* went up the stairs toward his own room.

Grey shut the door of his chamber behind him and leaned against it, in the manner of a man pursued. Tom Byrd, curled up asleep on the hearth rug, sat up and blinked at him.

'Me lord?'

'Who else?' Grey asked, made jocular from the fatigues and excitements of the evening. 'Did you expect a visit from the succubus?'

Tom's face lost all its sleepiness at that, and he glanced uneasily at the window, closed and tightly shuttered against the dangers of the night.

'You oughtn't jest that way, me lord,' he said reproachfully. 'It's an Englishman what's dead now.'

'You are right, Tom; I beg pardon of Private Bodger.' Grey found some justice in the rebuke, but was too much overtaken by events to be stung by it. 'Still, we do not know the cause of his death. Surely there is no proof as yet that it was occasioned by any sort of supernatural interference. Have you eaten?'

'Yes, me lord. Cook had gone to bed, but she got up and fetched us out some bread and dripping, and some ale. Wanting to know all about what I found in the churchyard,' he added practically.

Grey smiled to himself, the faint emphasis on 'I' in this statement indicating to him that Tom's protests on behalf of the late Private Bodger sprang as much from a sense of proprietariness as from a sense of propriety.

Grey sat down, to let Tom pull off his boots and still-damp stockings. The room he had been given was small, but warm and bright, the shadows from a well-tended fire flickering over striped damask wallpaper. After the wet cold of the churchyard and the bleak chill of the Schloss's stone corridors, the heat upon his skin was a grateful feeling – much enhanced by the discovery of a pitcher of hot water for washing.

'Shall I come with you, me lord? In the morning, I mean.' Tom undid the binding of Grey's hair and began to comb it, dipping the comb occasionally in a cologne of bay leaves and hyssop, meant to discourage lice.

'No, I think not. I shall ride over and speak to Colonel Ruysdale first; one of the servants can follow me with the body.' Grey closed his eyes, beginning to feel drowsy, though small jolts of excitement still pulsed through his thighs and abdomen. 'If you would, Tom, I should like you to talk with the servants; find out what they are saying about things.' God knew, they would have plenty to talk about.

Clean, brushed, warmed, and cozily ensconced in nightshirt, cap, and banyan, Grey dismissed Tom, the valet's arms piled high with filthy uniform bits.

He shut the door behind the boy, and hesitated, staring into the polished surface of the wood as though to look through it and see who might be standing on the other side. Only the blur of his own face met his gaze, though, and only the creak of Tom's footsteps were audible, receding down the corridor.

Thoughtfully, he touched his lips with a finger. Then he sighed, and bolted the door.

Stephan had kissed him before – kissed innumerable people, for that matter; the man was an inveterate *embrasseur*. But surely this had been somewhat more than the fraternal embrace of a fellow soldier. He could still feel the grip of Stephan's hand curled around his leg. Or was he deluded by fatigue and distraction, imagining more to it than there was?

And if he were right?

He shook his head, took the warming pan from his sheets, and crawled between them, reflecting that, of all the men in Gundwitz that night, he at least was safe from the attentions of any roving succubi.

Chapter 3

A Remedy for Sleeplessness

Regimental headquarters for the 52nd was in Bonz, a small hamlet that stood some ten miles from Gundwitz. Grey found Colonel Ruysdale in the central room of the largest inn, in urgent conference with several other officers, and indisposed to take time to deal with an enlisted body.

'Grey? Oh, yes, know your brother. You found what? Where? Yes, all right. See . . . um . . . Sergeant-Major Sapp. Yes, that's it. Sapp will know who . . .' The colonel waved a vague hand, indicating that Grey would doubtless find whatever assistance he required elsewhere.

'Yes, sir,' Grey said, settling his bootheels into the sawdust. 'I shall do so directly. Am I to understand, though, that there are developments of which our allies should be informed?'

Ruysdale stared at him, eyes cold and upper lip foremost.

'Who told you that, sir?'

As though he needed telling. Troops were being mustered outside the village, drummers beating the call to arms and corporals shouting through the streets, men pouring out from their quarters like an anthill stirred with a stick.

'I am a liaison officer, sir, seconded to Captain von Namtzen's Hanoverian Foot,' Grey replied, evading the question. 'They are at present quartered in Gundwitz; will you require their support?'

Ruysdale looked grossly offended at the notion, but a captain wearing an artillery cockade coughed tactfully.

'Colonel, shall I give Major Grey such particulars of the situation as may seem useful? You have important matters to deal with . . .' He nodded round at the assembled officers, who seemed attentive, but hardly on the brink of action.

The colonel snorted briefly and made a gesture somewhere between gracious dismissal and the waving-away of some noxious insect, and Grey bowed, murmuring, 'Your servant, sir.'

Outside, the clouds of last night's storm were making a hasty exodus, scudding away on a fresh, cold wind. The artillery captain clapped a hand to his hat, and jerked his head toward a pothouse down the street.

'A bit of warmth, Major?'

Gathering that the village was in no danger of imminent invasion, Grey nodded, and accompanied his new companion into a dark, smoky womb smelling of pigs' feet and fermented cabbage.

'Benjamin Hiltern,' the captain said, putting back his cloak and holding up two fingers to the barman. 'You'll take a drink, Major?'

'John Grey. I thank you. I collect we shall have time to drink it, before we are quite overrun?'

Hiltern laughed, and sat down across from Grey, rubbing a knuckle under a cold-reddened nose.

'We should have time for our gracious host' – he nodded at the wizened creature fumbling with a jug – 'to hunt a boar, roast it, and serve it up with an apple in its mouth, if you should be so inclined.'

'I am obliged, Captain,' Grey said, with a glance at the barman, who upon closer inspection appeared to have only one leg, the other being supported by a stout peg of battered aspect. 'Alas, I have breakfasted but recently.'

'Too bad. I haven't. *Bratkartoffeln mit Ruhrei,*' Hiltern said to the barman, who nodded and disappeared into some still-more-squalid den to the rear of the house. 'Potatoes, fried with eggs and ham,' he explained, taking out a kerchief and tucking it into the neck of his shirt. 'Delicious.'

'Quite,' Grey said politely. 'One would hope that your troops are fed as well, after the effort I saw being expended.'

'Oh, that.' Hiltern's cherubic countenance lost a little of its cheerfulness, but not much. 'Poor sods. At least it's stopped raining.'

In answer to Grey's raised brows, he explained.

'Punishment. There was a game of bowls yesterday, between a party of men from Colonel Bampton-Howard's lot and our lads – local form of skittles. Ruysdale had a heavy wager on with Bampton-Howard, see?'

'And your lot lost. Yes, I see. So your lads are—'

'Ten mile run to the river and back, in full kit. Keep them fit and out of trouble, at least,' Hiltern said, half-closing his eyes and lifting his nose at the scent of frying potatoes that had begun to waft through the air.

'I see. One assumes that the French have moved, then? Our last intelligence reported them as being a few miles north of the river.'

'Yes, gave us a bit of excitement for a day or two; thought they might come this way. They seem to have sheered off, though – gone round to the west.'

'Why?' Grey felt a prickle of unease go down his spine. There was a bridge at Aschenwald, a logical crossing point – but there was another several miles west, at Gruneberg. The eastern bridge was defended by a company of Prussian artillery; a detachment of grenadiers, under Colonel Bampton-Howard, presumably held the western crossing.

'There's a mass of Frenchies beyond the river,' Hiltern replied. 'We think they have it in mind to join up with that lot.'

That was interesting. It was also information that should have been shared with the Hanoverian and Prussian commanders by official dispatch – not acquired accidentally by the random visit of a liaison officer. Sir Peter Hicks was scrupulous in maintaining communications with the allies; Ruysdale evidently saw no such need.

'Oh!' Hiltern said, divining his thought. 'I'm sure we would have let you know, only for things here being in a bit of confusion. And truly, it didn't seem urgent; scouts just said the French were shining their gear, biffing up the supplies, that sort of thing. After all, they've got to go *somewhere* before the snow comes down.'

He raised one dark brow, smiling in apology – an apology that Grey accepted, with no more than a second's hesitation. If Ruysdale was going to be erratic about dispatches, it would be as well for Grey to keep himself informed by other means – and Hiltern was obviously well-placed to know what was going on.

They chatted casually until the host came out with Hiltern's breakfast, but Grey learned no more of interest – save that Hiltern was remarkably *un*interested in the death of Private Bodger. He was also vague about the 'confusion' to which he had referred, dismissing it with a wave of the hand as a 'bit of a muddle in the commissary – damned bore.'

The sound of hooves and wheels, moving slowly, came from the street outside, and Grey heard a loud voice with a distinctly Hanoverian accent, requesting direction '*Zum Englanderlager.*'

'What is *that*?' Hiltern asked, turning on his stool.

'I expect that will be Private Bodger coming home,' Grey replied, rising. 'I'm obliged to you, sir. Is Sergeant-Major Sapp still in camp, do you know?'

'Mmm . . . no.' Hiltern spoke thickly, through a mouthful of potatoes and eggs. 'Gone to the river.'

That was inconvenient; Grey had no desire to

hang about all day, waiting for Sapp's return in order to hand over the corpse and responsibility for it. Another idea occurred to him, though.

'And the regimental surgeon?'

'Dead. Flux.' Hiltern spooned in more egg, concentrating. 'Mmp. Try Keegan. He's the surgeon's assistant.'

With most of the men emptying out of camp, it took some time to locate the surgeon's tent. Once there, Grey had the body deposited on a bench, and at once sent the wagon back to the Schloss. He was taking no chances on being left in custody of Private Bodger.

Keegan proved to be a scrappy Welshman, equipped with rimless spectacles and an incongruous mop of reddish ringlets. Blinking through the spectacles, he bent close to the corpse and poked at it with a smudgy exploratory finger.

'No blood.'

'No.'

'Fever?'

'Probably not. I saw the man several hours before his death, and he seemed in reasonable health then.'

'Hmmm.' Keegan bent and peered keenly up Bodger's nostrils, as though suspecting the answer to the private's untimely death might be lurking there.

Grey frowned at the fellow's grubby knuckles and

the thin crust of blood that rimmed his cuff. Nothing out of the way for a surgeon, but the dirt bothered him.

Keegan tried to thumb up one of the eyelids, but it resisted him. Bodger had stiffened during the night, and while the hands and arms had gone limp again, the face, body, and legs were all hard as wood. Keegan sighed and began tugging off the corpse's stockings. These were greatly the worse for wear, the soles stained with mud; the left one had a hole worn through and Bodger's great toe poked out like the head of an inquisitive worm.

Keegan rubbed a hand on the skirt of his already grubby coat, leaving further streaks, then rubbed it under his nose, sniffing loudly. Grey had an urge to step away from the man. Then he realized, with a small sense of startlement mingled with annoyance, that he was thinking of the Woman. Fraser's wife. Fraser had spoken of her very little – but that reticence only added to the significance of what he *did* say.

One late night, in the governor's quarters at Ardsmuir Prison, they had sat longer than usual over their chess game – a hard-fought draw, in which Grey took more pleasure than he might have taken in victory over a lesser opponent. They usually drank sherry, but not that night; he had a special claret, a present from his mother, and had insisted that Fraser must help him to finish it, as the wine would not last once opened.

It was a strong wine, and between the headiness

of it and the stimulation of the game, even Fraser had lost a little of his formidable reserve.

Past midnight, Grey's orderly had come to take away the dishes from their repast, and stumbling sleepily on the threshold in his leaving, had sprawled full-length, cutting himself badly on a shard of glass. Fraser had leapt up like a cat, snatched the boy up, and pressed a fold of his shirt to the wound to stop the bleeding. But then, when Grey would have sent for a surgeon, Fraser had stopped him, saying tersely that Grey could do so if he wished to kill the lad, but if not, had best allow Fraser to tend him.

This he had done with great skill and gentleness, washing first his hands, and then the wound, with wine, then demanding needle and silk thread – which he had astonished Grey by dipping into the wine, as well, and passing the needle through the flame of a candle.

'My wife would do it so,' he'd said, frowning slightly in concentration. 'There are the wee beasties, called germs, d'ye see, and if they—' He set his teeth momentarily into his lip as he made the first stitch, then went on.

'—If they should be getting into a wound, it will suppurate. So ye must wash well before ye tend the wound, and put flame or alcohol to your instruments, to kill them.' He smiled briefly at the orderly, who was white-faced and wobbling on his stool. 'Never let a surgeon wi' dirty hands touch ye, she said. Better to bleed to death quickly than die slow of the pus, aye?'

Grey was as skeptical of the existence of germs as of succubi, but ever afterward had glanced automatically at the hands of any medical man – and it did seem to him that perhaps the more cleanly of the breed tended to lose fewer patients, though he had made no real study of the matter.

In the present instance, though, Mr. Keegan offered no hazard to the late Private Bodger, and in spite of his distaste, Grey made no protest as the surgeon undressed the corpse, making small interested 'Tut!' noises in response to the post-mortem phenomena thus revealed.

Grey was already aware that the private had died in a state of arousal. This state appeared to be permanent, even though the limbs had begun to relax from their rigor, and was the occasion of a surprised 'Tut!' from Mr. Keegan.

'Well, he died happy, at least,' Keegan said, blinking. 'Sweet God almighty.'

'Is this a . . . normal manifestation, do you think?' Grey inquired. He had rather expected Private Bodger's condition to abate postmortem. If anything, it seemed particularly pronounced, viewed by daylight. Though of course that might be merely an artifact of the color, which was now a virulent dark purple, in stark contrast to the pallid flesh of the body.

Keegan prodded the condition cautiously with a forefinger.

'Stiff as wood,' he said, unnecessarily. 'Normal?

Don't know. Mind, what chaps I see here have mostly died of fever or flux, and men what are ill aren't mostly of a mind to . . . Hmm.' He relapsed into a thoughtful contemplation of the body.

'What did the woman say?' he asked, shaking himself out of this reverie after a moment or two.

'Who, the woman he was with? Gone. Not that one might blame her.' Always assuming that it had been a woman, he added to himself. Though given Private Bodger's earlier encounter with the gypsy, one *would* assume . . .

'Can you say what caused his death?' Grey inquired, seeing that Keegan had begun to inspect the body as a whole, though his fascinated gaze kept returning to . . . Color notwithstanding, it really was remarkable.

The assistant surgeon shook his ringlets, absorbed in wrestling off the corpse's shirt.

'No wound that I can see. Blow to the head, perhaps?' He bent close, squinting at the corpse's head and face, poking here and there in an exploratory fashion.

A group of men in uniform came toward them at the trot, hastily doing up straps and buttons, hoicking packs and muskets into place, and cursing as they went. Grey removed his hat and placed it strategically abaft the corpse, not wishing to excite public remark – but no one bothered to spare a glance at the tableau by the surgeon's tent; one dead man was much like another.

Grey reclaimed his hat and watched them go,

grumbling like a miniature thunderstorm on the move. Most of the troops were already massed on the parade ground. He could see them in the distance, moving in a slow, disorderly mill that would snap into clean formation at the sergeant-major's shout.

'I know Colonel Ruysdale by reputation,' Grey said, after a thoughtful pause, 'though not personally. I have heard him described as "a bit of a Gawd-'elp-us," but I have not heard that he is altogether an ass.'

Keegan smiled, keeping his eyes on his work.

'Shouldn't think he is,' he agreed. 'Not altogether.'

Grey kept an inviting silence, to which invitation the surgeon acquiesced within moments.

'He means to wear them out, see. Bring them back so tired they fall asleep in their suppers.'

'Oh, yes?'

'They been a-staying up all night, you see? Nobody wanting to fall asleep, lest the thing – a sucky-bus, is it? – should come round in their dreams. Mind, it's good for the tavern owners, but not so good for discipline, what with men falling asleep on sentry-go, or in the midst of drill . . .'

Keegan glanced up from his inspections, observing Grey with interest.

'Not sleeping so well yourself, Major?' He tapped a dirty finger beneath his eye, indicating the presence of dark rings, and chuckled.

'I kept rather late hours last night, yes,' Grey

replied equably. 'Owing to the discovery of Private Bodger.'

'Hmm. Yes, I see,' Keegan said, straightening up. 'Seems as though the sucky-bus had her fill of him, then.'

'So you do know about the rumors of a succubus?' Grey asked, ignoring the attempt at badinage.

'Of course I do.' Keegan looked surprised. 'Everybody knows. Aren't I just telling you?'

Keegan did not know how the rumor had reached the encampment, but it had spread like wildfire, reaching every man in camp within twenty-four hours. Original scoffing had become skeptical attention, and then reluctant belief, as more stories began to circulate of the dreams and torments suffered by men in the town – and had become outright panic, with the news of the Hanoverian soldier's death.

'I don't suppose you saw that body?' Grey asked, interested.

The Welshman shook his head. 'The word is that the poor bugger was drained of blood – but who's to know the truth of it? Perhaps it was an apoplexy; I've seen 'em taken so, sometimes – the blood comes bursting from the nose, so as to relieve the pressure on the brain. Messy enough to look at.'

'You seem a rational man, sir,' Grey said, in compliment.

Keegan gave a small, huffing sort of laugh, dismissing it, and straightened up, brushing his palms once more against his coat skirts.

'Deal with soldiers for as long as I have, Major, and you get used to wild stories, that's all I can say. Men in camp, 'specially. Not enough to keep them busy, and a good tale will spread like butter on hot toast. And when it comes to dreams . . . !' He threw up his hands.

Grey nodded, acknowledging the truth of this. Soldiers put great store in dreams involving Jamie Fraser. A faint warmth in the belly reminded him of one of his own dreams, but he put the memory firmly aside.

'So you can tell me nothing regarding the cause of Private Bodger's death?'

Keegan shook his head, scratching at a row of fleabites on his neck as he did so.

'Don't see a thing, sir, I'm sorry to say. Other than the . . . um . . . obvious.' He nodded delicately toward the corpse's mid-region. 'And that's not generally fatal. You might ask the fellow's friends, though. Just in case.'

This cryptic allusion made Grey glance up in question, and Keegan coughed.

'I did say the men didn't sleep, sir? Not wanting to give any sucky-bus an invitation, so to speak. Well, some went a bit further than that, and took matters – so to speak – into their own hands.'

A few bold souls, Keegan said, had reasoned that if what the succubus desired was the male essence, safety lay in removing this temptation – 'so to speak, sir.' While most of those choosing this expedient had presumably chosen to take their precautions in privacy, the men lived in very close quarters. It was in fact complaints from more than one citizen of gross mass indecency by the soldiers quartered on his premises that had provoked Colonel Ruysdale's edict.

'Only thinking, sir, as a wet graveyard is maybe not the place I'd choose for romance, was the opportunity to come my way. But I could see, maybe, a group of men thinking they'd face down the sucky-bus on her own ground, perhaps? And if Private . . . Bodger, you said was his name, sir? . . . was to have keeled over in the midst of such proceedings . . . well, I expect his comrades would have buggered off smartly, not hung about to answer questions.'

'You have a very interesting turn of mind, Mr. Keegan,' Grey said. 'Highly rational. I don't suppose it was you who suggested this particular . . . precaution?'

'Who, me?' Keegan tried – and failed – to exhibit outrage. 'The idea, Major!'

'Quite,' Grey said, and took his leave.

In the distance, the troops were departing the parade ground in orderly fashion, each rank setting off in turn, to the clank and rattle of canteens and muskets and the staccato cries of corporals and sergeants. He stopped for a moment to watch them, enjoying the warmth of the autumn sun on his back.

After the fury of the night's storm, the day had dawned clear and calm, and promised to be mild. Very muddy underfoot, though, he noted, seeing the churned earth of the parade ground and the spray of clods flying off the feet of the runners, spattering their breeches. It would be heavy going, and the devil of a sweat to clean up afterward. Ruysdale might not have intended this exercise principally as punishment, but that's what it would be.

Artilleryman that he had been, Grey automatically evaluated the quality of the terrain for the passage of caissons. Not a chance. The ground was soft as sodden cheese. Even the mortars would bog down in nothing flat.

He turned, eyeing the distant hills where the French were said to be. If they had cannon, chances were that they were going nowhere for the moment.

The situation still left him with a lingering sense of unease, loath though he was to admit it. Yes, the French likely were intending to move toward the north. No, there was no apparent reason for them to cross the valley; Gundwitz had no strategic importance, nor was it of sufficient size to be worth a detour to loot. Yes, Billman's troops were between the French and the town. But he looked at the deserted parade ground, and the troops vanishing in the distance, and felt a tickle between the shoulder blades, as though someone stood behind him with a loaded pistol.

I should feel happier if a few more of Ruysdale's troops were to move to defend the bridge. Hicks's words echoed in memory. So Sir Peter felt that itch, as well. It was possible, Grey reflected, that Ruysdale *was* an ass.

Chapter 4

The Gun Crew

It was past midday by the time he reached the river. From a distance, it was a tranquil landscape under a high, pale sun, the river bordered by a thick growth of trees in autumn leaf, their ancient golds and bloody reds a-shimmer, in contrast to the black-and-dun patchwork of fallow fields and meadows gone to seed.

A little closer, though, and the river itself dispelled this impression of pastoral charm. It was a broad, deep stream, turbulent and fast-moving, much swollen by the recent rains. Even at a distance, he could see the tumbling forms of uprooted trees and bushes, and the occasional carcass of a small animal, drowned in the current.

The Prussian artillery were placed upon a small rise of ground, concealed in a copse. Only one ten-pounder, he saw, with a sense of unease, and a small mortar – though there were sufficient stores of shot and powder, and these were commendably well-kept, with a Prussian sense of order, tidily sheltered under canvas against the rain.

The men greeted him with great cordiality; any

diversion from the boredom of bridge-guarding was welcome – the more welcome if it came bearing beer, which Grey did, having thoughtfully procured two large ale skins before leaving camp.

'You will with us eat, Major,' said the Hanoverian lieutenant in charge, accepting both beer and dispatches, and waving a gracious hand toward a convenient boulder.

It was a long time since breakfast, and Grey accepted the invitation with pleasure. He took off his coat and spread it over the boulder, rolled up his sleeves, and joined companionably in the hard biscuit, cheese, and beer, accepting with gratitude a few bites of chewy, spicy sausage, as well.

Lieutenant Dietrich, a middle-aged gentleman with a luxuriant beard and eyebrows to match, opened the dispatches and read them while Grey practiced his German with the gun crew. He kept a careful eye upon the lieutenant as he chatted, though, curious to see what the artilleryman would make of von Namtzen's dispatch.

The lieutenant's eyebrows were an admirable indication of his interior condition; they remained level for the first moments of reading, then rose to an apex of astonishment, where they remained suspended for no little time, returning to their original position with small flutters of dismay, as the lieutenant decided how much of this informa- tion it was wise to impart to his men.

The lieutenant folded the paper, shooting Grey a

sharp interrogative glance. Grey gave a slight nod; yes, he knew what the dispatch said.

The lieutenant glanced round at the men, then back over his shoulder, as though judging the distance across the valley to the British camp and the town beyond. Then he looked back at Grey, thoughtfully chewing his mustache, and shook his head slightly. He would not mention the matter of a succubus.

On the whole, Grey thought that wise, and inclined his head an inch in agreement. There were only ten men present; if any of them had already known of the rumors, all would know. And while the lieutenant seemed at ease with his command, the fact remained that these were Prussians, and not his own men. He could not be sure of their response.

The lieutenant folded away his papers and came to join the conversation. However, Grey observed with interest that the substance of the dispatch seemed to weigh upon the lieutenant's mind, in such a way that the conversation turned – with no perceptible nudge in that direction, but with the inexorable swing of a compass needle – to manifestations of the supernatural.

It being a fine day, with golden leaves drifting gently down around them, the gurgle of the river nearby, and plenty of beer to hand, the varied tales of ghosts, bleeding nuns, and spectral battles in the sky were no more than the stuff of entertainment. In the cold shadows of the night, it would be different – though the stories would still be told. More than cannon shot, bayonets, or disease, boredom was a soldier's greatest enemy.

At one point, though, an artilleryman told the story of a fine house in his town, where the cries of a ghostly child echoed in the rooms at night, to the consternation of the householders. In time, they traced the sound to one particular wall, chipped away the plaster, and discovered a bricked-up chimney, in which lay the remains of a young boy, with the dagger which had cut his throat.

Several of the soldiers made the sign of the horns at this, but Grey saw distinct expressions of unease on the faces of two of the men. These two exchanged glances, then looked hurriedly away.

'You have heard such a story before, perhaps?' Grey asked, addressing the younger of the two directly. He smiled, doing his best to look harmlessly engaging.

The boy – he could be no more than fifteen – hesitated, but such was the press of interest from those around him that he could not resist.

'Not a story,' he said. 'I – we' – he nodded at his fellow – 'last night, in the storm. We heard a child crying, near the river. We went to look, with a lantern, but there was nothing there. Still, we heard it. It went on and on, though we walked up and down, calling and searching, until we were wet through, and nearly frozen.'

'Oh, is that what you were doing?' a fellow in his twenties interjected, grinning. 'And here we thought you and Samson were just buggering each other under the bridge.'

Blood surged up into the boy's face with a suddenness that made his eyes bulge, and he launched himself at the older man, knocking him off his seat and rolling with him into the leaves in a ball of fists and elbows.

Grey sprang to his feet and kicked them apart, seizing the boy by the scruff of the neck and jerking him up. The lieutenant was shouting at them angrily in idiomatic German, which Grey ignored. He shook the boy slightly, to bring him to his senses, and said, very quietly, 'Laugh. It was a joke.'

He stared hard into the boy's eyes, willing him to come to his senses. The thin shoulders under his hands vibrated with the need to strike out, to hit something – and the brown eyes were glassy with anguish and confusion.

Grey shook him harder, then released him, and under the guise of slapping dead leaves from his uniform, leaned closer. 'If you act like this, they will know,' he said, speaking in a rapid whisper. 'For God's sake, laugh!'

Samson, experienced enough to know what to do in such circumstances, was doing it – pushing at joking comrades, replying to crude jests with cruder ones. The young boy glanced at him, a flicker of awareness coming back into his face. Grey let him go, and turned back to the group, saying loudly, 'If I were going to bugger someone, I would wait for good weather. A man must be desperate, to swive *anything* in such rain and thunder!'

'It's been a long time, Major,' said one of the soldiers, laughing. He made crude thrusting gestures with his hips. 'Even a sheep in a snowstorm would look good now!'

'Haha. Go fuck yourself, Wulfie. The sheep wouldn't have you.' The boy was still flushed and damp-eyed, but back in control of himself. He rubbed a hand across his mouth and spat, forcing a grin as the others laughed.

'You *could* fuck yourself, Wulfie – if your dick is as long as you say it is.' Samson leered at Wulf, who stuck out an amazingly long tongue in reply, waggling it in derision.

'Don't you wish you knew!'

The discussion was interrupted at this point by two soldiers who came puffing up the rise, wet to the waist and dragging with them a large dead pig, fished out of the river. This addition to supper was greeted with cries of approbation, and half the men fell at once to the work of butchery, the others returning in desultory fashion to their conversation.

The vigor had gone out of it, though, and Grey was about to take his leave, when one of the men said something, laughing, about gypsy women.

'What did you say? I mean – *was ist das Du hast sprechen*?' He groped for his German. 'Gypsies? You have seen them recently?'

'Oh, *ja*, Major,' said the soldier obligingly. 'This morning. They came across the bridge, six wagons with mules. They go back and forth. We've seen them before.'

With a little effort, Grey kept his voice calm.

'Indeed?' He turned to the lieutenant. 'Does it not seem possible that they may have dealings with the French?'

'Of course.' The lieutenant looked mildly surprised, then grinned. 'What are they going to tell the French? That we're here? I think they know that, Major.'

He gestured toward a gap in the trees. Through it, Grey could see the English soldiers of Ruysdale's regiment, perhaps a mile away, their ranks piling up on the bank of the river like driftwood as they flung down their packs and waded into the shallows to drink, hot and mud-caked from their run.

It was true; the presence of the English and Hanoverian regiments could be a surprise to no one; anyone on the cliffs with a spyglass could likely count the spots on Colonel Ruysdale's dog. As for information regarding their movements . . . well, since neither Ruysdale nor Hicks had any idea where they were going or when, there wasn't any great danger of that intelligence being revealed to the enemy.

He smiled, and took gracious leave of the lieutenant, though privately resolving to speak to Stephan von Namtzen. Perhaps the gypsies were harmless – but they should be looked into. If nothing else, the gypsies were in a position to tell anyone who cared to ask them how few men were guarding that bridge. And somehow, he thought that Ruysdale was not of a mind to consider Sir Peter's request for reinforcement.

He waved casually to the artillerymen, who took little notice, elbow-deep in blood and pig guts. The boy was by himself, chopping green wood for the spit.

Leaving the artillery camp, he rode up to the head of the bridge and paused, reining Karolus in as he looked across the river. The land was flat for a little way, but then broke into rolling hills. Above, on the cliffs, the French presumably still lurked. He took a small spyglass from his pocket, and scanned the clifftops, slowly. Nothing moved on the heights; no horses, no men, no swaying banners – and yet a faint gray haze drifted up there, a cloud in an otherwise cloudless sky. The smoke of campfires; many of them. Yes, the French were still there.

He scanned the hills below, looking carefully – but if the gypsies were there, as well, no rising plume of smoke betrayed their presence.

He should find the gypsy camp and question its inhabitants himself – but it was growing late, and he had no stomach for that now. He reined about and turned the horse's head back toward the distant town, not glancing at the copse that hid the cannon and its crew.

The boy had best learn – and quickly – to hide his nature, or he would become in short order bumboy to any man who cared to use him. And many would. Wulf had been correct; after months in the field, soldiers were not particular, and the boy was much more appealing than a sheep, with those soft red lips and tender skin.

Karolus tossed his head, and he slowed, uneasy. Grey's hands were trembling on the reins, gripped far too tightly. He forced them to relax, stilled the trembling, and spoke calmly to the horse, nudging him back to speed.

He had been attacked once, in camp somewhere in Scotland, in the days after Culloden. Someone had come upon him in the dark, and taken him from behind with an arm across his throat. He had thought he was dead, but his assailant had something else in mind. The man had never spoken, and was brutally swift about his business, leaving him moments later, curled in the dirt behind a wagon, speechless with shock and pain.

He had never known who it was: officer, soldier, or some anonymous intruder. Never known whether the man had discerned something in his own appearance or behavior that led to the attack, or had only taken him because he was there.

He *had* known the danger of telling anyone about it. He washed himself, stood straight and walked firmly, spoke normally and looked men in the eye. No one had suspected the bruised and riven flesh beneath his uniform, or the hollowness beneath his breastbone. And if his attacker sat at meals and broke bread with him, he had not known it. From that day, he had carried a dagger at all times, and no one had ever touched him again against his will.

The sun was sinking behind him, and the shadow of horse and rider stretched out far before him, flying, and faceless in their flight.

Chapter 5

Dark Dreams

Once more he was late for dinner. This time, though, a tray was brought for him, and he sat in the drawing room, taking his supper while the rest of the company chatted.

The princess saw to his needs, and sat with him for a time, flatteringly attentive. He was worn out from a day of riding, though, and his answers to her questions brief. Soon enough, she drifted away and left him to a peaceful engagement with some cold venison and a tart of dried apricots.

He had nearly finished, when he felt a large, warm hand on his shoulder.

'So, you have seen the gun crew at the bridge? They are in good order?' von Namtzen asked.

'Yes, very good,' Grey replied. No point – not yet – in mentioning the young soldier to von Namtzen. 'I told them more men will come, from Ruysdale's regiment.'

'The bridge?' The dowager, catching the word, turned from her conversation, frowning. 'You have no need to worry, Landgrave. The bridge is safe.'

'I am sure it will be safe, madam,' Stephan said,

clicking his heels gallantly as he bowed to the old lady. 'You may be assured, Major Grey and I will protect you.'

The old lady looked faintly put out at the notion.

'The bridge is safe,' she repeated, touching the religious medal on the bodice of her gown, and glancing pugnaciously from man to man. 'No enemy has crossed the bridge at Aschenwald in five hundred years. No enemy will ever cross it!'

Stephan glanced at Grey, and cleared his throat slightly. Grey cleared his own throat and made a gracious compliment upon the food.

When the dowager had moved away, Stephan shook his head behind her back, and exchanged a brief smile with Grey.

'You know about that bridge?'

'No, is there something odd about it?'

'Only a story.' Von Namtzen shrugged, with a tolerant scorn for the superstition of others. 'They say that there is a guardian, a spirit of some kind that defends the bridge.'

'Indeed,' Grey said, with an uneasy memory of the stories told by the gun crew stationed near the bridge. Were any of them local men, he wondered, who would know the story?

'*Mein Gott,*' Stephan said, shaking his massive head as though assailed by gnats. 'These stories! How can sane men believe such things?'

'I collect you do not mean that particular story?' Grey said. 'The succubus, perhaps?'

'Don't speak to me of that thing,' von Namtzen

said gloomily. 'My men look like scarecrows and jump at a bird's shadow. Every one of them is scared to lay his head upon a pillow, for fear that he will turn it and look into the night hag's face.'

'Your chaps aren't the only ones.' Sir Peter had come to pour himself another drink. He lifted the glass and took a deep swallow, shuddering slightly. Billman, behind him, nodded in glum confirmation.

'Bloody sleepwalkers, the lot.'

'Ah,' said Grey thoughtfully. 'If I might make a suggestion . . . not my own, you understand. A notion mentioned by Ruysdale's surgeon . . .'

He explained Mr. Keegan's remedy, keeping his voice discreetly low. His listeners were less discreet in their response.

'What, Ruysdale's chaps are all boxing the Jesuit and begetting cockroaches?' Grey thought Sir Peter would expire from suffocated laughter. Just as well Lieutenant Dundas wasn't present, he thought.

'Perhaps not all of them,' he said. 'Evidently enough, though, to be of concern. I take it you have not experienced a similar phenomenon among your troops . . . yet?'

Billman caught the delicate pause and whooped loudly.

'Boxing the Jesuit?' Stephan nudged Grey with an elbow, and raised thick blond brows in puzzlement. 'Cockroaches? What does this mean, please?'

'Ahhh . . .' Having no notion of the German equivalent of this expression, Grey resorted to a briefly graphic gesture with one hand, looking over his shoulder to be sure that none of the women was watching.

'Oh!' Von Namtzen looked mildly startled, but then grinned widely. 'I see, yes, very good!' He nudged Grey again, more familiarly, and dropped his voice a little. 'Perhaps wise to take some such precaution personally, do you think?'

The women and the German officers, heretofore intent on a card game, were looking toward the Englishmen in puzzlement. One man called a question to von Namtzen, and Grey was fortunately saved from reply.

Something occurred to him, though, and he grasped von Namtzen by the arm, as the latter was about to go and join the others at a hand of favo.

'A moment, Stephan. I had meant to ask – that man of yours who died – Koenig? Did you see the body yourself?'

Von Namtzen was still smiling, but at this, his expression grew more somber, and he shook his head.

'No, I did not see him. They said, though, that his throat was most terribly torn – as though a wild animal had been at him. And yet he was not outside; he was found in his quarters.' He shook his head again, and left to join the card game.

Grey finished his meal amid cordial conversation with Sir Peter and Billman, though keeping an inconspicuous eye upon the progress of the card game.

Stephan was in dress uniform tonight. A smaller man would have been overwhelmed by it; Hanoverian taste in military decoration was grossly excessive, to an English eye. Still, with his big frame and leonine blond head, the Landgrave von Erdberg was merely . . . eye-catching.

He appeared to have caught the eye not only of the Princess Louisa, but of three other young women. These surrounded him like a moony triplet, caught in his orbit. Now he reached into the breast of his coat and withdrew some small object, causing them to cluster round to look at it.

Grey turned to answer some question of Billman's, but then turned back, trying not to look too obviously.

He had been trying to suppress the feeling Stephan roused in him, but in the end, such things were never controllable – they rose up. Sometimes like the bursting of a mortar shell, sometimes like the inexorable green spike of a crocus pushing through snow and ice – but they rose up.

Was he in love with Stephan? There was no question of that. He liked and respected the Hanoverian, but there was no madness in it, no yearning. Did he *want* Stephan? A soft warmth in his loins, as though his blood had begun somehow to simmer over a low flame, suggested that he did.

The ancient bear's skull still sat in its place of honor, below the old prince's portrait. He moved slowly to examine it, keeping half an eye on Stephan.

'Surely you have not eaten enough, John!' A delicate hand on his elbow turned him, and he looked down into the princess's face smiling up at him with pretty coquetry. 'A strong man, out all day – let me call the servants to bring you something special.'

'I assure you, Your Highness . . .' But she would have none of it, and tapping him playfully with her fan, she scudded away like a gilded cloud, to have some special dessert prepared for him.

Feeling obscurely like a fatted calf being readied for the slaughter, Grey sought refuge in male company, coming to rest beside von Namtzen, who was folding up whatever he had been showing to the women, who had all gone to peer over the card player's shoulders and make bets.

'What is that?' Grey asked, nodding at the object.

'Oh—' Von Namtzen looked a little disconcerted at the question, but with only a moment's hesitation, handed it to Grey. It was a small leather case, hinged, with a gold closure. 'My children.'

It was a miniature, done by an excellent hand. The heads of two children, close together, one boy, one girl, both blond. The boy, clearly a little older, was perhaps three or four.

Grey felt momentarily as though he had received an actual blow to the pit of the stomach; his mouth opened, but he was incapable of speech. Or at least he thought he was. To his surprise, he heard his own voice, sounding calm, politely admiring.

'They are very handsome indeed. I am sure they are a consolation to your wife, in your absence.'

Von Namtzen grimaced slightly, and gave a brief shrug.

'Their mother is dead. She died in childbirth when Elise was born.' A huge forefinger touched the tiny face, very gently. 'My mother looks after them.'

Grey made the proper sounds of condolence, but had ceased to hear himself, for the confusion of thought and speculation that filled his mind.

So much so, in fact, that when the princess's special dessert – an enormous concoction of raspberries, brandy, sugar, and cream – arrived, he ate it all, despite the fact that raspberries made him itch.

He continued to think, long after the ladies had left. He joined the card game, bet extensively, and played wildly – winning, with Luck's usual perversity, though he paid no attention to his cards.

Had he been entirely wrong? It was possible. All of Stephan's gestures toward him had been within the bounds of normalcy – and yet . . .

And yet it was by no means unknown for men such as himself to marry and have children. Certainly men such as von Namtzen, with a title and estates to bequeath, would wish to have heirs. That thought steadied him, and though he scratched occasionally at chest or neck, he paid more attention to his game – and finally began to lose.

The card game broke up an hour later. Grey

loitered a bit, in hopes that Stephan might seek him out, but the Hanoverian was detained in argument with Kaptain Steffens, and at last Grey went upstairs, still scratching.

The halls were well lit tonight, and he found his own corridor without difficulty. He hoped Tom was still awake; perhaps the young valet could fetch him something for itching. Some ointment, perhaps, or – he heard the rustle of fabric behind him, and turned to find the princess approaching him.

She was once again in nightdress – but not the homely woolen garment she had worn the night before. This time, she wore a flowing thing of diaphanous lawn, which clung to her bosom and rather clearly revealed her nipples through the thin fabric. He thought she must be very cold, in spite of the lavishly embroidered robe thrown over the nightgown.

She had no cap, and her hair had been brushed out but not yet plaited for the night; it flowed becomingly in golden waves below her shoulders. Grey began to feel somewhat cold, too, in spite of the brandy.

'My Lord,' she said. 'John,' she added, and smiled. 'I have something for you.' She was holding something in one hand, he saw; a small box of some sort.

'Your Highness,' he said, repressing the urge to take a step backward. She was wearing a very strong scent, redolent of tuberoses – a scent he particularly disliked.

'My name is Louisa,' she said, taking another step toward him. 'Will you not call me by my name? Here, in private?'

'Of course. If you wish it – Louisa.' Good God, what had brought this on? He had sufficient experience to see what she was about – he was a handsome man, of good family, and with money; it had happened often enough – but not with royalty, who tended to be accustomed to taking what they wanted.

He took her outstretched hand, ostensibly for the purpose of kissing it; in reality, to keep her at a safe distance. What did she want? And why?

'This is – to thank you,' she said, as he raised his head from her beringed knuckles. She thrust the box into his other hand. 'And to protect you.'

'I assure you, madam, no thanks are necessary. I did nothing.' Christ, was that it? Did she think she must bed him, in token of thanks – or rather, had convinced herself that she must, because she wanted to? She did want to; he could see her excitement, in the slightly widened blue eyes, the flushed cheeks, the rapid pulse in her throat. He squeezed her fingers gently and released them, then tried to hand back the box.

'Really, madam – Louisa – I cannot accept this; surely it is a treasure of your family.' It certainly looked valuable; small as it was, it was remarkably heavy – made either of gilded lead or of solid gold – and sported a number of crudely cut cabochon stones, which he feared were precious.

'Oh, it is,' she assured him. 'It has been in my husband's family for hundreds of years.'

'Oh, well, then certainly—'

'No, you must keep it,' she said vehemently. 'It will protect you from the creature.'

'Creature. You mean the—'

'*Der Nachtmahr,*' she said, lowering her voice and looking involuntarily over one shoulder, as though fearing that some vile thing hovered in the air nearby.

Nachtmahr. 'Nightmare,' it meant. Despite himself, a brief shiver tightened Grey's shoulders. The halls were better lighted, but still harbored drafts that made the candles flicker and shadows flow like moving water down the walls.

He glanced down at the box. There were letters etched into the lid, in Latin, but of so ancient a sort that it would take close examination to work out what they said.

'It is a reliquary,' she said, moving closer, as though to point out the inscription. 'Of St. Orgevald.'

'Ah? Er . . . yes. Most interesting.' He thought this mildly gruesome. Of all the objectionable popish practices, this habit of chopping up saints and scattering their remnants to the far ends of the earth was possibly the most reprehensible.

She was very close, her perfume cloying in his nostrils. How was he to get rid of the woman? The door to his room was only a foot or two away; he had a strong urge to open it, leap in, and slam it shut, but that wouldn't do.

'You will protect me, protect my son,' she murmured, looking trustfully up at him from beneath golden lashes. 'So I will protect you, dear John.'

She flung her arms about his neck, and glued her lips to his in a passionate kiss. Sheer courtesy required him to return the embrace, though his mind was racing, looking feverishly for some escape. Where the devil were the servants? Why did no one interrupt them?

Then someone did interrupt them. There was a gruff cough near at hand, and Grey broke the embrace with relief – a short-lived emotion, as he looked up to discover the Landgrave von Erdberg standing a few feet away, glowering under heavy brows.

'Your pardon, Your Highness,' Stephan said, in tones of ice. 'I wished to speak to Major Grey; I did not know anyone was here.'

The princess was flushed, but quite collected. She smoothed her gown down across her body, drawing herself up in such a way that her fine bust was strongly emphasized.

'Oh,' she said, very cool. 'It's you, Erdberg. Do not worry, I was just taking my leave of the major. You may have him now.' A small, smug smile twitched at the corner of her mouth. Quite deliberately, she laid a hand along Grey's heated cheek, and let her fingers trail along his skin as she turned away. Then she strolled – curse the woman, she *strolled*! – away, switching the tail of her robe.

There was a profound silence in the hallway.

Grey broke it, finally.

'You wished to speak with me, Captain?'

Von Namtzen looked him over coldly, as though deciding whether to step on him.

'No,' he said at last. 'It will wait.' He turned on his heel and strode away, making a good deal more noise in his departure than had the princess.

Grey pressed a hand to his forehead, until he could trust his head not to explode, then shook it, and lunged for the door to his room before anything else should happen.

Tom was sitting on a stool by the fire, mending a pair of breeches that had suffered injury to the seams while Grey was demonstrating saber lunges to one of the German officers. He looked up at once when Grey came in, but if he had heard any of the conversation in the hall, he made no reference to it.

'What's that, me lord?' he asked instead, seeing the box in Grey's hand.

'What? Oh, that.' Grey put it down, with a faint feeling of distaste. 'A relic. Of St. Orgevald, whoever he might be.'

'Oh, I know him!'

'You do?' Grey raised one brow.

'Yes, me lord. There's a little chapel to him, down the garden. Ilse – she's one of the kitchen maids – was showing me. He's right famous hereabouts.'

'Indeed.' Grey began to undress, tossing his coat across the chair and starting on his waistcoat buttons. His fingers were impatient, slipping on the small buttons. 'Famous for what?'

'Stopping them killing the children. Will I help you, me lord?'

'What?' Grey stopped, staring at the young valet, then shook his head and resumed twitching buttons. 'No, continue. Killing what children?'

Tom's hair was standing up on end, as it tended to do whenever he was interested in a subject, owing to his habit of running one hand through it.

'Well, d'ye see, me lord, it used to be the custom, when they'd build something important, they'd buy a child from the gypsies – or just take one, I s'pose – and wall it up in the foundation. Specially for a bridge. It keeps anybody wicked from crossing over, see?'

Grey resumed his unbuttoning, more slowly. The hair prickled uneasily on his nape.

'The child – the murdered child – would cry out, I suppose?'

Tom looked surprised at his acumen.

'Yes, me lord. However did you know that?'

'Never mind. So St. Orgevald put a stop to this practice, did he? Good for him.' He glanced, more kindly, at the small gold box. 'There's a chapel, you say – is it in use?'

'No, me lord. It's full of bits of stored rubbish. Or, rather – 'tisn't in use for what you might call devotions. Folk do go there.' The boy flushed a bit, and frowned intently at his work. Grey deduced that Ilse might have shown him another use for a deserted chapel, but chose not to pursue the matter.

'I see. Was Ilse able to tell you anything else of interest?'

'Depends upon what you call interesting, me lord.' Tom's eyes were still fixed upon his needle, but Grey could tell from the way in which he caught his upper lip between his teeth that he was in possession of a juicy bit of information.

'At this point, my chief interest is in my bed,' Grey said, finally extricating himself from the waistcoat, 'but tell me anyway.'

'Reckon you know the nursemaid's still gone?'

'I do.'

'Did you know her name was Koenig, and that she was wife to the Hun soldier what the succubus got?'

Grey had just about broken Tom of calling the Germans 'Huns,' at least in their hearing, but chose to overlook this lapse.

'I did not.' Grey unfastened his neckcloth, slowly. 'Was this known to all the servants?' More importantly, did Stephan know?

'Oh, yes, me lord.' Tom had laid down his needle, and now looked up, eager with his news. 'See, the soldier, he used to do work here, at the Schloss.'

'When? Was he a local man, then?' It was quite usual for soldiers to augment their pay by doing work for the local citizenry in their off hours, but Stephan's men had been *in situ* for less than a month. But if the nurserymaid was the man's wife—

'Yes, me lord. Born here, the both of them. He

141

joined the local regiment some years a-gone, and came here to work—'

'What work did he do?' Grey asked, unsure whether this had any bearing on Koenig's demise, but wanting a moment to encompass the information.

'Builder,' Tom replied promptly. 'Part of the upper floors got the woodworm, and had to be replaced.'

'Hmm. You seem remarkably well informed. Just how long did you spend in the chapel with young Ilse?'

Tom gave him a look of limpid innocence, much more inculpatory than an open leer.

'Me lord?'

'Never mind. Go on. Was the man working here at the time he was killed?'

'No, me lord. He left with the regiment two years back. He did come round a week or so ago, Ilse said, only to visit his friends among the servants, but he didn't work here.'

Grey had now got down to his drawers, which he removed with a sigh of relief.

'Christ, what sort of perverse country is it where they put starch in a man's smallclothes? Can you not deal with the laundresses, Tom?'

'Sorry, me lord.' Tom scrambled to retrieve the discarded drawers. 'I didn't know the word for starch. I thought I did, but whatever I said just made 'em laugh.'

'Well, don't make Ilse laugh too much. Leaving

the maidservants with child is an abuse of hospitality.'

'Oh, no, me lord,' Tom assured him earnestly. 'We was too busy talking to, er . . .'

'To be sure you were,' Grey said equably. 'Did she tell you anything else of interest?'

'Mebbe.' Tom had the nightshirt already aired and hanging by the fire to warm; he held it up for Grey to draw over his head, the wool flannel soft and grateful as it slid over his skin. 'Mind, it's only gossip.'

'Mmm?'

'One of the older footmen, who used to work with Koenig – after Koenig came to visit, he was talkin' with one of the other servants, and he said in Ilse's hearing as how little Siegfried was growing up to be the spit of him. Of Koenig, I mean, not the footman. But then he saw her listening and shut up smart.'

Grey stopped in the act of reaching for his banyan, and stared.

'Indeed,' he said. Tom nodded, looking modestly pleased with the effect of his findings.

'That's the princess's old husband, isn't it, over the mantelpiece in the drawing room? Ilse showed me the picture. Looks a proper old bugger, don't he?'

'Yes,' said Grey, smiling slightly. 'And?'

'He ain't had – hadn't, I mean – any children more than Siegfried, though he was married twice before. And Master Siegfried was born six months to the day after the old fellow died. That kind of thing always causes talk, don't it?'

'I should say so, yes.' Grey thrust his feet into the proffered slippers. 'Thank you, Tom. You've done more than well.'

Tom shrugged modestly, though his round face beamed as if illuminated from within.

'Will I fetch you tea, me lord? Or a nice syllabub?'

'Thank you, no. Find your bed, Tom, you've earned your rest.'

'Very good, me lord.' Tom bowed; his manners were improving markedly, under the example of the Schloss's servants. He picked up the clothes Grey had left on the chair, to take away for brushing, but then stopped to examine the little reliquary, which Grey had left on the table.

'That's a handsome thing, me lord. A relic, did you say? Isn't that a bit of somebody?'

'It is.' Grey started to tell Tom to take the thing away with him, but stopped. It was undoubtedly valuable; best to leave it here. 'Probably a finger or a toe, judging from the size.'

Tom bent, peering at the faded lettering.

'What does it say, me lord? Can you read it?'

'Probably.' Grey took the box, and brought it close to the candle. Held thus at an angle, the worn lettering sprang into legibility. So did the drawing etched into the top, which Grey had to that point assumed to be merely decorative lines. The words confirmed it.

'Isn't that a . . . ?' Tom said, goggling at it.

'Yes, it is.' Grey gingerly set the box down.

They regarded it in silence for a moment.

'Ah . . . where did you get it, me lord?' Tom asked finally.

'The princess gave it me. As protection from the succubus.'

'Oh.' The young valet shifted his weight to one foot, and glanced sidelong at him. 'Ah . . . d'ye think it will work?'

Grey cleared his throat.

'I assure you, Tom, if the phallus of St. Orgevald does not protect me, nothing will.'

Left alone, he sank into the chair by the fire, closed his eyes, and tried to compose himself sufficiently to think. The conversation with Tom had at least allowed him a little distance, from which to contemplate matters with the princess and Stephan – save that they didn't bear contemplation.

He felt mildly nauseated, and sat up to pour a glass of plum brandy from the decanter on the table. That helped, settling both his stomach and his mind.

He sat slowly sipping it, gradually bringing his mental faculties to bear on the less personal aspects of the situation.

Tom's discoveries cast a new and most interesting light on matters. If Grey had ever believed in the existence of a succubus – and he was sufficiently honest to admit that there had been moments, both in the graveyard and in the dark-flickering halls of the Schloss – he believed no longer.

The attempted kidnapping was plainly the work of some human agency, and the revelation of the relationship between the two Koenigs – the vanished nursemaid and her dead husband – just as plainly indicated that the death of Private Koenig was part of the same affair, no matter what hocus-pocus had been contrived around it.

Grey's father had died when he was twelve, but had succeeded in instilling in his son his own admiration for the philosophy of reason. In addition to the concept of Occam's razor, his father had also introduced him to the useful doctrine of *cui bono*.

The plainly obvious answer there was the princess Louisa. Granting for the present that the gossip was true, and that Koenig had fathered little Siegfried . . . the last thing the woman could want was for Koenig to return and hang about where awkward resemblances could be noted.

He had no idea of the German law regarding paternity. In England, a child born in wedlock was legally the offspring of the husband, even when everyone and the dog's mother knew that the wife had been openly unfaithful. By such means, several gentlemen of his acquaintance had children, even though he was quite sure that the men had never even thought of sharing their wives' beds. Had Stephan perhaps—

He caught that thought by the scruff of the neck

and shoved it aside. Besides, if the miniaturist had been faithful, Stephan's son was the spitting image of his father. Though painters naturally would produce what image they thought most desired by the patron, in spite of the reality—

He picked up the glass and drank from it until he felt breathless and his ears buzzed.

'Koenig,' he said firmly, aloud. Whether the gossip was true or not – and having kissed the princess, he rather thought it was; no shrinking violet, she! – and whether or not Koenig's reappearance might threaten Siggy's legitimacy, the man's presence must certainly have been unwelcome.

Unwelcome enough to have arranged his death?

Why, when he would be gone again soon? The troops were likely to move within the week – surely within the month. Had something happened that made the removal of Private Koenig urgent? Perhaps Koenig himself had been in ignorance of Siegfried's parentage – and upon discovering the boy's resemblance to himself on his visit to the castle, determined to extort money or favor from the princess?

And bringing the matter full circle . . . had the entire notion of the succubus been introduced merely to disguise Koenig's death? If so, how? The rumor had seized the imagination of both troops and townspeople to a marked extent – and Koenig's death had caused it to reach the proportions of a panic – but how had that rumor been started?

He dismissed that question for the moment, as there was no rational way of dealing with it. As for the death, though . . .

He could without much difficulty envision the princess Louisa conspiring in the death of Koenig; he had noticed before that women were quite without mercy where their offspring were concerned. Still . . . the princess had presumably not entered a soldier's quarters and done a man to death with her own lily-white hands.

Who had done it? Someone with great ties of loyalty to the princess, presumably. Though, upon second thought, it need not have been anyone from the castle. Gundwitz was not the teeming boil that London was, but the town was still of sufficient size to sustain a reasonable number of criminals; one of these could likely have been induced to perform the actual murder – if it was a murder, he reminded himself. He must not lose sight of the null hypothesis, in his eagerness to reach a conclusion.

And further . . . even if the princess had in some way contrived both the rumor of the succubus *and* the death of Private Koenig – who was the witch in Siggy's room? Had someone truly tried to abduct the child? Private Koenig was already dead; clearly he could have had nothing to do with it.

He ran a hand through his hair, rubbing his scalp slowly to assist thought.

Loyalties. Who was most loyal to the princess? Her butler? Stephan?

He grimaced, but examined the thought carefully. No. There were no circumstances conceivable under which Stephan would have conspired in the murder of one of his own men. Grey might be in doubt of many things concerning the Hanoverian, but not his honor.

This led back to the princess's behavior toward himself. Did she act from attraction? Grey was modest about his own endowments, but also honest enough to admit that he possessed some and that his person was reasonably attractive to women.

He thought it more likely, if the princess had indeed conspired in Koenig's removal, that her actions toward himself were intended as distraction. Though there *was* yet another explanation. One of the minor corollaries to Occam's razor that he had himself derived suggested that quite often, the observed result of an action really was the intended end of that action. The end result of that encounter in the hallway was that Stephan von Namtzen had discovered him in embrace with the princess, and been noticeably annoyed by said discovery.

Had Louisa's motive been the very simple one of making von Namtzen jealous?

And if Stephan *was* jealous . . . of whom? And what, if anything, did Bodger's death have to do with any of this?

The room had grown intolerably stuffy, and he rose, restless, and went to the window, unlatching the shutters. The moon was full, a great, fecund yellow orb that hung low above the darkened fields and cast its light over the slated roofs of Gundwitz and the paler sea of canvas tents that lay beyond.

Did Ruysdale's troops sleep soundly tonight, exhausted from their healthful exercise? He felt as though he would profit from such exercise himself. He braced himself in the window frame and pushed, feeling the muscles pop in his arms, envisioning escape into that freshening night, running naked and silent as a wolf, soft earth cool, yielding to his feet.

Cold air rushed past his body, raising the coarse hairs on his skin, but his core felt molten. Between the heat of fire and brandy, the nightshirt's original grateful warmth had become oppressive; sweat bloomed upon his body, and the woolen cloth hung limp upon him.

Suddenly impatient, he stripped it off, and stood in the open window, fierce and restless, the cold air caressing his nakedness.

There was a whir and rustle in the ivy nearby, and then something – several somethings – passed in absolute silence so close and so swiftly by his face that he had not even time to start backward, though his heart leapt to his throat, strangling his involuntary cry.

Bats. The creatures had disappeared in an instant, long before his startled mind had collected itself sufficiently to put a name to them.

He leaned out, searching, but the bats had disappeared at once into the dark, swift about their hunting. It was no wonder that legends of succubi abounded, in a place so bat-haunted. The behavior of the creatures indeed seemed supernatural.

The bounds of the small chamber seemed at once intolerably confining. He could imagine himself some demon of the air, taking wing to haunt the dreams of a man, seize upon a sleeping body and ride it – could he fly as far as England? he wondered. Was the night long enough?

The trees at the edge of the garden tossed uneasily, stirred by the wind. The night itself seemed tormented by an autumn restlessness, the sense of things moving, changing, fermenting.

His blood was still hot, having now reached a sort of full, rolling boil, but there was no outlet for it. He did not know whether Stephan's anger was on his own behalf – or Louisa's. In neither case, though, could he make any open demonstration of feeling toward von Namtzen now; it was too dangerous. He was unsure of the German attitude toward sodomites, but felt it unlikely to be more forgiving than the English stance. Whether stolid Protestant morality or a wilder Catholic mysticism – he cast a brief look at the reliquary – neither was likely to have sympathy with his own predilections.

The mere contemplation of revelation and the loss of its possibility, though, had shown him something important.

Stephan von Namtzen both attracted and aroused him, but it was not because of his own undoubted physical qualities. It was, rather, the degree to which those qualities reminded Grey of James Fraser.

Von Namtzen was nearly the same height as Fraser, a powerful man with broad shoulders, long legs, and an instantly commanding presence. However, Stephan was heavier, more crudely constructed, and less graceful than the Scot. And while Stephan warmed Grey's blood, the fact remained that the Hanoverian did not burn his heart like living flame.

He lay down finally upon his bed, and put out the candle. Lay watching the play of firelight on the walls, seeing not the flicker of wood flame, but the play of sun upon red hair, the sheen of sweat on a pale bronzed body . . .

A brief and brutal dose of Mr. Keegan's remedy left him drained, if not yet peaceful. He lay staring upward into the shadows of the carved wooden ceiling, able at least to think once more.

The only conclusion of which he was sure was that he needed very much to talk to someone who had seen Koenig's body.

Chapter 6

Hocus-Pocus

Finding Private Koenig's last place of residence was simple. Thoroughly accustomed to having soldiers quartered upon them, Prussians sensibly built their houses with a separate chamber intended for the purpose. Indeed, the populace viewed such quartering not as an imposition, but as a windfall, since the soldiers not only paid for board and lodging and would often do chores such as fetching wood and water – but were also better protection against thieves than a large watchdog might be, without the expense.

Stephan's records were of course impeccable; he could lay hands on any one of his men at a moment's notice. And while he received Grey with extreme coldness, he granted the request without question, directing Grey to a house toward the western side of the town.

In fact, von Namtzen hesitated for a moment, clearly wondering whether duty obliged him to accompany Grey upon his errand, but Lance-Korporal Helwig appeared with a new difficulty – he averaged three per day – and Grey was left to carry out the errand on his own.

The house where Koenig had lodged was nothing out of the ordinary, so far as Grey could see. The owner of the house was rather remarkable, though, being a dwarf.

'Oh, the poor man! So much blood I have before not seen!'

Herr Hückel stood perhaps as high as Grey's waist – a novel sensation, to look down so far to an adult conversant. Herr Hückel was nonetheless intelligent and coherent, which was also novel in Grey's experience; most witnesses to violence tended to lose what wits they had and either to forget all details or to imagine impossible ones.

Herr Hückel, though, showed him willingly to the chamber where the death had occurred, and explained what he had himself seen.

'It was late, you see, sir, and my wife and I had gone to our bed. The soldiers were out – or at least we supposed so.' The soldiers had just received their pay, and most were busy losing it in taverns or brothels. The Hückels had heard no noises from the soldiers' room, and thus assumed that all four of the soldiers quartered with them were absent on such business.

Somewhere in the small hours, though, the good folk had been awakened by terrible yells coming from the chamber. These were not produced by Private Koenig, but by one of his companions, who had returned in a state of advanced intoxication, and stumbled into a blood-soaked shambles.

'He lay here, sir. Just so?' Herr Hückel waved his hands to indicate the position the body had occupied at the far side of the cozy room. There was nothing there now, save irregular dark blotches that stained the wooden floor.

'Not even lye would get it out,' said Frau Hückel, who had come to the door of the room to watch. 'And we had to burn the bedding.'

Rather to Grey's surprise, she was not only of normal size, but quite pretty, with bright, soft hair peeking out from under her cap. She frowned at him in accusation.

'None of the soldiers will stay here now. They think the *Nachtmahr* will get them, too!' Clearly, this was Grey's fault. He bowed apologetically.

'I regret that, madam,' he said. 'Tell me, did you see the body?'

'No,' she said promptly, 'but I saw the night hag.'

'Indeed,' Grey said, surprised. 'Er . . . what did it – she – it look like?' He hoped he was not going to receive some form of Siggy's logical but unhelpful description, *Like a witch.*

'Now, Margarethe,' said Herr Hückel, putting a warning hand up to his wife's arm. 'It might not have been—'

'Yes, it was!' She transferred the frown to her husband, but did not shake off his hand, instead putting her own over it, before returning her attention to Grey.

'It was an old woman, sir, with her white hair in

braids. Her shawl slipped off in the wind, and I saw. There are two old women who live nearby, this is true – but one walks only with a stick, and the other does not walk at all. This . . . thing, she moved very quickly, hunched a little, but light on her feet.'

Herr Hückel was looking more and more uneasy as this description progressed, and opened his mouth to interrupt, but was not given the chance.

'I am sure it was old Agathe!' Frau Hückel said, her voice dropping to a portentous whisper. Herr Hückel shut his eyes with a grimace.

'Old Agathe?' Grey asked, incredulous. 'Do you mean Frau Blomberg – the bürgermeister's mother?'

Frau Hückel nodded, face fixed in grave certainty.

'Something must be done,' she declared. 'Everyone is afraid at night – either to go out, or to stay in. Men whose wives will not watch over them as they sleep are falling asleep as they work, as they eat . . .'

Grey thought briefly of mentioning Mr. Keegan's patent preventative, but dismissed the notion, instead turning to Herr Hückel to inquire for a close description of the state of the body.

'I am told that the throat was pierced, as with an animal's teeth,' he said, at which Herr Hückel made a quick sign against evil and nodded, going a little pale. 'Was the throat torn quite open – as though the man were attacked by a wolf? Or—' But Herr Hückel was already shaking his head.

'No, no! Only two marks – two holes. Like a

snake's fangs.' He poked two fingers into his own neck in illustration. 'But so much blood!' He shuddered, glancing away from the marks on the floorboards.

Grey had once seen a man bitten by a snake, when he was quite young – but there had been no blood that he recalled. Of course, the man had been bitten in the leg, too.

'Large holes, then?' Grey persisted, not liking to press the man to recall vividly unpleasant details, but determined to obtain as much information as possible.

With some effort, he established that the tooth marks had been sizable – perhaps a bit more than a quarter inch or so in diameter – and located on the front of Koenig's throat, about halfway up. He made Hückel show him, repeatedly, after ascertaining that the body had shown no other wound when undressed for cleansing and burial.

He glanced at the walls of the room, which had been freshly whitewashed. Nonetheless, there was a large dark blotch showing faintly, down near the floor – probably where Koenig had rolled against the wall in his death throes.

He had hoped that a description of Koenig's body would enable him to discover some connection between the two deaths – but the only similarity between the deaths of Koenig and Bodger appeared to be that both men were indeed dead, and both dead under impossible circumstances.

He thanked the Hückels and prepared to take his

leave, only then realizing that Frau Hückel had resumed her train of thought and was speaking to him quite earnestly.

'. . . call a witch to cast the runes,' she said.

'I beg your pardon, madam?'

She drew in a breath of deep exasperation, but refrained from open rebuke.

'Herr Blomberg,' she repeated, giving Grey a hard look. 'He will call a witch to cast the runes. Then we will discover the truth of everything!'

He will do *what*?' Sir Peter squinted at Grey in disbelief. 'Witches?'

'Only one, I believe, sir,' Grey assured Sir Peter. According to Frau Hückel, matters had been escalating in Gundwitz. The rumor that Herr Blomberg's mother was custodian to the succubus was rampant in the town, and public opinion was in danger of overwhelming the little bürgermeister.

Herr Blomberg, however, was a stubborn man, and most devoted to his mother's memory. He refused entirely to allow her coffin to be dug up and her body desecrated.

The only solution, which Herr Blomberg had declared out of desperation, seemed to be to discover the true identity and hiding place of the succubus. To this end, the bürgermeister had summoned a witch, who would cast runes—

'What are those?' Sir Peter asked, puzzled.

'I am not entirely sure, sir,' Grey admitted. 'Some object for divination, I suppose.'

'Really?' Sir Peter rubbed his knuckles dubiously beneath a long, thin nose. 'Sounds very fishy, what? This witch could say anything, couldn't she?'

'I suppose Herr Blomberg expects that if he is paying for the . . . er . . . ceremony, the lady is perhaps more likely to say something favorable to his situation,' Grey suggested.

'Hmm. Still don't like it,' Sir Peter said. 'Don't like it at all. Could be trouble, Grey, surely you see that?'

'I do not believe you can stop him, sir.'

'Perhaps not, perhaps not.' Sir Peter ruminated fiercely, brow crinkled under his wig. 'Ah! Well, how's this, then – you go round and fix it up, Grey. Tell Herr Blomberg he can have his mumbo jumbo, but he must do it here, at the Schloss. That way we can keep a lid on it, what, see there's no untoward excitement?'

'Yes, sir,' Grey said, manfully suppressing a sigh, and went off to execute his orders.

By the time he reached his room to change for dinner, Grey felt dirty, irritable, and thoroughly out of sorts. It had taken most of the afternoon to track down Herr Blomberg and convince him to hold his – Christ, what was it? His rune-casting? – at the Schloss. Then he had run across the pest Helwig, and before he was able to escape, had been embroiled in an enormous controversy with a gang of mule drovers who claimed not to have been paid by the army.

This in turn had entailed a visit to two army camps, an inspection of thirty-four mules, trying interviews with both Sir Peter's paymaster and von Namtzen's – and involved a further cold interview with Stephan, who had behaved as though Grey were personally responsible for the entire affair, then turned his back, dismissing Grey in mid-sentence, as though unable to bear the sight of him.

He flung off his coat, sent Tom to fetch hot water, and irritably tugged off his stock, wishing he could hit someone.

A knock sounded on the door, and he froze, irritation vanishing upon the moment. What to do? Pretend he wasn't in was the obvious course, in case it was Louisa in her sheer lawn shift or something worse. But if it were Stephan, come either to apologize or to demand further explanation?

The knock sounded again. It was a good, solid knock. Not what one would expect of a female – particularly not of a female intent on dalliance. Surely the princess would be more inclined to a discreet scratching?

The knock came again, peremptory, demanding. Taking an enormous breath and trying to still the thumping of his heart, Grey jerked the door open.

'I wish to speak to you,' said the dowager, and sailed into the room, not waiting for invitation.

'Oh,' said Grey, having lost all grasp of German

on the spot. He closed the door, and turned to the old lady, instinctively tightening the sash of his banyan.

She ignored his mute gesture toward the chair, but stood in front of the fire, fixing him with a steely gaze. She was completely dressed, he saw, with a faint sense of relief. He really could not have borne the sight of the dowager *en dishabille.*

'I have come to ask you,' she said without preamble, 'if you have intentions to marry Louisa.'

'I have not,' he said, his German returning with miraculous promptitude. *'Nein.'*

One sketchy gray brow twitched upward.

'Ja? That is not what she thinks.'

He rubbed a hand over his face, groping for some diplomatic reply – and found it, in the feel of the stubble on his own jaw.

'I admire Princess Louisa greatly,' he said. 'There are few women who are her equal' – *And thank God for that,* he added to himself – 'but I regret that I am not free to undertake any obligation. I have . . . an understanding. In England.' His understanding with James Fraser was that if he were ever to lay a hand on the man or speak his heart, Fraser would break his neck instantly. It was, however, certainly an understanding, and clear as Waterford crystal.

The dowager looked at him with a narrow gaze of such penetrance that he wanted to tighten his sash further – and take several steps backward. He stood his ground, though, returning the look with one of patent sincerity.

'Hmph!' she said at last. 'Well, then. That is good.' Without another word, she turned on her heel. Before she could close the door behind her, he reached out and grasped her arm.

She swung round to him, surprised and outraged at his presumption. He ignored this, though, absorbed in what he had seen as she lifted her hand to the doorframe.

'Pardon, Your Highness,' he said. He touched the medal pinned to the bodice of her gown. He had seen it a hundred times, and assumed it always to contain the image of some saint – which, he supposed, it did, but certainly not in the traditional manner.

'St. Orgevald?' he inquired. The image was crudely embossed, and could easily be taken for something else – if one hadn't seen the larger version on the lid of the reliquary.

'Certainly.' The old lady fixed him with a glittering eye, shook her head, and went out, closing the door firmly behind her.

For the first time, it occurred to Grey that who-ever Orgevald had been, it was entirely possible that he had not originally been a saint. Some rather earthier ancient Germanic deity, perhaps? Pondering this interesting notion, he went to bed.

Chapter 7

Ambush

The next day dawned cold and windy. Grey saw pheasants huddling under the cover of shrubs as he rode, crows hugging the ground in the stubbled fields, and slate roofs thick with shuffling doves, feathered bodies packed together in the quest for heat. In spite of their reputed brainlessness, he had to think that the birds were more sensible than he.

Birds had no duty – but it wasn't quite duty that propelled him on this ragged, chilly morning. It was in part simple curiosity, in part official suspicion. He wished to find the gypsies; in particular, he wished to find *one* gypsy: the woman who had quarreled with Private Bodger soon before his death.

If he were quite honest – and he felt that he could afford to be, so long as it was within the privacy of his own mind – he had another motive for the journey. It would be entirely natural for him to pause at the bridge for a cordial word with the artillerymen, and perhaps see for himself how the boy with the red lips was faring.

While all these motives were undoubtedly sound,

though, the real reason for his expedition was simply that it would remove him from the Schloss. He did not feel safe in a house containing the princess Louisa, let alone her mother-in-law. Neither could he go to his usual office in the town, for fear of encountering Stephan.

The whole situation struck him as farcical in the extreme; still, he could not keep himself from thinking about it – about Stephan.

Had he been deluding himself about Stephan's attraction to him? He was as vain as any man, he supposed, but he could swear . . . His thoughts went round and round in the same weary circle. And yet, each time he thought to dismiss them entirely, he felt again the overwhelming sense of warmth and casual possession with which Stephan had kissed him. He had not imagined it. And yet . . .

Embrangled in this tedious but inescapable coil, he reached the bridge by mid-morning, only to find that the young soldier was not in camp.

'Franz? Gone foraging, maybe,' said the Hanoverian corporal, with a shrug. 'Or got homesick and run. They do that, the young ones.'

'Got scared,' one of the other men suggested, overhearing.

'Scared of what?' Grey asked sharply, wondering whether in spite of everything, word of the succubus had reached the bridge.

'Scared of his shadow, that one,' said the man he recalled as Samson, making a face. 'He keeps talking about the child; he hears a crying child at night.'

'Thought you heard it, too, eh?' said the Hanoverian, not sounding entirely friendly. 'The night it rained so hard?'

'Me? I didn't hear anything then but Franz's squealing.' There was a rumble of laughter at that, the sound of which made Grey's heart drop to his boots. *Too late,* he thought. 'At the lightning,' Samson added blandly, catching his glance.

'He's run for home,' the Hanoverian declared. 'Let him go; no use here for a coward.'

There was a small sense of disquiet in the man's manner that belied his confidence, Grey thought – and yet there was nothing to be done about it. He had no direct authority over these men, could not order a search to be undertaken.

As he crossed the bridge, though, he could not help but glance over. The water had subsided only a little; the flood still tumbled past, choked with torn leaves and half-seen sodden objects. He did not want to stop, to be caught looking, and yet looked as carefully as he could, half-expecting to see little Franz's delicate body broken on the rocks, or the blind eyes of a drowned face trapped beneath the water.

He saw nothing but the usual flood debris, though, and with a slight sense of relief, continued on toward the hills.

He knew nothing save the direction the gypsy wagons had been going when last observed. It was long odds that he would find them, but he searched doggedly, pausing at intervals to scan the countryside with his spyglass, or to look for rising plumes of smoke.

These last occurred sporadically, but proved invariably to be peasant huts or charcoal-burners, all of whom either disappeared promptly when they saw his red coat or stared and crossed themselves, but none of whom admitted to having heard of the gypsies, let alone seen them.

The sun was coming down the sky, and he realized that he must turn back soon or be caught in open country by night. He had a tinderbox and a bottle of ale in his saddlebag, but no food, and the prospect of being marooned in this fashion was unwelcome, particularly with the French forces only a few miles to the west. If the British army had scouts, so did the frogs, and he was lightly armed, with no more than a pair of pistols, a rather dented cavalry saber, and his dagger to hand.

Not wishing to risk Karolus on the boggy ground, he was riding another of his horses, a thickset bay who went by the rather unflattering name of Hognose, but who had excellent manners and a steady foot. Steady enough that Grey could ignore the ground, trying to focus his attention, strained from prolonged tension, into a last look round. The foliage of the hills around him faded into patch-work, shifting constantly in the roiling wind. Again and again, he thought he saw things – human figures, animals moving, the briefly seen corner of a wagon – only to have them prove illusory when he ventured toward them.

The wind whined incessantly in his ears, adding spectral voices to the illusions that plagued him. He rubbed a hand over his face, gone numb from the cold, imagining momentarily that he heard the wails of Franz's ghostly child. He shook his head to dispel the impression – but it persisted.

He drew Hognose to a stop, turning his head from side to side, listening intently. He was sure he heard it – but what was it? No words were distinguishable above the moaning of the wind, but there *was* a sound, he was sure of it.

At the same time, it seemed to come from nowhere in particular; try as he might, he could not locate it. The horse heard it, too, though – he saw the bay's ears prick and turn nervously.

'Where?' he said softly, laying the rein on the horse's neck. 'Where is it? Can you find it?'

The horse apparently had little interest in finding the noise, but some in getting away from it; Hognose backed, shuffling on the sandy ground, kicking up sheaves of wet yellow leaves. Grey drew him up sharply, swung down, and wrapped the reins around a bare-branched sapling.

With the horse's revulsion as guide, he saw what he had overlooked: the churned earth of a badger's sett, half hidden by the sprawling roots of a large elm. Once focused on this, he could pinpoint the noise as coming from it. And damned if he'd ever heard a badger carry on like that!

Pistol drawn and primed, he edged toward the bank of earth, keeping a wary eye on the nearby trees.

It was certainly crying, but not a child; a sort of muffled whimpering, interspersed with the kind of catch in the breath that injured men often made.

'Wer ist da?' he demanded, halting just short of the opening to the sett, pistol raised. 'You are injured?'

There was a gulp of surprise, followed at once by scrabbling sounds.

'Major? Major Grey? It is you?'

'Franz?' he said, flabbergasted.

'Ja, Major! Help me, help me, please!'

Uncocking the pistol and thrusting it back in his belt, he knelt and peered into the hole. Badger setts are normally deep, running straight down for six feet or more before turning, twisting sideways into the badger's den. This one was no exception; the grimy, tear-streaked face of the young Prussian soldier stared up at him from the bottom, his head a good foot below the rim of the hole.

The boy had broken his leg in falling, and it was no easy matter to lift him straight up. Grey managed it at last by improvising a sling of his own shirt and the boy's, tied to a rope anchored to Hognose's saddle.

At last he had the boy laid on the ground, covered with his coat and taking small sips from the bottle of ale.

'Major—' Franz coughed and spluttered, trying to rise on one elbow.

'Hush, don't try to talk.' Grey patted his arm

soothingly, wondering how best to get him back to the bridge. 'Everything will be—'

'But Major – the red coats! *Der Inglischeren!*'

'What? What are you talking about?'

'Dead Englishmen! It was the little boy; I heard him, and I dug, and—' The boy's story was spilling out in a torrent of Prussian, and it took no little time for Grey to slow him down sufficiently to disentangle the threads of what he was saying.

He had, Grey understood him to say, repeatedly heard the crying near the bridge, but his fellows either didn't hear or wouldn't admit to it, instead teasing him mercilessly about it. At last he determined to go by himself and see if he could find a source for the sound – wind moaning through a hole, as his friend Jurgen had suggested.

'But it wasn't.' Franz was still pale, but small patches of hectic color glowed in the translucent skin of his cheeks. He had poked about the base of the bridge, discovering eventually a small crack in the rocks at the foot of a pillar on the far side of the river. Thinking that this might indeed be the source of the crying, he had inserted his bayonet and pried at the rock – which had promptly come away, leaving him face to face with a cavity inside the pillar, containing a small, round, very white skull.

'More bones, too, I think. I didn't stop to look.' The boy swallowed. He had simply run, too panicked to think. When he stopped at last, completely out of breath and with legs like jelly, he had sat down to rest and think what to do.

'They couldn't beat me more than once for being gone,' he said, with the ghost of a smile. 'So I thought I would be gone a little longer.'

This decision was enhanced by the discovery of a grove of walnut trees, and Franz had made his way up into the hills, gathering both nuts and wild blackberries – his lips were still stained purple with the juice, Grey saw.

He had been interrupted in this peaceful pursuit by the sound of gunfire. Throwing himself flat on the ground, he had then crept forward, until he could see over the edge of a little rocky escarpment. Below, in a hollow, he saw a small group of English soldiers, engaged in mortal combat with Austrians.

'Austrians? You are sure?' Grey asked, astonished.

'I know what Austrians look like,' the boy assured him, a little tartly. Knowing what Austrians were capable of, too, he had promptly backed up, risen to his feet, and run as fast as he could in the opposite direction – only to fall into the badger's sett.

'You were lucky the badger wasn't at home,' Grey remarked, teeth beginning to chatter. He had reclaimed the remnants of his shirt, but this was insufficient shelter against dropping temperature and probing wind. 'But you said dead Englishmen.'

'I think they were all dead,' the boy said. 'I didn't go see.'

Grey, however, must. Leaving the boy covered with his coat and a mound of dead leaves, he untied the horse and turned his head in the direction Franz had indicated.

Proceeding with care and caution in case of lurking Austrians, it was nearly sunset before he found the hollow.

It was Dundas and his survey party; he recognized the uniforms at once. Cursing under his breath, he flung himself off his horse and scrabbled hurriedly from one body to the next, hoping against hope as he pressed shaking fingers against cooling cheeks and flaccid breasts.

Two were still alive: Dundas and a corporal. The corporal was badly wounded and unconscious; Dundas had taken a gun butt to the head and a bayonet through the chest, but the wound had fortunately sealed itself. The lieutenant was disabled and in pain, but not yet on the verge of death.

'Hundreds of the buggers,' he croaked breathlessly, gripping Grey's arm. 'Saw . . . whole battalion . . . guns. Going to . . . the French. Lloyd – followed them. Spying. Heard. Fucking succ – succ—' He coughed hard, spraying a little blood with the saliva, but it seemed to ease his breath temporarily.

'It was a plan. Got women – agents. Slept with men, gave them o-opium. Dreams. Panic, aye?' He was half sitting up, straining to make words, make Grey understand.

Grey understood, only too well. He had been given opium once, by a doctor, and remembered vividly the weirdly erotic dreams that had ensued. Do the same to men who had likely never heard of opium, let alone experienced it, and at the same time, start rumors of a demoness who preyed upon men in their dreams? Particularly with a flesh-and-blood avatar, who could leave such marks as would convince a man he had been so victimized?

Only too effective, and one of the cleverest notions he had ever come across for demoralizing an enemy before attack. It was that alone that gave him some hope, as he comforted Dundas, piling him with coats taken from the dead, dragging the corporal to lie near the lieutenant for the sake of shared warmth, digging through a discarded rucksack for water to give him.

If the combined force of French and Austrians was huge, there would be no need for such subtleties – the enemy would simply roll over the English and their German allies. But if the numbers were closer to equal, and it was still necessary to funnel them across those two narrow bridges . . . then, yes, it was desirable to face an enemy who had not slept for several nights, whose men were tired and jumpy, whose officers were not paying attention to possible threat, being too occupied with the difficulties close at hand.

He could see it clearly: Ruysdale was busy watching the French, who were sitting happily on the cliffs, moving just enough to keep attention diverted from the Austrian advance. The Austrians would come down on the bridge – likely at night – and then the French on their heels.

Dundas was shivering, eyes closed, teeth set hard

in his lower lip against the pain of the movement.

'Christopher, can you hear me? Christopher!' Grey shook him, as gently as possible. 'Where's Lloyd?' He didn't know the members of Dundas's party; if Lloyd had been taken captive, or – But Dundas was shaking his head, gesturing feebly toward one of the corpses, lying with his head smashed open.

'Go on,' Dundas whispered. His face was gray, and not only from the waning light. 'Warn Sir Peter.' He put his arm about the unconscious corporal, and nodded to Grey. 'We'll . . . wait.'

Chapter 8

The Witch

Grey had been staring with great absorption at his valet's face for some moments, before he realized even what he was looking at, let alone why.

'Uh?' he said.

'I *said*,' Tom repeated, with some emphasis, 'you best drink this, me lord, or you're going to fall flat on your face, and that won't do, will it?'

'It won't? Oh. No. Of course not.' He took the cup, adding a belated 'Thank you, Tom. What is it?'

'I told you twice, I'm not going to try and say the name of it again. Ilse says it'll keep you on your feet, though.' He leaned forward and sniffed approvingly at the liquid, which appeared to be brown and foamy, indicating the presence in it of eggs, Grey thought.

He followed Tom's lead and sniffed, too, recoiling only slightly at the eye-watering reek. Hartshorn, perhaps? It had quite a lot of brandy, no matter what else was in it. And he did need to stay on his feet. With no more than a precautionary clenching of his belly muscles, he put back his head and drained it.

He had been awake for nearly forty-eight hours, and the world around him had a tendency to pass in and out of focus, like the scene in a spyglass. He had also a proclivity to go intermittently deaf, not hearing what was said to him – and Tom was correct, that wouldn't do.

He had taken time, the night before, to fetch Franz, put him on the horse – with a certain amount of squealing, it must be admitted, as Franz had never been on a horse before – and take him to the spot where Dundas lay, feeling that they would be better together. He had pressed his dagger into Franz's hands, and left him guarding the corporal and the lieutenant, who by then was passing in and out of consciousness.

Grey had then donned his coat and come back to raise the alarm, riding a flagging horse at the gallop over pitch-black ground, by the light of a waning moon. He'd fallen twice, when Hognose stumbled, but luckily escaped injury either time.

He had alerted the artillery crew at the bridge, ridden on to Ruysdale's encampment, roused everyone, seen the colonel in spite of all attempts to prevent him waking the man, gathered a rescue party, and ridden back to retrieve Dundas and the others, arriving in the hollow near dawn to find the corporal dead and Dundas nearly so, with his head in Franz's lap.

Captain Hiltern had of course sent someone with word to Sir Peter at the Schloss, but it was necessary for Grey to report personally to Sir Peter and von

Namtzen when he returned at midday with the rescue party. After which, officers and men had flapped out of the place like a swarm of bats, the whole military apparatus moving like the armature of some great engine, creaking, groaning, but coming to life with amazing speed.

Which left Grey alone in the Schloss at sunset, blank in mind and body, with nothing further to do. There was no need for liaison; couriers were flitting to and from all the regiments, carrying orders. He had no duty to perform, no one to command, no one to serve.

He would ride out in the morning with Sir Peter Hicks, part of Sir Peter's personal guard. But there was no need for him now; everyone was about his own business; Grey was forgotten.

He felt odd; not unwell, but as though objects and people near him were not quite real, not entirely firm to the touch. He should sleep, he knew – but could not, not with the whole world in flux around him, and a sense of urgency that hummed on his skin yet was unable to penetrate to the core of his mind.

Tom was talking to him; he made an effort to attend.

'Witch,' he repeated, awareness struggling to make itself known. 'Witch. You mean Herr Blomberg still intends to hold his – ceremony?'

'Yes, me lord.' Tom was sponging Grey's coat, frowning as he tried to remove a pitch stain from the skirt. 'Ilse says he won't rest until he's cleared his mother's name, and damned if the Austrians will stop him.'

Awareness burst through Grey's fog like a pricked soap bubble.

'Christ! He doesn't know!'

'About what, me lord?' Tom turned to look at him curiously, sponging cloth and vinegar in hand.

'The succubus. I must tell him – explain.' Even as he said it, though, he realized how little force such an explanation would have upon Herr Blomberg's real problem. Sir Peter and Colonel Ruysdale might accept the truth; the townspeople would be much less likely to accept having been fooled – and by Austrians!

Grey knew enough about gossip and rumor to realize that no amount of explanation from him would be enough. Still less if that explanation were to be filtered through Herr Blomberg, whose bias in the matter was clear.

Even Tom was frowning doubtfully at him as he rapidly explained the matter. *Superstition and sensation are always so much more appealing than truth and rationality.* The words echoed as though spoken in his ear, with the same humorously rueful intonation with which his father had spoken them, many years before.

He rubbed a hand vigorously over his face, feeling himself come back to life. Perhaps he had one more task to complete, in his role as liaison.

'This witch, Tom – the woman who is to cast the

runes, whatever in God's name that might involve. Do you know where she is?'

'Oh, yes, me lord.' Tom had put down his cloth now, interested. 'She's here – in the Schloss, I mean. Locked up in the larder.'

'Locked up in the larder? Why?'

'Well, it has a good lock on the door, me lord, to keep the servants from – Oh, you mean why's she locked up at all? Ilse says she didn't want to come; dug in her heels entire, and wouldn't hear of it. But Herr Blomberg wouldn't hear of her *not,* and had her dragged up here, and locked up 'til this evening. He's fetching up the town council, and the magistrate, and all the bigwigs he can lay hands on, Ilse says.'

'Take me to her.'

Tom's mouth dropped open. He closed it with a snap and looked Grey up and down.

'Not like *that.* You're not even shaved!'

'Precisely like this,' Grey assured him, tucking in the tails of his shirt. 'Now.'

The game larder was locked, but as Grey had surmised, Ilse knew where the key was kept, and was not proof against Tom's charm. The room itself was in an alcove behind the kitchens, and it was a simple matter to reach it without detection.

'You need not come further, Tom,' Grey said, low-voiced. 'Give me the keys; if anyone finds me here, I'll say I took them.'

Tom, who had taken the precaution of arming himself with a toasting fork, merely clutched the keys tighter in his other hand, and shook his head.

The door swung open silently on leather hinges. Someone had given the captive woman a candle; it lit the small space and cast fantastic shadows on the walls, from the hanging bodies of swans and pheasants, ducks and geese.

The drink had restored a sense of energy to Grey's mind and body, but without quite removing the sense of unreality that had pervaded his consciousness. It was therefore with no real surprise that he saw the woman who turned toward him, and recognized the gypsy prostitute who had quarreled with Private Bodger a few hours before the soldier's death.

She obviously recognized him, too, though she said nothing. Her eyes passed over him with cool scorn, and she turned away, evidently engrossed in some silent communion with a severed hog's head that sat upon a china plate.

'Madam,' he said softly, as though his voice might rouse the dead fowl to sudden flight. 'I would speak with you.'

She ignored him, and folded her hands elaborately behind her back. The light winked gold from the rings in her ears and the rings on her fingers – and Grey saw that one was a crude circlet, with the emblem of St. Orgevald's protection.

He was overcome with a sudden sense of premonition, though he did not believe in premonition. He felt things in motion around him, things that he did not understand and could not control, things settling of themselves into an ordained and appointed position, like the revolving spheres of his father's orrery – and he wished to protest this state of affairs, but could not.

'Me lord.' Tom's hissed whisper shook him out of this momentary disorientation, and he glanced at the boy, eyebrows raised. Tom was staring at the woman, who was still turned away, but whose face was visible in profile.

'Hanna,' he said, nodding at the gypsy. 'She looks like Hanna, Siggy's nursemaid. You know, me lord, the one what disappeared?'

The woman had swung round abruptly at mention of Hanna's name, and stood glaring at them both.

Grey felt the muscles of his back loosen, very slightly, as though some force had picked him up and held him. As though he, too, was one of the objects being moved, placed in the spot ordained for him.

'I have a proposition for you, madam,' he said calmly, and pulled a cask of salted fish out from beneath a shelf. He sat on it and, reaching out, pulled the door closed.

'I do not wish to hear anything you say, *Schweinehund*,' she said, very coldly. 'As for you, piglet . . .' Her eyes darkened with no very pleasant light as she looked at Tom.

'You have failed,' Grey went on, ignoring this

digression. 'And you are in considerable danger. The Austrian plan is known; you can hear the soldiers preparing for battle, can't you?' It was true; the sounds of drums and distant shouting, the shuffle of many marching feet, were audible even here, though muffled by the stone walls of the Schloss.

He smiled pleasantly at her, and his fingers touched the silver gorget that he had seized before leaving his room. It hung about his neck, over his half-buttoned shirt, the sign of an officer on duty.

'I offer you your life, and your freedom. In return . . .' He paused. She said nothing, but one straight black brow rose, slowly.

'I want a bit of justice,' he said. 'I want to know how Private Bodger died. Bodger,' he repeated, seeing her look of incomprehension, and realizing that she had likely never known his name. 'The English soldier who said you had cheated him.'

She sniffed contemptuously, but a crease of angry amusement lined the edge of her mouth.

'Him. God killed him. Or the devil, take your choice. Or, no—' The crease deepened, and she thrust out the hand with the ring on it, nearly in his face. 'I think it was my saint. Do you believe in saints, pig-soldier?'

'No,' he said calmly. 'What happened?'

'He saw me, coming out of a tavern, and he followed me. I didn't know he was there; he caught me in an alley, but I pulled away and ran into the churchyard. I thought he wouldn't follow me there, but he did.'

Bodger had been both angry and aroused, insisting that he would take the satisfaction she had earlier denied him. She had kicked and struggled, but he was stronger than she.

'And then—' She shrugged. 'Poof. He stops what he is doing, and makes a sound.'

'What sort of sound?'

'How should I know? Men make all kinds of sounds. Farting, groaning, belching . . . pff.' She bunched her fingers and flicked them sharply, disposing of men and all their doings with the gesture.

At any rate, Bodger had then dropped heavily to his knees, and still clinging to her dress, had fallen over. The gypsy had rapidly pried loose his fingers and run, thanking the intercession of St. Orgevald.

'Hmm.' A sudden weakness of the heart? An apoplexy? Keegan had said such a thing was possible – and there was no evidence to belie the gypsy's statement. 'Not like Private Koenig, then,' Grey said, watching carefully.

Her head jerked up and she stared hard at him, lips tight.

'Me lord,' said Tom softly behind him. 'Hanna's name is Koenig.'

'It is not!' the gypsy snapped. 'It is Mulengro, as is mine!'

'First things first, if you please, madam,' Grey said, repressing the urge to stand up, as she leaned glowering over him. 'Where *is* Hanna? And what is she to you? Sister, cousin, daughter . . . ?'

'Sister,' she said, biting the word off like a thread. Her lips were tight as a seam, but Grey touched his gorget once again.

'Life,' he said. 'And freedom.' He regarded her steadily, watching indecision play upon her features like the wavering shadows on the walls. She had no way of knowing how powerless he was; he could neither condemn nor release her – and nor would anyone else, all being caught up in the oncoming maelstrom of war.

In the end, he had his way, as he had known he would, and sat listening to her in a state that was neither trance nor dream; just a tranquil acceptance as the pieces fell before him, one upon one.

She was one of the women recruited by the Austrians to spread the rumors of the succubus – and had much enjoyed the spreading, judging from the way she licked her lower lip while telling of it. Her sister Hanna had been married to the soldier Koenig, but had rejected him, he being a faithless hound, like all men.

Bearing in mind the gossip regarding Siegfried's paternity, Grey nodded thoughtfully, motioning to her with one hand to go on.

She did. Koenig had gone away with the army, but then had come back, and had had the audacity to visit the Schloss, trying to rekindle the flame with Hanna. Afraid that he might succeed in seducing her sister again – 'She is weak, Hanna,' she said with a shrug, 'she *will* trust men!' – she had gone to visit Koenig at night, planning to drug him with wine laced with opium, as she had done with the others.

'Only this time, a fatal dose, I suppose.' Grey had propped his elbow upon his crossed knee, hand under his chin. The tiredness had come back; it hovered near at hand, but was not yet clouding his mental processes.

'I meant it so, yes.' She uttered a short laugh. 'But he knew the taste of opium. He threw it at me, and grabbed me by the throat.'

Whereupon she had drawn the dagger she always carried at her belt and stabbed at him – striking upward into his open mouth, and piercing his brain.

'You never saw so much blood in all your life,' the gypsy assured Grey, unconsciously echoing Herr Hückel.

'Oh, I rather think I have,' Grey said politely. His hand went to his own waist – but, of course, he had left his dagger with Franz. 'But pray go on. The marks, as of an animal's fangs?'

'A nail,' she said, and shrugged.

'So, was it him – Koenig, I mean – was it him tried to snatch little Siggy?' Tom, deeply absorbed in the revelations, could not keep himself from blurting out the question. He coughed and tried to fade back into the woodwork, but Grey indicated that this was a question which he himself found of some interest.

'It can't have been; Koenig was already dead. But I assume that it was you the boy saw in his chamber?' *What did this witch look like?* he had asked. *Like a witch,* the child replied. Did she? She did not look like Grey's conception of a witch – but what was that, save the fabrication of a limited imagination?

She was tall for a woman, dark, and her face mingled an odd sexuality with a strongly forbidding aspect – a combination that many men would find intriguing. Grey thought it was not something that would have struck Siggy, but something else about her evidently had.

She nodded. She was fingering her ring, he saw, and watching him with calculation, as though deciding whether to tell him a lie.

'I have seen the dowager princess's medal,' he said politely. 'Is she an Austrian, by birth? I assume that you and your sister are.'

The woman stared at him, and said something in her own tongue, which sounded highly uncomplimentary.

'And you think *I* am a witch!' she said, evidently translating the thought.

'No, I don't,' Grey said. 'But others do, and that is what brings us here. If you please, madam, let us conclude our business. I expect someone will shortly come for you.' The Schloss was at dinner; Tom had brought Grey a tray, which he was too tired to eat. No doubt the rune-casting would be the after-dinner entertainment, and he must make his desires clear before that.

'Well, then.' The gypsy regarded him, her awe at his perspicacity fading back into the usual derision. 'It was your fault.'

'I beg your pardon?'

'It was Princess Gertrude – the dowager. She saw Louisa – that slut' – she spat casually on the floor, almost without pausing, and went on – 'making sheep's eyes at you, and was afraid she meant to marry you. Louisa thought she would marry you and go to England, to be safe and rich. But if she did, she would take with her her son.'

'And the dowager did not wish to be parted from her grandson,' Grey said slowly. Whether the gossip was true or not, the old woman loved the boy.

The gypsy nodded. 'So she arranged that we would take the boy – my sister and me. He would be safe with us, and after a time, when the Austrians had killed you all, we would bring him back.'

Hanna had gone down the ladder first, meaning to comfort Siggy if he woke in the rain. But Siggy had wakened too soon, and bollixed the scheme by running out of the room. Hanna had no choice but to flee when Grey had tipped the ladder over, leaving her sister to hide in the Schloss and make her way out at daybreak, with the help of the dowager.

'She is with our family,' the gypsy said, with another shrug. 'Safe.'

'The ring,' Grey said, nodding at the gypsy's circlet. 'Do you serve the dowager? Is that what it means?'

So much confessed, the gypsy evidently felt now at ease. Casually, she pushed a platter of dead doves aside, and sat down upon the shelf, feet dangling.

'We are Rom,' she said, drawing herself up proudly. 'The Rom serve no one. But we have known the Trauchtenbergs – the dowager's family – for generations, and there is tradition between us. It was her great-grandfather who bought the child who guards the bridge – and that child was the younger brother of my own great-grandfather. The ring was given to my great-grandfather then, as a sign of the bargain.'

Grey heard Tom grunt slightly with confusion, but took no heed. The words struck him as forcibly as a blow, and he could not speak for a moment. The thing was too shocking. He took a deep breath, fighting the vision of Franz's words – the small, round white skull, looking out at him from the hollow in the bridge.

Sounds of banging and clashing dishes from the scullery nearby brought him to himself, though, and he realized that time was growing short.

'Very well,' he said, as briskly as he could. 'I want one last bit of justice, and our bargain is made. Agathe Blomberg.'

'Old Agathe?' The gypsy laughed, and in spite of her missing tooth, he could see how attractive she could be. 'How funny! How could they suppose such an old stick might be a demon of desire? A hag, yes, but a night hag?' She went off into peals of laughter, and Grey jumped to his feet, seizing her by the shoulder to silence her.

'Be quiet,' he said. 'Someone will come.'

She stopped then, though she still snorted with amusement.

'So, then?'

'So, then,' he said firmly. 'When you do your hocus-pocus – whatever it is they've brought you here to do – I wish you particularly to exonerate Agathe Blomberg. I don't care what you say or how you do it – I leave that to your own devices, which I expect are considerable.'

She looked at him for a moment, looked down at his hand upon her shoulder, and shrugged it off.

'That's all, is it?' she asked sarcastically.

'That's all. Then you may go.'

'Oh, I may go? How kind.' She stood smiling at him, but not in a kindly way. It occurred to him quite suddenly that she had required no assurances from him, had not asked for so much as his word as a gentleman – though he supposed she would not have valued that, in any case.

She did not care, he realized, with a small shock. She had not told him anything for the sake of saving herself – she simply wasn't afraid. Did she think the dowager would protect her, for the sake either of their ancient bond, or because of what she knew about the failed kidnapping?

Perhaps. Perhaps she had confidence in something else. And if she had, he chose not to consider what that might be. He rose from the cask of fish, and pushed it back under the shelves.

'Agathe Blomberg was a woman, too,' he said.

She rose, too, and stood looking at him, rubbing her ring with apparent thought.

'So she was. Well, perhaps I will do it, then. Why should men dig up her coffin and drag her poor old carcass through the streets?'

He could feel Tom behind him, vibrating with eagerness to be gone; the racket of the dinner-clearing was much louder.

'For you, though—'

He glanced at her, startled by the tone in her voice, which held something different. Neither mockery nor venom, nor any other emotion that he knew.

Her eyes were huge, gleaming in the candlelight, but so dark that they seemed void pools, her face without expression.

'You will never satisfy a woman,' she said softly. 'Any woman who shares your bed will leave after no more than a single night, cursing you.'

Grey rubbed a knuckle against his stubbled chin, and nodded.

'Very likely, madam,' he said. 'Good night.'

Epilogue

Among the Trumpets

The order of battle was set. The autumn sun had barely risen, and the troops would march within the hour.

Grey was in the stable block, checking Karolus's tack, tightening the girth, adjusting the bridle, marking second by second the time until he should depart, as though each second marked an irretrievable and most precious drop of his life.

Outside the stables, all was confusion, as people ran hither and thither, gathering belongings, searching for children, calling for wives and parents, strewing away objects gathered only moments before, heedless in their distraction. His heart beat fast in his chest, and intermittent small thrills coursed up the backs of his legs and curled between them, tightening his scrotum.

The drums were beating in the distance, ordering the troops. The thrum of them beat in his blood, in his bone. Soon, soon, soon. His chest was tight; it was difficult to draw full breath.

He did not hear the footsteps approaching through the straw of the stables. Keyed up as he was, though, he felt the disturbance of air nearby, that intimation of intrusion that now and then had saved his life, and whirled, hand on his dagger.

It was Stephan von Namtzen, gaudy in full uniform, his great plumed helmet underneath one arm – but with a face sober by contrast to his clothing.

'It is nearly time,' the Hanoverian said quietly. 'I would speak with you – if you will hear me.'

Grey slowly let his hand fall away from the dagger, and took the full breath he had been longing for.

'You know that I will.'

Von Namtzen inclined his head in acknowledgment, but did not speak at once, seeming to need to gather his words – although they were speaking German now.

'I will marry Louisa,' he said, finally, formally. 'If I live until Christmas. My children—' He hesitated, free hand flat upon the breast of his coat. 'It will be good they should have a mother once more. And—'

'You need not give reasons,' Grey interrupted. He smiled at the big Hanoverian, with open affection. Caution was no longer necessary. 'If you wish this, then I wish you well.'

Von Namtzen's face lightened. He ducked his head a little, and took a breath.

'*Danke*. I say, I will marry if I am alive. If I am not . . .' His hand still rested on his breast, above the miniature of his children.

'If I live, and you do not, then I will go to your home,' Grey said. 'I will tell your son what I have known of you. Is this your desire?'

The Hanoverian's graveness did not alter, but a deep warmth softened his gray eyes.

'It is. You have known me, perhaps, better than anyone.'

He stood still, looking at Grey, and all at once, the relentless marking of fleeting time stopped. Confusion and danger still hastened without, and drums beat loud, but inside the stables, there was a great peace.

Stephan's hand left his breast, and reached out. Grey took it, and felt love flow between them. He thought that heart and body must be entirely melted – if only for that moment.

Then they parted, each drawing back, each seeing the flash of desolation in the other's face, both smiling ruefully to see it.

Stephan was turning to go when Grey remembered.

'Wait!' he called, and turned to fumble in his saddlebag.

'What is this?' Stephan turned the small, heavy box over in his hands, looking puzzled.

'A charm,' Grey said, smiling. 'A blessing. My blessing – and St. Orgevald's. May it protect you.'

'But—' Von Namtzen frowned with doubt, and tried to give the reliquary back, but Grey would not accept it.

'Believe me,' he said in English, 'it will do you more good than me.'

Stephan looked at him for a moment longer, then nodded, and, tucking the little box away in his pocket, turned and left. Grey turned back to Karolus, who was growing restive, tossing his head and snorting softly through his nose.

The horse stamped, hard, and the vibration of it ran through the long bones of Grey's legs.

'Hast thou given the horse strength?' he quoted softly, hand stroking the braided mane that ran smooth and serpentlike down the great ridge of the stallion's neck. 'Hast thou clothed his neck with thunder? . . . He paweth in the valley, and rejoiceth in his strength: he goeth on to meet the armed men. He mocketh at fear, and is not affrighted; neither turneth he back from the sword.'

He leaned close and pressed his forehead against the horse's shoulder. Huge muscles bulged beneath the skin, warm and eager, and the clean musky scent of the horse's excitement filled him. He straightened then, and slapped the taut, twitching hide.

'He saith among the trumpets, Ha, ha; and he smelleth the battle afar off, the thunder of the captains, and the shouting.'

Grey heard the drums again, and his palms began to sweat.

Historical Note: In October of 1757, the forces of Frederick the Great and his allies moved swiftly, crossing the country to defeat the gathering French and Austrian army at Rossbach, in Saxony. The town of Gundwitz was left undisturbed, the bridge at Aschenwald never crossed by an enemy.

'Lord John and the Haunted Soldier'

'Haunted Soldier' was actually written specifically for this collection, and has (so far) not been published anywhere else.

The chronology of Lord John Grey stories (to date) is as follows:

'Lord John and the Hellfire Club' (short story)
Lord John and the Private Matter (novel)
'Lord John and the Succubus' (novella)
Lord John and the Brotherhood of the Blade (novel)
'Lord John and the Haunted Soldier' (novella)

So, if you have this volume and the two novels, you're in great shape!

There is a third Lord John novel to come – titled *Lord John and the Scottish Prisoner* – but this is not yet written.

LORD JOHN
and the
Haunted Soldier

Part I

Inquisition

November, 1758
Tower Place, the Arsenal at Woolwich

Hell was filled with clocks, he was sure of it. There was no torment, after all, that could not be exacerbated by a contemplation of time passing. The large case clock at the end of the corridor had a particularly penetrating *tick-tock*, audible above and through all the noises of the house and its inhabitants. It seemed to Lord John Grey to echo his own inexorable heartbeats, each one a step on the road toward death.

He shook off that grisly notion and sat bolt upright, his best hat balanced upon his knee. The house had once been a mansion; doubtless the clock was a remnant of those gracious days. Pity none of the chairs had made the transition to government service, he thought, shifting gingerly on the niggardly stool he'd been given.

A spasm of impatience brought him to his feet. Why would they not bloody call him in and get on with it?

Well, there was a rhetorical question, he thought, tapping the hat against his leg with soft impatience.

If *The mills of God grind slowly, but they grind exceeding small* was not the official motto of His Majesty's government, it was surely that, *de facto*. It had taken months for the Royal Commission of Inquiry to be convened, still longer for it to sit, and longer yet for inquisition to stretch out its hand in his direction.

His arm and ribs were quite healed now, the furrow through his scalp no more than a thin white scar beneath his hair. The freezing rain of November beat upon the roof above; in Germany the thick grass around the ninth station of the cross must lie now brown and dead, and the lieutenant who lay beneath that grass food for worms long since. Yet here Grey sat – or stood – a small, hard kernel yet awaiting the pressure of the grindstone.

Grimacing, he sought respite from the clock's ticking by striding up and down the corridor, returning the censorious looks of the row of portraits hung upon the wall as he passed them – early governors of the Arsenal.

The portraits were mediocre in execution for the most part, save the one near the end, done by a more talented hand. Perhaps a Dutchman by his looks – a black-browed gentleman whose fiercely rubicund features radiated a jolly determination. Probably a good attitude for one whose profession was explosion.

As though the Dutchman agreed with this sentiment, a tremendous boom rattled the casement at the end of the corridor and the floor heaved suddenly under Grey's feet.

He flung himself flat, hat flying, and found himself hugging the shabby hall-runner, sweating and breathless.

'My lord?' A voice from which any trace of astonishment or curiosity had been carefully removed spoke above him. 'The gentlemen are ready.'

'Are they? In . . . deed.' He rose, stilling the trembling of his limbs by main effort, and brushed the dust from his uniform with what nonchalance could be managed.

'If you will follow me, my lord?' The functionary, a small, neatly wigged person of impeccable politeness and indeterminate aspect, bent to pick up Grey's hat, and handing it to him without comment, turned to lead him back down the corridor. Behind them, the clock ticked imperturbably on, the passage of time undisturbed by such ephemera as explosion or death.

There were three of them, seated behind a long table, a weighty thing of carved dark wood. To one side, a clerk sat at a small desk, quill and paper at the ready to record his testimony. A single chair was placed, stark and solitary, in the space before the table.

So it really was an inquisition, he thought. His brother Hal had warned him. His sense of unease grew stronger. The trouble with an inquisition was that it seldom went hungry to bed.

The black-coated functionary accompanied him to the chair, hovering at his elbow as though afraid he might bolt, and left him there with a murmured 'Major Grey' and a discreet bow in the direction of the Commission of Inquiry. They did not bother to introduce themselves. The tall, thin-faced fellow was vaguely familiar; a nobleman, he thought – knight, perhaps a minor baronet? Expensively tailored in gray superfine. The name escaped him, though perhaps it would come of itself in time.

He did recognize the military member of the tribunal: Colonel Twelvetrees, of the Royal Artillery Regiment, wearing his dress uniform and an expression that spoke of habitual severity. From what Grey knew of his reputation, the expression was well earned. That could be dealt with, though; *yes, sir, no, sir, three bags full, sir.*

The third was less forbidding in aspect, a middle-aged gentleman, plump and neat in purple, with a striped waistcoat and a small decoration; he went so far as to smile politely at Grey. Grey removed his hat and bowed to His Majesty's Royal Commission of Inquiry, but did not sit 'til he was bidden to do so.

The colonel cleared his throat then and began without preamble.

'You are summoned here, Major, to assist us in an inquiry into the explosion of a cannon whilst under your command during the battle at Crefeld in

Prussia, on twenty-third June of this year. You will answer all questions put to you, in as much detail as may be required.'

'Yes, sir.' He sat bolt upright, face impassive.

A sort of rumble ran through the building, felt rather than heard, and the droplets on a small crystal chandelier tinkled gently overhead. The huge proving grounds of the Arsenal lay somewhere beyond the Tower Place house, he knew – how far away?

The plump gentleman put a pair of spectacles on his nose and leaned forward expectantly.

'Will you tell us, please, my lord, the circumstances in which you came to take charge of the gun and its crew?'

Obediently, he told them, in the words he had prepared. Colorless, brief, exact. Allowing of no doubt. Had any of them ever set foot on a battlefield, he wondered? If they had, they would know how little resemblance his words held to the truth of that day – but it hardly mattered. He spoke for the record, and was therefore careful.

They interrupted now and then, asking trivial questions about the position of the gun upon the field, the proximity of the French cavalry at the time, the weather – what in God's name might the weather have had to do with it? he wondered.

The clerk scratched industriously away, recording it all.

'You had had previous experience in fighting a gun of this type?' That was the roundish gentleman with the striped waistcoat and the discreet decoration. The baronet had called him Oswald, and suddenly he realized who the man must be – the Honorable Mortimer Oswald, Member of Parliament. He'd seen the name on posters and banners during the last election.

'I had.'

Oswald cocked an eyebrow, plainly inviting him to elaborate, but he kept silent.

Twelvetrees fixed him with a cold eye.

'With which regiment, when, how long?'

Blast.

'I served informally with the Forty-sixth, sir – my brother's regiment – Lord Melton, that is – during the Jacobite campaign in Scotland under General Cope. Was detailed to a gun crew belonging to the Royal Artillery after taking up my commission, and trained there for six months before coming back to the Forty-sixth. More recently, I was seconded to a Hanoverian regiment in Germany, and saw service there with a Prussian artillery company.'

He saw no need to add that this service had consisted largely of eating sausages with the gun crew. And as for his so-called service with Cope . . . the less said about that, the better. He had, however, actually commanded the firing of cannon, which the members of the board very likely had not, Twelvetrees included.

'Cope?' said the baronet, seeming to rouse a bit at the name. 'Gentleman Johnny?' He laughed, and the colonel's hatchet face tightened.

'Yes, sir.' *Oh, God.* Please God, he hadn't heard the story.

Apparently not; the man merely hummed a snatch of that mocking Scotch song, 'Hey, Johnny Cope, are ye walkin' yet?' and broke off, looking amused.

'Cope,' he repeated, shaking his head. 'You must have been very young at the time, Major?'

'Sixteen, sir.' He felt his blood rise and his cheeks flush. Nearly half a lifetime. Dear God, how long would he have to live, in order to escape the memory of Prestonpans, and goddamned Jamie Fraser?

Twelvetrees was not amused, and cast a cold glance at the nobleman.

'Had you commanded a gun in battle, prior to Crefeld?' Bloody-minded sod.

'Yes, sir,' Grey replied, keeping his voice calm. 'At Falkirk.' They'd put him in charge of a gun and allowed him to fire several shots at an abandoned church before retreating, for the sake of practice.

Oswald emitted a hum of interest.

'And what sort of gun did you command on that occasion, Major?'

'A murderer, sir,' he replied, naming a small and very old-fashioned cannon, left over from the last century.

'Not quite so murderous as Tom Pilchard, though, eh, Major?'

He must have looked as blank as he felt, for Oswald kindly elaborated.

'The gun you served at Crefeld, Major. You did not know its name?'

'No, sir,' he said, and could not help adding, 'we were not formally introduced, owing to the circumstances.'

He knew before he said it that it was a mistake, but nerves and irritation had got the best of him; the constant thumping from the proving ground beyond the house made the floor shake every few minutes, and sweat was running down his sides inside his shirt. The price of his momentary lapse was a blistering ten-minute lecture from Twelvetrees on respect for the army – in the person of himself, he gathered – and the dignity of His Majesty's commission. All the while Grey sat upright as a ramrod, saying, 'Yes, sir,' and 'No, sir,' with a countenance of perfect blankness, and Oswald wheezed with open amusement.

The baronet waited through the colonel's tirade with ill-concealed impatience, stripping the barbs from his quill one by one, so that tiny feathers strewed the table and flew up in a cloud as he drummed his fingers.

From the corner of his eye, Grey saw the clerk lean back, looking faintly entertained. The man rubbed his ink-stained fingers, clearly grateful for the momentary break in the proceedings.

When at last the colonel subsided – with a final ugly jab at his brother, his brother's regiment, and Grey's late father – the baronet cleared his throat with a menacing growl and sat forward to take his own turn.

Grey was inclined to think that the growl was aimed as much at Twelvetrees as at himself – noblemen did not like to hear others of their ilk rubbished in public, regardless of circumstance. The lack of amity among the members of the commission had become increasingly apparent during the questioning, but that observation was of little value to him personally.

The clerk, seeing the end of his brief vacation, picked up his quill again with an audible sigh.

Marchmont – that was it! Lord Marchmont – he *was* a baronet – set about a brisk dissection of Grey's experience, background, education, and family, ending with a sudden pointed inquiry as to when Grey had last seen Edgar DeVane.

'Edgar DeVane?' Grey repeated blankly.

'Your brother, I believe?' Marchmont said, with elaborate patience.

'Yes, sir,' Grey said respectfully, thinking, *What the devil . . . ? Edgar?* 'I beg pardon, sir. Your question took me unexpectedly. I believe I last saw my half brother' – he leaned a little on the words – 'near Christmas last.' He remembered the occasion, certainly; Edgar's wife, Maude, had badgered her husband into bringing the family to London for a month, and Grey had accompanied her and her two daughters in their raids on the Regent and Bond Street shops, in the capacity of native bearer. He recalled thinking at the time that Edgar's affairs must be prospering markedly; either that, or he would return to Sussex bankrupt.

He waited. Marchmont squinted at him, tapping the mangled quill on the papers in front of him.

'Christmas,' the baronet repeated. 'Have you been in correspondence with DeVane since then?'

'No,' he replied promptly. While he assumed that Edgar was in fact literate, he'd never seen anything of a written nature purporting to emanate from his half brother. His mother kept up a dutiful correspondence with all four of her sons, but the Sussex half of that particular exchange was sustained entirely by the efforts of Maude.

'Christmas,' Marchmont repeated again, frowning. 'And when had you last seen DeVane, prior to that?'

'I do not recall, sir; my apologies.'

'Oh, now, I am afraid that won't do, my lord.' Oswald was still looking genial, but light glittered from his spectacles. 'We must insist upon an answer.'

A louder than usual boom from beyond the house made the clerk start in his seat and grab for his inkwell. Grey might easily have started likewise, were he not so taken aback by this sudden insistence upon his half brother's whereabouts and relations with himself. He could only conclude that the commission had lost its collective mind.

Twelvetrees added his own bit to this impression, glowering at him under iron-gray brows.

'We are waiting, Major.'

Ought he to choose some date at random? he wondered. Would they investigate to discover whether he told the truth?

Knowing what sort of response it might provoke, he replied firmly, 'I am sorry, sir. I see Edgar DeVane very infrequently; prior to last Christmas, I suppose that it might have been more than a year – two, perhaps – since I have spoken to him.'

'Or written?' Marchmont pounced.

He didn't know that, either, but there was much less chance that anyone could prove him wrong.

'I think that I may have written to him when—' His words were drowned out by the whistle of some large missile, very near at hand, followed by a tremendous crash. He kept himself in his chair only by seizing the seat of it with both hands, and gulped air to keep his voice from shaking. '—when I was seconded to the Graf von Namtzen's regiment. That – that would have been in – in – '57.'

'Can they not still that infernal racket?' Marchmont's nerves seemed also to have become frayed by the bombardment. He sat upright and slapped a hand on the table. 'Mr. Simpson!'

The black-coated functionary appeared in the doorway with an inquiring look.

'Tell them to stop banging away out there, for God's sake,' the baronet said peevishly.

'I am afraid that the Ordnance Office is a power unto itself, my lord,' Simpson said, shaking his head sadly at the thought of such intransigence.

'Perhaps we might dismiss the major until a more

congenial time—' Oswald began, but Twelvetrees snapped, 'Nonsense!' at him, and turned his minatory gaze on Grey once more.

The colonel said something, but was drowned out by a barrage of bangs and pops, as though the Ordnance fellows proposed to emphasize their independence. Grey's blood was roaring in his ears, his leather stock tight round his throat. He dug his fingers hard into the wood of the chair.

'With all respect, sir,' he said, as firmly as he might, disregarding whatever it was that Twelvetrees had asked. 'I have little regular contact with my half brother. I cannot tell you more than I have.'

Marchmont uttered an audible 'hmp!' of disbelief, and Twelvetrees glared as though he wished to order Grey strung up to a triangle and flogged on the spot. Oswald, though, peered closely at him over the tops of his spectacles, and in a sudden, blessed silence from the proving ground, changed the subject.

'Were you intimately acquainted with Lieutenant Lister prior to the occasion at Crefeld, my lord?' he asked mildly.

'I am not familiar with that name at all, sir.' He could surmise who Lister was, of course, who he must have been.

'You surprise me, Major,' said Oswald, looking not at all surprised. 'Philip Lister was a member of White's, as you are yourself. I should think you must have seen him there now and then, whether you knew his name or not?'

Grey wasn't surprised that Oswald knew that he belonged to White's club; all of London had heard about his last visit there. He didn't haunt the place, though, preferring the Beefsteak.

Rather than endeavor to detail his social habits, he merely replied, 'That is possible. However, the lieutenant had been struck by a cannonball, sir, which unfortunately removed his head. I had no opportunity of examining his features in order to ascertain whether he might be an acquaintance.'

Marchmont glanced at him sharply.

'Are you being impertinent, sir?'

'Certainly not, sir.' All three of them looked suddenly at him as one, like a phalanx of owls eyeing a mouse. A drop of sweat wormed its slow way down his back, itching.

Twelvetrees coughed explosively and the illusion was broken. With bewildering suddenness, they resumed questioning him about the battle.

'How long had you been fighting the gun when it exploded?' Marchmont asked, drumming his fingers on the table.

'Roughly half an hour, sir.' *No idea, sir. Seemed all day, sir.* Couldn't have been, though; the battle itself had taken no more than three or four hours. So he'd been told, later.

He realized, with a faint sense of nightmare, that his hands were beginning to tremble, and as unobtrusively as possible, curled them into fists on his knees.

They returned to the battle, making him go

through it again, and once more, and then again: the number of men in the gun crew, their separate offices, how the gun was aimed – a pause, while he explained to a frowning Marchmont exactly what quoins were and that, no, the placement of these wooden wedges beneath the cannon's trunnions affected nothing more than the altitude of the barrel, and could not possibly have contributed to the explosion – what shot had they been using – grapeshot, for the most part – what was the fucking weather like, which member of the crew had been killed – the loader, he didn't know the man's name – and exactly who had put the linstock to the touchhole during that last, fateful firing?

He clung to the colorless, rehearsed words of his testimony, a feeble shield against memory.

A faint haze of smoke from the proving ground had seeped through the cracks of the windows and hung near the egg-and-dart molding of the ceiling, gray as the rain clouds outside.

His left arm ached where it had been broken.

Sweat ran over his ribs, slow as seeping blood.

The ground shook under him, and he felt in his bones the invisible presence of Prussian dragon-riders.

He wished to God they had not told him Lister's name.

The thump and rumble of distant explosion had resumed. He began to try to identify the sounds as a means of distraction, wondering, *An eight? Or a coehorn?* at a series of regular, hollow thumps, or

thinking with more confidence, *Twenty-four pounder,*
when the chandelier rattled overhead.

'It rained in the night,' he repeated for the fourth
time, 'but it was not raining heavily during the
battle, no, sir.'

'Your vision was not obscured, then?'

Only by the sweat burning in his eyes and the
billows of black powder smoke that drifted like
thunderclouds over the field.

'No, sir.'

'You were not distracted in mind?'

He gripped his knees.

'No, sir.'

'So you claim,' Marchmont said, with distinct
skepticism. 'Do you not think it possible – or even
likely, Major – that in the heat of battle, you might
conceivably have ordered your crew to load a second
charge before firing the first? I think such an
eventuality would have provided an explosion of
sufficient force as to rupture the cannon, would it
not, Colonel?' He leaned a little forward, raising an
interrogative brow at Twelvetrees, who looked more
po-faced than usual, but nodded.

A small smirk of satisfaction oiled Lord
Marchmont's lips, as he looked back at Grey.

'Major?'

Grey felt a sharp jolt in the pit of his stomach.
He'd come expecting official tedium, the meticulous
dissection of accident required by those whose
business such things were. He hadn't looked
forward either to the endless questions or to the

inescapable reliving of the events at Crefeld – but the last thing he'd expected was this.

'Do I understand you aright, my lord?' he asked carefully. 'Do you insinuate – do you *dare* to insinuate – that I . . . that my actions *caused* the explosion which—'

'Oh, no, oh, no!' Oswald leapt in hurriedly, seeing Grey draw himself up. 'I am quite sure his lordship insinuates nothing.' But Grey was already on his feet.

The clerk looked up, startled. There was a smut on his nose.

'Good day, my lord, gentlemen.' Grey bowed, jammed the hat on his head, and turned on his heel.

'Major! You have not been dismissed!'

Ignoring the outbreak of exclamations and orders behind him, he strode beneath the trembling chandelier and out the door.

Grey was so exercised in mind that he took no notice at all of his surroundings. Emerging into the portrait hallway, he did not wait to be shown out, but stamped off via the most direct route that presented itself. In consequence, he found himself a few moments later outside the house, in the midst of a raging downpour, but with Bell Street, where he had come in, nowhere in sight.

He paused, breathing heavily, thought of skulking back into the manor house to ask direction, dismissed that notion instanter, and looked round for an alternate means of egress.

He was surrounded by a cluster of smaller buildings, mostly wet brick, roofed with rain-slick slates, and with a profusion of small, muddy lanes leading to and fro among them.

No wonder they called the bloody place 'the Warren,' he thought grimly, and was inclined to find his present confusion merely a continuation of the morning's aggravation. He chose a direction at random and set off, cursing the Arsenal and all its works.

Ten minutes of tramping through rain and mud left his clothes wet, his boots fouled, and his temper fouler, but he was no closer to escape. A shattering *boom!* from very close at hand made him veer suddenly sideways, fetching up against one of the myriad brick buildings, heart thundering in his chest. He pressed a hand hard over it, and tried without effect to calm his breathing.

His hands and feet were chilled to the bone, but he felt fresh sweat trickle down his ribs, further dampening his already clammy linen. Not that it mattered; he would be soaked to the skin in another few minutes.

'Oh, the devil with it,' he muttered to himself, and seizing the nearest door handle in sight, shoved it open.

He found himself in a low-ceilinged room that smelt strongly of sulfur, hot metal, and other noxious substances. It did, however, have a fire in the hearth, and he headed for this like a racing pigeon homing to its cot.

He slung his cloak forward over his shoulder and closed his eyes in momentary bliss at the feel of heat on his legs and backside.

A sound caused him to open his eyes, and he saw that the noise of his entry had attracted a young man, presently gaping at him from a door on the far side of the room.

'Sir?' said the young man tentatively, taking in Grey's uniform. The young man himself was in shirtsleeves and breeches, a slender chap with dark, curly hair and a face of almost girlish delicacy, perhaps a few years younger than himself.

'I beg your pardon for my unseemly intrusion,' Grey said, letting his cloak fall and forcing a smile. 'I am Major John Grey. I was unfortunately—' He had begun some explanation of his presence, but the young man's eyes forestalled him with an exclamation of surprise.

'Major Grey! Why, I know you!'

'You do?' For some reason, this made Grey somewhat uneasy.

'But of course, of course! Or rather,' the young man corrected himself, 'I know your name. You were called before the commission this morning, were you not?'

'I was,' Grey said shortly, fury returning at the memory.

'Oh – but I forget myself; your pardon; sir. I am Herbert Gormley.' He bobbed an awkward bow, which Grey returned, with mutual murmurs of 'your servant, sir.'

Glancing round, he saw that the strong odors came from an assortment of pots and glass vessels scattered higgledy-piggledy across an assortment of tables and benches. Wisps of steam rose from a small earthen pot on the table nearest him.

'Could that be *tea*?' Grey asked dubiously.

It could. Gormley, clearly grateful for the opportunity to be hospitable, snatched up a filthy cloth, and using this as a pot holder, poured hot liquid into a pottery mug, which he handed to Grey.

The tea was the same grayish color as the mud on his boots, and the smell led him to suspect that the mug was not employed strictly as a drinking vessel – but it was hot, and that was all that mattered.

'Er . . . what is this place?' Grey inquired, emerging from the mug and waving at their surroundings.

'This is the Royal Laboratory, sir!' Gormley said, straightening his back with an air of pride. 'If you please, sir? I'll fetch someone directly; he will be so excited!'

Before Grey could speak to stop him, Gormley had darted back into the recesses of the building.

Grey's uneasy feeling returned. Excited? The revelation that everyone in the Warren seemed to have heard about his appearance before the commission was sufficiently sinister. That anyone should be excited about it was unsettling.

In Grey's not inconsiderable experience, for a

soldier to be talked about was a good thing only if the conversation were in reference to some laudable feat of arms. Otherwise, a prudent man kept his head down, lest it be – this unwary thought evoked a sudden memory of Lieutenant Lister, and he shuddered convulsively, slopping hot tea over his knuckles.

He set the cup down and wiped his hand on his cloak, debating the wisdom of absquatulating before Gormley returned with his 'someone' – but the rain was now slashing ferociously at the shutters, driven by a freezing east wind, and he hesitated an instant too long.

'Major Grey?' A dark, burly soldier in a Royal Artillery captain's uniform emerged, a look of mingled welcome and wariness upon his heavy face. 'Captain Reginald Jones, sir. May I welcome you to our humble abode?' He offered his hand, tilting his head in irony toward the cluttered room.

'I am obliged to you, sir, both for shelter from the storm and for the kind refreshment,' Grey replied, taking both the offered hand and advantage of the pounding rain to indicate his reason for intrusion.

'Oh, you did not come in response to my invitation?' Jones had thick brows, like woolly caterpillars, which arched themselves in inquiry.

'Invitation?' Grey repeated, the sense of unease returning. 'I received no invitation, Captain, though I assure you—'

'I did tell you, sir,' Gormley said reproachfully to the captain. 'When I took your note across to the manor, they said I had just missed the major, who had already left.'

'Oh, so you did, so you did, Herbert,' Jones said, smacking himself theatrically on the forehead. 'Well, then, it seems good luck or Providence has delivered you to us, Major.'

'Indeed,' Grey said warily. 'Why?'

Captain Jones smiled warmly at him.

'Why, Major, we have something to show you.'

He had no time to dwell upon the Commission, at least.

It was a long gallop from the laboratory, through a maze of smaller outbuildings and sheds, then into what Gormley – shouting to be heard above the noise of rain and hammering – told him was the Royal Brass Foundry, a large, airy stone and brick building, through whose archways Lord John glimpsed strange marvels: casting pits, boring machines, a gigantic beam scale large enough to weigh a horse . . . and a horse. Two, to be accurate, their wet flanks gleaming as they backed a wagon filled with barrels of clay and burlap bags of sand in through the high vestibule door.

The air was thick with the scents of wet rope, drying clay, hot wax, tallow, fresh manure, and the acrid, fiery odors of an unseen forge somewhere in the recesses of the place. Gormley shouted brief descriptions of the various activities they passed, but Jones was leading the way at the double-quick, and Grey had barely time to inhale the fascinating aromas of gun-founding before he found himself propelled once more into the open air and the cold smell of rain on stone, tinged with a miasma of rot and ordure from the prison hulks on the river nearby.

The air shivered periodically with explosion; they were drawing nearer to the proving grounds. The bangs echoed in the hollow of his stomach. Jesus, they weren't going to try to make him reenact the events leading up to the demise of Tom Pilchard, surely?

The pitted landscape of the proving grounds stretched away to the left; he could see it now. Acres of open ground punctuated by earthen bunkers, outposts of heaped sandbags, and tents of various shapes and sizes, canvas darkened by the rain. Here and there, the glint of muted light on the barrels of the bigger guns.

To his relief, though, Jones veered right and down a muddy path lined with the dismounted carcasses of ruined guns, neatly laid out like dead bodies.

He had no time to study them, but was impressed by both their number – there must be fifty, at least – and by the size of some. There must be half a dozen cannon royal, whose monstrous barrels weighed eight thousand pounds or more and must be drawn by a dozen horses.

Ahead lay a very large, open-sided shelter, roofed with canvas. Long tables lay bleak under the canvas, covered with debris. Here lay half a Spanish culverin, the breech blown off. There the twisted remains of a short gun he could not identify.

The thump of a fresh explosion reached him, muffled only slightly by the rain that drummed on the canvas overhead as he followed Gormley into the shelter.

'Why do they test ordnance in the rain?' he asked, to cover his unease, and by way of making conversation.

'Do you not sometimes fight in the rain, my lord?' Gormley sounded amused. 'Useful to have bombs and grenades that will still explode when the casing is wet, don't you think?'

'Ah . . . quite.' The Commission's harping insistence upon the weather at Crefeld seemed suddenly to acquire some meaning. Likewise their insistent questioning regarding his perceptions of the powder . . . Edgar. Goddammit, Edgar!

It was the juxtaposition of his half brother with the notion of gunpowder that finally triggered realization.

Rain would certainly dampen the firing powder, no matter what precautions were taken. Normally, damp was less of a problem with the bombs and grapeshot cartridges, they being well wrapped, but even these would now and then fail to explode. A certain number of them simply failed to explode in any case, weather notwithstanding. And when this happened, the dummy charge must be removed from the breech before a fresh load was rammed down the barrel. Otherwise, the impact itself might cause the faulty load to go off. Or – he remembered Marchmont's accusation with a fresh surge of fury – a hasty or incompetent gun crew occasionally *did* neglect to remove the faulty load, ram a fresh one, and then touch off both charges together, which might indeed fracture a gun.

And Edgar owned a powder mill. The insinuation, he supposed, was that Edgar's mill had supplied dud powder, which had by coincidence been used to make the grapeshot cartridges he had used in Crefeld. One of these failing to go off, his own inattention or stupidity had . . . But this was the sheerest idiocy, even for someone like Marchmont. What—

But these fevered speculations were interrupted as Jones came to an abrupt halt beside one of the tables and turned, looking expectant.

The table was littered with shattered chunks of verdigrised and blackened brass. It had been a large cannon, a twenty-four pounder; most of the barrel forward of the trunnions was intact. And it was an English cannon – the royal cypher of George the Second showed clearly, though the reinforcing band upon which it was stamped had cracked through and the breech of the gun lay in a rubble of twisted pieces, blackened with powder.

'Do you recognize it, Major?' Gormley asked.

Grey felt an odd sense of shock, and something strangely like sorrow, as he might for an unknown soldier blown to bits beside him. Would he care, he wondered, if he didn't now know the gun by name?

'Tom Pilchard, is it?' He reached out and touched the broken barrel, gently.

'Yes, sir.' The young man seemed to share his sense of loss; he bowed his head respectfully, and spoke with lowered voice, as one might at the bier of a friend. 'I thought you might wish to see him, sir – or what's left.'

Grey glanced at Gormley, rather surprised – and caught sight of Captain Jones on the far side of the table, staring at him intently. Blank puzzlement was succeeded by a fresh wave of anger, as realization struck him. God damn them, they'd brought him to view the carcass in order to see whether he might betray some manifestation of guilt!

He hoped no sign of his fury showed on his face. Heart thumping, he moved slowly down the table, examining the wreckage.

They had laid out the broken chunks in rough order, a giant bronze clutter of jagged pieces. Near the shattered butt, he caught sight of an oddly curved piece, and despite his awareness of Jones's scrutiny, put out a hand to it.

It was what remained of a leopard, couchant, part of the ornamentation from one of the cannon's dolphins. No more than the head remained, split right through. The face snarled intact on one side of the small chunk of metal, ear laid back. The other side was broken, the pitted brass already greening.

'My lord?' Gormley's voice was questioning. Paying no attention, Grey reached into his pocket and drew out a small piece of bronze, smoothly cast on one side, rough on the other. It was heavy in his hand, dark, clean, and cold. The last time he'd held it thus, it had been still warm from his body, and darker yet, slick with his blood.

There was a murmur of interest and excitement. Gormley leaned close to see, and Captain Jones, in his haste to look, too, caught his hip a wallop on the corner of the table, making the pieces of the cannon rumble and clang. Grey hoped it would leave a bruise.

'Where did you get that, Major?' Jones asked, rubbing his hip as he nodded at the fragment Grey held.

'The surgeon who removed it from my chest gave it me,' Grey answered, very cool. 'A memento of my survival.'

'May I?' Gormley extended a hand, face eager.

Grey wished to refuse, but a glimpse of Jones's hard interest prevented him. He tightened his lips and handed the cat's face to Gormley. Cupping the larger remnant in his hand, the young man fitted the smaller one to it, restoring the leopard's head.

Gormley made a small noise of pleasure at adding this bit to his jagged puzzle. Grey was more interested at what was still missing.

There was a dark crack between the halves of the leopard's head, where a two-inch sliver of metal was still missing. Missing, but not gone. He still retained *that* small souvenir of his brief acquaintance with

Tom Pilchard – lodged somewhere in the depths of his chest. He was interested to see the dimensions of it – longer than he'd thought, but very slender – no more than a hair's width at the narrower end.

The surgeon, digging through his chest with urgent fingers, had touched the end of the bronze splinter but been unable to take hold of it with forceps in order to draw it out – and after prolonged consultation with his learned German colleague, had decided that to leave it *in situ* was less risk than to attempt removal by cutting through his ribs and opening his chest.

Grey had been in no condition to contribute to that debate, nor did he remember everything they'd done to him, but he recalled – and with no sense of shame whatever – the warmth of tears running down his face at the news that they did not propose to hurt him any more.

He hadn't wept through all that terrible day, nor the ones that went before it. The dissolution, when it came, had been a blessing, acknowledgment of mourning for the lost, acceptance of what remained of his life.

'Major Grey?' He became aware that Gormley was squinting curiously at him, and shook off his memories abruptly.

'I beg your pardon?'

'I only asked, sir – when the gun blew up, did you hear anything?'

The question was so incongruous that he actually laughed.

'Did I *hear* anything? Beyond the explosion, you mean?'

'Well, what I mean, sir . . .' Gormley struggled for clarity. 'Did you hear just a loud bang, same as you would when the gun was fired? Or perhaps *two* bangs, right close together? Or a bang, and then a . . . clang? Metal, I mean.' He hesitated. 'I mean . . . did you hear the sound of the gun breaking?'

Grey looked at him, arrested.

'Yes,' he said slowly. 'I believe I did. A bang and a clang, as you put it. So close together, though . . . I couldn't swear . . .'

'Well, they would be,' Gormley said eagerly. 'Now, what I understand, sir – this wasn't your regular gun?'

Grey shook his head.

'No. I'd never seen it before.'

Gormley – Grey could not help thinking of him as 'Gormless,' the name was so the opposite of his small, quick cleverness – creased his narrow brow in a frown.

'How many times did it fire before it exploded?'

'I have no idea,' Grey answered shortly. This was beginning to echo the bloody inquisition he'd been through half an hour before, and he had no intention of repeating himself *ad infinitum* to a series of questioners of descending seniority. To forestall more questions, he seized the moment to ask his own.

'What are those?' He pointed to the broken barrel where several half circles scalloped the edge,

226

quite unlike the jagged shear of the rest.

To his surprise, Gormley stiffened and glanced uneasily at Jones, who gave the young man a flat, blank sort of look.

'Oh. That's . . . nothing, sir.'

The devil it is, thought Grey. But he had had enough of mystifications and dark hints. Moved by impulse, he picked up the smaller fragment of the leopard's head, restored it to his pocket, and bowed to Jones and Gormley.

'I have business elsewhere, gentlemen. I bid you good day.'

He turned on his heel, ignoring cries of protest. To his surprise, Captain Jones positively sprinted after him, catching him by the sleeve at the edge of the shelter.

'You can't take that!'

Grey glanced at the captain's hand on his sleeve, keeping his eyes fixed there, until Jones's grip relaxed.

'I beg your pardon, Major,' Jones said stiffly, standing back. 'But you must leave that bit of metal here.'

'Why?' Grey lifted a brow. 'The fragments will be melted down, surely?' Such a small bit of brass couldn't be worth the tenth part of a farthing.

Jones looked taken aback for an instant, but rapidly regained his confidence.

'That bit of metal,' he said in severe tones, 'is the property of His Majesty!'

'Of course it is,' Grey agreed cordially. 'And when

His Majesty likes to ask me for it, I shall be quite happy to give it to him. For the moment, though, I shall keep it safe.'

Taking a deep breath in preparation, he wrapped the edges of his cloak around himself, pulled his hat well down, and dived into the rain. Jones didn't follow.

He had a decent sense of direction and was used to finding his way through foreign towns and open country alike. Keeping in mind the directions Gormley had given him as they sped through the Warren, he was able to find his way back past the maze of the proving grounds to the foundry, pausing only now and then to take his bearings.

The din in the foundry seemed almost welcoming, a cheerful, self-absorbed racket that was completely uninterested in Major Grey and his experiences on the battlefield at Crefeld. He paused for a moment to watch a moulder beating with an iron rod at a great heap of clay that sat on a bench before him, while an assistant shoveled handsful of horse dung and wool clippings into the mix, counting as he did so.

In the next bay, men were winding rope carefully round a tapered wooden spindle, some ten feet long, that sat in a sort of large trough, suspended in notches at either end – the cannon mould to which the clay would be applied, he supposed.

'Beg pardon, sir.' A young man appeared out of

nowhere, pushing him politely aside in order to retrieve a bucket of soft soap, which he then rushed back and began daubing onto the tight-packed grooves of the rope with a large brush.

He would have liked to loiter and watch, but he was clearly in the way; already, men were glancing at him, curiosity mingled with a mild hostility at his unuseful presence.

The rain had at least slackened; he walked out of the main foundry building, his hand curled round the fragment of brass in his pocket, thinking of that missing sliver.

For the most part, he was unaware of it, and often forgot its presence altogether. Now and then, though, some postural shift would send a brief, piercing pain through his chest, freezing him in place. The English surgeon, Dr. Longstreet, had told him that there might remain some harmless irritation of the nerves, but that the spasms would eventually pass.

The German surgeon, evidently unaware of Grey's fluency in that language, had agreed, but remarked in his own tongue that there was of course a slight possibility of the sliver's turning suddenly, in which case it might pierce the pericardium, whatever that was.

But no need to think of that, he had concluded cheerfully, *as if so, he will be dead almost at once.*

He had recalled Gormley's directions aright; directly ahead was what the young man had called Dial Arch. Beyond that lay Dial Square, and beyond that in turn he should find the exit he sought to Bell Street, where, no doubt, his long-suffering valet was still waiting for him.

He smiled wryly at thought of Tom Byrd. He had insisted that there was no need for his valet to accompany him all the way out to Woolwich – it was ten miles, at least – but Byrd would not hear of his going out alone. Tom, bless him, had scarcely let him go anywhere alone since his return from Germany, fearing – and with some reason, Grey was grudgingly forced to admit – that he might collapse on the street.

He was much better now, though; quite restored, he told himself firmly. Hand still curled round the tiny leopard's head, he paused under the arch to brush and shake himself into order before facing the critical eye of Tom Byrd, aged eighteen.

A huge stone sundial lay in the center of the square, giving it its name. It was of course not working at the moment, but it did remind Grey of time. He had been engaged to his mother and step-father, General Stanley, for supper, but it was already growing dark; there was no hope of making the long and dangerous carriage ride in time. He'd have to spend the night in Woolwich.

Unpleasant as that prospect was, it carried with it a sense of relief. He'd seen the general since the 'unfortunate occurrence,' as Hal so tersely termed it, but only briefly. He hadn't been looking forward to a long tête-à-tête.

A movement on the other side of the sundial

made him look up. A man was standing there, regarding him with a faintly puzzled, somewhat offended look, as though considering his appearance exceptionable in some way.

Grey might have been offended in turn, were he not taken aback in his turn by the other's appearance, which was most certainly exceptionable.

He wore an unfamiliar uniform, old-fashioned in appearance, of a regiment that Grey did not recognize. The hilt of a dress sword showed beneath his coat – this a full-skirted garment, blue with scarlet facings, and two antique pistols were thrust through his belt. Below were breeches of a grossly unfashionable cut, baggy at the knee and so loose through the leg as to swim about his figure, stocky as it was. His wig, though, was the most remarkable thing, this being unpowdered, long, and curled upon his shoulders in a glossy profusion of dark brown. It was a most unmilitary sight, and Grey frowned at the man.

The soldier appeared no more impressed with Grey; he turned upon his heel without a word and walked toward the opening at the other side of the square. Grey opened his mouth to hail the fellow, then stood with it open. The soldier was gone, the archway empty. Or, no – not empty. A young man was there, looking into the square. Another soldier, an artillery officer by his dress – but certainly not the gentleman in the old-fashioned wig.

'Did you see him?' A voice at Grey's elbow

turned him; it was a short, middle-aged man in uniform, faintly familiar. 'Did you see him, sir?'

'The strange gentleman in the ancient wig? Yes.' He frowned at the man. 'Do I know you?' Memory supplied the answer, even as the soldier knuckled his forehead in salute.

'Aye, sir, though little wonder should you not recognize me. We met—'

'At Crefeld. Yes. You were part of the gun crew serving Tom Pilchard, were you not? You were – yes, you were the rammer.' He was sure of it, though the neat soldier before him bore little resemblance to the black-stained, sweat-soaked wretch whose half-toothless savage grin was the last image he recalled of the battle of Crefeld.

'Aye, sir.' The rammer appeared less interested in picking up the threads of past acquaintance, though, than in the old-fashioned gentleman who had so abruptly departed. 'Did you see him, sir?' he repeated, clearly excited. 'It was the ghost!'

'The what?'

'The ghost, sir! 'Twas the Arsenal ghost, I'm sure it was!' The rammer – Grey had never known his name – looked at once terrified and thrilled.

'Whatever are you talking about, Private?' Grey asked sharply. His tone brought the rammer up short, and he stood stiff at attention.

'Why, sir, it's the Arsenal ghost,' he said, and despite his pose, his eyes sought the opposite side of the square, where the apparition – if that's what it was – had vanished. 'Everybody knows about the

Arsenal ghost – but damn few has seen it!'

He sounded almost gloating, though his face was still pale.

'Folk say as he's the ghost of an artillery officer was killed on the proving ground, fifty years or more ago. It's good luck, they say, for an artilleryman to see him – not so good, maybe, was you not of his h'occupation.'

'Good luck,' Grey repeated, a little bleakly. 'Well, and I'm sure we can all use a bit of that. Come to that, Private, how do you come to be here?'

The ghost – if that's what he was – had raised not a hair on Grey's head, but the rammer's presence had set the back of his neck to prickling.

'Oh.' The man's look of avid interest faded a little. 'I'm summoned, sir. They's a Commission of Inquiry, regarding the h'explosion. Poor old Tom Pilchard,' he said, wagging his head mournfully. ' 'E were a noble gun.'

The rammer glanced at the sundial, gleaming with rain.

'But I come *here*, sir, for to see was there enough light to tell the time by the dial, see, sir, not to be late.'

A sense of movement on the other side of the square made Grey look up quickly. It was not the ghost, though – if it had been a ghost – but the small, black-coated functionary who had taken him before the commission, wearing a large handkerchief spread over his wig against the rain, and an annoyed expression.

'I believe this will be your summons now,' Grey said, nodding toward the functionary. 'Good luck!'

The rammer hurriedly straightened his hat, already moving across the square.

'Thank'ee, sir!' he called. 'The same to you!'

Grey lingered for a moment after the rammer's departure, looking into the walkway beyond the square. It was growing late in the afternoon, and the light was beginning to darken, but the space beyond was perfectly visible – and perfectly empty.

Grey found himself profoundly uneasy, and seized of a sudden urge to be gone. The artilleryman's ghost – if that's what it was – had not disturbed him in the slightest. What troubled him was the glimpse he had had of the other artilleryman, the young soldier standing in the walkway, watching.

He had told Oswald that he had had no opportunity of studying Philip Lister's face, and that was true enough. He *had*, however, seen it, in the instant before the cannonball struck. And he suffered now from a most unsettling conviction that he had just seen it again.

Drawing his cloak more closely round him, he crossed the square and went to find Tom Byrd, feeling a certain coldness near his heart.

Tom Byrd was waiting patiently for him in Bell Street, sheltering from the rain in a doorway.

'All right, me lord?' he inquired, putting on his broad-brimmed hat.

'Yes, fine.'

Byrd narrowed his eyes at Grey, who reflected – not for the first time – that Byrd's round and essentially guileless young face did not in any way prevent his exhibiting the sort of penetrating suspicion more suitable to an officer in charge of a court-martial – or to a nanny – than to a valet.

'Fine,' Grey repeated, more firmly. 'Mere formalities. As I said.'

'As you said,' Byrd echoed, with a trifle more skepticism than was entirely becoming. 'Covering their arses, I expect.'

'Certainly that,' Grey agreed dryly. 'Let us find a little food, Tom. And we must find a bed, as well. Do you know anywhere suitable?'

'To be sure, me lord.' Tom squinted in consideration, and after a moment's consultation with the detailed map of London he carried in his head, pointed off toward the east.

'The Lark's Nest; decent house round the corner,' he suggested. 'Do a nice oyster pie, and the beer's good. Dunno about the beds.'

Grey nodded.

'We'll chance the fleas for the sake of the beer.'

He gestured to Tom to lead the way, and pulled down his hat against the steady drizzle. He *was* hungry – ravenous, in fact – having eaten neither breakfast nor dinner, his appetite suppressed by thought of the coming interview.

He had been pushing that interview to the back of his mind, in hopes of distancing the

Commission's remarks sufficiently to deal rationally with them later. Now relieved of other distraction, though, there was no escape, and the Commission's questions replayed themselves uncomfortably in his mind as he splashed through darkening puddles after Tom.

He was still angered by Marchmont's insinuations regarding his own possible culpability in the explosion – but not so angered as not to try to examine them honestly.

The baffling taradiddle regarding Edgar he dismissed, seeing no way to make sense of it, save to suppose that Marchmont had intended to goad him and thus perhaps to drive him into unwary admission of fault.

Could the explosion have been in any way his fault? He felt a natural resistance to the suggestion, strong as the involuntary jerk of a knee. But he could not dismiss Marchmont's insinuations – or deal with them, if they could not be dismissed – if he was not clear in his own mind about the matter.

Be the devil's advocate, he told himself, hearing his father's voice in memory. *Assume that it. was your fault – in what way might it have happened?*

Only two possibilities that he could see. The most likely, as Marchmont had implied, was that the gun crew might, in the excitement of the moment, have double-loaded the cannon, not pausing for the first round to be touched off. When the linstock was put to the touchhole, both rounds would have exploded together, thus blowing the cannon apart.

The second possibility was that a faulty round might have been loaded, and properly touched off, but failed to explode. It should by rights have then been cleared from the barrel before a fresh load was inserted – but it was far from uncommon for this step to be overlooked in the heat of battle. If the aim did not require to be adjusted, the process of loading and firing developed an inexorable, mind-less rhythm after a time; nothing existed save the next motion in the complex process of serving the gun.

It would be simple; no one would notice that the charge had not gone off, and a fresh load would simply be tamped in on top of the faulty one. Stimulated by the explosion of the second, fresh charge, the faulty one might then explode, as well. He'd seen that happen once, himself, though in that instance, the cannon had merely been damaged, not destroyed.

Neither instance was rare, he knew. It was there-fore the responsibility of the officer commanding the gun to see that every member of the crew performed each step of his duty, to discover such errors in process and correct them before they became irrevocable. Had he done that?

For the hundredth time since he heard of the Commission of Inquiry, he reviewed his memories of the battle of Crefeld, looking for any indication of an omission, any half-voiced protest by some member of the gun crew . . . but they had been completely demoralized by the sudden death of their lieutenant, in no frame of mind to concentrate. They might so easily have made an error.

But the Commission had called the rammer. Had they already interviewed the other surviving members of the gun crew, he wondered suddenly? If so . . . but if some member of the gun crew had testified to double-loading, Grey would have been facing more than insinuations.

'Here we are, me lord!' Tom called over his shoulder, turning in to a sturdy, half-timbered house.

They had arrived at the Lark's Nest, and the smell of food and beer drew him momentarily from his broodings. Even oyster pie, sausage rolls, and good beer, though, could not keep recollection at bay. Once summoned, Crefeld remained with him, the smell of black powder, slaughtered pigs, and rain-soaked fields overpowering the scents of tobacco smoke and fresh-baked bread.

He had so many impressions of the day, the battle, many of them sharp as crystal – but able, like broken bits of crystal shaken in a dish, to fall suddenly into new and baffling patterns.

What, exactly, had he done? He recalled some things clearly – seizing the sword from Lister's fallen body, beating the crew back to the gun – but later? He could not be sure.

Neither could he be sure of the Commission's motives. What in bloody *hell* had Marchmont meant by dragging Edgar in? Twelvetrees's hostility was more understandable; there was bad blood between the Royal Artillery Regiment and his brother Hal, a feud of long standing, that had not been improved by last month's – Christ, was it only a month past? It seemed years – revelations.

And Oswald . . . he had seemed sympathetic by contrast with Marchmont and Twelvetrees, but Grey knew better than to trust such spurious sympathy. Oswald was an elected politician, hence by definition untrustworthy. At least until Grey knew more about who owned him.

'You *are* going to eat that, me lord, aren't you?' He looked up to find Tom Byrd focusing a stern look upon the neglected sausage roll in his hand.

And beyond Tom Byrd, at a table in the corner, sat a uniformed artilleryman, talking with two friends over pint-pots of the excellent beer. The man looked familiar, though he knew he did not know him. Another member of Tom Pilchard's crew?

'I haven't an appetite,' he said abruptly, laying down the roll. 'I believe I'll chance the fleas.'

The next morning, he and Tom returned to London by the post coach, arriving at his rooms – officers' quarters at the regimental barracks – by mid-afternoon. He sent a note of apology to his mother, looked at a pile of unopened mail, decided that it could continue in that state indefinitely, picked two or three random lice from his body, bathed, shaved, and then, dressed in a fresh suit of clothes, set out on foot for the Beefsteak Club in Curzon Street.

He hadn't set foot in the Beefsteak in months. In part, it was a simple disinclination for society; he had needed time apart to heal, before facing the companionship and curiosity – no matter how kindly meant – of his fellows.

The greater reason, though, was one which he scarcely admitted to himself. He had wished the Beefsteak to remain what it had always been for him – a place of peace and refuge. He could withstand the buffeting of circumstance, comforted by the thought that there was somewhere to which he could retire, if the pressures of the world became too much to bear.

If he did not go to the Beefsteak, his sense of it would be unchanged; his refuge was safe. But to go was to risk discovering that it was not, and he stepped across the threshold with a racing heart.

For an instant, he suffered the delusion that the dark red medallions of the Turkey runner in the entrance hall were blotches of blood, that some unsuspected catastrophe had befallen the place, and that he would enter the library to find bodies strewn in careless butchery.

He closed his eyes, and put out a hand to the doorjamb to steady himself. Breathed deep, and smelt the incense of tobacco and brandy, aged leather and the musk of men, spiced with the scents of fresh linen, lavender, and bergamot.

'My lord?' It was the chief steward's voice. He opened his eyes to find the man squinting at him in consternation, the library behind him its usual soft brown self, glowing like paradise in the late-afternoon light that filtered through the lace curtains of the tall windows and suffused the rising wisps of pipe smoke from the smoking room.

'Will you take a glass of brandywine, my lord?' the steward asked, stepping back to open the way to his favorite chair, a wingbacked object upholstered in a dark-green damask, sagging in the seat and much worn about the arms.

'If you please, Mr. Bodley,' he said, and peace filled his soul.

He returned to the Beefsteak again the next day, and spent a pleasant hour sipping good brandy in the Hermits' Corner – a trio of chairs set apart, facing the windows, backs turned to the room, for the use of those who had no appetite for company. One of the other chairs was occupied by a man he knew slightly, named Wilbraham; they nodded to each other as Grey sat down, and then studiously ignored each other's presence.

Behind them came the soothing murmur of masculine conversation, punctuated by laughter and suffused with the odors of linen, sweat, cologne, and brandy, spiced with a hint of tobacco from the smoking room down the hall. Fiber by fiber, Grey felt his clenched muscles relax.

As he had known it must, though, his tranquillity came to an abrupt end with the descent of a large, meaty hand on his shoulder. He turned to look into

Harry Quarry's grinning face, smiled despite himself, and rose, leaving Wilbraham in solitary contemplation of Curzon Street.

'You look like death warmed over,' Quarry said without preamble, after a briefly searching look at him. This annoyed Grey, as Tom Byrd had taken considerable pains with his appearance, and he had thought he looked quite well, inspecting himself in the glass before setting out.

'You're looking well, too, Harry,' he replied equably, finding no quick riposte. In fact, he did. War agreed with Quarry, lending a fine edge to a body and a character otherwise somewhat inclined to sloth, gluttony, cigars, and other appetites of the flesh.

'Melton said you'd had a bad time since Germany.' Quarry ushered him to the dining room and into a chair with an annoying solicitude, all but tucking a napkin under Grey's chin.

'Did he,' Grey replied shortly. How much had Hal told Quarry – and how much had he heard on his own? Rumor spread faster in the army than it did among the London salons.

Luckily, Quarry seemed disinclined to inquire after the particulars – which probably meant he'd already heard them, Grey concluded grimly.

Quarry looked him over and shook his head. 'Too thin by half! Have to feed you up, I suppose.' This assessment was followed by Quarry's ordering – without consulting him – thick soup, game pie, fried trout with grapes, lamb with a quince preserve and roast potatoes, and a broccoli sallet with radishes and vinegar, the whole to be followed by a jelly trifle.

'I can't eat a quarter of that, Harry,' Grey protested. 'I'll burst.'

Quarry ignored this, waving a hand to urge the waiter to ladle more soup into Grey's bowl.

'You need sustenance,' he said, 'from what I hear.'

Grey looked askance at him over his half-raised spoon.

'What you hear? What *do* you hear, may I ask?'

Quarry's craggily handsome face adopted the look that he normally wore when intending to be discreet, the fine white scar across his cheek pulling down the eye on that side in a knowing leer.

'Heard they knocked you about a bit at the Arsenal day before yesterday.'

Grey put down the spoon and stared at him.

'Who told you that?'

'Chap named Simpson.'

Grey racked his brain for anyone named Simpson whom he had met in the course of his visit to the Arsenal, but drew a complete blank.

'Who the hell is Simpson?' To show his general unconcern over the matter, he took an unwary gulp of soup, and burnt his tongue.

'Don't recall his actual title – under-under-sub-secretary to the assistant something-or-other, I suppose. He said he picked you up off the floor –

physically. Didn't know royal commissions resorted to cudgeling their witnesses.' Harry raised an interrogative brow.

'Oh, him.' Grey touched his singed tongue gingerly to the roof of his mouth. 'He did not pick me up; I rose quite without assistance, having caught my foot in the carpeting. Mr. Simpson happened merely to be present.'

Quarry looked at him thoughtfully, nodded, and inhaled a vast quantity of soup.

'Might easily happen to anyone,' he said mildly. 'Ratty old thing, that carpet, full of holes. Know it well.'

Recognizing this for the cue it was, Grey sighed and picked up his spoon again.

'You know it well. Right, Harry. Why are you haunting the Arsenal, and what is it you want to know?'

'Haunting,' Quarry repeated thoughtfully, signaling the waiter to remove his soup plate. 'Interesting choice of words, that. Our Mr. Simpson said he rather thought you'd met the ghost.'

That rattled him more than he wished to show. He waved away the soup, affecting indifference.

'So the Arsenal has its own ghost, has it? Would that be an artilleryman, wearing an ancient uniform?'

'Oh, you *did* see him, then.' Harry's eyes sharpened with interest. 'The artilleryman, was it? Some see him as a Roman centurion – there's a Roman cemetery under the Arsenal, did you know?'

'No. How do you know whether it's a ghost with a taste for fancy dress, or two ghosts – or whether it's a ghost at all?'

'Never seen him myself. I'm not the sort who sees phantoms,' Quarry said, with a sort of smugness that Grey found irritating.

'And I am, I suppose?' Not waiting for an answer, he picked up a bread roll. 'Did you set this Simpson to watch me, Harry?'

'Someone should be watching you,' Quarry said. 'Have you any notion what kind of trouble you're in?'

'No, but I suppose you're going to tell me. Is it mutiny to walk out on the questions of a royal commission? Am I to be shot at dawn tomorrow?'

He was not sure whether to be grateful for Harry's concern, or annoyed at his solicitude. The one thing he did know was that he required someone to discuss the matter with, though, and so he kept his tone light.

'Too simple.' Quarry's face twitched, and he waved the steward with the wine bottle over to refill their glasses. 'Twelvetrees wants Melton's balls, but failing that, he'll have yours. His assumption being, I suppose, that it would discredit Melton to have his younger brother accused of negligence and forced – at the least – to resign his commission amidst a sea of talk.'

'They can accuse all they like,' Grey said hotly. 'They can't prove a damn thing.' Or he hoped they couldn't. What in God's name might the rammer have told them? Or the other man from Tom Pilchard's crew?

Quarry raised a thick brow.

'I doubt they'd have to,' he said bluntly, 'if they can raise enough doubt about your actions, and get enough talk started. Surely you know that.'

Grey felt blood starting to throb in his temples, and concentrated on keeping his hands steady as he buttered a bite of bread.

'What I know,' he said levelly, 'is that they cannot force me to resign my commission, let alone prosecute me for negligence or malfeasance, without evidence. And I am assuming that they have none, because if they did, the ubiquitous Mr. Simpson would have told you of it.' He raised a brow at Quarry. 'Am I right?'

Quarry's mouth twitched.

'It isn't only Twelvetrees, mind,' he said, lifting a monitory finger. 'I suppose you didn't know that the gentleman presently sitting in the Tower, accused of treason as the result of your recent industry, is Marchmont's cousin?'

Grey choked on the bite of roll he had taken.

'I'll take that as a "no," shall I?' Quarry sat back, allowing the waiter to serve his lamb, while Mr. Bodley imperturbably struck Grey between the shoulder blades, dislodging the roll, before continuing to pour the wine.

'Is this entire commission engineered for the purpose of discrediting me, then?' Grey asked, as soon as he had got his breath back.

''Strewth, no. It wasn't only your bloody gun that's blown up. Eight more of 'em, within the last ten months.'

Grey's jaw dropped with astonishment, and he belatedly recalled the shattered remnants laid out for autopsy behind the proving grounds. Certainly more broken guns lay on those tables than the mortal remains of Tom Pilchard.

'This, naturally, is not something the Ordnance Office wants talked about. Might put the wind up the Germans – to say nothing of the Dutch – who are paying through the nose for cannon from the Royal Foundry, under the impression that these are the best armament available anywhere.

'Not that this is entirely a bad thing,' he added, shoveling a judicious quantity of quince preserve over his lamb. 'It's what's keeping them from trying harder than they are to have you drawn and quartered. You might have blown up one cannon, but you can't have done nine.'

'I did not blow it up!'

Harry blinked, surprised, and Grey felt his cheeks flush. He looked down into his plate and saw that the fork in his hand was shaking, ever so slightly. He laid it carefully down, and taking his wineglass in both hands, drank deep.

'I know that,' Quarry said, quietly.

Grey nodded, not trusting himself to speak. *But do I know it?* he thought.

Quarry coughed, delicately separating a forkful of succulent meat from its gristle.

'The word "sabotage" is being breathed – though the Ordnance Office is doing its level best to stifle any such breathing. Yet another reason to make a scapegoat of you, you see: make enough noise about Tom Pilchard, and perhaps the grubs of Fleet Street will be so busy baying at your heels, they won't hear about the other ruptured guns.'

'Sabotage,' Grey repeated blankly. 'How can you – Oh, Jesus. It's bloody Edgar, isn't it? They honestly suspect Edgar DeVane of – of – Christ, what on earth do they think he's done?'

'It hasn't got so far as thinking,' Harry assured him drily. 'And I've no idea whether they actually suspect your half brother of anything personally. Might only have been dragging him in in order to rattle you and make you do something injudicious – like walk out of the inquiry.'

He chewed, closing his eyes in momentary bliss.

'By God, that's good. Anyway,' he went on, swallowing and opening his eyes. 'I've had nothing to do with artillery, myself. But I suppose it *would* be possible to blow up a cannon with a bomb of some sort, disguised as a canister of ordinary shot?'

'I suppose so.' Grey picked up his fork, then laid it down again and clenched his hands together in his lap.

'Well. Have you any useful suggestions to make, Harry?'

'I think you should eat your trout while it's

still hot.' Quarry prodded his own fish approvingly in illustration. 'Beyond that . . .' He eyed Grey, chewing.

'There is a certain opinion in the regiment, to the effect that perhaps you should be seconded to the Sixty-fifth, or possibly the Seventy-eighth. Temporarily, of course; let things blow over and quiet down.'

The Sixty-fifth was presently stationed in the West Indies, Grey knew; the Seventy-eighth was a Highland regiment somewhere in the American colonies – the Northwest Territory, perhaps, or some other outlandish place.

'Thus allowing Twelvetrees and Marchmont to claim that I've fled to avoid prosecution, thus lending credence to their preposterous insinuations. I think not.'

Harry nodded, matter-of-fact.

'Of course. Which leaves us with my original suggestion.'

Grey raised an eyebrow at him.

'Eat your trout,' Quarry said. 'And the devil with your hands. Mine would shake, too, in your position.'

Hal was, of course, with the part of the regiment presently in winter quarters in Prussia. Harry had wanted to send word to him, but Grey declined.

'There is little Hal can do, and his presence would merely inflame feelings further,' he pointed out. 'Let me see what I can do alone; time enough to advise him if anything drastic should happen.'

'And what *do* you propose to do?' Quarry asked, giving him a narrow look.

'Go down to Sussex and see Edgar DeVane,' Grey replied. 'He ought at least to know that his name is being put forward as a suspected saboteur. And if there should be anything whatever to the matter . . .'

'Well, that will at least get you out of Town and out of sight for a bit,' Quarry agreed dubiously. 'Can't hurt. And you could be back within two or three days, should anything – you will pardon my choice of words, I trust – blow up.'

Grey's departure for Sussex was delayed, however, by receipt of a note in the morning post.

'What is it, me lord?' Tom, attracted by Grey's muttered blasphemies, stuck his head out of the pantry, where he had been cleaning boots.

'A Mr. Lister, from Sussex, is in Town. He wishes to call upon me, should I find that convenient.'

Tom shrugged. 'You might have found it convenient to be already gone, me lord,' he suggested.

'I would, but I can't. He's the father of Lieutenant Lister, the officer who was killed at Crefeld. He's heard that I have his son's sword, and while he's much too polite to say he wants it back, that is his obvious desire.'

Grey reached for ink and paper with a sigh.

'I'll tell him to come this afternoon. We'll leave tomorrow.'

Mr. Lister had a slight stammer, made worse by emotion, and a small, pale face, overwhelmed by a very new and full-bottomed wig, from whose depths he peeped out like a wary field mouse.

'Lord John G-Grey? I intrude intolerably, sir, but I – Colonel Quarry said . . . that is, I do hope I am not . . .'

'Not in the slightest,' Grey said firmly. 'And it is I who must beg pardon of you, sir. You should not have put yourself to the trouble of coming; I should have been most pleased to wait upon you.' Lord John bowed him to a chair, flicking a glance at Tom, who promptly vanished in search of refreshment.

'Oh, no, n-not at all, my lord. I – it is most gracious in you to receive me so s-suddenly. I know I am . . .' He waved a small, neat hand in a gesture that encompassed social doubt, self-effacement, and abject apology – and conveyed such a sense of helplessness that Grey felt himself obliged to take Mr. Lister's arm and lead him physically to a seat.

'I must apologize, sir,' he said, having seen his guest settled. 'I ought to have made an effort to inquire for Lieutenant Lister's family long before this.'

A faint approximation of a smile touched Mr. Lister's face.

'That is kind in you to say, sir. But there is no reason, really, why you should. Philip' – his lips twitched at speaking his dead son's name – 'Philip was not of your regiment, nor in any way under your command.'

'He was a fellow officer,' Grey assured him. 'And thus has claim to both my duty and respect – as does his family.' Having been drenched to the skin in Philip Lister's blood seemed an even more immediate claim upon his interest, but he thought he would not mention the fact.

'Oh.' Mr. Lister drew a deep breath, and seemed a little easier. 'I – Thank you.'

'Will you take something, sir? A little wine, perhaps?' Tom had appeared, manfully lugging an enormous tray equipped with a rattling array of bottles, decanters, glasses, and an immense seed cake. Where had he got that? Grey wondered.

'Oh! No, I thank you, my lord. I d-do not take spirits. We are Methodist, you understand.'

'Of course,' Grey said. 'We'll have tea, Tom, if you please.'

Tom gave Mr. Lister a disapproving look, but decanted the cake onto the table, hoisted the tray, and rattled off into the recesses of the apartment.

There was an awkward pause, which a little port or Madeira would have covered admirably. Not for the first time, Grey wondered at a religion which rejected so many of the things that made life tolerable. Perhaps it sprang from an intent to make heaven seem that much more desirable by contrast to a life from which pleasure had been largely removed.

But he must admit that his own attitudes toward Methodists perhaps lacked justice, having been badly colored by – He choked off that line of thought before it could reach its natural conclusion, and picking up the knife Tom had brought, waved it inquiringly in the direction of the seed cake.

Mr. Lister accepted the offer with alacrity, but obviously more in order to have something to do than from appetite, for he merely poked at his allotted portion, breaking off small bits and mashing them randomly with his fork.

Grey did his best to conduct a conversation, making courteous inquiries regarding Mr. Lister's wife and other family, but it was hard going, with the shade of Philip Lister perched like a vulture over the seed cake on the table between them.

At last, Grey put down his cup and glanced at Tom, hovering discreetly near the door.

'Tom, do you have Lieutenant Lister's sword convenient?'

'Oh, yes, me lord,' Tom assured him, with an air of relief. Mr. Lister was getting on his nerves, too. 'Cleaned and polished, kept quite proper!'

It was. Grey doubted that the sword had ever achieved such a blinding state of propriety while in the care of its original owner.

Grey felt an unexpected pang as he took the sheathed sword from Tom and presented it to Mr. Lister. He had no thought of keeping it, of course, and in fact had barely thought of it in the days since his return to England. Seeing it, though, and holding it, brought back in a sudden rush the events surrounding the battle at Crefeld.

The fog of misery and terror he had felt on that day enveloped him again, miasmalike – and then, cutting through all that, the weight of the sword in his hand, the same as the feeling in him when he had seized it from Lister's body. In that moment, he had thrown all emotion and any sense of self-preservation to the wind, and flung himself howling on the deserting gun crew, shouting and beating them with the flat of the sword, forcing them back to their duty by the power of his will.

He had not realized it until much later, but that moment of abnegation had had the paradoxical effect of making him whole, as though the heat of battle had melted all the shattered bits of mind and heart and forged him anew – into something hard and adamant, incapable of being hurt.

Then, of course, Tom Pilchard had blown up.

His hand had grown damp on the leather of the scabbard, and it took an actual effort of will to relinquish it.

Mr. Lister looked at the sword for some time, holding it upon the palms of his hands as though it might be some holy relic. Finally, very gently, he set it upon his knees, and coughed.

'I th-thank you, Lord John,' he said. His face worked for a moment, formulating words with such effort as to suggest that each one must be individually molded of clay.

'I – that is, my wife. His m-mother. I d-do not wish to . . . cause offense. Certainly. Or – or discomfort. B-but it would be perhaps some s-solace, were she to know what . . . what . . .' He stopped abruptly, eyes closed. He sat thus for some moments, absolutely still, seeming not even to breathe, and Grey exchanged an uneasy look with Tom, not sure whether his guest was merely overcome with emotion, or suffering a fit of some kind.

At last, Mr. Lister drew breath, though he did not open his eyes.

'Did he speak?' he asked hoarsely. 'Did you talk . . . talk to him? His last – his last w-words . . .' Tears had begun to course down Mr. Lister's pale face.

Methodist be damned, Grey thought. Prayer doubtless had its place, but when you were right up against it, there was no substitute for alcohol.

'Brandy, please, Tom,' he said, but it was there already, Tom nearly spilling the glass in his haste.

'Mr. Lister. Please, sir.' He leaned forward, tried to take Lister's hands in his, but they were clenched into fists.

He remembered the lieutenant's last words, vividly. Likewise, Philip Lister's expression of openmouthed astonishment as the cannonball had struck the ground, hit a stone, and soared up into the air – an instant later decapitating the lieutenant and rendering his last words ironically prophetic.

'Fuck me!' the lieutenant had said, in wonderment.

Mr. Lister was so much overcome with emotion that he made little protest at the brandy, and while he coughed and spluttered, Grey managed to pour sufficient into him as to induce a semblance of calm at last.

He had had it in mind, seeing his guest's distress, to compose some suitably noble speech in lieu of Philip Lister's actual exit line, but found that he could not bring himself to do this.

'I saw your son for the first time only moments before his death,' he said, as gently as he could. 'There was no time for talk. But I can assure you, sir, that he died instantly – and he died bravely, as a soldier of the king. You – and your wife, of course – may be justly proud of him.'

'May we?' The brandy had calmed Mr. Lister, and had the salutary effect of relieving his stammer, but had also brought a hectic flush to his pale cheeks.

'I thank you for your words, sir. And seeing that you share the profession of arms, I suppose you mean them.'

'I do,' Grey said, somewhat surprised.

Lister mopped at his face with the handkerchief Tom had discreetly provided, and looked directly at Grey for the first time.

'You will think me ungrateful, my lord, and I assure you I am not. But I must tell you that we – my wife and I – were completely opposed to Philip's choice of career. We – fell out over the matter, I regret to say. In f-fact . . .' He swallowed heavily. 'We had not spoken to Philip since he took up his commission.'

And now he was dead, as a direct result of having done so. Grey took a deep breath and nodded.

'I see, sir. You have my sympathy. A bit more brandy, perhaps? Purely for medicinal purposes.'

Mr. Lister looked at the bottle with a certain longing, but shook his head.

'No, my lord. I . . . no.'

He fell silent, looking down at the sword, which he now clutched tightly, one hand wrapped around the scabbard.

'May I ask a great favor of you, my lord?' he said abruptly.

'Certainly,' Grey replied, willing to do almost anything, firstly to relieve Lister's distress, secondly to get him out of Grey's sitting room.

'I said that we were opposed to Philip's pursuing a career with the army. He bought his commission with a small inheritance, and left almost immediately for London.' The hectic flush had faded a little; now it came back, washing up Mr. Lister's throat in a tide of shame. 'He – he t-took . . .' The words dried in his throat, and he looked down, fumbling with the ring of the scabbard.

Took what? Grey wondered. The family silver? Was he to be asked to comb pawnshops for bartered heirlooms? With a sense of resignation, he poured more tea, picked up the brandy bottle and added a healthy dollop, then firmly handed the cup to Mr. Lister.

'Took what?' he asked bluntly.

Mr. Lister took the tea with trembling hands and,

with an obvious effort, went on, looking down into its aromatic depths.

'He had formed an . . . attachment. To the daughter of our minister – a most suitable young woman; my wife and daughters were terribly fond of her.'

The minister had been, if not fond of Philip Lister, at least amenable to the match – until Philip had declared his intention of becoming a soldier.

The upshot of this had been that the minister had broken off the attachment – evidently it had not reached the stage of betrothal – and forbade Philip the house. Whereupon the new lieutenant, inflamed, had come round by night with a ladder, and in the best romantic tradition, induced his love to elope with him.

The little he had heard from Quarry of Philip Lister had already convinced Grey that perhaps the son was not so religious in outlook as were his parents; thus this revelation was not quite the shock to him that it plainly had been to his family.

'The scandal,' Mr. Lister whispered, and, gulping tea, shuddered convulsively. 'The disgrace of it nearly killed m-my wife. And the Reverend Mr. Thackeray, of course . . . The things he preached . . .'

Familiar with the ways of scandal, Grey had no difficulty in envisioning the aftermath of Lieutenant Lister's elopement. The religious aspects of the matter had – as they usually did, he reflected – merely magnified the damage.

The Lister family had been summarily dismissed from the congregation, even though they had already publicly disowned Philip. Their dismissal had in turn caused dissent and schism in the congregation – which had, naturally, spread throughout the village of which Mr. Lister was squire, resulting in general bad feeling, fisticuffs in the pub, the burning of someone's hayrick, and specific and personal denunciation of the Listers and their supporters from the pulpit.

'It is not that I consider the practice of arms immoral in itself, you understand,' Mr. Lister said, wiping his nose – which had gone bright red with emotion and brandy – with a napkin. 'Only that we had hoped for better things for Philip. He was our only son.'

Grey was conscious of Tom Byrd on the opposite side of the room, prickling like a hedgehog, but was careful not to catch his eye.

'I quite understand, sir,' he said, meaning only to be soothing.

'Do you, my lord?' Lister gave him a look of puzzled anguish. He seemed intent that Grey *should* understand. His brow drew down and he turned the sword over in his hand, seeming to search for some means of making himself clearer.

'It is such – such a *brutal* occupation, is it not?' he burst out at last.

Grey stared at him, thinking, *Yes. And so?*

Before he could formulate something polite in

reply, Tom Byrd, bending over the table to retrieve the seed cake, leapt in.

'I daresay,' he said hotly. 'And if it wasn't, you'd be saying what you just said in bleedin' French, wouldn't you?'

Lister regarded him, openmouthed. Grey coughed and motioned Tom hastily out of the room. The young valet went, with a last glower of disapproval at their guest.

'I must apologize for my valet, sir,' Grey said, feeling a terrible urge to laugh. 'He is . . .' A faint rattle from the cup and saucer he held made him realize that his hands had begun to shake, and he set them carefully down, grasping his knees with both hands.

'He is honest,' Lister said bleakly.

Outspoken honesty was not a virtue generally prized in a valet, but it was a virtue for all that – and Grey prized it. He nodded, and cleared his throat.

'A, um, favor, I believe you said?'

'Yes, my lord.' The recounting of his woes – and the recollection of the Reverend Mr. Thackeray's most iniquitous sermon – had revived Mr. Lister more than brandy. He sat bolt upright, cup clutched to his bosom, his dead son's sword across his knees, and fixed Grey with a burning gaze.

'I wish your help, my lord, in finding the girl. Anne Thackeray. I have some reason to suppose she was with child – and if so, I want the babe.'

'I am completely insane.'

'You've a very kind heart, me lord,' Tom Byrd said reprovingly. 'Not the same thing at all.'

'Oh, I am reasonably sure that it is – at least in this instance. Kind of you to give me the benefit of the doubt, though, Tom.'

'Of course, me lord. Lift your chin a bit, if you please.' Tom breathed heavily through his nose, frowning in concentration as he drew the razor delicately up the side of Grey's neck.

'Not as I know why you said you'd do it, mind,' Byrd remarked.

Grey shrugged one shoulder, careful not to move his head. He wasn't sure why he'd said he'd do it, either. In part, he supposed, because he felt some guilt over not having made an effort to return Lister's sword to his father sooner. In part because the Listers' village was no more than an hour's ride from his brother Edgar's place in Sussex – and he anticipated that having some excuse to escape from Maude might be useful.

And, if he were honest, because the prospect of dealing with other people's trouble was a welcome distraction from his own. Of course, he reflected, none of these considerations proved that he was *not* insane.

Tom Byrd's considerations were of another sort, though.

'*Brutal occupation,* is it?' he muttered. Lister's words of the day before had clearly rankled. 'I'll brutalize him and he don't mind his manners summat better. To say such a thing to *you,* and half a minute later ask you a bleedin' great favor!'

'Well, the man was upset. I daresay he didn't think—'

'Oh, he thought, all right! Me lord,' Tom added as an afterthought. 'Reckon he's done nothing *but* think since his son was killed,' he added, in less vehement tones.

He laid down the razor and subjected Grey's physiognomy to his usual searching inspection, hazel eyes narrowed in concentration. Satisfied that no stray whisker had escaped him, he took up the hairbrush and went round to complete the chore of making his employer fit for public scrutiny.

He snorted briefly, pausing to work out a tangle with his fingers. Grey's hair was like his mother's – fair, thick and slightly wavy, prone to disorder unless tightly constrained, which it always would be, if Tom Byrd was given his way. Actually, Tom would be best pleased if Grey would consent to have his head polled and wear a good wig like a decent gentleman, but some things were past hoping for.

'You've not been sleeping proper,' Byrd said accusingly. 'I can tell. You've been a-wallowing on your pillow; your hair's a right rat's nest!'

'I do apologize, Tom,' Grey said politely. 'Perhaps I should sleep upright in a chair, in order to make your work easier?'

'Hmp,' Byrd said. And added, after a few moment's strenuous brushing, 'Ah, well. P'r'aps the country air will help.'

Tom Byrd, always suspicious of the countryside, was not reassured by his first sight of Mudling Parva.

'Rats,' he said darkly, peering at the charmingly thatched rooves of the cottages they passed. 'I'll wager there's rats up in them thatches, to say nothing of bugs and such nastiness. My old granny come from a village like this. She told stories, how the rats would come down from the thatch at night and eat the faces off babies. Right in their cradles!' He looked accusingly at Lord John.

'There are rats in London,' Lord John pointed out. 'Probably ten times more of them than in the countryside. And neither you nor I, Tom, are babes.'

Tom hunched his shoulders, not convinced.

'Well, but. In the city, you can see things coming, like. Here . . .' He glanced round, his disparaging look taking in not only the muddy lane of the village and the occasional gaping villager, but also the tangled hedgerows, the darkly barren fallow fields, and the shadowed groves of leafless trees, huddled near the distant stream. 'Things might sneak up on you here, me lord. Easy.'

Part II

Family Matters

Blackthorn Hall, Sussex

Grey knew that his mother's first husband, Captain DeVane, had been a most impressive man to look at – tall, handsome, dark, and dashing, with an aristocratically prominent nose and hooded gray eyes that gave him the aspect of a poet; Grey had seen several portraits.

Edgar, like his elder brother, Paul, exhibited these same characteristics, to a degree that caused young women to stare at him in the village, their mouths half open, despite the fact that he was well into his forties.

Filial respect caused Grey to hesitate in passing *ex post facto* opinions on his mother's judgment, but after half an hour in the company of either Paul or Edgar, he could not escape a lurking suspicion that a just Providence, seeing the DeVanes so well endowed with physical beauty, had determined that there was no reason to spoil the work by adding intelligence to the mix.

'What?' Edgar frowned at him in incomprehension. 'Somebody thinks I might have blown up a *cannon*? Bloody cheek!'

Of course, Grey reflected with an inner sigh, his mother *had* been only fifteen when she married DeVane.

'Not you, personally, no,' he assured Edgar. 'The question—'

'Wasn't even *there*, was I?' Edgar's high cheekbones flushed with indignation.

'I'm sure I should have noticed if you had been,' Grey assured him gravely. 'The question—'

'Who's this Marchmont fellow, anyway? Piddling Irish title, not more than two generations out of the muck, what does he think he's about, insulting *me*?' The DeVanes boasted nothing more than the odd knighthood, but could – and Maude often tiresomely did – trace their lineage back to well before the Conquest.

'I'm sure no insult was—' Well, actually, he was convinced of exactly the opposite; Marchmont's purpose had been specific and blatant insult – and he did wonder why. Was it only to rattle Grey himself – or had he been *meant* to convey Marchmont's remarks to Edgar, all along? Well, that was a question to be turned over later.

For the moment, he dropped any further attempts at soothing his half brother and asked bluntly, 'Who oversees your powder mill, Edgar?'

Edgar looked at him blankly for an instant, but then the mist of anger in the hooded eyes lifted. Cleverness and intuition were not his strongest suits, but he could be depended on for straightforward facts.

'William Hoskins. Bill, he goes by. Decent man, got him from Waltham, a year ago. You think he's something to do with this?'

'As I've never heard of the man 'til this moment, I've no idea, but I should like very much to speak with him, if you have no objection.'

'Not the slightest.' They were standing in the orchard behind the manor house; Grey had waited for an opportunity to speak to Edgar in privacy after breakfast.

'Come now,' said Edgar, turning with an air of decision. 'We'll cut across the fields; it's quicker than fetching horses and going round by the road.'

It was rough going across the autumn fields, some already turned under by the plow, some still thick with stubble and the sharp, ragged ends of corn-stalks, but Grey didn't mind. The day was cold and misty, the sky gray and very low, so the air seemed still around them, wrapping them in silence, unbroken save for the occasional *whir* of a pheasant rising, or the distant calling of crows among the furrows.

It was a good two miles from the house to the powder mill, located on a bend of the river, and the brothers kept to their own thoughts for some time. At a stile, though, Grey caught his foot coming down and twisted awkwardly to save himself falling. The movement sent a sharp hot wire lancing through his chest, and he froze, trying not to breathe. He had made an involuntary noise, though, and Edgar turned, startled.

Grey lifted a hand, indicating that he would be all right – he hoped he would – but couldn't speak.

Edgar's brow creased with concern, and he put out a hand, but Grey waved him off. It had happened several times before, and generally the pain passed within a few moments; Dr. Longstreet's irritation of the nerves, quite harmless. There was always the possibility, though, that it might indicate a shift of the sliver of iron embedded in his chest, in which case he might be dead within the next few seconds.

He held his breath until he felt his ears ring and his vision gray, then essayed the slightest breath, found it possible, and slowly relaxed, the nightmare feeling of suffocation vanishing as his lungs expanded without further incident.

'Are you quite all right, John?' Edgar was surveying him with an expression of worried concern that moved him.

'Yes, fine.' He straightened himself, and gave Edgar a quick grimace of reassurance. 'Nothing. Just . . . taken queer for a moment.'

Edgar gave him a sharp look that reminded him for an unsettling instant of their mother.

'Taken queer,' he repeated, eyes passing up and down Grey's body as though inspecting him for damage, like a horse that had come up suddenly lame. 'Melton's wife wrote to Maude that you'd been injured in Germany; she didn't say it was serious.'

'It isn't.' Grey spoke lightly, feeling pleasantly giddy at the realization that he wasn't going to die just this minute.

Edgar eyed him for a moment longer, but then nodded, patted him awkwardly and surprisingly on the arm, and turned toward the river.

'Never could understand why you went to the army,' Edgar said, shaking his head in disapproval. 'Hal . . . well, of course. But surely there was no need for *you* to take up soldiering.'

'What else should I do?'

Grey wasn't offended. He felt suffused with a great lightness of being. The stubbled fields and clouded sky embraced him, immeasurably beautiful. Even Edgar seemed tolerable.

Oddly enough, Edgar seemed to be considering his question.

'You've money of your own,' he said, after a moment's thought. 'You could go into politics. Buy a pocket borough, stand for election.'

Just in time, Grey recalled his mother mentioning that Edgar himself had stood for Parliament in the last by-election, and refrained from saying that personally, he would prefer to be shot outright than to have anything to do with politics.

'It's a thought,' he said agreeably, and they spoke no more, until the powder mill came in sight.

It was a brick building, a converted grain mill, and outwardly tranquil, its big waterwheel turning slowly.

'That's for the coarse grinding,' Edgar said,

nodding at the wheel. 'We use a horse-drawn edge runner for the finer bits; more control.'

'Oh, to be sure,' Grey replied, having no idea what an edge runner might be. 'A very aromatic process, I collect?'

A gust of wind had brought them an eye-watering wave of feculent stink, and Edgar coughed, pulling a handkerchief from his coat and putting it over his nose in a practiced manner.

'Oh, that. That's just the jakesmen.'

'The what?' Grey hastily applied his own handkerchief in imitation.

'Saltpeter,' Edgar explained, taking obvious satisfaction in knowing something that his clever-arse younger brother did not. 'One requires brimstone – sulfur, you know – charcoal, and saltpeter for gunpowder, of course—'

'I did know that, yes.'

'—We can produce the charcoal here, of course, and sulfur is reasonably cheap; well, saltpeter is not so expensive, either, but most of it is imported from India these days – used to get it from France, but now – Well, so, the more of it we can obtain locally—'

'You're digging it out of your tenants' manure piles?' Grey felt a strong inclination to laugh.

'And the privies. It forms in large nuggets, down at the bottom,' Edgar replied seriously, then smiled. 'You know there's a law, written in Good Queen Bess's time, but still on the books, that allows agents of the Crown to come round and dig out the jakes of any citizen, in time of war? A local lawyer found it for me; most useful.'

'I should think your tenants might find having their privies excavated to be a positive benefit,' Grey observed, laughing openly.

'Well, that part's all right,' Edgar admitted, looking modestly pleased with all this evidence of his business acumen. 'They're less delighted at our messing about their manure piles, but they do put up with it – and it lowers the cost amazingly.'

He waved briefly as they passed within sight of the jakesmen, two muffled figures unhitching a morose-looking horse from a wagon piled high with irregular chunks of reddish-brown, but kept his handkerchief pressed firmly to his nose until they had moved upwind.

'Anyway, it all goes there' – he pointed at a small brick shed – 'to be melted and cleaned. Then there, to the mixing shed' – another brick building, somewhat larger – 'and then to one of the milling sheds, for the grinding and corning. Oh, but here's Hoskins; I'll leave you to him. Hoskins!'

Bill Hoskins proved to be a ruddy, healthy-looking man of thirty or so – young for an overseer, Grey thought. He bowed most respectfully when introduced, but had no hesitation in meeting Grey's eyes. Hoskins's own were a striking blue-gray, the irises rimmed with black; Grey noticed, then felt an odd clench in the pit of his stomach at the realization that he *had* noticed.

In the course of the next hour, he learned a great

many things, among them what an edge runner was – this being a great slab of stone that could be drawn by horses over a flat trough of gunpowder – what raw sulfur smelled like – rotten eggs, as digested by Satan; 'the devil's farts,' as Hoskins put it, with a smile – how gunpowder was shipped – by barge down the river – and that Bill Hoskins was a noticeably well-built man, with large, clean, remarkably steady hands.

Trying to ignore this irrelevant observation, he asked whether powder of different grades was produced.

Hoskins frowned, considering.

'Well, can be, of course. That's what the corning's for—' He nodded at one of the flimsily built wooden sheds. 'The finer the powder's ground and corned into grains, the more explosive it is. But then, the finer it's corned, the riskier it is to handle. That's why the milling sheds are built like that' – he nodded at one – 'roofs and walls nobbut sheets of wood, cobbled together, loose-like. If one should go up, why, then, it's easy to pick up the bits and put them back together.'

'Indeed. What about anyone who might have been working in the shed when it . . . went up?' Grey asked, feeling his mouth dry a little at the thought.

Hoskins smiled briefly, eyes creasing.

'Not so easy. What you asked, though – in practice, we make only the one grade of powder at this mill, as it's all sold to the Ordnance Office for artillery. Hard enough to pass their tests; we do better than most mills, and even so, a good quarter of some batches turns out dud when they test it at Woolwich. Not that any o' that is *our* fault, mind. Some others is mebbe not so careful, naming no names.'

Grey recalled the incessant thuds from the proving grounds.

'Oh, pray do,' he said. 'Name names, I mean.'

Hoskins laughed. He was missing a tooth, far back on one side, but for the most part, his teeth were still good.

'Well, there's the three owners in the con-sortium—'

'Wait – what consortium is this?'

Hoskins looked surprised.

'Mr. DeVane didn't tell you? There's him, and Mr. Trevorson, what owns Mayapple Farm, down-river—' He lifted his chin, pointing. 'And then Mr. Fanshawe, beyond; Mudlington, his place is called. They went in together to bid the contracts for powder with the government, so as to be able to hold their own with the bigger powder mills like Waltham. So the powder's kegged and shipped all as one, marked with the consortium's name, but it's made separate at the three mills. And as I say, not everyone's as careful as what we are here.'

He looked over the assemblage of buildings with a modest pride, but Grey paid no attention.

'Marked with the consortium's name,' he repeated, his heart beating faster. 'What name is that?'

'Oh. Just *DeVane,* as your brother's the principal owner.'

'Indeed,' Grey said. 'How interesting.'

Edgar had gone on about his own business, offering to send back a horse for Grey. He had refused this offer, not wishing to seem an invalid – and feeling that he might profit from the solitary walk back across the fields, having considerable new information to think about.

The news of the consortium of powder-mill owners put a different complexion on the matter altogether.

We make only the one grade of powder at this *mill,* Hoskins had said. Grey had overlooked the slight emphasis at the time, but in retrospect, was sure it had been there.

The implication was plain; one or another of the consortium's mills *did* make the higher grades of black powder required for grenades, muskets, and rifle cartridges. He thought of turning back to ask Hoskins which mill might provide the more explosive powder, but thought better of it. He could check that with Edgar.

He must also ask Edgar to invite the other mill owners to Blackthorn Hall. He should speak with them in any case, and it was likely best to do that *en masse,* so that none of them should feel personally accused, and thus wary. He might also be able to gain some information from seeing them together, watching to see what the relations among them were.

Could there possibly be truth behind Lord Marchmont's insinuations of sabotage? If so – and he was still highly inclined to doubt it – then it became at least understandable why Marchmont should have mentioned Edgar by name.

No matter which mill had actually produced it, any suspicious powder would have been identified simply with the DeVane mark – a simplified version of Edgar's family arms, showing two chevrons quartered with an odd heraldic bird, a small, foot-less thing called a martlet. Hoskins had shown him the half-loaded barge at anchor in the river, stacked with powder kegs, all branded with that mark.

The sun was still obscured, but faintly visible; a small, hazy disk directly overhead. Seeing it, and becoming aware from interior gurglings that it had been a long time since breakfast, he considered what to do next.

There was time to ride to Mudling Parva. The obvious first step in doing as he had promised Mr. Lister was to interview the Reverend Mr. Thackeray, for any indications he might be able to provide of his errant daughter's whereabouts.

He could, though, reasonably leave that errand for the morrow, and return to Blackthorn Hall for luncheon. He must speak to Edgar about the con-sortium. And Maude had mentioned at breakfast that a friend or two from the county would be joining them.

'Hmm,' he said.

His relations with his elder half brothers had always been distant but cordial – save for the occasion when, aged ten, he had unwisely expressed the opinion that Edgar's fiancée was an overbearing doggess, and been clouted halfway across the room in consequence. His opinion of his sister-in-law had not altered in subsequent years, but he *had* learned to keep his opinions to himself.

Perhaps he would leave a note for Edgar and find some sort of sustenance on his way to the village.

He walked on, enjoying the spongy give of the earth beneath his boots, and returned to his contemplation of black powder. Or tried to. Within a few moments, though, he became aware that he was not thinking so much of the consortium, or of his new knowledge of the process of powder-making . . . but of Bill Hoskins.

The realization unsettled him. He had not responded in that visceral way to a man's physical presence since – well, since before Crefeld.

He hadn't really supposed that that part of him was dead, but had been content to leave it dormant, preoccupied as he had been with other matters, such as survival. If anything, though, he had expected that it might return slowly, healing gradually, as the rest of his body did.

Nothing gradual about it. Sexual interest had sprung up, sudden and vivid as a steel-struck spark, ready to ignite anything flammable in the vicinity.

Not that anything *was*. There was not the

slightest indication that Hoskins had any such proclivities – and even had Hoskins been giving him a blatantly rolling eyeball of invitation, Grey would in no case approach someone in his brother's orbit, let alone his employ.

No, it was nothing but simple appreciation.

Still, when he came to the stile where he had been stricken on the way out, he did not climb it, but seized the rail of the fence and vaulted over, then walked on, whistling 'Lilibulero.'

Upon due consideration, Grey left Tom Byrd at the ordinary in Mudling Parva, with enough money to render half a dozen men indiscreet, if not outright insensible, and instructions to gather whatever tidbits of local gossip might be obtained under these circumstances. He himself proceeded, in his soberest clothes, to the home of the Reverend Mr. Thackeray, where he introduced himself by title, rather than rank, as a club acquaintance of Philip Lister's, interested in the welfare of Anne Thackeray.

From Mr. Lister's description of the minister, Grey had been expecting something tall and cadaverous, equipped with piercing eye and booming voice. The reality was something resembling a pug dog belonging to his friend Lucinda, Lady Joffrey: small, with a massively wrinkled face and slightly bulging eyes at the front, the impression of a wagging curly tail at the back.

The Reverend Mr. Thackeray's air of effusive welcome diminished substantially, however, when informed of Lord John's business.

'I am afraid I cannot tell you anything regarding my late daughter, sir,' he said, repressed, but still courteous. 'I know nothing of her movements since her departure from my house.'

'Is your daughter . . . deceased?' Grey asked cautiously. 'I was unaware . . .'

'She is dead to *us*,' the minister said, shaking his head dolefully. 'And might better be dead in all truth, rather than to be living in a state of grievous sin. We can but hope.'

'Er . . . quite.' Grey sipped at the tea he had been offered, pausing to regroup, then essayed a different sally. 'Should she be alive, though – perhaps with a child . . .'

The Reverend Mr. Thackeray's eyes bulged further at the thought, and Grey coughed.

'I hesitate to voice the observation for fear of seeming crude, and I can but trust to your courtesy to overlook my presumption – but Lieutenant Lister actually *is* dead,' he pointed out. 'Your daughter – and perhaps her offspring – is therefore presumably left without protection. Would you not wish to receive news of her, perhaps to offer aid, even if you feel unable to accept her home again?'

'No, sir.' Mr. Thackeray spoke with regret, but most decidedly. 'She has chosen the path of ruin and damnation. There is no turning back.'

'You will pardon my ignorance, sir – but does

your faith not preach the possibility of redemption for sinners?'

The minister's amiably wrinkled countenance contracted, and Grey perceived the small, sharp teeth behind the upper lip.

'We pray for her soul,' he said. 'Of course. And that she will perceive the error of her ways, repent, and thus perhaps be allowed at last to enter the kingdom of God.'

'But you have no desire that she should receive forgiveness while still alive?' Grey had intended to remain aloofly courteous throughout the interview, no matter what was said, but found himself becoming irritated – whether with the Reverend Mr. Thackeray's sanctimony or his illogic, he was not sure.

'Certainly we should attempt to emulate Our Lord in forgiving,' the minister said, twitching the bands of his coat straight and drawing himself as upright as his diminutive stature would permit. 'But we cannot be seen to suffer licentiousness and lewd behavior. What example would I be to my congregation, were I to accept into my home a young woman who had suffered such public and flagrant moral ruin, the fruit of her sin apparent for all to see?'

'So she *has* borne a child?' Grey asked, pouncing upon this last injudicious phrase.

All of the reverend's wrinkles flushed dark red and he stood abruptly.

'I fear that I can spare you no more time, Lord

John. I have a great many engagements this afternoon. If you will—'

He was interrupted by the parlor maid who had brought tea, who bobbed a curtsy from the doorway.

'Your pardon, sir; it's Captain Fanshawe come.'

The choler left the Reverend's face at once.

'Oh,' he said. He glanced quickly at Grey, then at the doorway. Grey could see the figure of a tall man, standing in the hallway just beyond the maid.

'Captain Fanshawe . . . would that be Captain Marcus Fanshawe, perhaps?' Grey asked politely. 'I believe we are members of the same club.' He'd met the man briefly on that last, riotous visit to White's, he thought.

The minister nodded like a clockwork doll, but looked back and forth between Grey and the doorway, exhibiting marked perplexity and what looked like embarrassment.

Grey was somewhat perplexed himself. He was also angry with himself for having allowed his personal opinions to intrude on the conversation. No help now but to retreat in good order, perhaps leaving enough goodwill to provide for another visit later. He rose and bowed.

'I thank you for receiving me, sir. I can show myself out.'

The Reverend Mr. Thackeray and the maid both gave sharp gasps as he strode through the door, and the minister made a brief movement as though to prevent him, but Grey ignored it.

The man in the hall was dressed in ordinary riding clothes, his hat in his hand. He turned sharply at Grey's appearance, surprised.

Grey nodded toward the newcomer, hoping that his face did not reveal the shock he felt at Fanshawe's appearance. It was the sort of face that drew both men and women, dark and arresting in its beauty – or had been. One eye remained, sapphire-colored, dark-lashed, and framed by an arch of black brow, a perfect jewel.

The other was invisible, whether injured or destroyed, he had no idea. A black silk scarf was bound across Fanshawe's brow, a bar sinister whose starkness cut across a mass of melted, lividly welted flesh. The nose was mostly gone; only the blunt darkness of the nostrils remained. He had the horrid fancy that they stared, inviting him – almost *compelling* him – to look through them into Fanshawe's brain.

'Your servant, sir,' he heard himself say, bowing automatically.

'And yours.'

Had he ever heard Fanshawe's voice before? It was colorless, correct, with the slightest tinge of Sussex. Fanshawe turned at a sound from the parlor door, and Grey felt suddenly faint. Part of the captain's head had been caved in, leaving a shocking depression above the ear, nearly a quarter of the skull . . . gone. How had he lived?

Grey bowed again, murmuring something meaningless, and escaped, finding himself in the

280

road without noticing how he had got there.

His heart was beating fast and he felt the taste of bile at the back of his throat. He tried to erase the vision of Fanshawe's head from his mind, but it was no use. The ruined face was terrible to look upon, and filled him with a piercing regret for the loss of beauty – though he had seen such things before. But that sickening place, where the eye expected a solid curve of skull and found emptiness instead, was peculiarly shocking, even to a professional soldier.

He stood still, eyes closed, and breathed slowly, concentrating on the sharp autumnal odors round him: chimney smoke and the sweet scent of windfall apples, rotting in the grass; damp earth and dead leaves, the bitter smell of hawthorn fruits, cut straw, used to mulch the flower beds in Thackeray's garden. Soap—

Soap? His eyes flew open and he saw that the branches of the hedgerow beside him were heaving.

'Psst!' said the hedge.

'I beg your pardon?' he replied, leaning to look closer. Through the spiny branches of a hawthorn, he made out the anxious face of a young woman, perhaps eighteen or so, whose large, prominent eyes and upturned nose betrayed a close resemblance to the puglike Mr. Thackeray.

'May I speak to you, sir?' she said, eyes imploring.

'I believe you are, madam, but if you wish to continue doing so, perhaps it would be easier were I to meet you yonder?' He nodded down the road, to a gap where there was a gate set into the hedge.

The clean-smelling young woman met him there, her face pink with cold air and flusterment.

'You will think me forward, sir, but I – Oh, and I *do* apologize, sir, but I couldn't help overhearing, and when you spoke to Father about Annie . . .'

'I collect you are . . . Miss Thackeray?'

'Oh, I am sorry, sir.' She bobbed him an anxious curtsy, her ruffled cap clean and white, like a fresh mushroom. 'I am Barbara Thackeray. My sister is Miss Thackeray – or – or was,' she corrected, blushing deeply.

'Is your sister deceased, then?' Grey inquired, as gently as possible. 'Or married?'

'Oh, sir!' She gave him a wide-eyed look. 'I do *hope* she is married, and not – not the other. She wrote to me, and said she and Philip meant to be married ever so soon as they might. She is a good girl, Annie; you must not pay attention to anyone who tells you otherwise, indeed you must not!' She looked quite fierce at this, like a small pug dog seizing the edge of a carpet in its teeth, and he nearly laughed, but stopped himself in time.

'She wrote to you, you say?' He glanced involuntarily back at the house, and she correctly interpreted the look.

'She sent a letter in care of Simon Coles, the lawyer. He is – a friend.' Her color deepened. 'It was but a brief note, to assure me of her welfare. But I have heard nothing since. And when we heard that

Philip – that Lieutenant Lister – was killed . . . Oh, my fears for her will destroy me, sir, pray believe me!'

She looked so distressed that Grey had no difficulty in believing her, and so assured her.

'May I – may I ask, sir, why you have come?' she asked, pinkening further. 'You do not *know* anything of Anne, yourself?'

'No. I came in hopes of learning something regarding her whereabouts. You are familiar with Lieutenant Lister's family, I collect?'

She nodded, brows knit.

'Well, Mr. Lister is most desirous of discovering your sister's current circumstances, and offering what assistance he might, for his son's sake,' he said carefully. He really did not know whether Lister would be interested in helping the young woman if she had *not* given birth to Philip Lister's child, but there was no point in mentioning that possibility.

'Oh,' she breathed, a slight look of hope coming into her face. 'Oh! So you are a friend of Mr. Lister's? It was wise of you not to tell Father so. He holds the Listers responsible entirely for my sister's disgrace . . . and in all truth,' she added, with a trace of bitterness, 'I cannot say he is wrong to do so. If only Marcus . . . *He* would have quit the army for Anne's sake, I know he would. And of course now he is invalided out, but . . .'

'Captain Fanshawe was an – a suitor of Miss Thackeray's?' Grey said, hastily substituting that term for the more vulgar 'admirer.'

Barbara Thackeray nodded, looking troubled.

'Oh, yes. He and Philip both wished to marry her. My sister could not choose between them, and my father disliked them equally, because of their profession. But then—' She glanced back at the house, involuntarily. 'Did you *see* Marcus?'

'Yes,' Grey said, unable to repress a small shiver of revulsion. 'What happened to him?'

She shuddered in sympathy.

'Is it not terrible? He will not allow me or my younger sisters to see him, save he is masked. But Shelby – the parlor maid – told me what he is like. It was an explosion.'

'What – a cannon?' Grey asked, with a certain feeling of nightmare. She shook her head, though.

'No, sir. The Fanshawes own a powder mill, by the river. One of the buildings went – they do, you know, every so often; we hear the bang sometimes, in the distance, so dreadful! Two workmen were killed; Marcus lived, though everyone says it would have been a mercy had he not.'

Shortly after this tragedy, Philip Lister had eloped with Anne Thackeray, and bar that one short note, evidently nothing further was known of her whereabouts.

'She said that Philip had found her a suitable lodging in Southwark, and that the landlady was most obliging. Is that a help?' Barbara asked hopefully.

'It may be.' Grey tried not to imagine how many obliging landladies there might be in Southwark. 'Do you know – did your sister take away any jewelry with her?' The first – perhaps the only – thing a young woman left suddenly destitute might do was to pawn or sell her jewelry. And there might be fewer pawnbrokers in Southwark than landladies.

'Well . . . yes. At least . . . I suppose she did.' She looked doubtful. 'I could look. Her things . . . Father wished to dispose of them, and had them packed up, but I – well, I could not bear to part with them.' She blushed, looking down. 'I . . . persuaded Simon to speak to the drover who took away the boxes; they are in his shed, I believe.'

A distant shout made her look over her shoulder, startled.

'They are looking for me. I must go,' she said, already gathering her skirts for flight. 'Where do you stay, sir?'

'At Blackthorn Hall,' Grey said. 'Edgar DeVane is my brother.'

Her eyes flew wide at that, and he saw her look closely at him for the first time, blinking.

'He is?'

'My half brother,' he amended dryly, seeing that she was taken slightly back by his appearance.

'Oh! Yes,' she said uncertainly, but then her face changed as another shout came from the direction of the house. 'I must go. I will send to you about the jewelry. And thank you, sir, ever so much!'

She gave him a quick, low curtsy, then picked up her skirts and fled, gray-striped stockings flashing as she ran.

'Hmm!' he said. Used as he was to general approbation of his person, he was amused to discover that his vanity was mildly affronted at her plain astonishment that such an insignificant sort as himself should be brother to the darkly dramatic Edgar DeVane. He laughed at himself, and turned back toward the spot where he had left Edgar's horse, swishing his stick through the hedge as he passed.

Despite her rather prominent eyes and her lack of appreciation for his own appearance, he liked Barbara Thackeray. So, obviously, did Simon Coles. He hoped Coles was a more acceptable candidate for marriage than Lister or Fanshawe had been, for the young woman's sake.

He rather thought he must go and speak to lawyer Coles. Because while Barbara had received only the one note from her sister, both her father and Mr. Lister appeared to believe that Anne had later borne a child. It was possible, he thought, that Simon Coles knew why.

He was not sure what he had expected of Simon Coles, but the reality was different. The lawyer was a slight young man, with sandy hair, a sprinkling of freckles across a thin, homely face, and a withered leg.

'Lord John Grey . . . *Major* Grey?' he exclaimed, leaning eagerly forward over his desk. 'But I know you – know *of* you, I should say,' he corrected himself.

'You do?' Once again, Grey found himself uneasy at being the unwitting subject of conversation. Perhaps Edgar had mentioned his impending arrival; he *had* sent a note ahead to Blackthorn Hall.

'Yes, yes! I am sure of it! Let me show you.' Reaching for the padded crutch that leaned against the wall, he tucked it deftly beneath one arm and swung himself out from behind the desk, heading so briskly for the bookshelves across the room that Grey was obliged to step out of the way.

'Now where . . . ?' the lawyer murmured, running a finger across a row of books. 'Ah, yes, just here, just here!'

Pulling down a large double folio, he bundled it across to the desk, where he flung it open and flicked the pages, revealing it to be a sort of compendium, wherein Grey recognized accounts from various newspapers, carefully cut out and pasted onto the pages. For variety, he glimpsed a number of illustrated broadsheets, and even a few ballad sheets, tucked amongst the pages.

'There! I knew it must be the same, though Grey is not an uncommon name. The circumstances, though – I daresay you found those sufficiently uncommon, did you not, Major?' He looked up with sparkling eyes, his finger planted on a cutting.

Unwilling, Grey felt still compelled to look, and was mortified to read a recently published and highly colored account of his saving a cannon – the gun reported as being named 'Tod Belcher' – from the hands of a ravening horde of Austrians after the tragic and untimely demise of the gun's captain. He, Grey, having personally swept an oncoming Austrian cavalry officer from his saddle, then pinned him to the ground with his sword through the officer's coat, demanded and accepted his surrender, and then (by report) had fought the gun virtually single-handed, the rest of the crew having been slain by the accident which took the life of 'Philbert Lester,' the doomed captain, whose detached limbs had been scattered to the four winds, and his bowels torn out. Rather oddly, the explosion of the cannon that had concluded this remarkable passage at arms was treated in a single offhand sentence.

Whoever had written this piece of bombast *had* managed, to Grey's amazement, both to spell his own name correctly – scarcely a blessing, in the circumstances – and to note that the event had occurred in Germany.

'But Mr. Coles!' Grey said, aghast. 'This – this – it is the most arrant poppycock!'

'Oh, now, Major, you must not be modest,' Coles assured him, wringing him by the hand. 'You must not seek to lessen the honor your presence grants to my office, you know!'

He laughed merrily, and Grey, with a feeling of helplessness, found himself obliged to smile and bow in an awkward parody of graciousness.

Coles's clerk, a youth named Boggs, was summoned in to meet the hero of Crefeld, then sent off in a state of wide-eyed excitement to fetch refreshment – against Grey's protests – from the local ordinary. Where, Grey reflected grimly, he was no doubt presently recounting the whole idiotic story to anyone who would listen. He resolved to finish his business in Mudling Parva as quickly as possible, and decamp back to London before Edgar and Maude got wind of the newspaper story.

As it was, he had considerable trouble in getting Mr. Coles to attend to the matter in hand, as the lawyer wished to ask him any number of questions regarding Germany, his experiences in the army, his opinion of the current political situation, and what it was like to kill someone.

'What is it like . . .' Grey said, thoroughly taken aback. 'To – In battle, I suppose you mean?'

'Well, yes,' said Coles, his eagerness slightly – though only slightly – abating. 'Surely you have not been slaughtering your fellow citizens in cold blood, Major?' He laughed, and Grey joined – politely – in the laughter, wondering what in God's name to say next.

He was fortunately saved by Coles's own sense of propriety – evidently he did have one, overborne though it was by gusts of enthusiasm.

'You must forgive me, Major,' Coles said, sobering a little. 'I am sure the matter is a sensitive one. I should not have asked – and I beg pardon for so intruding upon your feelings. It is only that I have always had a strong and most . . . abiding *admiration* for the profession of war.'

'You do?'

'Yes. Oh, there you are, Boggs! Thank you, thank you . . . yes, you will have some wine, I hope, Major? Allow me, please. Yes,' he repeated, settling back in his chair and waving his reluctant clerk firmly out of the room. 'Many of the men of my family in previous generations have taken up commissions – my great-grandfather fought in Holland – and I should no doubt have pursued the same career myself, were it not for this.' He gestured ruefully toward his leg.

'Thus my fascination with the subject. I have made a small study of military history' – this was obviously modesty speaking, Grey thought, judging by the impressive collection on the shelves behind him, which seemed to include everyone from Tacitus and Caesar to King Frederick of Prussia – 'and have even been so bold as to compose a brief essay upon the history of siege warfare. I, um, do not suppose you have ever been involved personally in a siege, have you, Major?'

'No, no,' Grey said hurriedly. He had been penned up in Edinburgh Castle with the rest of the government troops during the Jacobite occupation of the city, but it was a siege in name only; the Jacobites had had no thought of battering their way into the castle, let alone of starving out the inhabitants.

'Mr. Coles,' he said, inspired by thought of battering rams, and seeing that the only way of progressing in his own interest was by bluntness, 'I collect that you are acquainted with the

Thackeray family – specifically, with a Miss Barbara Thackeray?'

Coles blinked, looking almost comically nonplussed.

'Oh! Yes,' he said, a little uncertain. 'Of course. I, er, have the honor to consider myself a friend of the family.' Meaning, Grey thought, that Mr. Thackeray was probably unaware of Coles's friendship with Barbara.

'I flatter myself that I may count myself a friend to them, as well,' Grey said, 'though our acquaintance is so new.' He smiled, and Coles, sunny by disposition, smiled back.

An understanding thus established, there seemed no reason to avoid mention of Mr. Lister with Coles, and so Grey put the matter before him straightforwardly.

'Miss Barbara said that she had had a note from her sister, forwarded by your kind offices,' Grey said carefully, and Coles blushed.

'I should have taken it to her father, I know,' he said awkwardly. 'But . . . but . . . she . . . I mean, Miss Barbara Thackeray is . . .'

'A friend,' Grey finished for him, echoing Barbara Thackeray's own words – spoken, he noted, with precisely the same blushing intonation. 'Of course.'

Skating away from that delicate subject, he said, 'Mr. Lister believes there is a possibility that Anne Thackeray is or was with child. From something that Mr. Thackeray let slip during our conversation, I believe he may have the same impression. I wonder, Mr. Coles, whether you can shed any light on this possibility?'

For the first time, Coles looked uneasy.

'I have no idea,' he said. Grey thought it was as well the young lawyer was a country solicitor; someone with so little talent for lying would fare ill before the Bench.

'Mr. Coles,' he said, letting a bit of steel show in his voice, 'it is a question of the young woman's life.'

The lawyer paled a little, the freckles on his cheeks standing out.

'Oh. Well . . . I, er . . .'

'Did you receive any further communications from Anne Thackeray?'

'Yes,' Coles said, succumbing with a distinct air of relief. 'Just the one. It was addressed to me, rather than to Barbara – I should not have read it, else. It was written just before the news came of Philip's death; she did not know of it.'

Grey noted the familiarity of the Christian name, and thought that Coles must have known Philip Lister personally – but of course he did. This was not London; everyone knew everyone – and very likely, everything about them.

Anne Thackeray had written in desperation, saying that she had recently discovered herself to be with child, had exhausted the money Philip had left for her, and was near the end of her resources. She had appealed to Simon Coles to intercede for her with her father.

'Which I did – or tried to.' Coles wiped his nose

with a crumpled handkerchief, which, Grey noted, he wore in his sleeve, like a soldier. 'My efforts were not, alas, successful.'

'The Reverend Mr. Thackeray does seem a trifle . . . strict in his views,' Grey observed.

Coles nodded, tucking away the handkerchief.

'You must not think too hardly of him,' he said earnestly. 'He is a good man, a most excellent minister. But he has always been very . . . firm . . . with his family. And his daughters' virtue is naturally a matter of the greatest importance.'

'Greater than their physical well-being, evidently,' Grey observed caustically, but then dismissed that with a wave. 'So, when Mr. Thackeray refused to listen, you naturally went to Mr. Lister.'

Coles looked embarrassed.

'It was professionally quite wrong of me, I know. Indiscreet, at best, and most presumptuous. But I really did not know what else to do, and I thought that perhaps the Listers would be more inclined to . . .'

But they hadn't. Mr. Lister had sent the young lawyer away with a flea in his ear. But that, of course, was before Philip Lister had been killed.

'What was the address on the letter?' Grey asked. 'If she expected help, surely she must have given an address to which it could be sent.'

'She did give an address, in Southwark.' Coles took up his neglected glass of wine and swallowed, avoiding Grey's gaze. 'I – I could not ignore her plea, you see. I – we – that is, I prevailed upon a mutual friend to take some money to her, and to see how she fared. I would have gone myself, but . . .' He indicated his crutch.

'Did he find her?'

'No. He came back in some agitation of mind, and reported that she was gone.'

'Gone?' Grey echoed. 'Gone where?'

'I don't know.' The young lawyer looked thoroughly miserable. 'He inquired in every place he could think of, but was unable to discover any clue to her whereabouts. Her landlady said that Anne – Miss Thackeray – had been unable to pay her account, and had thus been put out of her room. The woman had no idea where she had gone then.'

'Not very obliging of her,' Grey observed.

'No. I – I tried to make further inquiries. I hired a commercial inquiry agent in London, but he made no further discoveries. Oh, if only I had sent to her at once!' Coles cried, his face contorting in sudden anguish.

'I should not have wasted so much time in thinking how to approach her father, in screwing up my courage to go to the Listers, but I was afraid, afraid to speak to them, afraid of failing – and yet I did fail. I am a coward, and whatever has become of Anne is all my fault. How am I to look her sister in the face?'

It took Grey some time to console and reassure the young lawyer, and his efforts were only partially successful. In the end, Coles was restored to some semblance of resolution by Grey's recounting of his conversation with Barbara regarding her sister's jewelry.

'Yes. Yes! I do have Anne's boxes, safely in my shed. I will look them out this afternoon. We must make some pretext, Barbara and I, to meet and examine them—'

'I am sure that such a challenge will prove no bar to someone with your extensive study of strategy and tactics,' Grey assured him, rising from his chair. 'If you or Miss Barbara will then send me a note, describing any trinkets that may be missing . . ?'

He took his leave, and was nearly out the door when Coles called after him.

'Major?'

He turned to see the young lawyer leaning on his desk, his quicksilver face for once settled into seriousness.

'Yes, Mr. Coles?'

'What I asked you . . . what it feels like to have killed someone in battle . . . that was mere vulgar curiosity. But it makes me think. I hope I have not killed Anne Thackeray. But if I have – you will tell me? I think I would prefer to know, rather than to fear.'

Grey smiled at him.

'You would have made a good soldier, Mr. Coles. Yes, I'll tell you. Good day.'

Any joy, Tom?'

'Dunno as I'd go so far, me lord.' Tom looked dubious, and put a hand to his mouth to stifle a belch. 'I will say as the Goose and Grapes has very good beer. Grub's not so good as the Lark's Nest, but not bad. Did you get summat to eat, me lord?'

'Oh, yes,' Grey said, dismissing the matter. In fact, his sole consumption since breakfast had been half a slice of fruitcake at Mr. Thackeray's, and a considerable quantity of wine, taken in Mr. Coles's company. It had come, he was sure, from the Goose and Grapes, but had not shared the excellent quality of the beer. It had, however, been strong, and his head showed a disturbing disposition to spin slightly if he moved too suddenly. Luckily the horse knew the way home.

'Were you able to hear anything about the Thackerays, the Listers, the Fanshawes, the Trevorsons – or for that matter, the DeVanes?'

'Oh, a good bit about all of 'em, me lord. Especially about Mrs. DeVane.' He grinned.

'I daresay. Well, perhaps we can save that for entertainment on our journey back to London,' Grey said dryly. 'What about the Fanshawes and Trevorsons?'

Tom squinted, considering. He had declined to share Grey's horse, and was walking alongside.

'Squire Trevorson's a sporting man, they say. Gambling, aye?'

'In debt?'

'To his eyeballs,' Tom said cheerfully. 'They didn't know for sure, but the talk is his place – Mayapple Farm, it's called, and there's an unlucky name for you – is mortgaged to the eaves.'

'What the hell is unlucky about it?'

Tom glanced up at Grey's unaccustomed sharpness, but answered mildly.

'A mayapple's a thing grows in the Americas, me lord. The red Indians use it for medicine, they say, but it's poison otherwise.'

Grey digested this for a moment.

'Has Trevorson got connexions in America, then?'

'Yes, me lord. An uncle in Canada, and two younger brothers in Boston and Philadelphia.'

'Indeed. And does popular knowledge extend to the politics of these connexions?' It seemed far-fetched, but if sabotage were truly involved in the cannon explosions – and Quarry seemed to think it might be – then the loyalties of Trevorson's family might become a point of interest.

The denizens of the Goose and Grapes had not possessed any knowledge on that point, though – or at least had volunteered none. About the Fanshawes, talk had been voluble, but centered about the terrible misfortune that had befallen Marcus; nothing to the discredit of his father, Douglas Fanshawe, seemed to be known.

'Captain Fanshawe got himself blown up in one o' the milling sheds,' Tom informed Grey. 'Tore off half his face, they said!'

'For once, public comment is understated. I saw the captain at the Thackerays.'

'Cor, you saw him?' Tom was awed. 'Was it as bad as they say, then?'

'Much worse. Did anyone talk about the accident? Do they know what happened?'

Tom shook his head.

'Nobody knows but Captain Fanshawe. He's the only one that lived, and he doesn't talk to anybody save the Reverend Mr. Thackeray.'

'He does talk to Thackeray?'

'Aye, me lord. He goes there regular to visit, but nowhere else. It'll be weeks on end when no one sees him – and folk don't speak when they do; he's a proper creepy sight, they say, going about in a black silk mask and everybody a-knowing what's behind it. The reverend treats him very kind, though, they say.'

Grey remembered Coles, young and earnest, saying, *You must not think too hardly of him. He is a good man, a most excellent minister.* Evidently Thackeray did have some bowels of compassion, even if not for his daughter.

'Speaking of Thackeray, did you learn anything there?'

'Well, there was a deal of gossip,' Tom said doubtfully. 'Not really what you'd call information, like. Just folk arguing was Miss Anne a wicked trollop or was she se-dyuced' – he pronounced it carefully – 'by Lieutenant Lister.'

'One side or the other prevalent?'

Tom shook his head.

'No, me lord. Six of one, half a dozen o' the other.'

Opinion had been likewise divided as to the schism in the local Methodist congregation that had culminated in the Listers being ousted. Comment had been prolonged and colorful, but there appeared to be no useful kernels of information in it.

News exhausted, silence fell between them. The sun had long since set, and cold darkness crept up from the fallow fields on either side. Tom Byrd was no more than a shadow, pacing by his stirrup, patient as de— Grey drew himself up in the saddle, shaking his head to drive off the thought.

'You all right, me lord?' Tom asked, suspicions at once aroused. 'You're not a-going to fall off that nag, are you?'

'Certainly not,' Grey said crisply. In fact, he was desperately tired, hunger and unaccustomed exertion weighting his limbs.

'You been overdoing. I knew it,' Tom said, with gloomy relish. 'You'd best go straight to bed, me lord, with a bit o' bread and milk.'

Grey did not, of course, go to bed, dearly as he would have liked to.

Instead, hastily washed, brushed, and changed by a disapproving Tom Byrd, he went down to supper to meet the consortium, all hastily summoned by Edgar at his request.

Matters did not proceed as smoothly as he had

hoped. For one thing, Maude was present, and loud in her disbelief that anyone could suppose that the sacred name of DeVane could be disparaged in this wanton fashion.

Edgar, bolstered by support from the distaff side, kept thwacking a metaphorical riding crop against his leg, clearly imagining the prospect of thrashing Lord Marchmont or Colonel Twelvetrees with it. Grey admitted the charming nature of the notion, but found the repetition of the sentiment wearing.

As for Fanshawe and Trevorson, both appeared to be exactly as described – an honest, rather dull farmer, and a slightly reckless country squire, given to ostentatious waistcoats. Both were bug-eyed with shock at news of what had been said at the Commission of Inquiry, and both professed complete bewilderment at what the commission could possibly have been thinking.

Ignorance did not, of course, prevent their speculating.

'Marchmont,' Trevorson said, in tones of puzzlement. 'I confess I do not understand this at all. If it had been – you did say Mortimer Oswald was a member of this . . . body?'

'Yes,' Grey said, though he forbore nodding, fearing that his head might fall off. 'Why?'

Trevorson humphed into his claret cup.

'Snake,' he said briefly. 'No doubt he put Marchmont up to it. Feebleminded collop.'

Grey tried to form some sensible question in response to this information, but could make no connexion between Marchmont's feeblemindedness, Oswald's presumably serpentlike nature, and the problem at hand. The hell with it, he decided, glassy-eyed. He'd ask Edgar in the morning.

'Ridiculous!' Fanshawe was saying. 'What idiocy is this? Explode a cannon by loading it with tricky powder? A thousand times more likely that the gun crew made some error.' He smacked a hand down on the table. 'I'll wager you a hundred guineas, some arsehole panicked and double-loaded the thing!'

'What odds?' Trevorson drawled, making the table rock with laughter. Grey felt the muscles near his mouth draw back, miming laughter, but the words echoed in the pit of his stomach, mixing uneasily with the roast fowl and prunes.

Some arsehole panicked . . .

'John, you haven't touched the trifle! Here, you must have some, it is my own invention, made with gooseberry conserve from the gardens. . . .' Maude waved the butler in his direction, and he could not find will to protest as a large, gooey mass was dolloped onto his plate.

Exercised by his revelations, the members of the consortium kept him late, the brandy bottle passing up and down the table as they argued whether they should go in a body to London to refute this monstrous allegation, or send one of their membership as representative, in which case ought it be DeVane, as the largest mill owner—

'I believe that to make such a formal representation would merely inflame a matter that is at present not truly serious,' Grey said firmly, suffering nightmare visions of Edgar striding into Parliament, armed with a horsewhip.

'A letter, then!' Fanshawe suggested, red-faced with brandy and indignation. 'We cannot let such scurrilous insinuations pass unaddressed, surely!'

'Yes, yes, must compose a letter of complaint.' Trevorson was slurring his words, but his oxlike eyes swiveled toward Grey. 'You would take it, aye? She . . . *see*' – he wiped a dribble of saliva from the corner of his mouth – 'that it is delivered to this iniqui-tous Commission of In-qui-ree.'

That motion passed by acclamation, Grey's attempts at reason being shouted down and drowned in bumpers of brandy.

At last, he dragged himself upstairs, leaving the consortium to the amiable exercise of composing insulting epithets amid shouts of laughter, Edgar – as the only one still sober enough to write – being charged with committing these to paper.

Head pounding and clothes reeking of tobacco smoke, he pushed open the door to his room, to find Tom reclining in a chair by the hearth, immersed in *The Adventures of Peregrine Pickle*. The young valet hopped up at once, put by his book, and came to take Grey's coat and waistcoat.

Having briskly stripped his master and draped him in a clean nightshirt, he went to retrieve Grey's banyan, which had been hung to warm on the fire screen. He held this ready, peering closely at Grey in concern.

'You look like . . .' he said, and trailed off, shaking his head as though the prospect before him was too frightful for words. This matched Grey's own impression of the situation, but he was too exhausted to say so, and merely nodded, turning to thrust his arms into the comforting sleeves.

'Go to bed, Tom,' he managed to say. '*Don't* wake me in the morning. I plan to be dead.'

'Very good, me lord,' Tom said, and lips pressed tight, went out, holding Grey's wine-stained, sweat-damp, tobacco-smelling shirt at arm's length before him.

He had intended to fall directly upon his bed, but found that he could not. He was in that irritating state where one is exhausted beyond bearing, but so frayed of nerve as to find the mere thought of sleep unimaginable.

He sat down by the fire and picked up Tom's book, but found the words swim before his eyes and put it down again. Liquor surged through his veins, weariness clung to his limbs like spring mud, and it seemed an impossible effort to rise. Still, he did it, and wandered slowly round the room, touching things at random, as though in hopes of anchoring his thoughts, which – in distinct contrast to his body – were scuttling round in circles at a high rate of speed.

He opened the window; fresh air might clear his head. The smell of dark, cold earth rushed in, chilling him with its menace, and he shut the window hastily, fumbling at the catch. He leaned his head against the cold glass then for a time, staring at the moon, which was at the half, large and yellow as a cheese.

Below, the raucous shouts of the consortium came through the floor. Now they were arguing over the date of their putative letter, as to whether it must be dated today or tomorrow, and whether today was the twenty-first or the twenty-second of November.

November. He was late. Normally, if he was not in the field or on duty, he made his quarterly visit to Helwater in late October, before the roads in the Lake District began to succumb to the autumn rains.

But of course, after what had happened . . . Quite without warning, he found himself back in the stable at Helwater, blood pounding through his body and the sound of his own unforgivable words ringing in his ears.

Seized by impulse, he went to the secretary, snatched a sheet of paper, and flipped open the inkwell.

Dear Mr. Fraser,

I write to inform you that I shall not visit Helwater this quarter; official affairs detain me.

Your servant

He frowned at the paper. He could not possibly sign a letter to a prisoner *Your servant*, no matter that the prisoner in question had once been a gentleman. Something more formal . . . yet this *was* the usual formal closure, between gentlemen – and whether Jamie Fraser was now a groom or not . . .

'Are you insane?' Grey asked himself, aloud. Why should he think to send a letter, something he had never done, something that would cause no end of curiosity and unwelcome attention at Helwater . . . and *how* could he contemplate the possibility of writing to Fraser at all, given the enormity of what had happened between them at their last meeting?

He rubbed hard at his brow, took the sheet of paper in his hand, and crumpled it. He turned to throw it into the fire, but instead stopped, holding the ball of paper in his hand . . . and then sat slowly down again, smoothing the paper upon the desk.

The simple act of writing Fraser's name had given him a sense of connexion, and he realized that the desperate need for such connexion was what had driven him to write it. He realized now that he would never send a letter. Yet that sense lingered – and if such sense was the product only of his need, still it was there.

Why not? If it was no more than talking to himself, perhaps the act of writing down his thoughts would bring them into better order.

'Yes, you are insane,' he muttered, but took up his quill. Firmly crossing out *Your servant*, he resumed.

These affairs concern an inquiry into the explosion of a

cannon in Germany, June last. I was summoned before an official Commission of Inquiry, which . . .

He wrote steadily, pausing now and then to compose a sentence, and found that the exercise did seem to bring his seething thoughts to earth.

He wrote of the commission, Marchmont, Twelvetrees, and Oswald, Edgar and his consortium, Jones, Gormley, the corpse of Tom Pilchard . . .

At this point, he was writing so quickly that the letters scrawled across the page, barely legible – and his thoughts, too, had deteriorated as badly as his penmanship. What had begun as a calm, well-reasoned analysis of the situation had become incoherent.

He flung down the quill and resumed his circuit of the room. Pausing before the looking glass, he glanced at it, then away – then back.

Frozen in place, he stared into the silvered glass, and seemed to see his own features overlaid by Marcus Fanshawe's ruined face. His stomach heaved, and he clapped a hand to his mouth to keep from vomiting. The illusion vanished with the movement, but a ripple of horror ran over him from crown to sole.

He whirled, hand fumbling at his side for an invisible sword, but there was nothing there.

'Oh, Jesus,' he said softly. He had – he was sure of it – seen something else in the glass: the vision of Philip Lister, standing behind him.

He closed his eyes, trembling, then opened them,

afraid of what he might see. But the room was vacant, quiet save for the hissing of the fire and the rumble of laughter from below.

He had a sudden impulse to dress and go downstairs, even the company of Edgar and his partners seeming welcome. But his legs were trembling, too, and he sat down abruptly in the chair at the desk, obliged to put his head in his hands, lest he faint.

He breathed, eyes shut, for what seemed a very long time, trying not to think of anything. When he opened them again, the scrawled sheets of his unfinished letter lay before him.

His hands were shaking badly, but he took up the quill and, ignoring blots and scratches, began doggedly to write. He had no idea what he wrote, only wanting to find some escape in the words, and found after a time that he was recounting Mr. Lister's visit and that gentleman's remarks anent the profession of arms.

It is a brutal occupation, he wrote, *and God help me, if I am no hero, I am damned good at it. You understand, I think, for I know you are the same.*

The quill had left marks on his fingers, so tightly as he'd gripped it. He laid it down briefly, rubbing his hand, then took it up again.

God help me further, he wrote, more slowly. *I am afraid.*

Afraid of what?

Some arsehole panicked. . . .

I am afraid of everything. Afraid of what I may have done, unknowing – of what I might do. I am afraid of death, of mutilation, incapacity – but any soldier fears these things, and fights regardless. I have done it, and—

He wished to write firmly, *and will do it again.* Instead, the words formed beneath his quill as they formed in his mind; he could not help but write them.

I am afraid that I might find myself unable. Not only unable to fight, but to command. He looked at that for a moment, and put pen tentatively to the paper once more.

Have you known this fear, I wonder? I cannot think it, from your outward aspect.

That outward aspect was vivid in his mind; Fraser was a man who would never pass unnoticed. Even during their most relaxed and cordial moments, Fraser had never lost his air of command, and when Grey had watched the Scottish prisoners at their work, it was plain that they regarded Fraser as their natural leader, all turning to him as a matter of course.

And then, there had been the matter of the scrap of tartan. He felt hot blood wash through him and his stomach clench with shame and anger. Felt the startling thud of a cat-o'-nine-tails on bare flesh, felt it in the pit of his stomach, searing the skin between his shoulders.

He shut his eyes in reflex, fingers clenching so tightly on the quill that it cracked and bent. He dropped the ruined feather and sat still a moment, breathing, then opened his eyes and reached for another.

Forgive me, he wrote. And then, hardly pausing, *And yet why should I beg your forgiveness? God knows that it was your doing, as much as mine. Between your actions and my duty . . .* But Fraser, too, had acted from duty, even if there was more to the matter. He sighed, crossed out the last bit, and put a period after the words Forgive me.

We are soldiers, you and I. Despite what has lain between us in the past, I trust that . . .

That we understand one another. The words spoke themselves in his mind, but what he saw was not the understanding of the burdens of command, nor yet a sharing of the unspoken fears that haunted him, sharp as the sliver of metal next his heart.

What he saw was that one frightful glimpse of nakedness he had surprised in Fraser's face, naked in a way he would wish to see no man naked, let alone a man such as this.

'I understand,' he said softly, the sound of the words surprising him. 'I wish it were not so.'

He looked down at the muddled mess of paper before him, blotched and crumpled, marked with spider blots of confusion and regret. It reminded him of that terse note, written with a burnt stick. Despite everything, Fraser had given him help when he asked it.

Might he ever see Jamie Fraser again? There was a good chance he would not. If chance did not kill him, cowardice might.

The mania of confession was on him; best make

the most of it. His quill had dried; he did not dip it
again.

I love you, he wrote, the strokes light and fast,
making scarcely a mark upon the paper, with no ink.
I wish it were not so.

Then he rose, scooped up the scribbled papers,
and, crushing them into a ball, threw them into the
fire.

He was unfortunately *not* dead when he woke in the
morning, but wished he were. Every muscle in his
body ached, and the ghastly residue of everything
he had drunk clung like dusty fur to the inside of his
throbbing head.

Tom Byrd brought him a tray, paused to view the
remains, and shook his head in a resigned manner,
but said nothing.

Oddly enough, his hands did not shake. Still, he
clasped them carefully round his teacup and raised
it cautiously to his lips. As he did so, he noticed a
letter on the tray, sealed with a blob of crimson
wax, in which the initials SC were incised. Simon
Coles.

He sat up, narrowly avoiding spilling the tea, and
fumbled open the missive, which proved to contain
a brief note from the lawyer and a sheet of paper
containing several drawings, with penciled
descriptions written tidily beneath. Descriptions of
the bits of jewelry that Anne Thackeray had taken
with her when she eloped with Philip Lister.

'Tom,' Grey croaked.

'Yes, me lord?'

'Go tell the stable lad to ready the horses, then pack. We'll leave in an hour.'

Both Tom's eyebrows lifted, but he bowed.

'Very good, me lord.'

He had hoped to escape from Blackthorn Hall unnoticed, and was in the act of depositing a gracious note of thanks – pleading urgent business as excuse for his abrupt removal – on Edgar's desk, when a voice spoke suddenly behind him.

'John!'

He whirled, guilt stamped upon his features, to find Maude in the doorway, a garden trug over one arm, filled with what looked like onions but were probably daffodil bulbs or something agricultural of the sort.

'Oh. Maude. How pleased I am to see you. I thought I should have to take my leave without expressing my thanks for your kindness. How fortunate—'

'You're leaving us, John? So soon?'

She was a tall woman, and handsome, her dark good looks a proper match for Edgar's. Maude's eyes, however, were not those of a poetess. Something more in the nature of a gorgon's, he had always felt; riveting the attention of her auditors, even though all instinct bade them flee.

'I . . . yes. Yes. I received a letter—' He had

311

Coles's note with him, and flourished it as evidence. 'I must—'

'Oh, from Mr. Coles, of course. The butler told me he had brought you a note, when he brought me mine.'

She was looking at him with a most unaccustomed fondness, which gave him a small chill up the back. This increased when she moved suddenly toward him, setting aside her trug, and cupped a hand behind his head, looking searchingly into his eyes. Her breath was warm on his cheek, smelling of fried egg.

'Are you sure you are quite well enough to travel, my dear?'

'Ahh . . . yes,' he said. 'Quite. Quite sure.' God in heaven, did she mean to kiss him?

Thank God, she did not. After examining his face feature by feature, she released him.

'You should have told us, you know,' she said reproachfully.

He managed a vaguely interrogative noise in answer to this, and she nodded toward the desk. Where, he now saw, the newspaper cutting referring to him as the Hero of Crefeld was displayed in all its glory, along with a note in Simon Coles's handwriting.

'Oh,' he said. 'Ah. That. It really—'

'We had not the slightest idea,' she said, looking at him with what in a lesser woman would have passed for doe-eyed respect. 'You are so modest, John! To think of all you have suffered – it shows so clearly upon your haggard countenance – and to say not a word, even to your family!'

It was a cold day and the library fire had not been lit, but he was beginning to feel very warm. He coughed.

'There is, of course, a certain degree of exaggeration—'

'Nonsense, nonsense. But of course, your natural nobility of character causes you to shun public acclaim, I understand entirely.'

'I knew you would,' Grey said, giving up. They beamed at each other for a few seconds; then he coughed again and made purposefully to pass her.

'John.'

He halted, obedient, and she took him by the arm. She was slightly taller than he was, which he found disquieting, as though she might drag him off to her lair at any moment.

'You will be careful, John?' She was looking at him with such earnest concern that he felt touched, in spite of everything.

'Yes, dear sister,' he said, and patted her hand gently. 'I will.'

Her hand relaxed, and he was able to detach himself without violence. In the moment's delay afforded by the action, though, a belated thought had occurred to him.

'Maude – a question?'

'To be sure, John. What is it?' She paused in the act of picking up her trug, expectant.

'Do you know, perhaps, what would lead Douglas

Fanshawe to describe a politician named Mortimer Oswald as a snake?'

She drew herself up, suffering a slight reversion to her former attitude toward him.

'Really, John. Can you possibly be in ignorance of Oswald's despicable behavior during the election last year?'

'I . . . er . . . believe I may have been abroad,' he said politely, with a nod at the cutting on the desk. Her face changed at once, expressing remorse.

'Oh, of course! I am so sorry, John. Naturally you would have been preoccupied. Well, then; it is only that Mr. Oswald simply *slithered* round the district, spreading loathsome insinuations and ill-natured gossip about Edgar – nay, absolute *lies,* though he took great care never to be caught out about them, the beast!'

'Er . . . what sort of insinuations? Other than being loathsome, I mean.'

'Hints meant to suggest that there was something . . . *corrupt*' – her lips writhed delicately away from the word – 'in the means by which Edgar and his partners gained their contracts with the government. Which of course there was not!'

'Of course not,' Grey said, but she was in full spate, eyes flashing magnificently in indignation.

'As though Oswald's own hands were clean, in that regard! Everyone knows that the man simply *battens* upon bribery! He is a perfect viper of depravity!'

'Indeed.' Grey was undergoing a swift process of

enlightenment, realizing belatedly that Oswald had clearly been Edgar's opponent in the recent election. Which explained very neatly the insinuations of sabotage directed at the DeVane consortium. A better way of removing any future political threat could scarcely be imagined.

Oswald's cleverness in the matter had been in leading Marchmont and Twelvetrees to make the accusations, virtuously avoiding any appearance of involvement himself. Yes, 'snake' seemed reasonably accurate as a description.

'Who bribes him?' he asked.

There, though, Maude was at a loss, able only to repeat that everyone knew – but not precisely *what* everyone knew. Meaning that if Oswald did take bribes, he was reasonably circumspect about it. A word with Harry Quarry might shed a bit more light on the matter, though.

Invigorated by this thought, and the more eager to return to London, he smiled warmly upon Maude.

'Thank you, Maude, my dear,' he said. 'You are a blessing and a boon.' Standing a-tiptoe, he kissed her startled cheek, then strode with great determination for the stables.

Part III

The Hero's Return

W'ould you say that I appear haggard, Tom?' he inquired. There was a looking glass upon his dresser, but he found himself reluctant to employ it.

'Yes, me lord.'

'Oh. Well, Colonel Quarry won't mind, I suppose. You know what to do?'

'Yes, me lord.' Tom Byrd hesitated, looking at him narrowly. 'You're sure as you'll be all right alone, me lord?'

'Certainly,' he said, with what heartiness he could muster. He waved a hand in dismissal. 'I'll be fine.'

Byrd eyed him in patent disbelief.

'I'll summon you a coach, me lord,' he said.

He resisted the suggestion for form's sake, in order not to alarm Tom, but once safely inside the coach, he sank gratefully into the dusty squabs, closing his eyes, and concentrated on breathing for the journey to the Beefsteak.

How many pawnshops might there be in Southwark? he wondered, as the coach rattled through the streets. Tom had made several careful copies of the list of Anne Thackeray's jewelry; he and his brothers would see whether any of the bits and bobs had been pawned.

He had a most uneasy feeling about Anne Thackeray, but hoped for her sister's sake that some trace of her could be found. He had gone himself to her last known address directly upon his return to London, but the landlady, a hard-faced bitch of a woman, had known nothing – or at least, nothing she would tell, even for a price.

He felt mildly feverish; after he'd seen Harry, perhaps he'd take a room at the Beefsteak for the night and go to bed. But he wanted to tell Quarry what he'd learned in Sussex, and set him on the trail of Mortimer Oswald. Granted, Maude DeVane was not an unbiased witness on the subject of the MP, but the way she had said, *Everyone knows,* so positive . . . If Oswald did take bribes, it was more than possible that Harry could find out. Harry's own half brother was Sir Richard Joffrey, an influential and canny politician who had survived a good many shifts in government over the course of the last fifteen years. No one did that without knowing where a few bodies were buried.

He paid the coach and turned to find the doorman holding open the Beefsteak's door, bowing with unusual respect.

'My lord!' the man said fervently.

'Are you quite all right, Mr. Dobbs?' he asked.

'Never better, sir,' the man assured him, bowing

him inside. 'Colonel Quarry's a-waiting on you in the library, my lord.'

His sense of unease grew as he passed through the hall. Mr. Bodley, the steward, stopped dead upon seeing him, eyes round, then vanished hurriedly into the dining room, presumably to fetch his tray.

He paused warily at the door to the library, but all seemed reassuringly as usual. Quarry's broad back was visible, bent over a table by the window. As Grey drew near, he saw that the table was covered with newspapers, one of which Harry Quarry was perusing, a look of absorption upon his face. At Grey's step, he looked up, his craggy face breaking into an ears-wide grin.

'Ho!' he said in greeting. 'It's the man himself! A bumper of your best brandy, Mr. Bodley, if you please, for the Hero of Crefeld!'

'Oh, *shit*!' said Grey.

In the end, he did spend the night at the Beefsteak, having been – despite his repeated protests, which went completely ignored by everyone – obliged to join in so many extravagant toasts in his honor that merely walking became problematic, let alone finding his way back to his quarters in the barracks.

An attempt at escape in the morning was frustrated by the baying hounds of Fleet Street, several of whom had got wind of his presence at the club and hovered outside, kept at bay by the indomitable Mr. Dobbs, who had survived being tomahawked by red Indians in America and thus was not intimidated by mere scribblers.

One of the most intransigent balladeers took up a station under the windows of the library and bellowed out a never-ending performance of a dramatic – and execrably rhymed – lay entitled 'The Death of Tom Pilchard,' to the general dis-edification of Mr. Wilbraham and the other inhabitants of the Hermit's Corner, all of whom glared at Grey, holding *him* responsible for the disturbance.

He escaped at last under cover of darkness, disguised in Mr. Dobbs's shabby greatcoat and laced hat, and made his way on foot through the streets, arriving hungry and exhausted – though finally sober – to find Tom Byrd and his elder brother Jack awaiting him impatiently at the barracks.

'I found it at a place called Markham's,' Jack told him, displaying his find. 'Pawned a month ago, by a lady. Young, the pawnbroker said, and summat of a pop-eyed look about her, though he didn't remember nothing else.'

'It's hers, isn't it, me lord?' Tom chipped in anxiously.

Grey picked up the trinket – a cheap silver locket, inscribed with the letter 'A.' He compared it for form's sake to the sheet Barbara had given him, but there could be little doubt.

'Excellent!' he said. 'You asked, of course, whether she had left an address.'

Jack nodded.

'No joy there, my lord. The only thing . . .' He glanced at his younger brother, who was, after all, Grey's valet, and thus had rights.

'The feller didn't want to sell it to us, me lord. He said he'd had other things from this lady, and there was a gent what would come by, asking particular for her things, and pay a very pretty price for 'em.'

'Aye, sir,' Jack said, nodding agreement. 'I thought it wasn't but a ruse to get more, and wouldn't have paid, but Tom said as how we must. I hope that was all right?'

'Yes, of course.' Grey waved that aside. 'The man – did the pawnbroker remember him?'

'Oh, yes, me lord,' Tom said. His hair was nearly standing on end with excitement at what he had to impart. 'He remembered *him* well enough. Said it was a man what always wore a mask – a black silk mask.'

Grey felt a surge of excitement equal to the Byrds'.

'Christ!' he said. 'Fanshawe!'

Tom nodded.

'I thought it must be, me lord. Is he looking for Miss Thackeray, too, d'ye suppose?'

'I can't think what else he might intend – though surely he is not pursuing her with any great determination, if he has not yet discovered her lodgings.'

'Perhaps he has,' Jack Byrd suggested, 'but he's not got up his nerve to see her, what with the face an' all – Tom told me what happened to him.' Jack shuddered reflexively at the thought.

Grey glanced at the window, black night showing through the half-drawn curtains.

'Well, we can do little about it tonight. I will write a note, though – if you will take it in the morning, Jack?'

'What, to Sussex?' Jack looked slightly non-plussed. 'Well, of course, my lord, if you like, but—'

'No, I think we needn't go that far,' Grey assured him. 'Plainly, Captain Fanshawe visits London regularly. He is a member at White's; leave the note there, to be delivered upon his arrival.'

The two Byrds bowed, for an instant looking absurdly alike, though they did not really resemble each other closely.

'Very good, me lord,' Tom said. 'Will you have a bit of supper, then?'

Grey nodded and sat down to compose his note. He had just trimmed his quill when he became aware that neither Byrd had departed; both were standing on the opposite side of the room, viewing him with approval.

'What?' he said.

'Nothing, me lord,' Tom said, smiling benefi-cently. 'I was just telling Jack, you aren't looking quite so hag-rid as you was.'

'You mean haggard?'

'That, neither.'

Grey had finally fallen into an uneasy sleep, in which he hurried endlessly through stubbled fields with crows cawing overhead, sure that he must reach a distant red-brick building in order to prevent some unspeakable disaster, but never drawing closer.

One crow dived low, shrieking, and he ducked, covering his head, then sat up abruptly, realizing that the crow had said, 'Wake up, me lord.'

'What?' he said blankly. He could not focus eyes or mind, but the terrible sense of urgency from his dream had not left him. 'Who . . . what?'

'There's a soldier come, me lord. I'd not have waked you, but he says it's a man's life.'

His eyes finally consenting to operate, he saw Tom Byrd, round face worried but alight with interest, shaking out his banyan before a hastily poked-up fire.

'Yes. Of course. He . . . did he . . .' He groped simultaneously for words and bedclothes. 'Name?'

'Yes, me lord. Captain Jones, he says.'

Scrambling out of bed, Grey thrust his arms into the sleeves of his banyan, but did not wait for Tom to find his slippers, padding quick and barefoot through the cold to the darkened sitting room.

Jones was stirring up the fire, a black and burly demon whose silhouette was limned by sparks. He turned at Grey's entrance, dropping the poker with a crash upon the hearth.

'Where is he?' He reached as though to seize Grey's arm, but Grey stepped aside.

'Where is who?'

'Herbert Gormley, of course! What have you done with him?'

'Gormless?' Grey was so startled that the name popped out of him. 'What's happened to him?'

Jones's clenched-fist expression, just visible by the glow of the fire, relaxed a trifle at that.

'Gormless? You call him that, too, do you?'

'Not to his face, certainly. Thank you, Tom.' Byrd, hurrying in, had placed his slippers on the floor, eyeing Jones with marked wariness.

'What has happened?' Grey repeated, thrusting his cold feet into the slippers and noting absently that they were warm; Tom had taken time to hold them over the bedroom fire.

'He's disappeared, Major – and so has Tom Pilchard. And I want to know what you have to do with the matter.'

He stared at Jones, unable for a moment to take this in. Still half in the grip of nightmare, his brain produced a vision of Herbert Gormley absconding by night, the remains of a massive cannon tucked tidily under one arm. He shook his head to clear it of this nonsense, and gestured Jones to the sofa.

'Sit. I assure you, sir, I have nothing "to do" with the matter – but I certainly wish to know who does. Tell me what you know.'

Jones's face worked briefly – Grey had the notion that he was grinding his teeth – but he nodded shortly and sat down, though he remained poised

323

upon the edge of the sofa, hands on his knees, ready to leap up at a moment's notice.

'He's gone – Herbert. When I found the cannon gone, I went to find him, ask what – but he was nowhere to be found. I've been searching for him since the day before yesterday. Do you know where he is?'

Tom had been building up the fire; the flame was high enough now to show Jones's heavy face, hollowed by worry and pouched with fatigue.

'No. You know where he lives?' Grey sat down himself, and scrubbed a hand over his face in an effort to rouse himself completely.

Jones nodded, massive fists clenching and unclenching unconsciously upon his thighs.

'He's not been home in two days. The last anyone saw of him was Wednesday evening, when he left the laboratory. You're quite sure he's not been here?' Dark eyes flicked suspiciously at Grey.

'You are entirely welcome to search the place.' Grey waved a hand toward the room and the door through which Tom Byrd had disappeared, presumably toward the barracks kitchen in search of refreshment. 'Why the devil would he come here?'

'For that bit of shrapnel.'

For a moment, Grey looked blank; then memory returned. His hand rose involuntarily toward his chest, but he altered the motion, pretending instead to stifle a yawn.

'The bit of iron from Tom Pilchard? The

leopard's head? What on earth would he – or you – want it for?'

Jones measured him for a long moment before replying, but answered at last, reluctant.

'With the cannon gone, that may be the only evidence.'

'Evidence of *what*, for God's sake? And what do you mean, the cannon's gone?' he added, belatedly realizing that he had overlooked the other bit of Jones's statement. 'Who in Christ's name would steal a burst cannon?'

'It wasn't stolen,' Jones answered shortly. 'The foundrymen took it – and the others. It's been melted down.'

This seemed an entirely reasonable thing to do, and Grey said as much, causing Jones's face to work again. He *was* grinding his teeth; Grey could hear it.

Jones abruptly shut his eyes, upper lip folded under his lower teeth in a way that reminded Grey of his cousin Olivia's bulldog, Alfred. It was an amiable animal, but remarkably stubborn.

The chiming clock on the mantelpiece struck the hour: two o'clock. The captain was likely telling the truth about searching everywhere else before coming to Grey's door.

Jones at length opened his eyes – they were bloodshot, enhancing the resemblance to Alfred – though the teeth remained fixed in his lip. At last he shook his head in resignation and sighed.

'I'll have to trust you, I suppose,' he said.

'I am distinctly honored,' Grey said, with an edge. 'Thank you, Tom.'

Byrd had reappeared with a tray hastily furnished with two cups of tea. The tea was stewed and black, undoubtedly from the urn kept for the night watch, but served in Grey's decent vine-patterned china. He took a cup gratefully, adding a substantial dollop of brandy from the decanter.

Jones stared at the cup of tea in his own hand, as though wondering where it had come from, but essayed a cautious sip, then coughed and rubbed the back of his hand across his mouth.

'The cannon. Herbert said he thought you knew nothing about the process of gun-founding; is that true?'

'Nothing more than he told me himself.' The hot tea and brandy were both comfort and stimulant; Grey began to feel more alert. 'Why?'

Jones blew out his breath, making a small cloud of steam; the air in the sitting room was still chilly.

'Without describing the entire process to you – you *do* know that the bronze of a cannon is an alloy, produced by—'

'Yes, I do know that.' Grey was sufficiently awake by now as to be annoyed. 'What does that—'

'I am sure that the burst cannon – all of them – had been cast from an inferior alloy, one lacking the proper proportion of copper.' He stared meaningfully at Grey, obviously expecting him to drop his tea, clutch his head, or otherwise exhibit signs of horrified comprehension.

'Oh?' Grey said, and reached for the brandy again.

Jones heaved a sigh that went all the way to his feet, and put out a hand for the decanter in turn.

'Not to put too fine a point upon the matter, Major,' he said, eyes on the amber stream splashing into his tea, 'I am a spy.'

Grey narrowly prevented himself saying, 'Oh?' again, and instead said, 'For the French? Or the Austrians?' Tom Byrd, who had been loitering respectfully in the background, stiffened, then bent casually to pick up the poker from the hearth.

'Neither, for God's sake,' Jones said crossly. 'I am in the employ of His Majesty's government.'

'Well, who the bloody hell are you spying *on*, then?' Grey said, losing patience.

'The Arsenal,' Jones replied, looking surprised, as though this should be obvious. 'Or rather, the foundry.'

There ensued a tedious ten minutes of extraction which brought Grey to the point of wishing to gnash his own teeth. At the end of it, though, he had managed to get Jones to admit – with extreme reluctance – that he was not in fact employed by the Arsenal, as Grey had assumed. He *was* a genuine captain in the Royal Artillery Regiment, though, and as such had been sent to nose unofficially about the Arsenal and see what he could discover regarding the matter of the exploding cannons – the Royal Artillery having an interest, as Grey might suppose.

'Couldn't be official, d'ye see,' Jones said, becoming more confidential. 'The Royal Commission had already been appointed, and it's their show, so to speak.'

Grey nodded, curious. Twelvetrees, who was a member of the Commission of Inquiry, belonged to the Royal Artillery; why ought the regiment be sending Jones to do surreptitiously what Twelvetrees was doing so overtly? Unless ... unless someone suspected Twelvetrees of something?

'To whom do you report your findings?' Grey asked. Jones began again to look shifty, and a small premonitory prickle ran suddenly down Grey's spine.

Jones's lips worked in and out in indecision, but at last he bit the bullet and blurted, 'A man named Bowles.'

As though cued by an invisible prompter, the teacup began to rattle gently in its saucer. Grey felt a monstrous sense of irritation; was he never going to be allowed to drink a full cup of tea in peace, for God's sake? Very carefully, he set down the cup and saucer, and wiped his hands upon the skirts of his dressing gown.

'Oh, you know him, do you?' Jones's red-rimmed eyes fixed on Grey, suddenly alert.

'I know of him.' Grey did not wish to admit to his relations with Bowles, let alone discuss them. He had met the mysterious Mr. Bowles once, and had no wish to repeat the experience.

'So you had no official standing at the laboratory?'

'No, that's why I needed Gormley.'

Herbert Gormley had no great authority within the hierarchy of the Ordnance Office, but he had the necessary knowledge to locate the remains of the exploded cannon, and sufficient administrative skill to have them quietly brought to the guns' graveyard near the proving grounds and sequestered there for autopsy.

'There are hundreds of broken guns there; they should have been safe!' Jones's teeth were clenched in frustration; in hopes of preventing further damage to the man's molars, Grey poured more brandy into his empty cup.

Jones gulped it and set down the cup, eyes watering.

'But they weren't,' he said hoarsely. 'They're gone. There were eight of them under my investigation – all gone. But *only* those eight – the ones Gormley found for me. Everything else is still there. And now Gormley's gone, too. You can't tell me that's coincidence, Major!'

Grey had no intention of doing so.

'You do not suppose that Gormless – Gormley – had anything to do with the removal of the exploded cannon?'

Jones shook his head violently.

'Not a chance. No, he's onto me. Has to be.'

'He? Whom do you mean?'

'I don't fucking *know*!' Jones's hands clenched together in an unconscious pantomime of neck-wringing. 'Not for sure. But I'll get him,' he added, giving Grey a fierce look, with a glimpse of clenched, bared fang. 'If he's harmed poor little Herbert, I'll – I'll—'

The man would be toothless before he was forty, Grey thought.

'We will find Mr. Gormley,' he said firmly. 'But wherever he is, I doubt that we can discover him before daylight. Compose yourself, Captain, if you please – and then tell me the goddamn truth about what's going on at the Arsenal.'

The truth, once extracted and divested of its encrustations of laborious speculation and deductive dead ends, was relatively simple: Gormley and Jones had concluded, on the basis of close examination, that someone at the foundry was abstracting a good part of the copper meant to be used in the alloy for casting. Result being that while new cannon cast with this alloy looked quite as usual, the metal was more brittle than it should be, thus liable to sudden failure under sustained fire.

'Those marks you noticed on Tom Pilchard,' Jones said, describing a series of semicircles in the air with a blunt forefinger. 'Those are the marks where holes left in the casting have been plugged later, then sanded flat and burnished over. You might get a hole or two in any casting – completely normal – but if the alloy's wanting, you'll get a lot more.'

'And a much higher chance of the metal's fracturing where you have several holes together, such as those I saw. Quite.'

He did. He saw himself and four other men, standing no more than a foot away from a cannon riddled like a cheese with invisible holes, each charge rammed down its smoking barrel one more throw of crooked dice. Grey was beginning to have a metallic taste in the back of his mouth. Rather than lift the cup and saucer again, he simply picked up the decanter and drank from it, holding it round the neck.

'Whoever is taking the copper – they're selling it, of course?' Copper was largely imported, and valuable.

'Yes, but I haven't been able to trace any of it,' Jones admitted, moodily. 'The damn stuff hasn't any identifying marks. And with the Dockyards so handy . . . might be going anywhere. To the Dutch, the French – maybe to someone private, the East India Company perhaps – wouldn't put it past the bastards.' He glanced at the window, where a slice of night still showed black between the heavy curtains, and sighed.

'We will find him,' Grey repeated, more gently, though he was himself by no means so sure of it. He coughed, and drank again.

'If you are correct – if copper has been abstracted – then surely whoever is responsible for the casting would know of it?'

'Howard Stoughton,' Jones said bleakly. 'The Master Founder. Yes, most likely. I've been watching him for weeks, though, and he's not put a foot wrong. No hint of any secret meetings with foreign agents; he scarcely leaves the foundry, and when he does, he goes home and stays there. But if it *is* the copper, and it *is* him, and Gormley's found some proof . . .'

Another thought occurred to Grey, and he felt obliged to put it, despite the risk to Jones's tooth enamel.

'We have two assumptions here, Captain, do we not? Firstly, that you and Mr. Gormley are correct in your assessment of the cause of the cannons' failure. And secondly, that Mr. Gormley is missing because he has discovered who is responsible for the abstraction of copper from the Arsenal and been removed in consequence. But these are assumptions only, for the moment.

'Have you considered the alternative possibility,' he said, taking a firmer hold of the brandy bottle in case he should require a weapon, 'that Mr. Gormley might himself have been involved in the matter?'

Jones's inflamed eyes swiveled slowly in Grey's direction, bulging slightly, and the muscles of his neck bunched. Before he could speak, though, a discreet cough came from the vicinity of the hearth.

'Me lord?' Tom Byrd, who had been listening raptly, poker in hand, now set it down and stepped diffidently forward.

'Yes, Tom?'

'Beg pardon, me lord. Only as I was in the Lark's Nest Wednesday – having stopped for a bite on my way back from the Arsenal, see – and the place was a-buzz, riled like it was a hornets' nest, rather than a lark's. Was a press gang going through the neighborhood, they said; took up two men was regulars, and there was talk about would they maybe go and try to get them back – but you could see there wasn't nothing in it but talk. They warned me to go careful when I left, though.'

The young valet hesitated, looking from one gentleman to another.

'I think they maybe got him, this Gormley.'

'A press gang?' Jones said, his scowl diminishing only slightly. 'Well, it's a thought, but—'

'Begging your pardon, sir, it's maybe summat more than a thought. I saw them.'

Grey's heart began to beat faster.

'The press gang?'

Tom turned a freckled, earnest face in his employer's direction.

'Yes, sir. 'Twas a heavy fog comin' in from the river, and so I heard them coming down the street afore they saw me, and ducked rabbity into an alleyway and hid behind a pile of rubbish. But they passed me by close, sir, and I did see 'em; six sailors and four men they'd seized, all roped together.'

He hesitated, frowning.

'It *was* foggy, sir. And I ain't – haven't – seen him before. But it was right near the Arsenal, and that what you called him – Gormless. It's only – would he maybe be a dark, small, clever-looking cove, with a pretty face like a girl's and dressed like a clerk?'

'He would,' Grey said, ignoring Jones, who had

made a sound like a stuck pig. 'Could you see anything to tell which ship they came from?'

Tom Byrd shook his head.

'No, sir. They was real sailors, though, the way they talked.'

Jones stared at him.

'Why wouldn't they be real sailors? What do you mean, boy?'

'Mr. Byrd has a somewhat suspicious mind,' Grey intervened tactfully, seeing Tom flush with indignation. 'A most valuable attribute, on occasion. On the present occasion, I presume that he means only that your initial supposition was that Mr. Gormley had been abducted by the person or persons responsible for the removal of copper from the foundry, but apparently that is not the case. By the way,' he added, struck by a thought, 'have you any indication that copper *is* missing from the foundry? That would be evidence in support of your theory.'

'Yes,' Jones said, a small measure of satisfaction lightening the anxiety in his face. 'We have got that, by God. When I reported our suspicions about the copper, Mr. Bowles undertook to introduce another of his subordinates, a man named Stapleton, into the foundry in the capacity of clerk and set him to inspect the accounts and inventory on the quiet. A good man, Stapleton,' he added with approval. 'Got the information in less than a week.'

'Splendid,' Grey said, and took a searingly large swallow of brandy. The hairs rose on his body at the mention of Neil Stapleton. Neil of the hot blue eyes

. . . and even more incendiary attributes. Known to his intimates – if not necessarily his friends – as Neil the Cunt.

He'd met Stapleton twice: initially, at a very private club called Lavender House, in such circumstances as to leave no doubt of either's private inclinations. And again when Grey had ruthlessly threatened to expose those inclinations to Hubert Bowles, in order to force Stapleton to obtain urgent information for him. Christ, how close had he come to meeting the man again? He shoved that thought hastily away and took another drink.

Jones was showing signs of impatience, tapping his feet back and forth in a soundless tattoo upon the carpet.

'It's got to be a ship anchored by the Dockyards. Soon as it's light, I'm going through them like a dose of salts, and then we'll be to the bottom of this!'

'I wish you the best of luck,' Grey said politely. 'And I do hope that the gentleman Tom saw in the custody of the press gang *was* Mr. Gormley. However – if he was, does this not rather obviate your conclusion that he was in possession of incriminating information regarding the perpetrator?'

Jones gave him a glassy look, and Tom Byrd looked reproving.

'Now, me lord, you know you oughtn't talk like that at this hour of the morning. You got to pardon his lordship, sir,' he said apologetically to Jones.

'His father – the duke, you know – had him schooled in logic. He can't really help it, like.'

Jones shook his head like a swimmer emerging from heavy surf, and reached wordlessly for the brandy, which Grey surrendered with a brief gesture of apology.

'I mean,' he amended, 'if Gormley's been taken by a press gang, it might be simple misfortune. It needn't have anything to do with your inquiries.'

Jones pressed his lips together, looking displeased.

'Perhaps. Perhaps not. But the first thing is to get Gormley back. Agreed?'

'Certainly,' Grey said, wondering privately just how complex a matter it might prove to pry a new seaman – no matter how unwillingly recruited – from the rapacious grasp of the navy.

Jones nodded, satisfied, and glanced at the clock. A few minutes until three; the sun would not be up for several hours yet. Tom Byrd yawned suddenly, and Grey felt his own jaw muscles creak in sympathy.

All conversation seemed to have ceased abruptly; there was nothing more to say, and they sat for some moments in silence. There were sounds from the distant barracks and the murmur of the fire, but these were muted, unreal. The night hung over them, heavy with possibilities – most of them threatening.

Grey began to be conscious of his heartbeat, and just behind each beat, a slight, sharp pain in his chest.

'I'm going to bed,' he said abruptly, gathering his feet under him. 'Tom, will you find Captain Jones somewhere to sleep?'

Disregarding the captain's muttered reply that he needn't bother, wouldn't sleep anyway, he stood and turned for the door, his brandy-clouded vision smearing light and shadow. Just short of the door, though, one final question occurred to him.

'Captain – you are positive that all the explosions are the result of weakened alloy, are you?' Grey asked, swinging round. 'No evidence of deliberate sabotage – as, for instance, by the provision of bombs packed with a higher grade of powder than they should be?'

Jones blinked at him, owl-eyed.

'Why, yes,' he said slowly. 'In fact, there is. That's what began the investigation; the Ordnance Office discovered two grapeshot cartridges packed with a great deal more powder than they should have been, and fine-ground, too – you know that's unstable, yes? But very explosive. Bombs, they were.'

Grey nodded, his hands curving in unconscious memory of the shape and the weight of the grapeshot cartridges he had handled at Crefeld, tossing them in careless hurry, as though they had been harmless as stones.

'This was just as they began to be aware of the destruction of the cannon,' Jones said, shrugging, 'and so they convened the Commission of Inquiry.'

Dry-mouthed, Grey licked his lips.

'How did they discover this?'

'Testing on the proving grounds. Came near to killing one of the proving crew. Gormley was almost sure that it had nothing to do with the cannons' fracturing, though.'

'Almost?' Grey echoed, with a skeptical intonation.

'He could prove it was the alloy, he said. He could assay the metal from the ruined cannon, and prove that it lacked the proper mix of copper. He couldn't do it openly, though; he had to wait on an opportunity to use the laboratory's facilities secretly.'

Jones's throat worked, whether with anger or grief, Grey couldn't tell. He swallowed his emotion, though, and went on.

'But they took the cannon before he could make his tests. That's why I was sure at first that he'd come to you, Major,' he added, fixing Grey with a gimlet eye.

'That bit of shrapnel you took away is the only metal from an exploded cannon that hasn't been melted down and lost. It's the only bit of proof that's left. You will take care of it, won't you?'

What do you mean, there are no press gangs operating near the Arsenal?'

Grey thought Jones would explode like a milling shed, walls and roof flying every which way. His heavy face quivered with rage, eyes bulging as he loomed over the diminutive harbormaster of the Royal Dockyards.

The harbormaster, accustomed to dealing with volatile sea captains, was unmoved.

'Putting aside the matter of courtesy – the navy would not normally so intrude upon the operations of another service—' he said mildly, 'there are no ships outfitting in the yards just at present. If they are not outfitting, they do not require additional crew. If they do not require seamen, plainly the captains do not send out press gangs to acquire them. *Quod erat demonstrandum,*' he added, obviously considering this the *coup de grâce.*

The captain seemed disposed to argue the point – or to assault the harbormaster. Feeling that this would be counter to their best interests, Grey seized him by the arm and propelled him out of the office.

'That whoreson is lying to us!'

'Possibly,' Grey said, urging Jones down the length of the dock by main force. 'But possibly not. Come, let us see whether Tom has discovered anything.'

Whether ships were outfitting in the yards or not, ships were most assuredly being built and repaired there. The ribs and keelson of a large ship rose like a whale's skeleton on one side, while on the other, a newly completed keel lay in the channel, swarms of men covering it like ants, laying deck in a racket of hammers and curses.

The shipyard was littered with timbers, planking, rolls of copper, hogsheads of nails, barrels of tar, coils of rope, heaps of sawdust, mallets, saws, drawknives, planes, and all the other bewildering impedimenta of shipbuilding. Men were everywhere; England was at war, and the dockyards buzzed like a hive.

Out in the river, small craft plied to and fro, sails white against the brown of the Thames and the dark shapes of the prison hulks anchored in the distance. Two larger ships lay at anchor, though, and these were the focus of Grey's attention.

Not sure precisely where Tom Byrd might be, he took Jones firmly by the arm and sauntered to and fro, whistling 'Lilibulero.' Passing workmen spared them a glance now and then, but the docks were thick with tradesmen and uniforms; they were not conspicuous.

Eventually his valet stepped cautiously out from behind a large heap of timbers, a small brass spyglass in hand.

'Yes, me lord?'

'For God's sake, put that away, Tom, or you'll be taken up as a French spy. I'd have the devil of a time getting you out of a naval prison.'

Seeing that his employer was not joking, Tom tucked the spyglass hastily inside his jacket.

'Have you seen anyone familiar?'

'Well, I can't be sure, me lord, but I *think* I've maybe spotted a cove as was one of the press gang I saw.'

'Where?' Jones's eyebrows bristled, eyes gleaming beneath them with readiness to strangle someone.

Byrd nodded toward the water.

'He was a-going out to one o' the big ships, sir. That un.' He nodded toward the vessel on the left, a three-masted thing with its canvas furled. 'Maybe half an hour gone; I've not seen him come back.'

Grey stood for a moment, gazing at the ships. He had vivid memories of his last venture on the high seas, and thus a marked disinclination to set foot on board a ship again. On the other hand, his involuntary voyage had been at the hands of the East India Company, and it did not appear that either of the ships presently at anchor intended any immediate departure.

Jones quivered at his side, like a hunting dog scenting pheasant on the wind.

'All right,' Grey said, resigned. 'No help for it, I suppose. Stick close, though, Tom. I don't want to see *you* pressed.'

Him, me lord.' Tom Byrd spoke under his breath, with the barest of nods toward a man who stood with his back to them, shouting something up into the rigging. 'I'm sure.'

'All right. See if you can find out who he is, without making too much of a stir. I think we'll have time.'

Turning his back, Grey strolled nonchalantly to the rail, where he stood looking toward the Woolwich shore. The Arsenal was no more than a splotch of dark buildings at this distance, set amid the ruffled acres of its proving grounds. Below, he could hear the sounds of Jones's impromptu search party.

Captain Hanson of the *Sunrise* had been surprised, to say the least, by their sudden appearance, and had reiterated the harbormaster's statement about press gangs. Still, he was not harried at present, was a young and naturally amiable man – and was acquainted with Grey's brother. He had therefore graciously invited Jones to search the ship if he liked – in case his Mister Gormley had somehow smuggled himself aboard – accompanied by the third lieutenant and two or three able seamen to open or lift anything he would like to look into or under.

It was apparent from this that there was nothing suspicious to be found aboard, but Jones had had little choice but to conduct his search, leaving Grey to converse with the captain – and Tom to circle warily about the decks, in hopes of spotting the man he had seen in the fog.

Captain Hanson had after a short time excused himself, offering Grey the use of his cabin – an offer Grey had politely declined, saying that he would prefer to take the air on deck until his friend was at liberty.

He turned his back to the rail, glancing casually over the deck. The man Tom had picked out was certainly one who invited recognition; he bore a strong resemblance to a Barbary ape, that part of his hair not tarred into a pigtail standing up in a ginger crest on his head.

He seemed also to be in a position of some authority; at the moment, he had one foot resting on a barrel, an elbow resting on the raised knee, and his chin upon the palm of his hand, squinting quizzically at something – the cut of the jib? The lie of the bilge? Grey knew nothing of nautical terms.

It wouldn't do to stare; he turned back to the shore, noting as he did so Tom, in cordial conversation with a young sailor near the back – well, aft, he did know that much – of the ship.

What next? He was sure that Jones would not find Gormley aboard the *Sunrise*. He supposed they would have to go and search the other ship, as well. He'd seen men shouting to and fro between the ships – the other lay not more than a few hundred yards away; doubtless the Barbary ape could have taken Gormley there without difficulty – though he had no idea why he should have done so.

The ape – Grey glanced covertly at the man again – was plainly part of the crew of the *Sunrise*. And yet Captain Hanson had said unequivocally that he had sent out no press gangs. Ergo, if Tom were correct in his identification – and a face like that one would be memorable, coming out of the fog – the ape had been conducting some private enterprise of his own.

Now, *that* was an interesting notion. And if they failed to find any trace of Gormley on the other ship, it might be worth having Tom brought face to face with both Captain Hanson and the ape, to tell his story. Grey supposed that any captain worth his salt would be interested to know if his crew were conducting a clandestine trade in bodies.

The thought gave him a faint chill. Christ, what if it *were* bodies? The ape and his cohorts might be augmenting their pay by dealing as resurrection men, providing cadavers to the dissection rooms.

No. He dismissed the grisly vision of a dead and eviscerated Gormless as both too dramatic and too complicated to be true. Back to Occam, then. Given multiple alternatives, the simplest explanation is most likely to be true. And the simplest explanation for the disappearance of Herbert Gormley was, firstly, that Tom had seen the Barbary ape but had *not* seen Gormley, being mistaken in his identification. Or secondly – and equally likely, he thought, knowing Tom – that his valet *had* seen them both, and the ape had done something unaccountable with his captives.

They were presently operating under the second assumption, but perhaps that had been reckless of him. If . . .

All thought was momentarily suspended, his eye caught by a small boat halfway out from the shore. Or, rather, by the glint of sunlight on yellow hair. Grey uttered an oath which caused the sailor nearest him to drop his jaw, and leaned out over the rail, trying for a better look.

'He's called Appledore,' said a voice in his ear, startling him.

'Who's called Appledore?'

'Him what we're watching, me lord – he's a

bosun's mate, they say. *And*' – Tom swelled a bit with excited importance – 'he was ashore Wednesday, and came back to the ship at . . . well, I don't quite know, the peculiar way they have of telling time on ships, all bells and watches and such, but it was late.'

'Excellent,' he said, scarcely listening. 'Tom, give me your spyglass.'

He clapped the instrument to his eye, catching wild swathes of river, sky, and clouds, until suddenly he brought the boat in view, its contents sharp and clear. There were two men in the boat. One of them was unfamiliar, a heavyset fellow muffled in a coat and cocked hat, a portmanteau at his feet. The man rowing in his shirtsleeves, though, yellow hair a-flutter in the wind, was Neil the Cunt. Which almost certainly meant that the other gentleman must be Howard Stoughton, master founder of the Royal Brass Foundry.

The small boat was not making for either of the two large ships, but steering a course a little way to the south. Following the direction of its bow, he saw a small, brisk-looking craft tacking slowly to and fro.

'Stay here.' Grey thrust the spyglass back into Tom's hands. 'See that small boat, with two men? Don't take your eyes off it!'

'Where you going, me lord?' Tom, startled, was trying to look at his employer and through the glass at the same time, but Grey was already halfway to the door that led below.

'To organize a boarding party!' he called over his shoulder, and plunged without hesitation into the bowels of the *Sunrise*.

The captain's gig hurtled over the river's chop, propelled by half a dozen burly sailors. The captain himself had come; Grey was shouting further explanation into his ear, clinging with one hand to the side of the boat, with the other to the impressive-looking cutlass the mate had shoved into his hand.

Tom Byrd and Captain Jones were likewise armed. Tom looked thrilled, Jones grimly dangerous.

The small boat was moving much more slowly, but had a substantial lead. It would undoubtedly reach the brig – Hanson said it was a brig – before they did, but that would not matter, so long as they were in time to prevent the brig's fleeing downriver.

As they drew closer, he saw Neil Stapleton turn a startled face toward them, then turn back, redoubling his efforts at the oars.

For an instant, he wondered whether Stapleton was indeed Bowles's man. But, no – he had caught a crab, as the sailors said, one oar skimming the surface and slewing his boat half round. Clever enough to look accidental, but slowing the smaller craft, while the gig cleaved the waters to the bosun's bark.

Hanson was kneeling, gripping Grey's shoulder to avoid being thrown from the boat, roaring something at the men on board the brig. They looked surprised, glancing from the oncoming gig to the smaller boat, struggling to reach them.

The small boat thumped the side of the brig; Grey heard it, and the cries of outrage from the men on deck. The impact had knocked the heavyset man into the bottom of the boat; he rose, cursing, and reached up, scrambling awkwardly over the rail of the brig, half-tumbling into the arms of the waiting sailors.

He gained his feet and turned back, reaching urgently over the rail for his portmanteau. But Stapleton had dug his oars and was pulling rapidly away, coming fast toward the gig.

' 'Vast rowing!' bellowed the bosun, and the crew of the gig shipped oars as one, letting the long, sleek boat glide up beside the smaller one. Hands reached out to grab the sides, and Stapleton let go his oars.

His face was scarlet with exertion and excitement, blue eyes bright as candle flames. Grey spared the space of one deep breath to admire his beauty, then grabbed him by the arm and yanked him head over arse into the gig.

'Is it Stoughton?' Jones was yelling. Grey barely heard him above the bellowing to and fro of Hanson and the men on the deck of the brig above.

Stapleton was on hands and knees, gasping for breath, his face nearly in Grey's lap, but managed to look up and nod. Other hands were grappling across the portmanteau; it fell with a thud into the bottom of the gig, and Jones lunged for it.

'Come on!' Hanson shouted. He was already reaching for the hands of the sailors on the brig.

Grey rose, lurching to keep his footing, was seized by several helpful pairs of hands and virtually thrown aboard the brig. He seized the rail to keep from falling back, and over his shoulder saw Stapleton's grinning face below.

He sketched a salute, then turned to deal with the matter at hand.

What do you mean, it's a naval vessel?' Jones looked disbelieving. *'This?'*

The captain of the *Ronson,* for so the small and elderly brig was named, looked displeased. He was very young, but conscious of the dignity of his service, his ship, and himself.

'We are one of His Majesty's ships,' he said stiffly. 'You are under the jurisdiction of the navy, Captain. And you will *not* take this man.'

The man, Stoughton, drew breath at this, and left off looking quite so terrified.

'He's right, you know.' Captain Hanson, crammed into the tiny cabin with Grey, Jones, and Stoughton, had been listening to all the arguments and counterarguments, an expression of bemused absorption on his face. 'His authority on his own vessel is absolute – save a senior naval officer should come aboard.'

'Well, bloody hell! Are you not a senior officer, then?' Jones cried. His eyes were bloodshot, he was soaked with river water, and his hair was standing on end.

'Well, yes,' Hanson said mildly. 'But the gentleman who wrote that letter is a good deal more senior still.' He nodded at the open letter on the desk, the sheet of paper that Stoughton had been carrying in his bosom.

It was crumpled and damp, but clearly legible. It was signed by a vice-admiral, and it gave one Howard Stoughton safe passage upon any of His Majesty's ships.

'But the man is a fucking traitor!' Jones was still holding his cutlass. He tightened his fist upon it and glared at the hapless Stoughton, who recoiled a little but stood his ground.

'I am not!' he said, sticking out his chin. ' 'Twasn't treason, whatever else you like to call it.'

The two sea captains glanced at each other, and Grey felt something unseen pass between them.

'A word with you, sir?' Hanson asked politely. 'If you will perhaps excuse us, gentlemen . . .'

Grey and Jones were obliged to leave, the *Ronson*'s mate escorting them up on deck and out of earshot.

'I don't frigging believe it. How can he . . .'

Grey wasn't listening. He went to the rail and leaned over, to see Stapleton engaged in argument with the gig's bosun, apparently over the portmanteau. The bosun had the case between his feet, and appeared to be resisting Stapleton's efforts to open it.

'What do you think is in there, Mr. Stapleton?' he called.

Neil looked up, face still flushed, and Grey caught the gleam of his teeth as he shouted back.

'Gold,' he said. 'Maybe papers. Maybe a name. I hope so.'

Grey nodded, then caught the bosun's eye.

'Don't let him open it,' he called, and turned away. Occam's razor said Stoughton had acted alone – all other things being equal. But someone had exerted considerable force upon the navy to produce that letter. And he did not think Stoughton possessed anything like that sort of influence.

Grey smelt a rat; a large one.

If he *hadn't* acted alone, Grey wanted the name of his confederate. And he had no faith at all that that name would ever come to light, once Hubert Bowles got his hands on it. Particularly not if that name had anything to do with His Majesty's navy.

The sound of the cabin door opening presaged the appearance on deck of Captain Hanson, who jerked his chin to summon Grey aside. He looked bemused.

'Right,' he said. 'I have thirty seconds, and this is between you and me. He is who you think he is, and he's done what you think he's done – and he's going to France in the *Ronson*. I'm sorry.'

Grey took a long, deep breath, and wiped a flying strand of hair out of his face.

'I see,' he said, calmly under the circumstances. 'He sold the copper to the navy.'

Hanson had the grace to look embarrassed.

'It is wartime,' he said. 'The lives of our men—'

'Is the life of a sailor worth more than that of a soldier?'

Hanson's lips set in a grimace, but he didn't reply.

Grey realized that his nails were cutting into the palms of his hands, and consciously unclenched his fists, breathing. Hanson was stirring, preparing to go.

'One thing,' Grey said, holding Hanson's eye.

The captain made a brief motion of the head, not quite agreement, but willingness to listen.

'One minute alone with that portmanteau. The price of the gunners' lives.'

Hanson's jaw worked for a moment.

'Not alone,' he said finally. 'With me.'

'Done,' said Grey.

It was nearly sunset when he emerged from Captain Hanson's cabin. Jones was sitting on a gun case by the rail. He had passed the point of apoplexy long since, and merely regarded Grey with a suspicious, bloodshot eye.

'Got it, did you?' he said.

Grey nodded.

'And you aren't going to tell me, are you?' Jones sounded bitter, but resigned.

Grey reached into his pocket, brought out the small lump of the leopard's head, cold and hard, and dropped it into Jones's open palm.

'You have the proof you sought. You and

Gormley were right; the cannons failed because of lack of copper, and it was Stoughton who stole it. You will make your report to that effect – and before you give it to your colonel in the Royal Artillery Regiment and to Bowles, you will send a copy to the Royal Commission of Inquiry into the explosion of the cannon Tom Pilchard.'

Seeing Jones's brow knit, he hardened his voice.

'That, Captain, is an order from a superior officer. Assuming you would prefer that your colonel continues in ignorance of your association with Mr. Bowles, I suggest you follow it.'

Jones made a small rumbling noise in his throat, but nodded reluctantly.

'Yes, all right. But that the bugger should escape altogether . . . and now you're going to let the other bugger escape, too, aren't you? The man who brokered this infernal transaction? I tell you, Major, it drives me mad!'

'I don't blame you.' Grey sat down beside him, suddenly exhausted. 'War may be a brutal occupation, but politics is far more so.'

They sat in silence for a moment, watching the sailors. Appledore was bellowing for the gig to be brought alongside. Hearing this, Jones sat bolt upright once more.

'But poor little Herbert Gormley – what of him? Tell me at least that you made Stoughton tell you what he did with Gormley! Is he dead?'

Fatigue of a not unpleasant sort blanketed Grey's limbs. He was tired, but not drained. And what was another hour or two, between him and the delightful prospect of supper and bed? The London end of the business could wait until tomorrow.

'No, he's in the hulks,' Grey said, nodding upriver at the distant prison ships. 'We're going to go and get him now.'

The navy was in it up to their necks!' Quarry said. 'Goddamned bloody sods!'

Grey had seldom seen Quarry so angry. The scar on his cheek stood out white and the eye on that side was pulled nearly shut.

'Not all of them.' He rubbed a hand across his face, still surprised to find it smooth. He felt seedy and grimy – but Tom Byrd had insisted upon shaving him before letting him go to the Beefsteak.

'Hanson didn't know; if he had, he would never have agreed to board the *Ronson*. And he was very angry at discovering that his bosun's mate – that was Appledore, the apelike fellow I told you of – was involved in such adventures without his knowledge. Had it not been for his indignation at being so practiced upon – his authority usurped without his knowledge or consent – I doubt he would have told me anything. As it was . . .'

As it was, the matter had become clear to Grey sometime before Hanson himself had realized the degree of the navy's involvement. For Appledore to have abducted Gormley – taking all the men he could find who matched Gormley's description –

obviously at Stoughton's instigation, but without the knowledge of his own captain . . .

'That argued the existence of someone *in* the navy, involved in the matter, whose authority superseded Hanson's. And when I saw the letter from the . . . gentleman of whom we spoke—' They were alone in the Beefsteak's smoking room, but there were people in the hallway, and discretion forbade his speaking the vice-admiral's name aloud in any case.

' "Gentleman." Pfaugh!' Quarry made as though to spit on the floor, but caught the eye of the steward coming in with brandy, and refrained. 'Scuttling sewer rat,' he muttered, instead.

'A bilge rat, surely, Harry?' Grey took the brandy glass from Mr. Bodley's tray with a nod of thanks, and waited until the steward had departed before continuing.

'Rat or no, such a highly placed gentleman wouldn't risk any direct association with Stoughton. The only such indication is that letter of immunity – and that was worded in such a way as to give no proof of anything. In fact, had Stoughton not reached the *Ronson* – damn Stapleton, for not contriving some means of stopping him in time! – the letter would have been valueless. It offered him nothing but safe passage, and if the matter became public, that could be dismissed as a simple courtesy to the Arsenal, allowing him to travel easily as his official business might demand.'

Quarry huffed into his drink, but gave a grudging nod.

'Aye, I see. And so you concluded rightly that there was a third rotten apple in that barrel – someone who stood between Stoughton and our elevated bilge rat.'

Grey nodded in turn, closing his eyes involuntarily at the pleasing burn of the liquor on his palate.

'Yes, and that consideration in turn focused my attention on the members of the commission. For it must be someone who had regular business with the Arsenal – and thus could consult with Stoughton without arousing suspicion. And likewise, it must be someone for whom consorting with a vice-admiral also would cause no remark.

'Beyond that,' he said, licking a sticky drop from his lower lip, 'the assumption that one of those three was involved in this matter would have explained their notably uncharitable behavior toward me in the course of the inquiry. Pinning responsibility for the death of Tom Pilchard to my coat would deflect any inquiry into other possible causes, *and* prevent the explosion being linked with the destruction of the other cannon, as well as having the salutary effect of discrediting one or both of my brothers. And any one of those three men could easily have influenced the other two, so as to guide the questioning as he desired.'

'Hmph.' Quarry frowned at the amber liquid in his glass, drank it off as though it were water, and set the glass aside. 'Well, if discrediting Melton were the principal motive of our wicked bugger, it would be Twelvetrees. Bad blood, there. I shouldn't be surprised if it comes to pistols at dawn between him and Melton, one of these days.'

'True,' Grey agreed. 'And Hal would shoot him like a dog, with pleasure. But it *wasn't* the principal motive. Twelvetrees is a sod, but an honorable sod. He's not merely a soldier, nor yet a colonel – he's a colonel of the Royal Artillery.'

Quarry nodded, purse-lipped, taking the point. 'Aye. Rob the army and take money from the naval bilge rat, to kill his own men? Never.'

'Exactly. Because bloody Stoughton was right – it *wasn't* treason, merely criminal. Ergo, the simplest motive is the most likely: money.'

'And Marchmont wipes his arse with cloth of gold; he doesn't need money. Whereas Oswald . . .'

'Is a politician of no particular means,' Grey finished. 'Thus by definition in constant need of money.'

'Thus by definition without conscience or honor? Quite. Oh, sorry, your half brother's one, too, isn't he? Steward!'

Mr. Bodley, well-acquainted with Quarry's habits, was already bringing in more brandy and a small wooden box of Spanish cigars. Quarry selected two with care, clipped the end of one, and handed it to Grey, who held it for Mr. Bodley's taper.

He seldom smoked, and the rush of tobacco through his blood made his heart pound. He felt a slight twinge in his chest, but ignored it.

Quarry blew a long, pleasurable stream of smoke through pursed lips.

'Can you prove it?' he asked, offhanded. '*I* believe you implicitly, of course. But beyond that . . .'

Grey squinted, trying to blow a smoke ring, but failed dismally.

'I don't suppose it would stand up in court,' he said. 'But I found this, in Stoughton's portmanteau. As I said, had Stoughton failed to reach the ship, he could expect no protection from the navy. If I were a villain, I'd want a bit of leverage upon my fellow villain, just in case.'

He reached into his pocket and removed a small medal, attached to a silk ribbon.

'I saw Oswald wearing this, at the inquiry. I don't know whether he gave it to Stoughton as acknowledgment of their connexion, or whether Stoughton simply stole it. Oswald would claim the latter, I suppose.'

Quarry frowned at the bit of metal, pretending that he did not require spectacles to make out the engraving, which he did.

'It's an army decoration, surely; Oswald's never been a soldier,' he said, handing it back. 'Could simply claim it isn't his, couldn't he?'

'Hardly. His father's name is engraved on the back. And Mortimer Montmorency Oswald – the Third, if you please – is not *quite* so common as "John Smith," I daresay.'

Quarry laughed immoderately, taking back the medal and turning it over in his hand.

'Montmorency, by God? So his father was in the army, was he? Decorated for valor?'

'Well, no,' Grey said. 'It's a medal for good conduct. As to what I propose to do,' he added, stubbing out his cigar and rising to his feet, 'I am going home to change my clothes. I have an engagement this evening – a masqued ball at Vauxhall.'

Quarry blinked up at him through a cloud of smoke.

'A masqued ball? What on earth do you propose to go as?'

'Why, as the Hero of Crefeld,' Grey said, taking back the medal and pocketing it. 'What else?'

In fact, he went as himself. Not in uniform, but attired in an inconspicuous suit of dark blue, worn with a scarlet domino. Those whom he sought would know him by sight.

They would have to, he thought, seeing the hordes of people streaming through the gates of the Vauxhall Pleasure Gardens. If those with whom he sought interview were disguised in any effective way – and one of them at least would certainly be masked – he would have little hope of distinguishing them among the throng.

'Oh,' breathed Tom, completely entranced at sight of the trees, largely leafless but strung with hundreds of glimmering lights. 'It's fairyland!'

'Something like,' Grey agreed, smiling despite the beating of his heart. 'Try not to be too enraptured by the local fairies, though; a good many of them would pick your pocket as soon as look at you, and the rest would give you fair value under a bush, with a dose of the clap thrown in for free.'

He paid admission for himself and Tom, and they walked into the maze of pathways that spread along the bank of the Thames, leading from grottoes where musicians played, muffled to the eyes against the autumn chill, to arbors where tables of luscious viands were spread, supper boxes piled high behind laboring servants dressed in livery. The great Rotunda, where dancing was held, rose like a bubble in the center of the Gardens, and laughter ran through the night like currents in a river, catching up the merrymakers and carrying them along from adventure to adventure.

'Enjoy yourself, Tom,' said Grey, handing Byrd some money. 'Don't stay too close; Oswald's a wary bird.'

'He won't see me, me lord,' Tom assured him, straightening the black domino he wore. 'But I'll not be far off, don't you worry!'

Grey nodded, and parting company with his servant, chose a path at random and strolled in the direction of the strains of Handel.

Sheltered by thick hedges and brick walls and thronged with bodies, it was scarcely cold in the gardens, despite the lateness of the season. The chill was pleasant, caressing face and hands – and any other bits of exposed flesh – enhancing the heat of the rest of the body by contrast.

There was a great deal of flesh exposed, to be

sure. It gleamed among the light and shadow, set off by the rich colors of the costumes – the scarlets, crimsons, and purples, greens and blues, the flaunting yellow of tropical birds. Here and there a woman – perhaps – who chose to dress in stark black and white by way of contrast. These came dramatic out of the shadows, seeming to emerge from the night itself. One gave him a languishing look as she passed, reached out a hand to him, and as he raised his own, involuntarily, took hold of it, drew one of his fingers into her mouth, and sucked hard.

She drew it slowly free, her teeth – *her* teeth? He could not tell – exquisite on his skin, then dropped his hand, flashed him a brilliant smile, and ran away, light-footed down the path. He stood a moment looking after her – or him – and then walked on.

He heard whoops of delight approaching, and stepped hastily aside in time to avoid being run down by a covey of girls, scantily clad and equipped with skates, these ingeniously mounted on tiny wheels, so that they whizzed down the path in a body, draperies flying, squealing with excitement. A clatter of applause made him glance aside; a series of spinning plates on rods appeared over a hedge – jugglers in an adjoining alcove.

Music, smoke, food, wine, beer, rum punch, and spectacle – all combined to induce an atmosphere of indulgence, not to say license. The Pleasure Gardens were liberally equipped with dark spaces, alcoves, grottoes, and secluded benches; most of these were being fully employed by couples of all sorts.

He was aware – as most of the merrymakers were not – of the mollies among the crowd. Some dressed as women, others in their own male garb surmounted by outlandish masks, finding each other by glance and grimace, by whatever alchemy of flesh enabled body to seek body, freed by disguise of their usual constraints.

More than one gay blade glanced at him, and now and then one jostled him in passing, a hand brushing his arm, his back, lingering an instant on his hip, the touch a question. He smiled now and then, but walked on.

Feeling hungry, he turned in to a supper table, bought a box, and found a place on the nearby lawn to eat. As he finished a breast of roast fowl and tossed the bones under a bush, a man sat down beside him. Sat much closer than was usual.

He glanced warily at the man, but did not know him, and deliberately looked away, giving no hint of invitation.

'Lord John,' said the man, in a pleasant voice.

It gave him a shock, and he choked, a bit of chicken caught in his throat.

'Do I know you, sir?' he said, politely, when he had finished coughing.

'Oh, no,' said the gentleman – for he was a gentleman, by his voice. 'Nor will you, I'm afraid. My loss, I am sure. I come merely as a messenger.'

He smiled, a pleasant smile beneath the mask of a great horned owl.

'Indeed.' Grey wiped greasy fingers on his handkerchief. 'On whose behalf are you come, then?'

'Oh, on behalf of England. I beg you will forgive the melodrama of that statement,' he said, deprecating. 'It is true, though.'

'Is that so?' The man wore no weapon – these were firmly discouraged in Vauxhall, but the odd knife was common, now and then a pistol.

'Yes. And the message, Lord John, is that you will abandon any efforts to expose Mortimer Oswald.'

'Will I?' he said, maintaining a tone of skepticism, though his stomach had clenched hard with the words. 'Are you from the navy, then?'

'No, nor from the army, either,' said the man, imperturbable. 'I am employed by the Ministry of War, if that information is of use to you. I doubt it will be.'

Grey doubted it, too – but he didn't doubt the man's assertion. He felt a low, burning anger growing, but this was tinged with a certain sense of fatality. Somehow, he was not truly surprised.

'So you mean Oswald to escape payment for his crimes?' he asked. 'His actions have meant the death of several men, the maiming of several more, and the endangerment – the ongoing endangerment, I might add – of hundreds. This means nothing to the government?'

The man turned to face him straight-on, the

painted eyes of his owl mask huge and fierce, obliterating the puny humanity of the man's own orbs.

'It will not serve the interests of the country for Oswald to be openly accused – let alone convicted – of corruption. Do you not realize the effect? Such accusations, such a trial, would cause widespread public anger and alarm, discrediting both the army and the navy, endangering relationships with our German allies, giving heart to our enemies . . . No, my lord. You will not pursue Oswald.'

'And if I do?'

'That would be most unwise,' the man said softly. His own eyes were closed; Grey could see the pale lids through the holes of his mask. Suddenly he opened them; they were dark in the flickering light; Grey could not tell the color.

'We will see that Mr. Oswald does no further harm, I assure you.'

'And it would suit the War Office's purposes so much better to have a member of Parliament who can be quietly blackmailed to vote as you like, rather than one being hanged in effigy and hounded in the broadsheets?' He had a grip on his anger now, and his voice was steady.

The owl inclined his head gravely, without speaking, and the man gathered his feet under him, preparing to rise. Grey stopped him with a hand on his arm.

'Do you know, I think I am not very wise?' he said conversationally.

The man became very still.

'Indeed?' he said, still polite, but noticeably less friendly.

'If I were to speak openly of what I know – to a journalist, perhaps? I have proof, you know, and witnesses; not enough for a trial by jury, perhaps, but more than adequate for a trial in the press. A Question in the House of Lords?'

'Your career means nothing to you?' A note of threat had entered the owl's voice.

'No,' Grey said, and took a deep breath, ignoring the harsh stab of pain in his chest. 'My honor means something, though.'

The man's mouth drew in at the corners, lips pressed tight. It was a good mouth, Grey thought; full-lipped, but not crude. Would he know the man by his mouth alone, if he saw it again? He waited while the man thought, feeling oddly calm. He'd meant what he said, and had no regrets, whatever might come of it now. He thought they would not try to kill him; that would accomplish nothing. Ruin him, perhaps. He didn't care.

At last the owl allowed his mouth to relax, and turned his head away.

'Oswald will resign quietly, for reasons of ill health. Your brother will be appointed to replace him for the remainder of his term. Will that satisfy you?'

Grey wondered for an instant whether Edgar might do the country more harm than Oswald. But England had survived stupidity in government for centuries; there were worse things. And if the War Office thought Grey as corrupt as themselves, what did that matter?

'Done,' he said, raising his voice a little, to be heard over the sound of violins from a strolling band of gypsies.

The owl rose silently and vanished into the throng. Grey didn't try to see where he went. All he would have to do was to remove the mask and tuck it under his arm to become invisible.

'Who was that?' said a voice near his ear.

He turned with no sense of surprise – it was that sort of night, where the unreality of the surroundings lent all experience a dreamlike air – to find Neil the Cunt seated beside him on the frosty grass, blue eyes glowing through the feathered mask of a fighting cock.

'Bugger off, Mr. Stapleton,' he said mildly.

'Oh, now, Mary, let us not bicker.' Stapleton leaned back on the heels of his hands, legs flung oh-so-casually apart, the better to display his very considerable assets.

'You can tell me,' he coaxed. 'He didn't look as though he wished you well, you know. It might be useful to you to have a friend with your best interests at heart to watch your back.'

'I daresay it would,' Grey said dryly. 'That would not, however, be Hubert Bowles. Or you. Were you following me, or the gentleman who has just left us?'

'If I'd been following him, I'd know who he was, wouldn't I?'

'Quite possibly you *do* know, Mr. Stapleton, and only wish to know whether I do.'

Stapleton made a sound, almost a laugh, and edged closer, so that his leg touched Grey's. Not for the first time, Grey was startled at the heat of Stapleton's body; even through the layers of cloth between them, he glowed with a warmth that made the red and yellow feathers of his mask seem about to burst into flames.

'Charming ensemble,' Neil drawled, eyes burning through his mask with a boldness far past flirtation. 'You have always such exquisite *taste* in your dress.' He reached out to finger the lawn ruffle of Grey's shirt, long fingers sliding slowly – very slowly – down the length of it, slipping between the buttons, his warm touch just perceptible on the bare, cool skin of Grey's breast.

Grey's heart gave a sudden bump, pain stabbed him, and he stiffened. He felt as though his chest were transfixed by an iron rod, holding him immobile. Tried to breathe, but was stopped by the pain. Christ, was he going to die in public, in a pleasure garden, in the company of a sodomite spy dressed like a rooster? He could only hope that Tom was nearby, and would remove his body before anybody noticed.

'What's that?' Stapleton sounded startled, drawing back his fingers as though burned.

Grey was afraid to move, but managed to bend his neck enough to look down. A spot of blood the size of a sixpence bloomed on his shirt.

He had to breathe; he would suffocate. He drew a breath and winced at the resultant sensation – but didn't die immediately. His hands and feet felt cold.

'Leave me,' he gasped. 'I'm unwell.'

Stapleton's eyes darted to and fro, doubtful. His mouth compressed in the shadow of the rooster's open beak, but after a long moment's hesitation, he rose abruptly and disappeared.

Grey essayed another breath, and found that his heart continued to beat, though each thump sent a jarring pain through his breast. He gritted his teeth and reached gingerly inside his shirt.

A tiny nub of metal, like the end of a needle, protruded half an inch from the skin of his chest. Breathing as shallowly as he dared, he pinched it tight between finger and thumb, and pulled.

Pulled harder, air hissing between his teeth, and it came, in a sudden, easing glide.

'Jesus,' he whispered, and took a long, deep, unhindered breath. 'Thank you.' His chest burned a little where it had come out, but his heart beat without pain. He sat for some time, fist folded about the metal splinter, his other hand pressing the fabric of his shirt against the tiny wound to stanch the bleeding.

He didn't know how long he sat there, simply feeling happy. Revelers went by in groups, in couples, here and there a solitary man on the prowl. Some of them glanced at him, but he gave no sign of acknowledgment or welcome, and they passed on.

Then another solitary man came round the

corner of the path, his shadow cast before him. Very tall, crowned with a mitre. Grey looked up.

Not a bishop. A grenadier in a high peaked cap, with his bomb sack slung over one shoulder, the brass tube at his belt glowing, eerie with the light of a burning slow match. At least it wasn't another frigging bird, Grey thought, but a feeling of cold moved down his spine.

The grenadier was moving slowly, plainly looking for someone; his head turned from side to side, his features completely hidden by a full-length black-silk mask.

'Captain Fanshawe.' Grey spoke quietly, but the blank face turned at once in his direction. The grenadier looked over his shoulder, but the path was vacant for the moment. He settled his sack more firmly on his shoulder and came toward Grey, who rose to meet him.

'I had your note.' The voice was the same, colorless, precise.

'And you came. I thank you, sir.' Grey pushed the splinter into his pocket, his heart beating fast and freely now. 'You will tell me, then?' He must; he would not have come, only to refuse. 'Where is Anne Thackeray?'

The grenadier unslung his sack, lowered it to the ground, and leaned back against a tree, arms folded.

'Do you come here often, Major?' he asked. 'I do.'

'No, not often.' Grey looked round and saw a low

brick wall, the river's darkened gleam beyond it. He sat down, prepared to listen.

'But you knew I would find the surroundings . . . comfortable. That was thoughtful of you, Major.'

Grey made no answer, but inclined his head.

The grenadier sighed deeply, and let his hands fall to his sides.

'She is dead,' he said quietly.

Grey had thought this likely, but felt still a pang of startled grief at the death of hope, thinking of Barbara Thackeray and Simon Coles.

'How?' he asked, just as quietly. 'In childbirth?'

'No.' The man laughed, a harsh, unsettling sound. 'Last week.'

'How?'

'By my hand – or as near as makes no never-mind, as the country people say.'

'Indeed.' He let the silence grow around them. Music still played, but the nearest orchestra was at a distance.

Fanshawe stood abruptly upright.

'Bloody hell,' he said, and for the first time, his voice was alive, full of anger and self-contempt. 'What am I playing at? If I've come to tell you, I shall tell you. No reason why not, now.'

He turned his blank, black face on Grey, who saw that there was a single eyehole pierced in it, but the eye within so dark that the effect was like talking to a wall.

'I meant to kill Philip Lister,' Fanshawe said. 'You've guessed that, I suppose.'

Grey made a small motion of the head – though in fact he had not.

'The powder?' he said, one small further puzzle piece falling into place. 'You made the unstable bomb cartridges. How did you mean to use them – and how in hell did they get to the battlefields?'

Fanshawe made a small snorting sound.

'Accident. Two of them, in fact. I meant to ask Philip to come with me, to have a look at something in the mill. It would have been a simple thing, to leave him to wait by one of the sheds, go inside and set a match, then leave and go away quietly, wait for the bang. That would have been simple. But, no, I had to be clever about it.'

Marcus Fanshawe was an expert, raised in the shadow of a gunpowder mill, fearless in the making and handling of the dangerous energy.

'What is it the Good Book says – *The guilty flee when no man pursueth?* I thought that if he died that way, people would wonder, ask questions. Anne' – there was a bitter pain in his voice at the name – 'she might suspect.'

And so he had begun the manufacture of high-grade powder, even finer than that required for rifle cartridges. An experimental batch; everyone knew about it, knew the potential risks of dealing with it. If *that* powder were to suddenly explode, no one would be surprised.

'I thought, you see, I knew what I was doing. I'd handled black powder since I was a lad; knew it all. And, in fact, I did. We'd made the powder, corned it with great care, got a number of the special cartridges made up, the rest mostly kegged. Not the slightest difficulty. And then a workman dropped a scraper.'

Not a wooden scraper, which would have done no harm; one of the heavy stone scrapers, whose weight was needed for the fine grinding. It should have made no difference; the granite used was inert. But some small inclusion in the stone was flint; it struck an iron fitment of a horse's harness, and made a spark.

'There was that one deadly instant when I saw it, saw the air filled with powder dust, and knew we were all dead,' Fanshawe said. 'And then the shed went up.'

'I see,' Grey said, dry-mouthed. He worked his tongue and swallowed. 'And the second accident?'

Fanshawe sighed.

'That one wasn't mine. Half the experimental batch was outside, packed in kegs, standing near the shed, where I'd carefully placed it – for Philip. But the explosion went the other way; the kegs didn't explode. And the overseer was one of the men killed in the explosion; the kegs weren't marked specially yet – someone simply loaded them onto the barge with the others. It was weeks before I recovered enough to speak, let alone act. By then, the high-grade powder had already gone to market, so to speak.'

'And Anne Thackeray had married Philip Lister.'

The peaked cap bent toward him in a nod.

'Eloped,' he corrected. 'They never had a chance to marry; Philip was called back to his regiment and sent to Prussia. He had just time to send a note to me, asking me to look after Anne. Idiot,' he added reflectively. 'Philip never could see what was under his nose.'

'Evidently not.' The brick wall was hard; Grey shifted his buttocks a little, seeking a more comfortable position, but none was to be found. 'But you didn't look after her.'

'No.' Fanshawe's voice had lost its momentary passion, gone back to its colorless normality. 'He died. I knew Philip wouldn't have left her well provided for – couldn't. And her father . . . Well, you've met him. So I waited.'

Waited, with the cold-blooded patience of one accustomed to handling explosive substances. Waited until Anne Thackeray had exhausted her resources.

'She wrote to that fool, Coles, who of course came bleating to me, money in hand. I took it, kept it.' And waited.

Anne, pregnant and destitute, had pawned her jewelry, bit by bit. And Marcus Fanshawe, following discreetly in her wake, had bought it, bit by bit.

'I meant, you see, to keep it for her,' he explained. 'When she had reached a state of complete desperation – then I should come to her, and she would have no choice but to accept me, even as I am. Something she would never do,' he added bitterly, 'save to escape from utter degradation.'

The grenadier was by now wreathed with floating smoke from the burning slow match at his waist, and Grey caught the whiff of brimstone as he moved. Fanshawe drew a length of the slow match from its tube and blew thoughtfully on it; the black silk fluttered, and the end of the slow match brightened like a spark.

'I waited too long, though,' he said. 'She gave birth, and I should have come then – but I was afraid that she wasn't yet so desperate that she'd have me. She'd taken refuge in a brothel, but with her belly big, they hadn't yet put her to work. I thought after *that* had happened once or twice . . .'

Grey felt incredulous revulsion form a ball in the pit of his stomach.

'That is the most . . . You – you are—' he said, but speech failed him.

'You cannot tell me anything about myself that I do not already know, Major.' Fanshawe bent and took what looked like an authentic grenade from the neck of his rucksack. He stood, tossing the small clay sphere casually in one hand.

'I waited too long,' he repeated, matter-of-factly. 'She took a fever and died. So there it is. Bloody Philip's won again.'

With an air of absolute calm, he held the slow match to the fuse of the grenade.

'What in the name of God do you expect to accomplish with this bit of theatrics?' Grey asked, contemptuous. 'And what of the child? Did the child live? If so – where is it?'

Fanshawe's head was bent, watching the slow creep of fire through the burning fuse. What was the maniac about? It couldn't be a real grenade.

Could it?

Uneasy, Grey got off the wall. His backside was chilled and his legs stiff.

'The child,' he repeated, more urgently. 'Where is the child?'

Fanshawe lifted the grenade, weighing it in his hand, and seemed to consider the burning fuse. How long did it take to burn down? Not more than seconds, surely. . . .

'Catch!' he said suddenly, and tossed the sphere at Grey.

Grey fumbled madly, the slippery thing bouncing off his hands, his chest, his stomach, finally trapped precariously against his thighs. Blood hammering in his ears, he carefully took a double-handed grip of the grenade and straightened up.

Fanshawe was laughing, his shoulders shaking silently.

'God damn you for a frigging buffoon!' Grey said, furious, and turning, flung the thing over the garden wall, toward the river.

The night flared red and yellow, blinding him, and a blast of hot air singed his cheeks. The sound of it was mostly drowned in the racket of music and conversation, but he heard a few voices near him, raised in awe or curiosity.

'Oh, fireworks!' someone exclaimed in rapture. 'I didn't know there were to be fireworks tonight!'

He sat down suddenly, all the strength in his legs gone to water. The place on his breast where the splinter had come out throbbed in time to his heart, and black-and-yellow spots floated before his eyes.

'Me lord! Are you all right?' He blinked, making out Tom Byrd's anxious face among the spots. Tom had acquired a comic hat somewhere, a huge thing of shoddy red sateen, equipped with a curling feather. This brushed against Grey's face as Byrd bent over him, and he sneezed.

'Yes,' he said, and swallowed, tasting sulfur. 'Where—' But the grenadier was gone, the space beneath the tree dark and empty.

Not quite empty.

'He's left his sack behind.' Tom bent, reaching for it, before Grey could shout a warning. He flung both hands over his head, curling into a ball in a futile attempt at self-protection.

'Oh,' said Tom, in tones of astonishment. He was holding up the flap of the bag, peering inside. 'Oh, my!'

'What?' Uncurling, Grey made his way on hands and knees to the sack. 'What is it?'

Tom reached gently into the sack and drew out the contents. A small baby, perhaps a month old, stirred in its wrappings and opened its amiably popping eyes.

'Oh,' said Grey, bereft of words. He held out his arms, and Tom Byrd carefully handed him the child, which was sopping wet but appeared not otherwise the worse for its recent adventures.

Somewhere in the night, there was a sudden, tearing sound above the music, and the air beyond the hedge flashed red and yellow. Grey paid no attention to the screams, the shouts of dismay. His whole being was focused on the bundle in his arms, for he was sure this would be his last vision of the face of Philip Lister.

It was very late, but John Grey was not yet asleep. He sat by the fire in his quarters in the barracks, the distant sounds of the night watch outside his window, writing steadily.

. . . and so it is ended. You may imagine the difficulties of discovering a wet-nurse in an army barracks in the middle of the night, but Tom Byrd has arranged matters and the child is cared for. I will send to Simon Coles tomorrow, that he may undertake the business of bringing the boy to his family – perhaps such an ambassage will pave the way for him in his courtship of Miss Barbara. I hope so.

I cling to the thought of Simon Coles. His goodness, his idealism – foolish though it may be – is a single bright spot in the dark quagmire of this wretched business.

God knows I am neither ignorant nor innocent of the ways of the world. And yet I feel unclean, so much evil as I have met tonight. It weighs upon my spirit; thus I write to cleanse myself of it.

He paused, dipped the pen, and continued.

I do believe in God, though I am not a religious man such as yourself. Sometimes I wish I were, so as to have the relief of confession. But I am a rationalist, and thus left to flounder in disgust and disquiet, without your positive faith in ultimate justice.

Between the cold consciencelessness of the government and the maniac passion of Marcus Fanshawe, I am left almost to admire the common, ordinary, self-interested evil of Neil Stapleton; he is so nearly virtuous by contrast.

He paused again, hesitating, bit the end of the quill, but then dipped it and went on.

A strange thought occurs to me. There is of course no point of similarity between yourself and Stapleton in terms of circumstance or character. And yet there is one peculiar commonality. Both you and Stapleton know. And for your separate reasons, cannot or will not speak of it to anyone. The odd result of this is that I feel quite free in the company of either one of you, in a way that I cannot be free with any other man.

You despise me; Stapleton would use me. And yet, when I am with you or with him, I am myself, without pretense, without the masks that most men wear in commerce with their fellows. It is . . . He broke off, thinking, but there really was no way to explain further what he meant.

. . . most peculiar, he finished, smiling a little despite himself.

As for the army and the practice of war, you will agree, I think, with Mr. Lister's assertion that it is a brutal occupation. Yet I will remain a soldier. There is hard virtue in it, and a sense of purpose that I know no other way of achieving.

He dipped the pen again, and saw the slender

splinter of metal that lay on his desk, straight as a compass needle, dully a-gleam in the candlelight.

My regiment is due to be reposted in the spring; I shall join them, wherever duty takes me. I shall, however, come to Helwater again before I leave.

He stopped, and touched the metal splinter with his left hand. Then wrote, *You are true north.*

Believe me ever your servant, sir,

John Grey

He sanded the letter and shook it gently dry, folded it, and taking the candlestick, dripped wax upon the edge and pressed his ring into the warm soft wax to seal it. The smiling crescent moon of his signet was sharp-cut, clear in the candlelight. He set down the candlestick, and after weighing the letter in his hand for a moment, reached out and touched the end of it to the flame.

It caught, flared up, and he dropped the flaming fragment into the hearth. Then, standing, shucked his banyan, blew out the candle, and lay down, naked in the dark.

Lord John and the Private Matter

Diana Gabaldon

For twenty years Claire Randall has kept her secrets. But now she is returning with her grown daughter to the majesty of Scotland's mist-shrouded hills. Here Claire plans to reveal a truth as stunning as the events that gave it birth: about the mystery of an ancient circle of standing stones, about a love that transcends the boundaries of time, and about James Fraser, a warrior whose gallantry once drew the young Claire from the security of her century to the dangers of his.

Now a legacy of blood and desire will test her beautiful daughter as Claire's spellbinding journey continues in the intrigue-ridden court of Charles Edward Stuart, in a race to thwart a doomed uprising and in a desperate fight to save both the child and the man she loves.

'Marvellous . . . It is a large canvas that Gabaldon paints, filled with strong passions and derring-do'
San Francisco Chronicle

'A triumph! A powerful tale layered in history and myth, at its core is a love so vivid and fierce . . . '
Nora Roberts

arrow books

Lord John and the Brotherhood of the Blade

Diana Gabaldon

It's 1758 and Europe is in turmoil – the Seven Years' War is taking hold and London is ripe with deceit. The enigmatic Lord John Grey, a nobleman and high-ranking officer in His Majesty's Army, pursues a clandestine love affair and a deadly family secret.

Grey's father, the Duke of Pardloe, shot himself just days before he was to be accused of being a Jacobite traitor. Now, seventeen years on, the family name has been redeemed; but an impending marriage revives the scandal.

From barracks and parade-grounds to the bloody battlefields of Prussia, Grey faces danger and forbidden passions in his search for the truth. But it is in the stony fells of the Lake District that he finds the man who may hold the key to his quest: the enigmatic Jacobite prisoner Jamie Fraser.

Eighteenth-century Europe is brought startlingly to life in this compelling adventure mystery.

arrow books

ALSO AVAILABLE IN ARROW

Drums of Autumn

Diana Gabaldon

How far will a woman travel to find a father – a lover – a destiny? Across seas – across time – across the grave itself

It began in Scotland, at an ancient stone circle. Claire Randall was swept through time into the arms of James Fraser whose love for her became legend – a tale of tragic passion that ended with her return to the present to bear his child. Two decades later, Claire travelled back again to reunite with Jamie, this time in frontier America. But Claire had left someone behind in her own time – their daughter Brianna.

Now Brianna has made a disturbing discovery that sends her to the stone circle and a terrifying leap into the unknown. In search of her mother and the father she has never met, she risks her own future to try to change history – and to save their lives. But as Brianna plunges into uncharted wilderness, a heartbreaking encounter may strand her forever in the past – or root her in the place she should be, where her heart and soul belong . . .

'A blockbuster hit!'
Wall Street Journal

arrow books

Dragonfly in Amber

Diana Gabaldon

For twenty years Claire Randall has kept her secrets. But now she is returning with her grown daughter to the majesty of Scotland's mist-shrouded hills. Here Claire plans to reveal a truth as stunning as the events that gave it birth: about the mystery of an ancient circle of standing stones, about a love that transcends the boundaries of time, and about James Fraser, a warrior whose gallantry once drew the young Claire from the security of her century to the dangers of his.

Now a legacy of blood and desire will test her beautiful daughter as Claire's spellbinding journey continues in the intrigue-ridden court of Charles Edward Stuart, in a race to thwart a doomed uprising and in a desperate fight to save both the child and the man she loves.

'Marvellous . . . It is a large canvas that Gabaldon paints, filled with strong passions and derring-do'
San Francisco Chronicle

'A triumph! A powerful tale layered in history and myth, at its core is a love so vivid and fierce . . . '
Nora Roberts

arrow books

A Breath of Snow and Ashes

Diana Gabaldon

**Their love has survived the test of time.
But can it survive fate?**

America, 1772. It is only a few years before the war of independence and the colony seethes with unrest. As battle lines are drawn up and loyalties tested, no one is safe in this new country.

Jamie Fraser receives a message from Governor Josiah Martin. He wants Jamie's help to keep the backcountry safe for King and Crown. But Jamie knows what's to come. His wife, Claire, has travelled back from the twentieth century and she knows what will happen to those loyal to the King of England. Exile or death. Neither prospect appeals to Jamie.

But Claire knows something else. From her own time she's read an article, dated 1776, reporting the destruction by fire of their home on Fraser's Ridge and the death of those who live there. Jamie hopes Claire is wrong, for once, about the future. But only time will tell . . .

arrow books